HANNAH LAKE was born
England. Having worked and
and London, she now lives i
Manifests Her Perfect Life, a comedy-romance, is her
novel.

Alice Carver Manifests Her Perfect Life

Hannah Lake

HQ

ONE PLACE. MANY STORIES

HQ
An imprint of HarperCollins*Publishers* Ltd
1 London Bridge Street
London SE1 9GF

www.harpercollins.co.uk

HarperCollins*Publishers*
Macken House, 39/40 Mayor Street Upper,
Dublin 1, D01 C9W8, Ireland

This edition 2025

1
First published in Great Britain by HQ,
an imprint of HarperCollins*Publishers* Ltd 2025

ISBN: 9780008769178

This book is set in 10.7/15.5 pt. Sabon by Type-it AS, Norway

This novel is entirely a work of fiction. The names, characters and incidents portrayed in it are the work of the author's imagination. Any resemblance to actual persons, living or dead, events or localities is entirely coincidental.

Printed and bound in the UK using 100% Renewable Electricity by CPI Group (UK) Ltd

MIX
Paper
FSC™ C007454

For more information visit: www.harpercollins.co.uk/green

For anyone else who has ever wondered:
what if it could actually work . . . ?

And for Nick. Of course.

The Guide

A Journal for Manifesting™

This Guide belongs to:

Alice Carver
....

Welcome to

The Guide
A Journal for Manifesting™

Manifesting is not the future.
Manifesting is NOW.

Seven days of the week
Seven heavens
Seven ages of man
Seven is your lucky number

*Begin by setting **seven** manifesting*
goals on the next page

Sign and date to mark your commitment

> *Manifest* /ˈmænɪˌfɛst/ – *to make what you want a reality*

1. *I manifest* . . . the perfect man (specifically, Guy Carmichael) falling in love with me
2. *I manifest* . . . having a gorgeous flat to live in from 4 January (if possible, central and cheap, or ideally free, and no rats)
3. *I manifest* . . . not getting fired (I may not *love* my job, but I need the money)
4. *I manifest* . . . getting a better job (more money, not boring, people bring me coffee rather than the other way round, no one gets my name wrong, etc.)
5. *I manifest* . . . respect and admiration from friends, colleagues and family (preferably with high levels of envy, veneration of my social media output, and general sense of shame for having ever doubted me)
6. *I manifest* . . . a perfect wedding (everyone whose wedding I've had to sit through can sit at mine and endure, knowing how much better mine is. Plus there will be many comments about how young and beautiful a bride I am)
7. *I manifest* . . . wiping that smug smile off Matthew Lloyd's face

Signed A.Carver

Date Sunday 25 December

*Congratulations! You've just taken the
first step towards securing your dreams!
Before we continue, let's take a minute to
REFLECT: what prompted you to invest in*

The Guide: A Journal for Manifesting™?

That one's easy:

My life. Total f**king disaster.

Okay. Well, unlike my sisters, I'm not the type to rehash childhood injustices (although if I was, the fringe Mum gave me when I was eight, and the 2002 archaeology 'holiday' in Tunisia would certainly feature), so I'm going to focus on the last couple of days, whilst the 'nudges' are fresh in my mind. Although I'm not sure 'nudges' is the right term. They were more like very unsubtle pokes but – on the plus side – it's galvanised me to take action. Like I said: my life is a total disaster.

Nudge 1: The Work Christmas Party
(Friday 23 December, 9pm)

I'd been looking forward to it for weeks: this was my chance to get the big boss, Guy Carmichael, to notice me, and ideally fall for me. Previously, he'd only spoken to me a couple of times in meetings (and called me by the wrong name), but I'm pretty sure that magnetic forces are equal and opposite so he will have felt it too (on some level). Problem was, I'm not the only one who's drawn to the MD of Carsons Children's Books Division. When Guy told us all off about the poor sales figures at last week's department meeting (children's books may have taken a hit nationally, but Carsons have dropped from market leaders to second place), it wasn't just me adjusting my collar; I saw Tina sit up straighter, and Charlotte actually licked her lips (that's Charlotte for you. *Shameless*). Anyway, the work Christmas party is the one opportunity to interact on an equal footing, and, even though Guy is notorious for putting in only a brief appearance, I intended to make the most of it.

So I pulled out all the stops, and despite having to re-use a Mango dress due to cash flow issues, I still looked good. But that was one of the few things that went right. The first thing that went wrong was that I got stuck with Sweater-vest Gareth from Accounts who asked me my age (that's how dull the conversation was) and misheard my answer of 'I'm *thirty*-seven' (we were standing near the speaker) and bloody Gareth 'kindly' replied, 'I wouldn't have put you over forty-five.'

Of course, Drunk Stephen found this hilarious and told me I should have a vodka jelly shot to cheer myself up and wasn't jelly a good source of collagen? I told him I shouldn't really drink because I was meant to be catching the early train home tomorrow morning for a wedding and not all of us have hollow legs (Drunk Stephen has, ironically, never, ever been drunk and he drinks shitloads – it's like a superpower). And he said, 'Who's rude enough to have a wedding on Christmas Eve? What a twat.' That's why he moved up the ranks from colleague to firm friend a long time ago: he's not afraid to call a twat a twat.

'Monty,' I answered flatly.

'As in your ex, Monty?'

I nodded, and Drunk Stephen sucked air through his teeth in a sympathetic way and proffered a jelly shot, which I ignored.

'Actually, I'm not bothered even though everyone thinks I am,' I announced, 'because I've got years left for that kind of thing – marriage, babies, etc.'

'Well . . . Maybe not *years*.' Flip side is, he's not afraid to *be* a twat either.

'Rude,' I said, snatching the jelly shot, downing it, and then another, just for the collagen, and Drunk Stephen laughed, saying I was far too easy to manipulate. But the jelly shots were delicious, so we had a couple more in order to benefit fully, and Drunk Stephen said my skin looked plumper already. I asked Drunk Stephen if he'd come to the wedding with me to make it more fun, and he said there was no way he was trekking over to Little Shagworth or whatever and that the Cotswolds was full of unimaginative bigots. Then, when I told him the wedding was at the newly refurbished Lamb Hotel *actually*, Drunk Stephen got all excited and said that apparently there was some seriously cool artwork there (that's designers for you) and that if he didn't have an overbearing mother to visit, he would have come with me.

And then the whole vibe in the room shifted. It wasn't that someone suddenly turned up the music volume, or that the lights dramatically dimmed, but they may as well have. Everyone felt it. Power. Then I realised why: over Drunk Stephen's shoulder I saw Guy Carmichael had finally arrived. That aura of potency instantly left the rest of the men seeming even more drab. It was as if he had a spotlight on him. I elbowed Drunk Stephen and we both watched as Guy paused by various people that he wouldn't normally stop for; they looked a little flustered and laughed a little too hard because who *wouldn't* want to impress Guy Carmichael? Especially when he was in party mode, rather than his default blunt mode (which totally does it for me – it's masterful and efficient and he gets to say things to people that I'd quite like to say like, 'That's shit, Jane. Don't show me shit covers like that again, Jane'). But just as they were starting to relax into it, he extricated himself and moved swiftly on to the next person – Guy Carmichael knew how to work the room. He must have managed to talk to about fifty people in not much more than twenty minutes.

'You have to admit he is seriously sexy,' I said.

Drunk Stephen, who doesn't really like Guy because he passed him over for promotion, acknowledged that for some-one old, he certainly had a whole big dick energy about him.

'I need to get him on his own,' I decided.

'Now's your chance,' said Drunk Stephen, 'he's crossing over to the bar . . .'

I asked Drunk Stephen to quickly check I didn't have panda eyes, and then I went over. However, Charlotte – with her 10k followers on TikTok and her Altuzarra dress – apparently had the same idea and arrived fractionally before me, angling herself so that her arse was practically in Guy Carmichael's face. And then I had to watch him notice. Like he had any choice. She swung round, whipping him with her freshly balayaged Beauty Cuts hair (she'd posted about it on Insta earlier) and I saw his eyes flash with appreciation. He didn't even register my arrival at his other side.

It was the closest I've ever been to Guy, and I could see a tiny bit of skin irritation at the nape of his neck; I wondered if he'd scratched it. When the barman asked me if I wanted ice, I laughed loudly, hoping to get Guy's attention – it didn't work. The barman looked (understandably) alarmed, and Guy remained fixated on Charlotte's breasts which she was pressing against his arm. Bloody Charlotte. She's always hitting on people. And getting them. For the last few months, it's been the GlowCycle instructor from her exclusive gym with endless sanctimonious posts about nutrition and clean living, and little videos of them muscled and sweaty together, frantically pedalling. But clearly she'd now set her sights on our boss. Tonight, her skin looked particularly luminescent and smooth and youthful. It was probably the soft lighting from the overhead pendants. Maybe mine looked good too, over here at the bar.

The barman pushed my drink towards me. 'You don't think I look old, do you?' I asked.

'No,' he said.

I gave him a smile and took a slow sip of the Moscow mule.

'But then again, to me, all you women over forty look the same – sort of mumsy.'

Over forty? Mumsy? A bit of raw ginger caught the back of my throat, and I inhaled and spluttered.

'Are you all right?' asked the barman, now concerned.

I waved my arm to reassure him, but he seemed to interpret this differently.

'Do you need help?'

I shook my head and tried desperately to look calm and casual as my eyes streamed with tears and I attempted to avoid coughing my drink everywhere. But Guy Carmichael had already turned around to check what was happening and was just in time to witness me snorting Moscow mule out of my right nostril and onto the barman's bow tie. *Then* I got to witness Guy Carmichael quietly leave the work Christmas party, with his hand on Charlotte's bum, less than half an hour after he'd arrived.

I was so depressed by all the unkind assumptions about my age from the barman and Gareth (and, if I'm honest, about Charlotte beating me to Guy) that after a couple more Moscow mules and a few more jelly shots I got Drunk Stephen to film me doing a little clip about age-shaming and pressure on women to get married and have kids (as Drunk Stephen pointed out, Gwyneth Paltrow got millions of likes for basically saying the same thing). Charlotte's not the only one who can have a social media side hustle.

Nudge 2: The Viral Video (Saturday 24 December, 9.37am)

I woke up on Christmas Eve with a horrific hangover and a text from Astrid asking if that was me on the Apple News feed. She said if it was, she hoped I didn't give consent, because she'd love to take on that legal battle. I clicked on the link, which took me to the headline 'Woman's Christmas Party Post Hilariously Backfires' and . . . to a clip of the video I recorded last night. Which turned out to have *incredibly* unflattering lighting.

The first thing I did was panic and call Drunk Stephen, but he didn't answer so I sent him a voice note. Then I saw an email from Harry Piles (total twat Children's Deputy MD) to the entire team saying 'this should cheer you up – at least you're not this woman' with a link to my video. It was almost immediately recalled, but goodness knows who else saw it. Then a further email arrived from Harry Piles apologising for any offence caused by the previous email which was sent in error to the whole team, and a reminder that Carsons are an equal opportunities publishing company.

I didn't know whether to vomit or run away to sea or both, so I tried Drunk Stephen again, and this time he answered.

'Why the fuck do you keep bothering me this early?'

'Why the fuck did you let me post it?' I screeched at him. 'It's gone fucking viral!'

'No one realises it's you.'

'But Harry Piles sent it to everyone!'

'He's a twat. And he hasn't twigged who it is in the video.'

'What makes you think that?'

'Honestly, *I* barely recognise you in it and I filmed it – you said your own sister didn't know for sure it was you.'

That was true. If Astrid *had* known it was me, she'd have dived straight in – I mean this was literally a gift from the mockery gods.

'Just delete it and move on. Although maybe invest in a ring light? If you're planning future videos . . . Now I'm hanging up because *I* take my skincare seriously and skin needs sleep.'

I opened the clip again. I was wearing a paper crown (we'd pulled crackers) which had slipped over one eye, and my make-up had run from the crying, and Drunk Stephen kept zooming in on my chin: it actually *was* quite hard to make out any identifying features.

So I deleted the video and messaged Astrid to tell her that of course it wasn't me and how could she even *think* that?

And she texted immediately to say, 'Phew: thank goodness I'm not related to that disaster!'

Never has the crying-with-laughter emoji I sent back been more appropriate.

Nudge 3: The Work Email (Saturday 24 December, 9.58am)

My phone buzzed: it was a text from Mum asking if I was sure it was a good idea to come to the wedding and to remember to empty the fridge and turn the heating off before I caught the train, and had I seen the email from Aunty Margaret?

I opened my emails but before I could find one from Aunty Margaret, I saw that one had appeared from Guy Carmichael marked 'high importance'. It was to everyone in our division telling us that Carsons are merging with Montague Place and that whilst they will be looking at head count this is unlikely to impact the majority, so not to worry and have a good Christmas.

What. The. Fuck?

I immediately messaged Drunk Stephen but he'd switched his phone off. And then I stupidly checked Charlotte's feed and she'd posted a picture of a swirled heart in her morning cappuccino and there, in the background, were Guy's hairy knuckles. I'd know them anywhere – I've spent a lot of time looking at his hands. All of us have. It's his tell: everyone knows when our MD is getting irritated in meetings because he drums those hairy-knuckled fingers lightly on the table, and you should see how much it makes people panic. So sexy. I'd love to command people like that. I'd love to be commanded like that. Who wouldn't? No wonder bloody Charlotte's showing off about it.

Then I remembered the email again and realised that now, most likely the only time I was going to experience Guy Carmichael commanding me was when he fired me. And however sexy he is (and if I'm honest, I wasn't finding this email very sexy), I'd rather keep my job.

Nudge 4: The House Email (Saturday 24 December, 10.04am)

Unsurprisingly, and as indicated by my mother, there was further misery in my inbox – that's why I don't check it that often. Rodentinators had finally got back to me saying they were short staffed and unable to change my rat boxes until 1 January (hardly rapid response, is it?) but reminding me that a slight odour is normal, to follow their pest-control guidelines and the situation would remain under control, and wishing me a very happy Christmas. I mean? If you've got decaying rats in your flat (well, strictly speaking, Aunty Margaret's flat), it's not going to be a very happy Christmas, is it? They told me the bait boxes were humane, but I can tell you, the smell coming from the one in the kitchen isn't humane at all, to me, as a human. Imagine if I were having people over in these circumstances? (I'm not having people over. I'm going home to Mum and Dad's like I have done every year, but maybe I would be inviting people over here for a grown-up Christmas if Rodentinators had got their act together.)

And directly underneath *that* was Aunty Margaret's email, telling me wonderful news – she'd finally found a new tenant for the flat and, on the proviso that they could move in quickly, they had paid three-months full rent on top of the deposit, which was very useful because she and Uncle Ted had an imminent tax bill. So I needed to make sure that I'd moved my stuff out by 2 January.

Second of January?

Unbelievable.

I mean I know she was *technically* doing me a favour letting me stay pretty much rent-free and that it was only ever temporary, etc., and meant to be a few weeks in between tenants, but as the months ticked by, I'd been hoping she'd sort of decided she liked having a family member in here. Clearly Aunty Margaret is more of a hard-nosed businesswoman than the family woman I'd assumed she was. Mind you, given that (a) we never actually see her and (b) she is Mum's sister, I should have known better.

I've been evicted a number of times, and lost a fair few jobs too, but never both together. On Christmas bloody Eve.

Nudge 5: The Wedding (Saturday 24 December, 3.30pm)

I mean, where do I start? Getting there was bad enough. I barely made the 11.08 train and very nearly puked on the platform (combination of running because late and committed consumption of vodka-based beverages through to early hours of this morning) and finally found a spare seat, only to discover Annabel and Hugh across the aisle. Annabel's eyes lit up in poorly disguised delight; what was unclear was whether her delight was due to how green I was looking or the gossip she'd get from chatting to the groom's ex. She cocked her head to one side, mock-sympathetically, and said, 'Alice, darling! How are you? I heard Monty had invited you to the *wedding*' – she mouthed the word – 'but so brave of you to *actually* come! Isn't it, Hugh?'

Lucky Hugh acted like he was engrossed in the *FT* (surely no one actually reads the *FT*?) whilst I (and everyone else) had to endure Annabel talking loudly about the Lamb and the artwork there and how she had an eye for art, until the conductor interrupted us. And then I got to watch Annabel's décolleté redden with pleasure as the conductor told me that my saver return wasn't valid in the first-class carriage.

Dad wasn't there to welcome me at the station, just my eldest sister Arrie honking at me to hurry up from the driver seat of her stinky, hairy Land Rover, which somehow was even filthier inside than out. She made me sit in the back on a slightly damp seat, squashed between the twins' booster seats, my knees hitting horse tackle, whilst her pregnant Vizsla, Maud, got to sit in the front because she 'doesn't like the back'. When I pointed out that I didn't like it much either, Arrie said, 'Yes, but you don't bark and urinate in protest.'

'No guarantees,' I said. 'I'm pretty hungover.'

She snorted derisively.

I thought about telling her that there was, in fact, a high

chance I was going to be sick if she continued to take the corners that fast but, knowing Arrie, rather than slow down, she'd just pull over and make me walk instead. Just because she was born five years before me, she's always thought it's her role as oldest sister to teach lessons.

As we hurtled down the High Street (definitely not a case of twenty's plenty for Arrie), we passed the entrance to the Lamb (with a very trendy slate-grey sign) and then our old house. 'Oh gosh,' I said, 'it's for sale again!'

'Give it up, Alice,' said Arrie. 'It's been ten years.'

I turned to watch the house for that bit longer; it looked even more beautiful in the low winter afternoon light. 'Do you remember how lovely Christmases there were, though? All that space for everyone. Do you think Mum and Dad could afford it again now?'

'No, Alice.' Arrie spoke slowly, like I was an idiot. 'Lost shares are lost. Surely even you understand that.'

'But the new house is so . . .'

'Practical,' said Arrie. 'It costs far less to heat and they don't need that much room for just the two of them. Not to mention how expensive it is to actually move.'

'Well, I miss it. Christmas isn't the same.'

'Then grow up, and get your own house, Alice, like the rest of us.'

'Some of us don't have husbands to buy farms for us, Arrie.'

'I bought that farm, not bloody Roger,' said Arrie.

Roger and Arrie have been married forever, and I'm not sure when she first started referring to him as 'bloody Roger' (probably after the twins) but she does it quite a lot. Often in front of him.

'*And* I bought this car that I'm currently giving you a free lift in.'

She did as well. So annoying having overachieving older siblings.

Then, despite having pretty much found fault with me since I'd got home (being late, not putting the phone charger back, spilling tea on the carpet) and even on the way up to the church (I'd used up too much hot water in the shower and everyone else had to have cold ones), Mum chose to wait until we were just about to enter the church, one hand holding the door ajar, to say loudly, 'Good golly, Alice, couldn't you have put some make-up on? You look positively haggard.'

The whole family turned to look at me, in their neat Noah's Ark pairs, in perfect descending order of age: Mum and Dad, Arrie and Roger, and Astrid and Aziz. Then me, on my own, at the back.

Aziz gave me a sympathetic look: nicest person in my family by far. I did warn him what we were all like, but he went ahead and married Astrid anyway.

And when I told Mum that I had, in fact, put make-up on, she just sighed and said, 'Well, I suppose working a junior desk job at a hardly junior age takes its toll.'

That's where Arrie gets it from: Mum is a big fan of 'constructive' criticism. Thank goodness she didn't see my viral post. And she firmly believes that working in children's publishing is for people who haven't managed to progress to adult publishing.

'As does years of alcohol abuse,' added Astrid. She's worse than Mum and Arrie because she knows full well what she's doing. Typical middle-child behaviour. Probably jealous of me because I was such a cute baby. 'No one better light a match near her; I think she's fifty per cent vodka.'

'Now, now, Astrid darling,' tried Dad gently, 'that's not even possible. In fact, the world record for highest recorded blood alcohol level was a mere 1.374 per cent. Held by a Polish chap apparently. Read all about it in—'

'Honestly, Alice!' Mum bulldozered over Dad. 'I despair. No one wants a drunk wife.'

'Who said I want to get married?' I said.

'Aunty Margaret's married,' said Astrid, to Mum. 'You said she drinks loads.' At least Astrid enjoys winding everyone up, not just me. That's why she's such a successful lawyer.

'Yes, well. She lives in Scotland. And she still had her looks when she met Ted. Tick tock, Alice,' said Mum stridently, pulling the church door fully open.

Where everyone was sitting in silence.

Except for Monty's mother, who was standing right by the door. And who, judging by the fact her bosom had increased two cup sizes with the grinning flush of schadenfreude, had heard every single word. From his uncharacteristic look of happiness, Joyless Julian had clearly overheard too (Monty must have deliberately chosen a wedding party full of people I'd disappointed).

The ceremony itself was, frankly, a merciful relief from people staring at me. The happy couple had written their own vows, which for the most part were very sweet; however, when Monty said how much he admired Minty's drive, self-sufficiency and insistence on standing on her own two feet, it felt a bit pointed. A feeling compounded by Monty's mother turning to catch my eye triumphantly.

*

The Lamb was absolutely stunning, once I'd made it past the intimidatingly cool and attractive staff on reception, who made me feel like I had to justify not only why I was there, but why I was worthy of being there. I thought about telling them that I actually spent a whole summer working here, back in the day but, given it was over a decade ago, it would probably have just made me seem old.

The wedding reception was as awful as I'd anticipated. The drinks reception part was a quagmire of congratulating old school 'friends' (Louise, Amira and Tara) – aka people I hadn't stayed in touch with for a reason – on the wonderful news of impending parenthood / increasing of broods / promotions / property acquisitions / awards, etc., and then navigating either sympathetic, troubled eyes about my continued unmarried, nonpregnant, homeless, crap-job state.

Or, worse still, enduring advice (from ghastly Shona): 'You'd better crack on and settle for someone, Alice, or there'll be no babies for you – none of us is getting any younger.'

And, worst of all, poorly disguised glee (from Fizz): 'Gosh, Alice, isn't it funny how life turns out in the end!'

It was all interspersed with endless, repetitive small talk about what a beautiful bride Minty made, the refurbished Lamb and much mentioning of wonderful artwork that I, to be entirely honest, didn't give a crap about.

Then the sit-down meal involved insult after insult. On the way to my table, I overheard one of Minty's bridesmaids saying, 'Oh no, not only was she was much older than Mints but according to Monty's mother, very directionless, which is why he had to end it.' And then I found out I'd been placed at the singles table, away from family and friends, with red-eyed Phoebe from two years below who seemed to have the same cold she had all through school. She still didn't talk about much other than chess and rabbits, and was still embarrassingly grateful for the fact I frequently stopped her getting bullied at school (but at least she appeared to actually like me). Unlike Minty's cousin Polly who kept shooting me filthy looks (while actually wearing a white dress). And I was *just* thinking, *God, this is a shit table*, when Joyless Julian turned up.

Then Astrid came over, and I thought it was to rescue me, but it was only to tell me to go easy on the champagne and remind me that I'd promised I wouldn't make a thing out of it, and how Mum and Dad still live here, and not to be selfish for once. 'Oh my god,' I said. 'What exactly do you think I'm going to do?'

Having struggled with the onglet (not good with a hangover) and the disappointment of lemon sorbet (how is that a dessert?), I then had to endure the incessant speeches. Not only did Minty's father sob his way through an entire photograph album of Minty's dull life including little video clips of her doing gymnastics (I mean you wouldn't even get away with this at a funeral), but the whole shitshow was punctuated with intermittent ear-splitting feedback from his clip-on microphone because he kept standing too close to the speaker.

Then, to top it all, just in case someone at the wedding hadn't clocked the party line, I was used as a prop by Monty and Minty (as the woman Monty rapidly rejects in favour of Minty) for their duet – 'You're the One That I Want' – from *Grease*.

Honestly, the only thing that could have made this debacle worse was if Matthew Lloyd had been there, witnessing it. I don't think I could have taken that. Me on the singles table and him smirking at me, with one of his ghastly identikit girlfriends. But I double-checked with Mum, just casually, and apparently the 'darling boy' was abroad doing his super-important serious job, so at least I wouldn't have to endure him being superior and mocking about yet another of my failed relationships, or pretend that he didn't get to me. Last time I'd seen Matthew Lloyd and I'd argued that Monty and I had loads in common, and that I found Monty's mother fascinating, Matthew had laughed so hard that his water went down the wrong way and Astrid, always his best friend, had to hit him on the back. I'd have left him to choke.

Nudge 6: The Library (Saturday 24 December, 7.05pm)

Whilst everyone was moving out of the restaurant and through to the bar for the harp recital, I took the opportunity to escape into the library. Skulking by the fire, I was taking a few breaths to steady myself when the door was pushed open: it was Aziz. 'Hey, Alice,' he said gently. 'How are you doing? I imagine this can't be easy for you.'

And I looked at his kind, questioning eyes, and felt my own begin to smart, so I quickly said that I was fine and that I needed to make a work call.

Aziz waited a moment, and I wondered if he was going to point out it was after 7pm and Christmas Eve and that

I never made work calls. But he nodded. 'Okay, if you're sure you're fine.'

And I said, 'Of course,' and we both knew I was lying but I think he could also tell that I didn't want his kindness right then, because my life was falling apart.

Then he said, 'I'd better get back to your sister and leave you to your call,' and I thought how unfair it was that bloody Astrid got him because, honestly, Aziz is far too nice for her: why can't I have someone supportive like that?

The library door had barely closed before it opened again. I glanced up in time to clock Monty's expression as he realised that I was already in there, all alone: he looked simultaneously haughty and guilty and fearful, rather like Arrie's dog Maud.

'I'm afraid one of us needs to leave this room forthwith,' he said.

'Why?' I asked. 'Congratulations, by the way.'

'Because I'm not allowed to be on my own with you. Minty's said you're not to be trusted.'

'Oh come on, Monts,' I said. 'I'm sure Minty's more confident of your relationship now you're married. What harm can it do? Besides, I haven't seen you in ages . . .'

'You shouldn't be in here anyway,' said Monty pompously. 'You should be through there listening to the harp.'

'So should you be,' I retorted, 'it's *your* wedding.'

'Yes, it is. We're going to cut the cake soon. It's cheese.'

'You do love cheese.'

'It's my weakness. Well, one of them.'

We both listened to the strains of the harpist playing Olivia Rodrigo.

'All a bit *Bridgerton*, isn't it?' I said.

'Costing me a bally fortune,' said Monty. 'The whole thing is. I mean the hotel alone. Even with the discount.'

'I bet,' I said, looking around. This hotel had received some serious investment.

'Hang on,' he said, 'when you worked here – didn't Matthew Lloyd work here too?'

'Yes.'

Monty shook his head in disbelief. 'How things change.'

He wasn't wrong. It felt like a lifetime ago, that summer we spent here as bar staff. Matthew and I had been friends. It *was* a lifetime.

'Enough to make a man weep,' said Monty. 'You see that bally great picture above the fireplace? It's a Banksy print.'

'Yes. I know.'

'Costs tens of thousands. Can't see why, personally. I'm basically paying for that bally picture, I tell you.'

'Hmm,' I said, remembering the vows. 'So Minty's letting you pay despite her fierce independence . . . ?'

Monty harrumphed. 'Still living in your aunt's flat, Alice?'

And suddenly I couldn't hold back. Monty was the one person who'd always adored me and now he was being snide. 'No, Monty, because my aunt wants it back so I'm not living anywhere actually. God. Talk about kicking someone when they're down! Honestly, I get that Minty's better than me. Everyone gets that. You prefer Minty. And that's fab – she's your wife. Your very young wife. You should prefer her. I just don't get why you're having to put me down in the process. I mean that duet? And telling everyone *you* dumped *me*?'

Monty wouldn't meet my eyes. 'Now you know how it feels.'

'Seriously? Is that what this is about? Is that why you invited me?' My voice broke on the last bit and I could feel my eyes stinging. 'You were always so kind, Monty. What did I *do* to you?'

Monty's sweet face crumpled. 'Don't cry, Alice,' he said. 'Please.' And then he pulled me close to him, suddenly, and hugged me.

He smelled of Floris and whisky and familiarity and even though I was cross with him, I couldn't help but hug him back.

'I thought you wanted to stay friends,' I said.

'I do,' said Monty.

'Well, friends don't treat each other like this!'

'You're right, Alice,' he said guiltily. 'I don't really want to hurt you. You know I don't.'

I sighed. 'I know.' I shifted uncomfortably, feeling something rigid digging into my shoulder. 'Ow. What is that?'

'Oh, it's the microphone,' he said, unclipping it with one hand and setting it on the side table. 'From the speeches earlier.'

'God, make sure it's off,' I said snottily.

'It's off.'

'Check it again. It would be just my luck.'

'Alice! You've watched too many films.'

'Please?' I said.

Monty reached over again and checked the switch. 'It's off, Alice.' He stroked the tears away from my cheeks and pulled me to him again. 'I'm sorry,' he said sadly.

'Well, I'm sorry too. I know I've said it many times, and I know it doesn't make it better, but I really didn't mean to hurt you.' He'd been so distraught when I ended things that he started trying to bargain, even offering to move his mother out. That hadn't gone down well, particularly as she was right there in the kitchen with us.

'You couldn't help the way you felt, Alice. Just like I couldn't help the way I felt.'

We stood for a moment and then I went to pull back, so I could blow my nose, but Monty held on.

'We were good together though, weren't we, Alice?' he whispered into my hair, breathing nasally. It reminded of when we used to have sex. 'I wish I'd been enough for you. Beautiful Alice,' he said, his voice cracking slightly.

I needed that after all the crap I'd had. I'd forgotten how nice Monty's adoration was.

'Beautiful, quite young-looking Alice?' I asked hopefully, thinking about the fact that Minty looks about twelve.

'No one else holds a candle to you. I still miss you, Alice,' he said hoarsely.

'You don't think I'm selfish, do you?' I asked, remembering Astrid's earlier accusations.

'I like giving to you, Alice. Always have. Your glorious body. God, I still think about what your face looks like when you—'

'Er, Monty.' I tried to disentangle myself slightly. 'I think someone may be a bit drunk.'

'Why, Alice?' he said, his face blotching with intensity. 'Why wasn't I enough for you? You know I cried myself to sleep every night for a whole year. I'd have given you anything. I'd have worshipped you every minute of every day if you'd let me. Physically.'

Golly. I'd forgotten how quickly the adoration could get quite intense. 'Come on,' I said, retreating. 'We've been through this. It's not that you weren't enough. We're just better suited to being friends. Let's get you back to your wedding.'

But Monty was on a one-way road. 'It should have been you, Alice, today. And clearly you know that too. Otherwise, why would you be here now? Giving me hope.'

And just as I was wondering how to get the fuck out of this situation, the library door opened and Joyless Julian and Astrid rushed in and grabbed the microphone off the table.

And *actually* switched it off.

'Monty!' I said in horror. 'You said it was off!'

Astrid's eyes were shining with fury. 'Seriously, Alice. What did I say? You *promised* not to make it all about you.'

Monty went sort of slush-coloured. 'Oh dear god. Who heard?'

'By some stroke of luck, Monty,' said Astrid, 'almost everyone else was in the bar listening to the harp recital. There were just the three of us left in the restaurant with the speaker. Me, Julian and . . .'

'Please god, not Mummy?' said Monty.

I could see Alice and Julian weren't expecting that. I was.

'*No*, not your mother,' said Astrid. 'And most importantly,' she said carefully, 'not *your wife* either. It was me, Julian and . . .'

And just when I thought maybe the universe wasn't out to get me after all, that's when the worst nudge, nay, shove from the universe happened . . . A tall, dark figure appeared at the doorway, very definitely male, and the room seemed to shrink.

Matthew.

Fucking.

Lloyd.

He leant against the library door. Christ. Were his shoulders always that broad? I broke out into a sweat.

'And me,' said Matthew drily.

*Sometimes we need to take a step back in order to take two steps forward. Nudges can feel bad but that's okay: that's the Universe giving you the motivation to change. Pick **one** of the above nudges that you found particularly difficult – ideally one that resulted in strongly negative feelings.*

Matthew Fucking Lloyd

Now take a few moments to relive it and record it <u>as it happened</u>.

Date: Saturday 24 December   **Time: 7.20pm**

It's a tableau of the library in a fine country house that would grace any am-dram flyer for an Agatha Christie play: we're temporarily immobilised in situ, our faces illuminated by the amber sconces; the plush, worn comfort of the armchairs and rugs at odds with the garish scene unfolding. I'm by the fire, Monty's gripping me with one arm, although he's backed off slightly, and I know I'm still alive because I can feel the heat from the flames hazing and licking, the dampness of sweat on my lower back, and the pressure of Monty's fingertips on my upper arm, but I feel like I'm watching it happen from a distance. Of all the people I'd least like to have overheard that conversation, I'd say Matthew Lloyd is probably top of the list. I mean, obviously I wouldn't want Monty's mother to have heard but let's face it – after this wedding it's not like we're going to spend much time together. Minty would have been awful – but mainly for Monty. Astrid hearing – well, that's annoying but it's happened and I'll cope. She was cross with me before this and she'll be even crosser now. But I'm used to that. My sisters don't know how to have fun, that's half the reason they're permanently pissed off with me. Besides, she'll get over this. She has to. She's my sister.

But Matthew Lloyd . . .

There are so many people at this bloody wedding. Everybody from school is here. Everybody from Little Minchcombe. Practically everybody from the whole bloody county. Why, oh why, out of everyone here, did it have to be Matthew Lloyd? *He* wasn't even meant to be coming. I checked with Mum. Twice. And then I checked once with Astrid. Actually, come to think of it – he *shouldn't* be here! I feel my vertebrae click back together in indignation and I break the silence.

'What the *fuck* are you doing here?' I demand.

Matthew doesn't blink, although Astrid shakes her head in despair, and Monty sort of whinnies slightly, like a horse, and applies more pressure to my arm. God. The Matthew Lloyd effect already. Everyone falling over themselves to ingratiate. Well, it doesn't work on me. Yes, he won all the prizes in the nature lottery and is objectively, provokingly good-looking (and he knows it) but he's scruffy and cocky and for people like me, who *aren't* shallow, it's what's on the inside that counts. Which, in his case, is an arrogant know-it-all who acts like he's your friend only to stab you in the back.

'Seriously. Were you even invited? I'm surprised they let you in here looking like that!'

'Alice!' reprimands Monty, pulling away from me like he's been scalded and walking over to Matthew. 'Of course he was invited. And thank you by the way, Matthew. Really. Thank you.'

Monty's not attractive when he's simpering. What's he thanking Matthew for anyway? Eavesdropping?

'You'd better get back to your wife, Monty,' says Matthew.

His voice has got gravelly. I bet he puts it on.

'Yes, yes, of course,' mutters Monty, making to go through the doorway. But of course he can't. Because Matthew Lloyd deliberately doesn't move. He just stands there, in his silly trainers, which I imagine are a total no-no nowadays in this place, taking up the space. So Monty has to wait.

'For goodness sake,' I say at last, patience deserting me. 'Matthew, just let Monty out, would you. And Julian too, whilst you're at it.'

Matthew turns slightly, so that Monty can technically access the door handle if he makes himself small, but Monty falters and looks back towards me. 'Please just tell me, if I weren't with Minty, would there have been any chance of you reconsidering us?'

'Oh come on, Monty!' Astrid says. 'Absolutely ridiculous.'

I give Astrid a sharp look. That stung. Especially in front of Matthew. 'Why do you have to be so mean? It's not ridiculous that someone might want me, you know.'

'He *just* got married!' says Astrid.

She has a point.

'Alice?' says Monty hopefully, breaking the silence.

I can hear the faint whistling of heightened emotion through his nostril hairs.

I shake my head. 'Sorry, Monts.' I feel pretty horrible watching his shoulders slump. 'You know we don't really work . . .'

'Well, Alice,' says Joyless Julian, 'you made me very happy during the dinner earlier when we had a very pleasant exchange about the beef, but after this little show, I'm certainly going to rethink the email I was planning to send you asking if we could rekindle.'

'Er, okay,' I say.

'Look, Monty,' says Julian, sounding uncharacteristically firm. 'You just need to stay away from Alice. She toys with one's feelings. Frankly, and I'm sorry to be blunt, Alice, but she's flighty. You're better off with Minty. You really are.'

He takes Monty's arm and steers him out of the library.

'Yes,' says Astrid. 'So much better off.' She flips me the finger as she follows them out the room, the oak and glass door shutting the chatter and laughter and music of the wedding party softly behind them.

And then it's just me and Matthew and the sound of the flames crackling and hissing.

So, Astrid's slated me and Joyless Julian has spoken his mind. Matthew's certainly not going to hold back. I brace myself for what he's going to say about me this time.

But he doesn't say anything. He doesn't even look at me.

I stand there waiting, carefully not looking at him either. His face is slightly in shadow and he's leaning against the stone door jamb. He's definitely filled out in the last few years. He always had that lean footballer strength thing, but now his shoulders and chest have got bigger, he looks more like a threat.

And then, after a while, he walks over to the sofa and flops down on it, occupying the space. He scratches his already messy hair, then yawns widely, not bothering to cover his mouth, and I notice his faded sweater's got a hole in the elbow.

Christ, he's rude. 'Aren't you going to say anything?' I ask.

'Nope.'

'Really? Don't you want to have a go at me for leading Monty on?'

'Not at all,' he says mildly, looking at the fire. 'Monty was clearly the one hitting on you. It's not your fault he can't keep away. Besides – he's the one who's married.'

For a moment, I'm quiet. *Is Matthew Lloyd being nice?*

Then he says, 'Although I would question what you were ever doing dating someone like Monty in the first place. He's a total idiot.'

'What?'

Matthew lazily gets off the sofa and wanders over to the fire, picking up the brass poker hanging in the mammoth stone hearth and stoking the fire. He keeps his back to me.

'I've always wondered . . .' says Matthew, and then tails off.

'What . . . ?' I say impatiently.

Matthew turns to face me. 'Does Monty breathe through his mouth like that when he's shagging? Or does the nose whistle turn you on? I wonder what first attracted you to him? The title? The castle? His love of cheese maybe? Yes, probably it was the cheese . . .'

He smiles at me.

'Fuck OFF, Matthew!' I say, going to kick him hard on the shin, but he moves to the side right at the last moment so I end up kicking the stupid log basket instead: a shooting pain sears up my foot as the basket tips, scattering logs over the hearth. 'Ow!' My eyes water. 'I think my toe's broken.'

Matthew just laughs, which makes me even crosser.

'Are you going to leave me in agony? At least Monty's a gentleman,' I say. 'Unlike you.'

'Every inch,' agrees Matthew. 'Minty's got herself a real catch.'

He grins, then turns away from me, bends down, rights the basket and retrieves the rolling logs. The pain is subsiding slightly, but he doesn't know that, which makes me hate him even more. Why's he messing around with the logs when I potentially have a fracture?

'Just leave the logs,' I snap. 'They have people to do that sort of thing here!'

He pauses, but doesn't turn round. 'People who will hold your drink for you, pick up for you, that sort of thing?' he says. 'Clear up *your* mess? I guess that's what staff are for.'

I feel my face getting hotter. Wanker. I don't get what his problem is. He knows I worked here just like he did: we were both bar staff that summer. Although I suppose he had to do more hours. And every holiday. But that was hardly my fault. 'Well, we're all suited to certain roles in life,' I say.

'Absolutely,' agrees Matthew, standing up. 'And you certainly seem to be sticking to the same old thing, don't you?'

What does that mean? I'm pretty sure he just insulted me. But now he's just staring at that painting above the fire, silhouetted against the flickering topaz light, like I'm not even there. I mean, I know it's art, and I'd never admit it in public, but I'm kind of with Monty here: it's not that interesting. But Matthew is seemingly fascinated. He moves closer to the painting, and then adjusts it.

Who the fuck adjusts a painting in a hotel?

'Careful,' I say. 'That's a Banksy print, and I happen to know it's exceedingly expensive.'

'It's not a print. It's an original.'

'Whatever.' I aim below the belt, but I don't care. He deserves it. 'If I were you, Matthew Lloyd, I'd keep my hands off things I couldn't afford.'

But he just chuckles.

'God, you're an arsehole,' I finally snap. At that precise moment, I feel the faint coldness of air from the door swishing shut, and hear the noise of the wedding, as someone politely clears their throat behind us. I swing round. It's one of the hotel managers who intimidated me earlier on reception; frankly she looks like she should be modelling, not working in a hotel. It's a clear power move from whichever cool fucker has taken over the Lamb.

'Sorry to interrupt,' she says smoothly.

'Not at all,' I say sweetly and politely. I may not be six feet tall like her, but I can play nice.

She gives me an appreciative smile: good manners cost nothing and I hope Matthew Lloyd has taken note.

Then she looks past me.

'That call's come through . . . ?' she says.

'Thanks, Rachel,' says Matthew, checking his watch and walking briskly towards the door. 'I'll take it in the office.'

What?

I think my mouth is still hanging open as the library door

35

shuts slowly. I turn to Rachel, who is following Matthew out.
'Hang on,' I say. 'Does he work here again or something?'

'Matthew?' she checks, pausing.

'Yes. Matthew.' I nod.

'Barely.' She tosses her glossy mane and smiles at me. 'Only
when he's in the country. Now he's got this place where he
wants it, he more or less leaves us to get on with it.'

'Got this place where he wants it?' I repeat inanely.

'It's even better than he told us it would be,' she says. 'But
it's not surprising. I mean it was his vision. Apparently he's
always imagined it since he was a boy – he grew up in the
village, you know? I've worked in some amazing hotels but
none of them were like this. And he doesn't pay me to say that
by the way.' Rachel laughs prettily.

'Sorry: are you saying Matthew Lloyd has become a hotel
manager?'

'No.' Rachel laughs again. 'He's the owner.'

Just as I realise that there's a small bit of saliva actually
coming out of the corner of my mouth, the library door opens
a fraction, a scuffed trainer toe appears and a deep voice says,
'Rachel?'

'Yes?' She swings to attention.

'I forgot to mention: this guest may well need assistance
to dial 999 on account of her horribly broken toe, and if you
could send Troy or Kate through to hold her drink as well,
that would be super.'

Rachel frowns.

'She's a code 44,' says Matthew. 'Standard princess treatment.'

Rachel stifles a snigger.

'Plus you may want to check the attire of the other guests,' says Matthew, 'in case it offends Alice. We wouldn't want that.'

Then he raises his eyebrows at me, flashes that smug smile and disappears.

I fucking HATE Matthew Lloyd.

Any time you need the motivation to commit to your journey towards a better you, read what you wrote above and recall how you felt. You do NOT want to feel that way again.

The Universe has spoken. And you listened. You decided to change your life. It's one thing to plan to change your life; it's another thing to actually change your life. People make plans all the time; plans are actionless.

But writing in this journal for manifesting,

The Guide™?

That is action. That is change. Remember:

I write; I act; I change . . .

Look at this journal,

The Guide: A Journal for Manifesting™

<u>*It was always meant to be in your hands.*</u>

How did the Universe bring you together?
Take the time to reflect and record the
story of this beautiful connection.

So . . . Mum and Dad give awful presents. Awful. It's Mum really – she doesn't believe in 'expectations' or the idea of getting something for nothing, which is quite ironic given what she inherited. (Although maybe the fact she lost most of her inheritance through unwise share investments has something to do with the expectations part.) She insists it's 'the thought that counts' when it comes to gift giving, which is clearly where she's going wrong. I've had my share of awful 'presents' over the years even if, according to Arrie (who's apparently scarred from the infamous 'bestowal' of NHS prescription glasses), I've been veritably 'spoilt' as the youngest with generous gifts such as the quilling set when I was eight ('I thought it would be fun, darling!') and the electric kettle for my eighteenth ('Think how popular it will make you at uni!').

But the worst part isn't even the presents, it's Mum's hurt

face when you're unable to feign gratitude for her latest offering (again, quite ironic given she doesn't believe in expectations).

Anyway, the year that Mum and Dad 'gave' me a donation to the RSPB was the year I snapped: I've never been a fan of birds. They're horrible pecky things. I told Mum this, and Mum told me I was an ingrate, and that birdsong was an absolute gift, and suggested that perhaps I'd like a cash donation instead, and I said, 'Yes, I bloody would – I'm absolutely broke and I've had to stop eating lunch this week – that donation could have fed your daughter and those birds could have eaten worms!'

And then Dad got upset (he's a real feeder) and said he knew I'd lost weight and this was the first rung on the ladder towards an eating disorder (he listens to *All in the Mind* on Radio 4 and drops in references to impress Aziz) and asked how much money I needed. I explained that basically £400 a month would really sort me out. So then, predictably, Arrie and Astrid started getting upset (because they wish Dad would give them some cash too but they're too twatty to admit it), saying that I was a freeloader and I'd never learn to stand on my own two feet if Dad was always bailing me out. Arrie monologued for a good five minutes about how she had her own business as well as the twins by the time she was my age, and that Astrid had been made a senior partner as a corporate lawyer. Dad pointed out that Arrie and Astrid had successful careers and wonderful homes, which not only did they own but which were shared with wonderful men, and that surely they should be concerned that their youngest sister was at risk of an eating disorder.

Astrid asked exactly how I was *at risk* and Dad explained that I was female, skipping meals, had low self-esteem and was a high achiever. Astrid snorted and said that I'd miss a lot more meals if I worked seventy-hour weeks like she did, and that anyone wearing *that outfit* had a pretty high opinion of themselves (she's always been jealous because I got my cup size from Granny Carver and Astrid's offerings are pure Mum – stingy) and was Dad really trying to claim that I was a 'high' achiever?

'Maybe not,' said Dad, 'but Alice said herself she wasn't eating. That's a warning, right, Aziz?'

Aziz had been trying to stay out of things, but he said whilst he wasn't unduly worried about me, I should come round to his and Astrid's if I was hungry.

'See,' said Dad triumphantly to Astrid, whilst I gave Aziz a hug because he's lovely, 'your husband is more concerned about your sister than you are!' You can imagine how well that went down.

Anyway, to cut a long story short, after a massive family argument – where Astrid ended up driving back to London in a pique (not helped by the fact Mum had given her a donation to a Cow Sanctuary), and Arrie went off on one about the NHS glasses again ('You were four years old, Arrie, and loved pink,' said Mum crossly. 'I thought you'd be delighted with the pink frames!') and how, unlike fucking Alice, she had to fund her own fucking therapy (and contact lenses) because she wasn't a spoilt freeloader and then bored us all by talking about the therapy – Mum saw the light and finally realised that her awful presents were just another source of discord in the Carver household.

Since that year, she's asked us what we want a couple of weeks before Christmas, and pretty much just got it for us. She puts a £50 limit on it, to ensure it is fair. It has improved things. Not that Arrie and Astrid have ever thanked me.

Fast forward to this year. I thought long and hard about the gift I wanted from Mum and Dad – really hard, because very few things in this day and age come in around £50 – and I asked for *The Guide* (RRP £99 but only £59 on Prime). All the best people have it – there's barely a post or a video from any mega influencer where you don't see this manifesting journal artfully placed. You can personalise the front cover and so I asked for it in pink moleskin like Radhi Devlukia-Shetty has got (that's +£45 but I'm hoping Mum won't notice the small font on her phone now her eyesight's fading), and honestly, the anticipation of receiving that gift is pretty much what kept me here, after the horror of the wedding yesterday. For a moment last night, I was tempted to call Drunk Stephen and ask if I could join him at his overbearing mother's for Christmas Day. But as Drunk Stephen and I have discussed numerous times when we're talking about the benefits of being single, other people's families are even worse than your own. Plus I got the twins nerf guns and I quite want to try them out.

Anyway, Christmas morning didn't get off to the best start: Mum woke me up, oblivious to my banging head, yanking back the pencil-pleat-gathered Laura Ashley monstrosities I mistakenly asked for when I was twelve and which she's since refused to replace, telling me it was after half-ten in the morning, everyone was due to arrive imminently, and I needed to get out of my single room because the twins would be sleeping here tonight, top to tail, and she needed to change the sheets quickly. If we were still in our old house with all its lovely bedrooms, I'd be able to sleep in.

'Merry Christmas to you too,' I muttered sarcastically. 'It's nice to know you still love me, your actual daughter, even though you've got grandchildren.'

'Get up,' she said, pulling the duvet off me whilst I was still scrolling through my feeds. (On a positive note, there was no further sign of Guy Carmichael in any of Charlotte's posts. Clearly she wasn't all that, sexually, despite the GlowCycle.) 'Up!' repeated Mum. 'I've still got the turkey to do and the cat's gone missing again.'

'So where exactly are you putting me?' I asked, shivering ostentatiously in my vest and pants. She didn't notice. 'To make way for Arrie's offspring? On the sofa bed downstairs?'

'No. Aziz and Astrid are taking that. You're in the spare room.'

'Oh.' I felt somewhat mollified. 'Nice. Fine. Don't get why the twins aren't in there though? Then I could stay in my room.'

'Not *that* spare room. Arrie and Roger are in there.'

'So where am I?' I sifted through some of the clothes in my wardrobe that were too shit to take to London, hoping to find something to put on.

'The other spare room,' she said, not looking at me.

'What? The garage? But it smells!'

'That's just the damp,' said Mum, stripping my duvet. 'It's fine in winter when the radiators are all on.'

'But it doesn't have a radiator.'

'You're right. That's why it's got all the black mould of

course. Silly me. Well, never mind. It's Christmas and we all have to muck in.'

'Hang on,' I said, my alcohol-addled brain kicking into gear. 'Who's in Arrie and Astrid's old room? Surely the twins can go in there?'

'No,' said Mum firmly. 'Maud's in there.'

'The *dog*? Can't she go in the garage?'

'Afraid not. Arrie says Maud's sensitive due to her pregnancy. She'll bark and urinate. And she doesn't like the whining noise of the freezer.'

'Gosh.' I shook my head in disbelief. 'Not just last born. I really am bottom of the pile.'

'Until you're a mother, Alice, you've no idea what bottom of the pile is. Stop moaning. Get up and dressed and get downstairs.'

I huffed and decided on an old baggy Christmas sweater from sixth form with a picture of puppies in Santa hats, which I pulled on crossly, but for some reason, it was horribly tight and I heard a rip under the armpit as it strained against my chest.

'What have you done to my top, Mum?' I asked.

'Oh I don't know,' she said. 'Washed it? Ironed it? Bought it?'

'Actually, *I* bought this sweater.' (I didn't. Hugh Winnington of Hugh and Annabel train ghastliness bought it for me when we were dating briefly, but that's not the moral point.) 'And it seems to have been ruined.'

'What's been ruined?' Astrid poked her head round the door, looking clear-eyed and sprightly. She'd probably been out for a run, written thirty emails and done an hour of yoga already. She's infuriatingly disciplined.

'My sweater. It's shrunk. Mum's clearly used that eco stuff again.'

'Maybe it's you.' Astrid looked at my chest pointedly. She withdrew her head and I heard her running down the stairs. 'You've missed breakfast by the way,' she called out. 'Dad's clearing it away.'

'What?' I shrieked, coming out of the bedroom sharpish. 'He can't clear away breakfast. It's Christmas bloody Day!'

'All gone,' said Astrid from below, slamming the kitchen door behind her.

I stomped down the stairs, calling, 'Dad? Dad! You know I like Christmas breakfast,' and yanked open the kitchen door, all ready to fight my corner, to find him still at the Aga, his Christmas apron on, humming along to the King's College Choir's carol service.

'Good morning, Alice,' said Dad, smiling at me, 'what's all the shouting about?'

'Nothing.' I was too relieved by the smells of sizzling bacon and warm bread to bother rising to Astrid's smirk, as she sat curled on the sagging sofa, crossword in one hand, a steaming mug of coffee in the other. 'Just hungry. Where's Aziz?'

'Out,' said Astrid shortly, not looking up.

'On Christmas morning? What's he doing?'

'Looking for the cat,' said Dad. 'Your mum's worried. You know Mitzy doesn't like loud noises and there was rather a lot of noise last night, wasn't there?' he added reproachfully.

I'd forgotten that I'd gone a bit high-pitched when we got home after the wedding and it became apparent that Astrid had told the rest of the family about the Monty thing. 'Just us three' indeed. Funny how she managed to share all that about

45

me with the family, but failed to share with *me* that Matthew Lloyd had gone and bought the Lamb Hotel. I was under the impression he had some dull consultancy company that sort of ticked over; you'd think someone might have mentioned he'd become Mr Monopoly.

'Yes, well, sorry about that, Dad.' I gave his cheek a kiss. 'But Mitzy wanders off at least once a week – it's hardly going missing. Besides it's Christmas Day, so hurrah, fresh start and all that.'

'Merry Christmas, my darling,' said Dad. 'Would you like everything?'

'And more.' I settled on the kitchen chair closest to the radiator, and watched Dad piling up my plate. 'When's Arrie's lot arriving?'

'Any moment,' said Dad. 'I'm sure the twins will have been up early with the excitement and you know poor Arrie's always up at the crack of dawn with the animals.'

'Yes, about that,' I said, taking advantage of Mum's absence. 'Did you know I've got to sleep in the garage because of Maud? What if it gives me asthma, Dad?' I gave a small cough. 'Could you tell Arrie that's not okay?'

Dad's forehead creased into its well-worn concern mode as he drizzled some maple syrup on my berries, trying to ascertain the lesser of two evils. 'We certainly don't want any asthma, Alice, but, well, your mother is usually in charge of that sort of thing . . .'

'What sort of thing?' said Mum briskly, coming into the room.

'The rooms,' said Dad. 'Poor Alice is asking nicely if Maud could have the—'

46

'Poor Alice?' said Mum crossly. 'Maud's pedigree and pregnant. And what about poor Arrie. She'll have been up at the crack of dawn.'

'Yes,' agreed Dad, shaking his head sadly. 'She will have. The crack of dawn.'

'Jesus,' I said. 'No one's *making* Arrie get up at dawn. The way you talk about her you'd think she was in prison.'

'Don't start, Alice,' said Mum, getting the broom out.

'If she doesn't like getting up so early, why doesn't she just have a bloody lie-in like the rest of us?'

Mum and Dad raised eyebrows at each other and Astrid said, 'Ha!' very loudly.

'What?' I said. 'What's so funny?'

'You're the only one who's had a lie-in,' said Astrid. 'As usual.'

'Well, why haven't you?'

'Because we've got shit to do,' said Astrid.

'On Christmas Day? No one does anything on Christmas Day.'

'Yes they flaming well do,' said Mum, sweeping quite viciously near my foot. 'Astrid doesn't get days off – she's a senior partner. And I've made beds, put on washing, peeled sprouts. Do you want Christmas lunch?'

'God. Not if you're going to make this much fuss. And anyway, Arrie's not making Christmas lunch. You are. So I don't see why she couldn't have a lie-in.'

'Because she's got children and animals, darling,' said Dad gently, setting down a plate of really delicious-looking fare in front of me.

'Yes, Alice,' mocked Astrid from behind the paper. 'Arrie is what we call a grown-up. Sometimes grown-ups have to do things they don't want to do. It will be hard for you to understand the concept.'

'Piss off, Astrid,' I said through a mouthful of croissant. 'I constantly do things I don't want to.'

'And sometimes you do things none of us want you to either,' said Mum.

'What's that meant to mean?'

'I just wish you'd left poor Monty alone, yesterday,' said Mum. 'Given him a chance.'

'I did! It was him, not me.'

'Poor boy,' said Mum. 'I had to comfort him. At his own wedding.'

'He's hardly a boy,' said Astrid. 'He's going bald.'

'That's hard for him too,' said Dad. 'Last thing he needs. Can really threaten your masculinity.'

'I don't get why you're all so worried about bloody Monty in all of this!' I said. 'I'm your daughter! Does no one care what it was like for me, having to watch him get married?'

'No,' said Astrid bluntly.

'Of course we do,' placated Dad. 'But you don't exactly seem to be pining, darling. More bacon?'

'Fallen off the vegan train already?' said Astrid.

'Actually,' I said. 'I'm following the 911 approach now.'

'Which is?'

'Nine days Paleo. One day fasting. One day break-out. Today's break-out.'

'So just a gentle 180 degree change,' said Astrid.

I ignored her.

'Wonderful, darling,' said Dad admiringly. 'I think I heard about this 911 diet on the Today show.'

'You certainly weren't fasting yesterday though, were you?' said Mum. 'You practically ate tier two of that cheese tower on your own. I've got to say – what a ghastly idea. Bad enough to get married on Christmas Eve but then to do cheese for a wedding cake? Mind you, clearly Alice loved it.'

'You're allowed extra break-out days for weddings and things,' I said defensively.

A lot of things in my case.

Astrid sniggered. 'For all that animal-based fat you've consumed, you'd think your skin would look a bit plumper. How's that sweater that Mum "shrunk" working out for you, Alice?'

'Shut up, Astrid. My generation isn't into body shaming. We're not all desperate for osteoporosis thighs.'

'Lucky for you,' said Astrid.

'Enough, girls,' Mum intervened. 'It's all in the genes anyway. Predetermined. Alice has Carver thighs.'

Astrid hooted with laughter.

'Mum!' I said.

'Grow up, Astrid,' said Mum. 'At this stage, there's very little to suggest Alice is going to end up with elephantitis of the legs like Great Granny Carver.'

'*What*?' I said.

'It's a compliment!' said Mum irritably, just as the back door swung open and the twins bundled in with Arrie and Roger, followed by a damp-looking Maud who made her way straight over to me, and stood there growling softly.

'Who were you complimenting, Mum?' asked Arrie, taking off the boys' hats, and removing her filthy wellies. 'Golly, Alice,' she did a double-take when she saw me. 'That top's

49

not really family friendly is it? Merry Christmas everyone by the way.'

'Not all of us want to dress like royals,' I muttered under my breath as Arrie shrugged off her gilet.

'I was telling Alice that despite having Granny Carver's thighs, I see no current signs, whatsoever, of elephantitis. Come in, Roger, you're making it cold,' said Mum briskly. 'Merry Christmas my darlings!'

Arrie looked at Mum and then at my thighs.

'I wouldn't exactly call that a compliment, Mum,' she said. 'Saying Alice doesn't have elephantitis.'

'What's elephantitis?' asked Edwin loudly.

'Massive swollen legs,' said Astrid.

Maud gave a small, shrill bark.

'Quiet, Maud!' ordered Arrie, pouring herself coffee from the pot Dad seems to manage to permanently have full, and leaving Roger to get his own.

'Who's got massive swollen legs?' asked Edwin, looking quite excited. 'I want to see them.'

'Not Aunty Alice,' said Mum firmly.

'Although, do you remember how we used to have to Vaseline up her thighs when she was little because they'd chafe?' said Arrie, unwinding her scarf.

'Ahem,' said Aziz, loudly and pointedly at the back door. 'Found the cat. And also found someone else . . .'

'Merry Christmas,' said another voice.

Oh great. Not *again*. What were the odds he'd choose to show up just when my family were mid-flow demeaning me? (Well, pretty high probably, considering how rude they all are. But it was particularly unfortunate timing considering our run-in yesterday.) He'd better not have heard that about the Vaseline . . .

'Hope you don't mind me popping in—' he began.

Yes I bloody did mind. I was planning to be incredibly intimidating and together when I next saw Matthew bloody Lloyd. Not wearing this crazily small top. Or looking like I just got out of bed. Oh god. I did just get out of bed. I haven't even looked in the mirror.

'—Matthew!' squealed my mum with delight, practically shoving poor Aziz and the supposedly beloved cat out of the way to get to him. 'You know you're family. Come in, darling boy. Merry Christmas!'

I noted Mum doesn't hug her actual family like that; I mean Roger hasn't even had a look in, but hey-ho.

'So what did I miss?' said Matthew.

'Nothing interesting,' said Astrid.

Maud eyed me aggressively and growled a little more intensely. What was her problem?

'Can I see Aunty Alice's elephant legs?' asked Ernie in a horribly loud whisper, his snotty hands pushing the table into my stomach and wedging me against the radiator as he tried to peer over the top.

'Manners!' admonished Roger.

'Sorry,' said Ernie. 'Can I see Aunty Alice's elephant legs, *please*?'

Maud suddenly barked several times, making me almost choke on my sausage, and I wasn't the only one: the cat startled and jumped out of Aziz's arms.

'Quiet!' roared Arrie, silencing everybody in the room.

The cat dived out the open window. Good move.

'Oh no!' said Mum. 'The cat's gone again. And it's Christmas Day!'

'She doesn't like Maud barking,' said Edwin.

'Why is she barking?' said Mum, looking over. Her brow clouded. 'Alice! What are you doing in Maud's chair?'

Everyone turned to look at me.

'Um. What?' I said, mid-sausage-chew.

'That's Maud's chair,' said Arrie. 'She likes the warmth of the radiator.'

'So do I.'

'She's pedigree!' said Mum.

'Alice knows all about class,' said Matthew.

Astrid giggled.

I rose above it.

'Move, Alice,' said Mum.

'I don't see why I have to move for the dog.'

Maud whined pitifully.

Everybody looked at me.

'Oh Alice,' said Dad reproachfully.

'What?!'

'Sometimes we have to do things we don't want to, don't we, Grandpa?' said Ernie. 'It's called being grown-up, isn't it?'

I'd obviously never say this to Arrie because she's extremely touchy about her youngest twin but I think Ernie needs to learn to be less of a twat. No wonder Edwin hits him a lot.

Then Edwin piped up.

'Grandma, why is Aunty Alice eating breakfast now? It's nearly lunch.'

God. I thought Edwin was the better one.

'Indeed,' said Mum. 'Aunty Alice could learn a thing or two from her sensible nephews.'

I'd had enough of the familial gaze. So glad Matthew Lloyd was here for this.

'Fine, fine,' I said. 'I'll move.'

I picked up my plate ready to stand up, but stupid Ernie had trapped me in with his desperation to look at my zoo-thighs. I couldn't even move my arms enough to push the table back because of the tight top. I floundered for a second as everyone watched.

'Aunty Alice can't get out,' said Ernie helpfully.

'Yeah,' said Matthew. 'You look like you're struggling there, Alice. Would you like me to go and fetch some Vaseline?'

Fucking Matthew Lloyd.

*

'I'm absolutely fine, thank you, Matthew,' I said stiffly, finally managing to shove the table back enough with my hip to edge out. 'Hadn't you better get back to your hotel? Hope you didn't cheat to get it like you always do at Monopoly!' I laughed at my own joke.

'Don't be silly, Alice,' said Arrie. 'Everyone knows you're the one who cheats. Because you can't cope with losing.'

'That's not true! It's Matthew. He's the cheat.'

'It's you, Alice,' said Astrid.

'It's not! Is it, Dad?'

'Well, darling,' said Dad. 'It did get a little heated last year, didn't it? With Scrabble? And Matthew wasn't even there.'

Matthew smiled.

'Yes, Matthew,' said Astrid. 'You missed a blinder last year.'

'And we missed you dreadfully, you naughty boy,' said Mum, her focus back on Matthew now that Maud was comfortably and victoriously sitting in my lovely warm seat. 'Where were you? Being terribly successful I suspect. Ken!' She poked my father in the ribs. 'Have you even congratulated Matthew, yet? The Lamb?'

'Oh goodness, yes!' Dad paused his washing-up to beam at Matthew. 'Absolutely wonderful, Matthew. Fantastic.'

'Fancy you buying your own hotel,' said Mum. 'You must have sunk everything into that. And I thought you had your own company working with all those big corporations – I didn't even know you were moving into hospitality!'

'I'm not,' said Matthew. 'I'm still doing the consultancy work.'

'Why have you got a hotel then?' asked Edwin.

Astute question from my nephew. Maybe he's not so bad after all.

'I thought it was a good opportunity. It's sort of a sideline, a hobby.'

'Daddy, can we have a hotel as a hobby?' asked Edwin.

'No,' said Roger shortly.

'What's your hobby, Daddy?' continued Edwin.

'Building up the model train track,' said Roger proudly. 'I just got a new docklands section and—'

'I'd rather have a hotel,' said Edwin sulkily.

Roger's right eyelid twitched. 'Hadn't you boys better check if there are any presents under the Christmas tree?'

I cast a quick look at Roger. His forehead was quite shiny. I reckoned it was getting to him too: Mum and Dad's open admiration of Matthew. If I wasn't finishing this last bit of bacon that Maud was eyeing up, I'd be tempted to follow the twins and escape the Matthew fan club in here.

'I don't understand,' said Mum, moving aside to let the twins out. 'How can a hotel be a sideline?'

Astrid looked up from her newspaper. 'Leave Matthew alone, Mum. It's an investment for him. You wouldn't understand.'

'Of course I understand investments,' insisted Mum. 'But surely Matthew isn't in the position where he can pop his pocket money in hotels? Are you, Matthew?'

'Umm . . .' Matthew looked slightly uncomfortable.

Astrid put down her paper and raised her eyebrows at Mum. 'So rude. You can't ask someone about their bank balance!'

'I wouldn't dream of asking Matthew about his bank balance!' said Mum. 'I care about him, that's all, and I want to check he's not going to end up in trouble and lose property. It happens you know. Shares go down as well as up.' She sounded both defensive and dispirited.

'You can ask anything you like, Nell,' said Matthew, smiling fondly. 'And thank you for caring. But you don't need to worry about me. Financially, anyway.'

Smug twat.

'Oh Matthew.' Mum tearfully patted his arm. 'You've come so far – your degrees, the business and now . . . sidelines too!'

'Yes,' agreed Dad. 'Remarkable achievements.'

'All on your own, too, Matthew,' said Mum. 'No handouts.' She looked meaningfully at me. Little bit hypocritical seeing as Mum got a lot of handouts from her family.

'Humbling,' said Dad. 'Reminds me of Oprah. You know

she grew up wearing potato sacks? And look at her now. That's perseverance. Something you've got, Matthew.'

'Yes. It's the work ethic. I wish you'd take a leaf out of his book, Alice,' said Mum.

Classic smooth transition on my parents' part: every commendation for Matthew Lloyd is a vehicle for finding fault with me. I should have seen this coming.

'What's that supposed to mean?' I asked, handing Dad my empty plate. 'I've always been a really hard worker!'

Astrid and Arrie and Mum all scoffed.

'How's that funny? I *do* work hard. I'm a self-starter. And I get stuff done. Everyone knows it. In fact, people have said, if a job needs doing, then Alice is the person to ask.'

Everyone seemed to find this hilarious, even Roger and Aziz, which was pretty insulting.

'Wow,' said Astrid. 'Which people?'

Well, technically me. On my CV. But this wasn't the time to get technical. 'I pull my weight,' I said breezily, casually getting out a tea towel from the drawer to help Dad dry, and to illustrate my point.

They all stared at me for a moment. Matthew folded his arms and leant back against the Aga like he was watching a show. I didn't know why everyone was making a fuss about my top – Matthew's looked pretty tight around the shoulders and chest to me – if he wasn't trying to get people to notice the fact he's all buff, then my name's not Alice Carver.

Gosh. It was a big tea towel. I quite struggled with it to be honest. Especially with Matthew watching me like that.

'Is anyone going to tell her it's a tablecloth?' said Astrid.

I knew there was something wrong with this tea towel.

'No,' said Matthew.

That arsehat actually enjoys watching me suffer. 'Some of us just see cloths,' I said loftily. 'We don't need to categorise them. I think this says more about your need to put labels on things. I'm sure Aziz, in his esteemed capacity, would agree?'

'No,' said Astrid firmly. 'It's a marker of just how infrequently you've ever dried up. You don't need to be a psychologist to know that.'

'There you go again: labelling. Poor Aziz is more than a psychologist. You're very reductionist, Astrid.' I could tell the family were impressed by my wise words.

'And you're a pain,' said Astrid. 'Tell her, Aziz.'

'Aziz?' I turned to my brother-in-law.

'Did someone say something about presents . . . ?' said Aziz.

'Ooh!' I put down the tablecloth. 'Good point, Aziz.' I was quite excited about the present I'd hoped Mum and Dad had got me.

Matthew checked his watch. 'I'm going to take off.'

I tried not to roll my eyes whilst everyone demurred and begged Matthew to stay, and instead distracted myself by having another quick check through Charlotte's posts. (Well actually, not everyone was persuading Matthew to stay. I noticed Roger was pretty silent too – apart from piping up, 'I'm sure the man has business to attend to what with his hotel hobby, haha,' and then laughing just a little too hard.)

Once Matthew had promised he'd return tomorrow (joy of joys) he was finally allowed to say goodbyes. I was nearly heaving a sigh of relief when he paused by me and whispered so no one else could hear (he's always been good at that – making out like he's nice when he's not), 'Tasteful top, Alice. Although quick heads-up: we wouldn't let you in at the Lamb looking like that. I'm sure you understand. Standards.' Then he said at normal volume, 'Bye, Alice,' gave my shoulder a squeeze and made his way to the kitchen door.

'Yeah, piss off,' I called after him.

'Alice!' Dad exclaimed.

'You didn't hear what he said!'

'We all heard him,' said Mum, shaking her head. 'He said goodbye. Sorry for Alice, Matthew.'

'Don't worry, Nell,' said smug Matthew. 'Merry Christmas, everyone!' he called as he left. 'Especially you, Alice!'

'Bye, love,' called Mum after him, as the door closed with a whoosh of cold air. 'He is a darling. Despite your rudeness, Alice.'

She held up my abandoned tablecloth and tutted. 'Dear lord. And to think of all those fees we spent on St Hilda's.'

'Well, at least I was trying to help,' I countered. 'Matthew never helps anyone except himself. To hotels.'

'Alice,' Mum sighed, 'do you realise that Matthew spent an entire day in A&E with your father a couple of months ago when his back went again? Drove him there, insisted on staying for the blood tests and then said he may as well wait, and drove him home. Eight hours later. That's help, Alice.'

'Well, it was probably nice for him to sit around a bit and drink tea with Dad,' I said, giving Dad a squeeze. 'I wish I'd got to be there with you.'

'You haven't tried the tea there.' Dad shuddered slightly. 'It comes out of an urn.'

'I'd have stopped at Starbucks on the way.'

'You didn't visit me in hospital once when I was stuck in after the twins, Alice,' said Arrie.

'That's different. I was at Glastonbury and Dolly Parton was playing. You wouldn't have wanted me to miss *that*!'

'Matthew missed collecting an award in person,' said Mum, 'just to keep your father company. We only found out afterwards. That's how thoughtful he is. He put your father's needs first.'

I rolled my eyes. 'Dad's a grown man. He'd have been fine on his own.'

'Fine on his own?!' Mum threw her hands up in despair. 'Who would have caught him when he fainted?'

'What?'

'Alice has forgotten her own father has a blood phobia. Thank goodness Matthew cares enough to remember!'

'Did he really have to catch you, Dad?'

'Yes, darling,' Dad told me. 'I've got to say, he's remarkably strong, Matthew. Gosh the muscles.'

'And so handsome—'

'Can I open *everything* under the tree?' shouted Ernie from the sitting room, saving me from this rabbit warren I'd fallen into, where every tunnel led back to a Matthew Lloyd love-fest.

Arrie and Roger exchanged a wide-eyed look. 'No! Don't open anything yet!'

'Oh.' Ernie was quiet for a moment, before yelling, 'Can I have some wrapping paper then? And tape?'

'I'll go.' Roger wearily downed the dregs of his coffee, and reluctantly began heaving himself more upright on the sofa. The problem with the sofa in the kitchen is that it sort of welcomes you to the extent where you can't leave – a bit like Mum and Dad with Matthew. It's so old and soft that you have to get physical purchase to exit. Unless you're some kind of squatting abdominal powerhouse. Roger's forehead developed more of a sheen. Arrie watched his efforts to free himself, her elbow on the table, chin resting on hand, face impassive.

'We'll all go through and join the boys – of course they're excited,' said Mum, reaching out a hand to help her eldest son-in-law. 'Come on, Roger. Give it some welly.'

'They've been excited since flipping September,' said Roger, finally making it off the sofa.

'Up since five.' Arrie sighed. 'Five.'

'So of course you were too, darling,' murmured Dad sympathetically.

'Please no one mention dawn's crack,' I grumbled under my breath, 'or I'm going back to bed.'

Astrid snorted, and got off the sofa with ease. Bloody show-off. I could see Roger was thinking the same thing.

'Come on, Alice,' she said, linking arms with me. 'I think someone else needs her Christmas to start too. Maybe a present and a little glass of something cold and fizzy . . . ?'

'It *might* help,' I agreed.

'Dad?' said Astrid. 'Can Aziz open a bottle of your finest? Alice here needs some Christmas champagne.'

That's the thing about Astrid – she's annoying and cross and mean so much of the time, but when she's nice, she totally gets it right.

I hadn't even set foot in the sitting room since I got back

because of the rush for the wedding yesterday, but it looked just like it always did every year – decorated Mum-style.

'Gosh.' I eyed the slightly wonky pine tree which was lush and bushy at the top and pretty sad and threadbare lower down. 'So you've gone top-heavy this year?'

'Matches you,' said Astrid, but as she handed me a glass of champagne at the same time, I let it go.

'Isn't it glorious?' said Mum proudly.

'That's one way of describing it,' Aziz answered politely. Goodness, he's good at navigating my family.

'And I got thirty per cent off. That's why you wait until Christmas Eve!'

'That's why *you* wait until Christmas Eve,' mumbled Arrie. She looked nostalgic. She was probably thinking of her own Christmas tree at home which would not have been discounted and would be decorated perfectly.

'Alice – you'll want a selfie with the tree, won't you,' continued Mum, 'for all your posting things.'

'Hmm,' I said thoughtfully.

I looked at the tree again. I don't know how Mum managed to arrange the lights quite so haphazardly that they ended up either bunched together or entirely absent. And it wasn't just the usual mismatch of colours and ornaments this year . . .

'What's happened to the decorations?' I asked.

'We think they may have been sat on,' said Mum. 'And sadly a couple of them have been affected by the black mould.'

'More than a couple,' said Arrie.

'Don't you like the tree, girls?' Mum sounded huffy. She took a similar stance to decorating as she did to gift giving. 'Why aren't you taking a photo, Alice?' She rounded on me, her eyes narrowing. 'You've got the glass of champers and the tree – what else do you need?'

Goodness, she's aggressive. It's probably because she's pedigree, like Maud. 'I might save the selfie in front of the tree until I've done my hair and stuff,' I told her.

'Great plan, Alice,' said Aziz smoothly. 'I can help you later. Let me top you up, Nell. And we can toast your tree-decorating.'

'Thank you, Aziz.' Mum graciously held out her glass, disarmed.

See. That's why I love Aziz.

'Please!' Ernie tugged at Arrie's top, sort of patting her on the boob, whilst we were all cheersing Mum. 'Please can we just open the presents?'

He had a trail of snot running from his left nostril down to his lip, his cheeks were scarlet, he looked dangerously close to bursting a blood vessel, and he was frankly quite gross, but you know, at that moment, I felt for him: the kid wanted his presents. So did I. When we were little, Mum had this whole thing about waiting until after lunch and I'd get crucified if I snuck in and opened one.

Arrie stood absolutely still and glared at him. So like Mum. No wonder she's a dog trainer. Eventually, Ernie got the message and took his hands off her, and stood there waiting, his bottom lip wobbling.

'One,' she assented at last.

'One more you mean,' said Roger wryly.

'But!' warned Arrie. 'You have to hand out one for everyone first.'

Ernie whooped and sprinted to the tree, shouting at Edwin

to help and within five seconds all the adults were holding a present and there was the sound of frantic ripping of paper from the twins.

I looked down at the package in my left hand. It was wrapped in brown paper – standard Mum-fare – and shaped promisingly. A5. I tested it. It felt the right weight. Yes. I set down my champagne flute on the oak sideboard and tested the parcel in two hands. I think it was what I asked for. The problem is you never knew with Mum. She set that limit at £50 which meant she may have bought me some knock-off version.

'Mum,' I said, 'Mum – is this what I think it is?'

'I said £50,' Mum reproved. 'And even you can count that high.'

'Great.' I began unwrapping it, ready for disappointment. It's what Mum specialises in.

It was face down when I first saw it, and yellow pleather, so I assumed it was just a cheap imitation of what I wanted. Then I turned it over and saw the words *The Guide: A Manifesting Journal*™ on the front; I got a little kick. Sure, Mum had obviously checked the price list and decided I didn't get the pink moleskin like Radhi Devlukia-Shetty. But she'd still spent £69. Progress. And, I mean, essentially it was the same thing, just a different cover.

Quite a tasteless cover. Amy Hart from *Love Island* also has it in the yellow pleather.

'Well?' prompted Mum. 'Don't you like it?'

'No, no, I do! Thanks, Mum.'

I took a sip of champagne.

'Careful!' she said. 'You're spilling champagne on that immorally expensive notebook.'

I took another swig of champagne and hastily wiped the cover with my sleeve. Came right off. I guess there are some advantages to pleather.

*It's time to begin the next stage of your journey: manifesting everything you want. And if you follow **The Guide**™, that's as easy as 1, 2, 3 . . .*

1. *Open yourself to the Universe*
2. *Believe*
3. *Use The Guide's tried and trusted journal format and enjoy extra Guide Posts™ to help you along your way*

Guide Post™

Both journey and journaling have identical roots stemming from the French word 'journee', meaning daily: remember that completing this journal daily is your transport towards the future life you want and deserve. So write in it as much and often as you can – your future is your priority!

My thoughts and reflections:

I'm in the 'other spare room' and if anything, it's even worse than I remembered. Not only does it smell of damp but there's some sort of acrid, pungent other odour too, almost like ammonia. Mum says she can't smell a thing but still came in and sprayed Febreze everywhere. Well, actually she sprayed oven cleaner everywhere 'because of the poor labelling and design', not because she's pissed, of course. She's quite a defensive drunk. The small side window won't open. Dad says it's because of the damp and the wood has swollen and stuck. Fabulous. Plus, I can't move without banging against all the paint pots, Astrid's old canoe, the rocking chair – in fact half the contents of our old house that won't fit in the new house – and now, in addition, the massive and extremely hard Peloton bike that I told Dad, correctly, he wouldn't want past January last year. The freezer whirs constantly and the camp bed creaks and I can feel the springs.

So here I am, getting bruises and breathing problems whilst the rest of the family and their husbands and offspring and pets lord it up in the nicer rooms. Basically I'm Harry Potter. The most annoying part is, I know if I had a better-paid job or my own flat, or a husband, I'd probably be in my own bed and the twins would be in here. Literally the minute Arrie got engaged to Roger, she never had to sit on the stool for meals. Ever. And Astrid and Aziz get the soft, matching Harrods towels if they stay over, and the unchipped mugs. It's so unfair that they move to 'guest' status just by being married.

Well, things are about to change.

I've spent the last twenty minutes or so watching Tammy from Wisconsin, who has a massive 2.5 million followers on TikTok, and although I originally mostly wanted this journal for the photos, I am increasingly inspired by this whole manifesting thing. Tammy manifested herself nice fingernails – you should see the transformation from those fungally little stumps she used to have – *and* a new car, which is unbelievable, but she swears it's true and she's been on the *Morning Show* and they fact-check everything, just by using the 3-6-9 method.

The more I research manifesting, the more I'm wondering why everyone isn't at it. You literally ask for stuff and you get it. I'm almost scared to start in case I'm the only one it doesn't work for, but Tammy from Wisconsin says that's just self-blocking. She was told by one nail technologist that she would never, ever have nice natural nails because the fungus was in the nail beds, and Tammy hit a proper low after that. Apparently she felt like ending it all. Then a friend who'd manifested her cheating husband's death (sounds like a basic case of murder to me) told her about the 3-6-9 method and Tammy's never looked back.

So I'm manifesting and I'm manifesting big.

But first of all I'm going to start small, with my social media output. I may as well be an influencer. Okay, it didn't go great the other night with that viral video – I deleted it before anyone

68

could twig it was me, let alone follow me – but I've learnt my lesson: don't freestyle. And choose good lighting. And don't be drunk. Charlotte clearly spends ages curating her videos. It's not like 10k followers is that many, but apparently she gets free juice cards from her GlowCycle gym on the back of that, plus she snared Guy Carmichael.

But I could do with a break already.

Because TikTok is flooded with people opening things left, right and centre and the biggest trend of all? Christmas morning (they're all in pyjamas) unboxing of *The Guide*. Why hadn't I got Aziz to film me when I opened mine earlier? That would have showed Charlotte.

I am letting go of:

- Those pictures of Tammy's nails. Well, I'm trying to.
- That viral video of mine – it's gone.

Guide Post™

Is it an obstacle?
Or is it an opportunity?

Look beyond the obvious and you'll soon see
the Universe is giving you an opening . . .

Date: Monday 26 December   **Time: 12.15am**

My thoughts and reflections:

Just realised I can turn an obstacle into an opportunity! Will get Aziz to film me *tomorrow* unboxing my journal! This means I can actually make the video way better – do hair, make-up, borrow nice pyjamas, etc. – and wrap the journal nicely (unlike Mum's economical efforts). Plus, I've now had the advantage of seeing which unboxing clips are the most popular (the ones with the super-attractive backgrounds / settings, and where they say, 'Oh my god – it works – I manifested *The Guide*!' #manifest #guidedmanifestation #dreamlife) which means I have a better chance of social media success.

My intention is:

- To get up super early – have set alarm for 7.30 – and enlist Aziz's help. Need to get it done before ML arrives.

My thoughts and reflections:

It's really quite marvellous how once you start seeing obstacles as opportunities, doors start opening. Literally. I just heard a scratching and mewing at the door and it pushed open and in came Mitzy. Mitzy's rarely shown me any affection, in fact normally she leaves a room if I'm there, but tonight she came straight in and started winding round my legs. She would never have come into my *actual* bedroom. She spent ages sniffing near the pipes and clawing the rug and now she's purring contentedly on the bottom of the camp bed, an embodiment of positive energy, and I'm starting to think the Universe is sending me a message. Mitzy may be old, way older than me if you calculate in cat years, but she's not worrying about how she looks or the fact she's single and the vet trashed her ovaries. Mitzy is a whole, confident cat who knows that she is enough as she is. I saw a clip from Oprah about how we can learn from the animal world, and tap into the animal within ourselves, and for the first time, I really get what that means.

I feel at one with Mitzy, my wonderful family and (even though I'm in the garage) my home – The Cotswolds – where I was born and raised.

I am grateful for:

Mitzy for teaching me. Here she is, purring, turning around occasionally and pawing the duvet, trusting in the Universe.

My thoughts and reflections:

If Mum knew that Mitzy was incontinent, you think she'd have mentioned it. And if she usually keeps the litter tray in the garage, you think she'd have mentioned that! And if Mitzy clawing and turning round was such a bloody obvious sign of imminent shitting, you'd think Mum could have maybe, just maybe told me.

I can't believe I'm stuck here, in a room where the only window is painted shut, and which now smells of cat shit. It's hardly Cotswolds living.

Also I'm worried about this 3-6-9 manifestation thing as not sure how it works, and how quickly you can trigger it. Tammy on TikTok says you just have to repeat out loud what you're manifesting – and I'm pretty sure I whispered to myself that I should be more like Mitzy a number of times. To be clear, I really don't want to manifest incontinence like Mitzy the cat. At all.

In one word:

Stinks

My thoughts and reflections:

Today did not start well.

Or end well.

I was woken up by the sound of Ernie bellowing, 'Mummy! Daddy! It's gone everywhere!' and then had to listen to Arrie and Roger arguing outside the downstairs loo about which of them should have to go in there and help Ernie, and whose fault it was that he'd had two helpings of trifle last night when they are both fully aware of his intolerance to dairy.

Arrie won. Predictably.

Anyway, no one wants to be woken up that way – it was disgusting and brought back memories of what happened last night. Then, when I tried to go back to sleep, Mitzy had the brazen cheek to start clawing at the door and mewing to be let in. No way was I falling for that.

I put the pillow over my head and tried not to think about my nephew in the loo, and to block out the muffled sounds of scratching from Mitzy, and the shouting and banging doors from my ridiculously noisy family; it was quite calming to inhale the scent of laundry detergent instead, and I must have drifted off again because when I went to check my phone, which had fallen under the bed, I found it was already 10am

– I'd completely slept through my alarm. So I bounded out of bed, keen to find Aziz and see if he'd help me with my unboxing video before Matthew Lloyd arrived; in my enthusiasm I bashed my arm against that doltish bike, which bloody hurt. As I was checking to see if it was bleeding, I heard more shouting and the front door slam. The voices faded. Then it was oddly silent.

I opened the door into the hallway and listened for a moment. 'Hello?' I called. Nothing. I poked my head into the dining room but it was empty, so I ran straight upstairs and no one was there either. I borrowed Arrie's dressing gown, and picked up her neatly folded White Company pyjamas – perfect – and headed down to the empty kitchen where I found a half pot of coffee steaming away invitingly. Things were looking up. All I needed was confirmation Matthew Lloyd wasn't going to turn up unexpectedly, and I could get on with my video and start my new life as a successful influencer, like Charlotte. I poured myself a mug of coffee and wandered through to the sitting room, where Aziz was standing staring out the bay window, his shoulders slightly hunched, hands in his pockets.

'Hey,' I said cheerfully.

He turned round and his brow unfurrowed when he saw it was me.

'What you looking at?' I asked, joining him at the window, unable to see what could possibly have been of such interest to him in our front garden, which really isn't all that unless the foxes have managed to tip the bin over.

'Nothing much,' said Aziz. 'Just . . . thinking.'

He didn't say anything else, or even smile, which isn't like him, so after a while I jostled his elbow to check he was okay, and then he did give me a jostle back.

'Where is everyone?' I asked.

'Gone for a walk.'

'Everyone?'

'Yep,' said Aziz.

'What about Matthew?'

'He arrived just as they were leaving, so he's gone with them.'

Well, things *were* looking up.

'Why haven't you gone?' I asked.

'Not in the mood,' said Aziz, walking off. 'I thought I'd catch up on some work. Might even go back to London.'

'No! Don't go back to London. You can't work on Boxing Day!' I said, following him back through to the kitchen. 'No one works on Boxing Day.'

'Not true, Alice,' said Aziz, going to pour himself the last of the coffee. 'Plenty of people have to work over Christmas.'

'Like who?' I asked, perching on the arm of the sofa.

'People who work in hotels, the fire service, vicars, nurses, doctors . . . I'm pretty sure the Co-op's open today.'

'Well, only proper doctors. No one's going to need therapy at this time of year.'

Aziz shook his head at me.

Hmm. Maybe I spoke before I thought there. On a couple of counts. 'Okay,' I conceded. 'You have a point. But I thought you said yesterday that you took this week off? Why would you head back to London already? Won't Astrid be pissed off?'

Aziz took a sip of his coffee, making his glasses steam up. 'I need some decent coffee.'

'You've never left on Boxing Day before!' I didn't want Aziz to go. Christmases have been better since he's been in the family.

'Yeah, maybe you're right. It was just a thought.'

'A terrible thought! What would we even do without you?'

We'd have a disgusting supper, that's what. Mum and Dad used to always give us 'cold cuts' but now, Aziz makes us a Boxing Day pie every year, which is pretty close to perfection.

'You're thinking about pie, aren't you?' said Aziz.

'A bit,' I admitted. 'But I'd miss you as well as the pie.'

Aziz smiled properly this time, and I clinked coffee mugs with him.

'So you'll stay?'

'Sure,' he said, settling back into the devouring sofa.

'Good. Make yourself comfortable.' I caught sight of the clock, and paused on my way to the sink. On second thought . . . 'Maybe not too comfortable, though . . .'

'Why?' said Aziz suspiciously.

'Nothing really. Just seeing as you and I are on our own and there's no Matthew Lloyd or Astrid or Arrie to be judge-y and you need a distraction from work, I thought we could hang out together . . . ?'

*

Aziz pushed the bridge of his glasses back up and sighed before speaking. 'You've used half a roll of paper opening and re-wrapping that journal and I've taken numerous videos of you pretending to be surprised by it. You don't like any of them. There's nothing I can do differently with you or this room. I'm done, Alice.'

I looked around the sitting room and felt a sense of panic. The reason I didn't like any of the videos was because of the state of the sitting room. The lighting was awful, as was that ridiculous tree. Plus, whilst I loved our ancient shabby furniture, on camera it looked more junk store than cosy chic; in the sitting room at the old house it had worked but here it looked cramped and haphazard. I was never going to get the kind of luxe vibe I needed in here. I needed somewhere like the library in the Lamb. Bloody Matthew Lloyd. How had he ended up with his own hotel? A video shot there would be perfect—

'Oh my goodness, Aziz, you're right!' I said, mentally thanking *The Guide* for that advice last night: *Every obstacle is a potential opportunity.* 'We need to go to the Lamb and film it there!'

'We do?' said Aziz. 'Are they going to let you in there wearing pyjamas?'

'I'll wear a long coat and no one will notice the pyjamas. But we need to go right now.' I reckoned I had less than an hour before they'd get back from that walk. There was no way I wanted to come across Matthew Lloyd whilst I was borrowing his hotel.

'Alice, I think I'm going to say no to this. I've had enough "hanging out".'

'Come on,' I cajoled. 'Look, I'll buy you a coffee there. A proper one.'

'I could really use an espresso,' deliberated Aziz. 'But not enough to do videos again.'

'Please. Just one . . . ?'

Aziz sighed. 'One video. No re-shoots. No re-wrapping. And a double espresso.'

'Done.'

*

We walked briskly along the street towards the Lamb, passing the huddle of honeyed stone houses that run up the rise of the hill, each one individual yet leaning comfortably together as if they had secrets to impart to one another. Leaded glass panes within the stone framed the twinkling lights of Christmas trees, decorated much more tastefully than Mum's, holly wreaths adorned doors painted in varying shades of Farrow & Ball muted neutrals, and, every now and again, a chimney ghosted up wisps of smoke into the grey skies to vanish there.

And I realised that however dead and dull Little Minchcombe may have seemed when I was growing up here, desperate for the excitement of city life, in terms of Instagrammable residential fantasy, it was pretty peerless.

Just before the Lamb, we passed our old house and I couldn't help but pause there for a moment. The recently departed previous owners had painted the door navy blue, which is just wrong for the stone, but they were philistines and they also put those white sheer blinds in all the windows, and there are a lot of those, so you can't look in now, plus they let the hedges at the front get really high, which means you can't see the whole of the house or the apple trees down the east side that were planted when Mum was a child. But it still made my heart beat faster. It was still my house. Our house. I used to have a swing in the middle apple tree.

'Alice?' interrupted Aziz. 'I could really use that coffee . . .'

'Sorry, Aziz. It just seems so sad that after all that time, our house is no longer in the family. What do you think?'

'I think,' said Aziz carefully, 'that perhaps you don't want my views on Britain's landed gentry. But I do get that you miss that house. Who wouldn't?'

*

The library was even more TikTok-able than I'd remembered: the fire was crackling merrily in the grate; articulate lighting highlighted beams and showcased the contents of gleaming oak bookcases; the golds and greens and reds of plumped cushions and deep sofas were a muted palate of taste and comfort amid the natural stone. It was almost like our sitting room in the old house, but even better. I sighed with pleasure. Surely anyone would aspire to receiving *The Guide* in a room like this.

I'd just got myself set up in the best position and was about to take my coat off, when a really attractive woman strode into the room. Oh great. It was Rachel from the other day. The one Matthew embarrassed me in front of. I pulled my coat around me more tightly.

'Hello,' she said warmly, adjusting a cushion which didn't need adjusting, and changing the whole ambience with her proprietary presence. 'Welcome to the Lamb.'

She was wearing a polo under her blazer and I was pretty sure it was Miu Miu.

'Would you like me to take your coat for you?' she said, leaning towards me.

It *was* Miu Miu. Matthew must be paying her seriously well.

'Er no, thanks,' I said. 'Can we just have coffees – a double espresso and a flat white?'

I saw a look of recognition cross her face and a small smile, which she quickly corrected.

'Someone will bring them through shortly,' she said. 'Please make yourselves at home.'

As soon as the library door had shut behind her I turned to Aziz. 'Do you think she's sleeping with Matthew?'

'What?' said Aziz.

'The model hotel woman with the expensive polo shirt.'

'She's his usual type, I suppose. But he's her boss. So I'd guess . . . no. Why?'

'I just feel she's a bit above her station.'

'How?'

'All that "make yourself at home" and plumping cushions.'

'Isn't that hospitality?' said Aziz, looking confused. Then he looked at me properly which is never a good sign. 'Is there something you want to talk about, Alice?'

'I mean yes, Aziz. There's loads I want to talk to you about – my life has gone to shit – but Astrid said she'll charge me.'

'Alice,' said Aziz gently. 'I can't be your therapist. Nothing to do with money and I'm sure Astrid didn't say that—'

'She did actually.'

'But you can talk to me as your brother-in-law if something is bothering you.'

My eyes flicked up to the carriage clock on one of the bookshelves. Time was running out.

We got the video filmed just before a man with floppy hair arrived with coffees, and although I hadn't managed to get my coat back on, apart from a slightly curious stare, he didn't comment on my attire. Aziz cheered up as soon as he'd downed his double espresso, which was helpful, because by now it was nearly midday, and I was keen to get home and changed before seeing the family. And Matthew bloody Lloyd.

'We'd better get back,' I said. 'Before they all do.'

'Okay.' Aziz reluctantly surrendered his seat on the wing-back armchair. 'Let's go. Don't forget you're paying.'

We made our way out of the library and along the generous flagstoned corridor to the spacious reception with its island desk and kidney-shaped velvet sofas that I think are from Heals, and obscenely large bunches of flowers. Gosh, it was gorgeous in here. I could happily spend all day just sitting in here.

'Can I settle our bill?' I asked the 'the woman behind the desk.

'Certainly,' she said, turning the screen to face me.

Bloody hell – £12 for two coffees? No wonder Matthew Lloyd was so rich.

'Aziz . . . ' I began.

'Seriously, Alice,' he said. 'You're buying.'

'I know! Absolutely. But can you lend me a tenner? And don't tell Astrid?'

*

We'd just made it out the front of the hotel and a few metres down the street towards our old house when I sensed danger.

I looked over and there were Astrid and Matthew, walking towards us on the opposite side of the street.

'Shit,' I said under my breath, as they also registered us. 'Just act normal, Aziz.'

'Er, yes. Why wouldn't I?' said Aziz, giving me a confused look.

'Hey, Aziz,' called Matthew, crossing over to us. 'Sorry for stealing your wife all morning.'

'Hey – fine by me,' said Aziz. 'Gave me a chance to help Alice—'

I elbowed him before he could continue.

'Ow,' said Aziz, looking at me indignantly.

'Gave us a chance to go for our own walk,' I said. 'Where's everyone else?'

'They went home to make a start on lunch and feed the cat. Anyway, why do you need help walking?' asked Astrid, frowning. She turned to Aziz. 'And if you wanted a walk then why didn't you come with us? Like I asked you to?' She didn't look happy with him.

'Oh it was a really short walk,' I said quickly.

'Where to?'

'Here.'

'That's not a walk!' said Astrid. 'It's five minutes from home.'

'Granny used to call it a walk.'

'Yeah, she only had one leg and thirty per cent lung capacity. What have you *actually* been doing?'

'Nothing!' I said.

'She's probably been in my hotel,' said Matthew. 'Is that what it is, Alice? Can't keep away?'

How could one person be this annoying?

'Of course I haven't been in your hotel. It's not my kind of thing if I'm honest.'

'That's news,' said Aziz, giving me a sharp elbow back. I was pretty sure therapists weren't allowed to shove people, but now wasn't the time to discuss that with Aziz.

'I thought you said you'd been desperate to go to the Lamb for ages,' said Astrid. 'You said everyone at work was talking about it.'

'Really?' Matthew looked revoltingly pleased with himself. 'No.'

'Yes,' continued Astrid. 'You even sent me a screenshot of the text from that work colleague of yours – you know the one who's mean about everyone and always has his ankles showing – telling you to get some photos?'

'Drunk Stephen was just letting me know about the art – that was all. We often share art tips.'

'Are you interested in art?' said Aziz, appearing baffled.

'Absolutely.'

'Since when?' said Astrid.

'Oh I don't know.' I really didn't know.

'So who's your favourite artist?' pushed Astrid.

I could see Matthew smirking. Cock.

'How do I choose just one?'

'So hard,' agreed Matthew. 'Maybe give us your top ten?'

Total cock. I had to think quickly. Then I remembered that ad from the tube about the exhibition at the Tate. 'I guess if I had to pick one . . .' I said.

'You don't,' said Matthew.

'If I had to settle on just one,' I continued, 'it would be Yayoi Kusama. He's super.'

'*She* really is,' said Matthew. 'And what a stroke of luck. I was just about to show Astrid round. Why don't you guys come too? Alice can spot the Kusama in my art collection – I'm sure she'll recognise it instantly. You can take a selfie with it, Alice.'

'No, thanks,' I said. 'I think I saw everything at the wedding. Great little venue, Matthew, but I'm not really into vanity projects.'

Just then the man with the floppy hair who served us coffee earlier came running out the hotel towards us.

'Oh, hi Matthew!' He put one hand to his hair to smooth it down, and blushed.

Typical Matthew. I bet he only hired people who fancied him deliberately.

'Problem, Tom?' said Matthew.

'No, it's just, the lady left this behind,' he said, slightly out of breath. Then he turned to me, 'You know, when you were videoing yourself in the library?' and held out my journal.

My yellow pleather *Guide*.

You've got to be shitting me.

How explicit do I have to be when I ask the Universe to help me out?

Matthew looked at me with glee in his eyes, before turning to Floppy Hair.

'Oh no, Tom. You must be mistaken. Can't have been Alice here. She hates the Lamb. And vanity projects.'

'No, Matthew, honestly,' said Floppy Hair, looking nervous. 'It was this lady. We don't have anyone else in pyjamas.'

Astrid laughed.

'Thanks, Tom.' Matthew reached out and took my journal from him. 'Good job.'

Floppy Hair tried not to look too pleased at the compliment as he went back in.

'I'll take that, thanks,' I said, holding out my hand.

'Oh, so it *is* yours?' said Matthew.

Shit.

Matthew angled himself slightly further away and scrutinised the front cover. '*The Guide* . . . why have I heard of that?'

'Because it's literally everywhere,' said Astrid.

'Not *everywhere* actually,' I said. 'It's very much for those in the know.'

'Yeah, that's not true,' said Astrid.

'*A Journal for Manifesting* . . . ' Matthew looked up with undisguised delight.

'What's manifesting?' asked Aziz.

'How do you not know?' said Astrid crossly. 'You're so out of touch.'

'As far as I can tell,' said Matthew, 'it's for crazy people who believe they can magic up whatever they want.'

'I'm not crazy!'

'You are wearing pyjamas outside,' said Astrid.

'I've got a coat on!'

'Have you written in it, Alice?' said Matthew.

'Of course she hasn't,' scoffed Astrid. 'She'll be using it as a prop. Even if she is stupid enough to borrow Arrie's white pyjamas and wear them outside – Arrie will kill you by the way – Alice is not stupid enough to believe in manifesting.'

'She's probably not.' Matthew stared at me for a moment. Then he smiled, and went to open my journal.

'No!' I screeched, shoving Astrid out the way and grabbing it back. 'That is private.'

'Amazing,' said Matthew. 'You *have* written in it.'

'Yes, I've written in it. And manifesting is not stupid.'

'God, Alice,' said Astrid. 'You're not really saying you believe in manifesting, are you?'

'Again, what is manifesting?' said Aziz.

'You ask for stuff you want and then you get it,' said Astrid.

'Gosh,' said Matthew. 'How marvellously simple.'

Condescending prick. 'Actually, manifesting is really quite complex,' I said. 'You ask for what you want and only get it if you believe you're going to get it.'

Matthew sniggered.

'So sorry,' said Astrid acerbically. 'Of course the believing would make all the difference.'

'To be fair,' interjected Aziz, 'it may well do.'

Hmm. Unlike Aziz to disagree with Astrid.

'Oh come on,' said Astrid. 'Are you saying, in your professional opinion, that if you believe in manifesting, it will work?'

'No, Astrid,' said Aziz. 'I'm saying it could make a difference to the outcomes.'

'Ha!' I turned to Matthew and Astrid. 'You heard the doctor. Manifesting works. He believes. I believe.'

'Not quite what I said,' said Aziz.

'Interesting,' said Matthew. 'Do you remember Lee Parker from primary school? Used to believe he was a dog? Insisted on eating out of a bowl on the floor? I assume, by that principle, Alice, Lee Parker now is a dog?'

Astrid laughed. 'I think he's actually a plumber.'

'It's easy to mock things that make you uncomfortable, Matthew,' I said, looking at his infuriatingly grinning face and Astrid laughing, and even Aziz smiling, and feeling like

I did when I was fifteen – like the butt of the joke – that familiar sting behind it, of being judged and found wanting. Always Matthew Lloyd. Why was I still letting him get away with it? 'Obviously you have a problem with thinking in new ways, and that's your prerogative, but we're not all stuck in the past.'

'I'm open-minded,' said Matthew mildly. 'And what do you mean, stuck in the past?'

'Well, you're mentioning people from primary school, and you've bought the hotel in the village you grew up in. Still coming round to ours on Boxing Day. It's not exactly branching out, is it? Moving on?'

Matthew surveyed me and then nodded slowly.

'What is your problem with Matthew, Alice?' said Astrid. 'Is this because Mum and Dad suggested you ask him if he could find you a proper job when you lose yours?'

'I'm not *definitely* losing my job and it *is* proper!' I snapped. 'You people don't understand creativity! And I'm not the one with the problem! Matthew is.'

'I do have a problem with stuff like that journal,' said Matthew. 'I don't like exploitation.'

'How is *The Guide* exploitative?'

'How much did it cost?' Matthew asked.

'I don't know.' Obviously I did. 'It was a gift.' If I'd hoped that would put him in his place, I was sorely mistaken.

'Well, it's just a notebook essentially – they likely have a ninety per cent plus profit margin on this. I saw that trademark on the front. Bet it's littered with them. Somebody is making a lot of money out of vulnerable people like you.'

'Says the man who charges £6 per coffee in his pretentious

hotel. Which is a sideline. And what do you mean vulnerable? I'm not vulnerable.'

'Okay,' said Matthew. 'Fine. You're not vulnerable. But you have spent a load of money on a promise. Only certain people are going to be open to buying magic beans, right? You don't see me or Astrid or Aziz "manifesting" relationships or jobs, do you?'

'No, genius, because you've already got them – *you* don't need to.'

Matthew raised his eyebrow slightly. 'Indeed. But perhaps vulnerable people *might* need them, or feel that they do. And luckily, *The Guide* can help! Does sound a bit like magic beans?'

Tosser.

Aziz winced like he was feeling sorry for me.

'It's not magic beans,' I said. 'Manifesting. It works actually.'

'If you say so.' Matthew smiled smugly. 'Whatever you feel the need to believe in for you, Alice.'

I would give anything, anything to wipe that smile off his face.

'I feel for you,' I said. 'That you find it hard to open your mind.'

'I *am* open minded,' said Matthew. 'I just know you're wrong.'

'And what if I'm right?'

'Then I'd be delighted.'

Liar. He can't lose at Scrabble. He can't lose at anything.

'Tell you what,' Matthew said. 'How about you prove it to me?'

'Fine. I will. And you'll have to admit you're wrong.'

'No, Alice,' said Astrid, sighing. 'You'll have to admit he's right. You can't manifest things. It's nonsense.'

'Yes, you can.'

'Okay,' said Matthew, 'so manifest a car.'

Jesus. I was thinking of something less concrete. 'I can't do that.'

'Thought not,' said Matthew. 'Bit too real, isn't it? And expensive. Because you can't manifest.'

'I could. But I'd have to want to. I don't want a car.'

'How about our old house then,' said Astrid. 'We all know how much you want that. And it's for sale.'

FFS. Why would Astrid do that to me? Doesn't she take down enough people in court? I look at them all, open-mouthed. Then I look at the house. Of course I want it. I can imagine myself in the kitchen right now, standing at the sink and looking out on the lawns at the back. I can imagine wandering into the huge sitting room with its triple aspect windows, a fire in the enormous grate, a splendid tree stretching up to the ceiling.

Matthew bit his lip. 'Let's just leave this argument now, shall we?'

'Yes,' said Astrid. 'I'm cold and I want a coffee. Give it up, Alice. You know you're losing this.'

'You should listen to your big sister.' Matthew patted me on the shoulder.

Oh god, I hate him so much. There has to be a way round this.

'Fine. I'll manifest our old house.'

Matthew gave me a hard stare. 'You'll manifest that house?'

'She can't manifest a house,' said Astrid. 'This is asinine.'

'Yes, I can,' I said. 'I will have that house. I manifest having that house.'

'Great,' said Matthew. 'Shall we pop in now?'

'It doesn't work like that. It will take me time. But I will live in that house. I will spend next Christmas in that house. And you will have to admit you're wrong.'

'You really want to do this?' said Matthew, his eyes gleaming.

'Alice,' warned Aziz.

'Absolutely.' I ignored Aziz and stared straight back at Matthew. 'I can't wait to hear you admit you were wrong.'

Matthew slowly smiled that smug smile.

'If you're living in that house by next Christmas,' said Matthew, 'not only will I admit I'm wrong, but I will give you that painting by your favourite artist. By way of an acknowledgement. What's her name again?'

Fuck, fuck, Alice. Remember. I watched him watch me panicking and saw his smile grow.

'Yayoi Kusama!' I said triumphantly. 'And only if you're sure you want to part with it?'

'Can't wait,' said Matthew. 'So. You genuinely believe you're going to manifest that house?' He extended his hand and waited.

I don't think I've ever been more determined.

'Absolutely,' I said without blinking.

His smile got wider.

I would do anything, anything to wipe that smile off his face.

As much as I didn't want to touch him, I put my hand in his. His grip was firm and strong and powerful and we both knew that he knew he had me. I was going to lose.

The tosser's smile didn't waver. Instead, he pulled me closer towards him so that his breath fleetingly brushed my ear, making me shiver. 'I always win, Alice,' he said, then turned back towards Astrid and Aziz, like I didn't even exist. 'Shall we?'

'About time,' said Astrid. 'Let's get inside; I'm freezing.'

'I could use another of those espressos, Matthew,' said Aziz.

As they walked into the hotel, talking together, none of them looking back, not even Aziz, I became all the more determined. I was going to manifest that house – it would be mine, and I *would* spend next Christmas there. But that wasn't the only thing. There was something even more important I needed to manifest too.

Something I know I can make happen.

One way or another, I *will* wipe that smile off Matthew Lloyd's face.

*

Although, as I settle into bed in the garage for another night, despite very distinctly asking the Universe *not* to sleep here tonight, and relive what happened earlier today, I do find my confidence waning somewhat. I keep thinking back to what ML said about *The Guide*. Obviously, he was being a wanker – I know that. But if I can't even manifest sleeping in a non-mouldy cat-toilet of a room, let alone achieve success as an influencer (only had seventeen views on that unboxing video so far), I do wonder how likely I am to successfully manifest keeping my job, or making Guy Carmichael fall for me. And when I think about the fact that I was goaded into saying I'd

93

manifest our old house, I feel hot with panic. I mean, even if I manage to keep my job, my current salary as a children's book editor barely covers rent; I wouldn't get a mortgage for this *garage,* let alone a house that my parents couldn't afford to keep. So, there is literally no chance of my winning that bet any other way than the Universe giving me our old house. I'm just going to have to believe that *The Guide* is as good as it claims to be.

But . . . it's *The Guide*™, technically. Fuck. Matthew Lloyd is getting in my head.

I am letting go of:

Posting videos – how come the one I looked awful in went viral and barely anyone has even glanced at my beautiful unboxing one? Plus, it takes ages. I'll just stick to selfies.

The notion that Arrie is a reasonable older sister: the White Company pyjamas are only slightly stained; they are certainly not brown. If she didn't want me to borrow them, she should have said. And crucially, why does she need to look good in nightwear anyway? She's married! That's the point of having a husband – Roger has to give it up regardless. Besides clearly Roger doesn't notice what she's wearing. Otherwise, he'd surely have said something about that gilet . . .

My thoughts and reflections:

I'm beginning to feel quite down about this process. I know I haven't journaled for a few days but my life has gone from bad to worse – which is, let's face it, a touch disheartening and not the right way round.

The weather is hideous – a grim, grey, wet misery like it has been since Boxing Day afternoon – and no one would take me to the station for this train from hell which is so busy that people are using the toilets for standing room. Mum said she couldn't because she was going to Pilates with Sue from next door and that Dad had to hand out leaflets about the New Year's Eve concert at the church because she'd forgotten to. Typical Mum. She gets Pilates and her jobs done for her and meanwhile her own daughter has to catch public transport to the public transport. To add insult to injury, Astrid and Aziz drove off to London this morning before I got up without even telling me. I could have gone with them! And when I mentioned this to Mum and Dad, Mum said, 'Well, precisely.'

I asked exactly what that meant. And she said that Astrid and Aziz didn't have time to be taxiing me around because they were busy professionals and I pointed out that they were driving to London anyway, how would it have put them out, and she told me I should be more respectful and no one has time to meet my expectations of door-to-door service. Which seriously pissed me off. I am respectful. They could have just dropped me *near* my flat. I don't expect door to door.

And then Dad inhaled and said carefully, 'But, darling, last time you wouldn't get out of Astrid's car until your Uber had arrived because it was raining. And then, darling, she was late for that rather important meeting.'

'Oh my god,' I said. 'One time.'

'No,' said Mum, 'there was also that time you made Aziz drop you directly at your flat so that he was late for that client of his with attachment problems and she ended up locking them both in until nearly midnight.'

'Dreadful business,' added Dad, shaking his head sadly. 'Poor Aziz, having to call the police . . . '

'How was I supposed to know she'd react so badly?'

(To be fair, Aziz did tell me that was what would happen, but I thought he was exaggerating. He really is a saint, putting himself on the line like that. Explains how he tolerates Astrid.)

So I had to stand opposite the Lamb with its inviting fires and sofas, in the rain and cold, shielding my Dior jacquard suitcase that I got for an absolute bargain on Vinted, and wait for the Stagecoach bus which was over twenty minutes late, and whilst I was standing there, the water running down the back of my neck and off the tip of my nose, feeling like the Little Match Girl, this luxurious brand-new Range Rover pulled up, with the Lamb logo on the side, and who should get out? Only bloody ML. He clambered out the back (he's got his own driver and I'm catching the Stagecoach – how things have changed) and walked leisurely into his hotel, like he owns the rain too and it knows not to fall on him. It was weird glimpsing him without him knowing. Weird seeing him full stop.

He hasn't been round to ours at all since I saw him on Boxing Day. Not once. Astrid and Aziz came back from the Lamb on their own and went on and on and on about how amazing it was and what a good job he'd done with it, etc., etc. Mum was all upset that he wasn't coming for lunch, but Astrid said he had loads of work stuff and that you don't end up being as successful as Matthew is without serious input. Of course Mum took that as an invitation to look my way and raise her eyebrows meaningfully.

Anyway, *I* was pleased that he'd stayed out the way – the only reason the last few days have felt so depressing is because of the shit, unseasonably wet weather. Plus, Astrid decided she wasn't drinking between Boxing Day and New Year's Eve which not only made her horrific company but resulted in my drinking her share. So I've been permanently either hungover or drunk since then – sometimes both – which frankly would make anyone feel a bit down.

I watched Matthew's back hoping he wouldn't turn round and see me and he didn't. That was a relief, at least. I could taste something bitter in my mouth. Probably acid rain mixing with my make-up.

After twenty minutes, the stuffy little bus pulled up. Then, not only did I suffer the indignity of trying to board with my suitcase, which the driver insisted I put in a tiny cage at the front of the bus – he did not offer to help – but also I was crammed in next to a behemoth of a child in a pushchair who kept ramming the metal footrest into my shin in what can only be described as a deliberate manner. And then, when I was getting off the bus at the station, my suitcase tipped on its side and fell into a muddy puddle so my clothes were probably all soaked, and the jacquard was ruined. Then the train was cancelled and I had to sit on the platform for fifty minutes with nothing to do apart from stalk Charlotte's Insta to check if there were any photos of Guy Carmichael, seeing as his own account is private and I don't dare send him a follow request, and he never changes his WhatsApp status so that's a dead loss.

And then eventually when the next train arrived, it turned out to be one of those horrific new swaying ones which make me feel sick and the only seat available was this one I'm in right now, sandwiched between the window and a man in a tight suit with a ghastly giant Breitling on his wrist, who is the world's most prolific cougher – I'm just waiting for some lung to shoot onto the ash-coloured melamine table (would it kill them to come up with less hideous furnishings?). Opposite us is a terrifying and beefy woman who has an equally terrifying and beefy dog on her lap. Either she or the dog has eaten something fucking unpleasant, because every few minutes or so, there is the type of noxious smell which would ordinarily result in everyone abandoning this carriage for another one. But now, there are so many standing passengers that it is simply not possible to move. And my phone battery died because of looking for Guy Carmichael, hence the move to put pen to paper.

So I'm staring out the train window as the pathetic daylight fades away and I catch sight of a dishevelled, miserable, worn-looking woman in the reflection, and it takes me a whole few beats before I realise it's me. Obviously it's the overhead lighting because I don't look like that normally, but it seems particularly cruel of the Universe to do that on the back of Sweater-vest Gareth's unintentional ageism the other day.

And what am I returning to? Job uncertainty. Imminent eviction. Rats.

So you can see why, all in all, I'm feeling down about things.

In fact, I don't mind admitting I am currently having serious doubts about the efficacy of *The Guide*.

Serious doubts.

My intention is:

- To suggest to Arrie that she invest in a light-therapy anti-ageing mask that I read about in *Vogue*.
- To borrow Arrie's new light-therapy anti-ageing mask.

My thoughts and reflections:

Oh god.

I remembered to empty the fridge before I left. I forgot, however, to empty the bin. It's carnage in there. And the smell is horrific.

At least the rats have had a good Christmas break.

Have called Drunk Stephen and he says I can stay for a few days because his flatmate is away in Scotland for Hogmanay, but an uncertain future looms. I've left a message with Rodentinators begging them to come before 1 January and explaining that the situation is not under 'control', and am now sitting on the stairs outside the flat, waiting for an Uber. I'm feeling sad and lost, like I'm being taught hard life lessons, and reminding myself of *The Water-Babies*.

Belts and braces as Mum would say.

At least things can't get any worse.

I am grateful for:

Drunk Stephen

My thoughts and reflections:

Things *can* get worse.

I have a horrible hangover, I slept badly in Drunk Stephen's flatmate's bed (his numerous Dungeons and Dragons figurines watching over me weren't conducive to repose), and Aunty Margaret has just called: apparently the new tenant has a life-threatening dust allergy, so I need to make sure the flat has been thoroughly and meticulously cleaned from top to bottom. When I asked if I should email or text the cleaning bill to her, it emerged she was expecting *me* to pay it and that it would be a 'drop in the ocean' in comparison to the rent I've saved for the last six months by living, for free, in her flat. She was pretty shirty really. I know that technically she has a point, but I'm starting to think I might be aligned with Aziz when it comes to the landed. I mean, Aunty Margaret has multiple properties and it's good to share. Universal fact. (When you have something someone else wants, at least.) Anyway, I decided it was safer not to update her on the rat situation.

When I told Mum that I was feeling rather like Sara from *A Little Princess*, Mum was incredibly unsympathetic, saying that it was time I started to appreciate the value of money; she clearly doesn't know me at all because I absolutely appreciate the value of nice things. That's precisely why I find it hard when I have to work with Chloe from Sales with her little Michael Kors cross-body bag and her Pandora bracelet dripping with charms and why I'm friends with Drunk Stephen despite his appalling rudeness because he has impeccable taste in shoes: he also appreciates the value of nice things. But Mum is not going to understand that. Not when she hangs out with people like Sue from next door who has black gravel. At least Mum did let it drop that Aunty Margaret is particularly bad-tempered at the moment because she has a painful cut on the septum from the nasal hair trimmers Uncle Ted bought her for Christmas, which according to Aunty Margaret's GP, should have come with a safety warning. Bloody hell. Who would want to be a GP?

Still, at least *now* things can't get any worse. Surely.

I am letting go of:

Getting my nails done for New Year's Eve – Drunk Stephen says I'll be looking at £180 plus VAT for the rats! Fucking outrageous.

My thoughts and reflections:

Turns out things can get still worse.

The man from Rodentinators says that the state of the kitchen made him feel queasy, and that's coming from someone who used to work in a chicken slaughterhouse. He says that because I didn't follow the Rodentinators guidelines and effectively 'courted rats', his work today will not be covered by the initial payment. The 'gold star' one-stop solution is £310 + VAT and he'd recommend leaving the apartment empty for a few days afterwards – and then having a professional company in to disinfect. When I asked how bad it could really be, he said he wouldn't even put his ex-wife in this health hazard of a flat. He says the entire place needs to be bleached. He's recommended a friend of his who would provide a discount and probably do it for £250, so long as I don't have a problem with supporting ex-cons.

I don't have a problem with supporting ex-cons but I do have a problem with supporting myself – no way I can afford £250 on top of the gold treatment. So, not only do I have nowhere to live, but I now won't be going out with Drunk Stephen to the party in Stratford after all. That £310 + VAT I've just paid the man is going to ruin me.

Basically, there's no way out of this. I'm going to have to message Aunty Margaret and tell her the news: her new tenants can't come and stay for another week because I've turned her flat into an uninhabitable environment. I don't think it's going to go down well.

I imagine things can get worse yet, so I won't make that mistake again.

I ask the Universe:

To stop being so unkind.

My thoughts and reflections:

I was just about to message Aunty Margaret when she messaged me to say that she's giving me £100 via Mum and Dad (she knows they're coming to London to see Astrid and Aziz who have clearly given up on the idea of proper fun plans for NYE, in the way that married people do), and could I use it to buy a nice bunch of flowers and some welcome groceries, etc., for the new tenants? She said that if the tenants are happy with the flat, perhaps we could look at some dates in the summer and see if there's a weekend available for me to spend a weekend at their other flat in Majorca, 'as a little thank you'.

Ooh!

So I think, on reflection it's probably better not to mention to Aunty Margaret what the Rodentinators man said. It'll only upset her and I've always wanted to go to their holiday apartment in Majorca – it's gorgeous – but she's very precious about it. I'm thinking that what I *could* do is use that £100 and buy some cleaning products and clean the flat myself tomorrow, and still have plenty left over for flowers, etc., and hopefully enough for a couple of drinks out with Drunk Stephen in Stratford tonight. How hard can it be to disinfect a flat? Bleach doesn't cost much. And I'm sure the tenants will be fine. After all, if they have such a serious dust allergy, they're used to playing roulette with life as it is. Plus Aunty Margaret only ever leaves Scotland to go to Majorca, so it's not like she'll be personally checking the flat.

Also, Astrid's just sent me a message inviting me along to an early supper tonight because she's found out Arrie and Roger are in London, too, visiting Roger's parents, which is perfect, as Astrid has a last-minute announcement she'd like to make to the whole family together. Bet she's pregnant. She's done two announcement suppers before – one when she got engaged to Aziz and one when she was made partner. So we'll all have to celebrate yet another win for Astrid. Whilst I am without partner, home or future. Fabulous.

On the plus side, at least Astrid has acknowledged that *I* am the fun sister, with NYE engagements that don't involve hanging out with retired parents: she said supper will be done by nine so it shouldn't interfere with whatever 'overpriced partying' I have planned. Also, I love their house, it's a free supper (that will be yummy if Aziz has cooked), there will be wine that hasn't been chosen simply because it's on offer, and once I tell Dad about what's been going on, he'll hopefully give me some cash.

My intention is:

To eat really well at Astrid's, to maybe borrow a couple of bottles of wine as a thank you to Drunk Stephen for letting me stay, and to resist being drawn into competitive or comparative (or combative) family dynamics.

Date: Sunday 1 January   **Time: 5.28am**

My thoughts and reflections:

Happy new year.

Happy fucking new fucking year. To me.

So, here I am, on the unpleasantly bouncy Ikea recliner in the sitting room of Drunk Stephen's flat because Drunk Stephen's flatmate came back early from Scotland due to a family crisis and kicked me out of his bedroom. I don't know what the family crisis is – maybe his mother's discovered his passion for painting weird little figurines. I do know that he's made it very clear that I can't sleep here for another night. He left all my stuff in the sitting room (apart from a couple of pairs of pants) with a rude note: *need you out by tomorrow morning and all underwear removed from my bedroom floor.* Not that I am sleeping. I am trying to ignore the muffled voices and giggles and occasional silences from Drunk Stephen and New Steven (the unbelievably hot guy Drunk Stephen met about six hours ago) who are also still very much not sleeping by the sounds of it, and trying to ignore the gnawing feeling of rising nausea that could be hunger or bitterness or trauma from the Dave-thing (I feel like I've still got the smell of pasties and paint thinners in my nostrils). More on this later, if I can bear to. Or it could be pancreatitis. And trying not to think about what a totally and utterly shit night this has been.

And so it is that on the first day of the new year I am awake but not having sex, not having fun, and anticipating the day ahead which holds . . . more not having sex, definitely not having fun, and a whole lot of hazardous deep cleaning. And for afters? I have nowhere to stay tonight, I'm back in the office the day after tomorrow to face potential redundancy, my whole family thinks I'm useless, and I made some pretty unwise decisions tonight. Including texting Monty. Just now. But then I deleted it.

All in all, I wouldn't say this has been a happy new year whatsofuckingever.

I began to manifest a better life over a week ago and whilst I didn't expect to see a steep upward trajectory immediately, I certainly didn't expect a steady deterioration. I may only have secured a C in maths GCSE but even I can tell the direction of a line and this line is going down. Down. Down. Down.

Honestly, I'm at the point where I may have to reconsider Monty. Maybe I'll message him again . . .

How has tonight ended up being so spectacularly awful?

Well. Let me break it down.

SUPPER *(Saturday 31 December, 7pm)*

Supper at Astrid and Aziz's *started* well, once I'd made the trek over to Chiswick. Arrie and Roger had left the twins with his parents and so were unusually light and sort of carpe diem in that sightly desperate free-pass way of trying to prove they were still fun. They're not. But they are less un-fun without the twins. Arrie doesn't do so much sudden shouting, and occasionally doesn't stare at Roger with contempt. And Roger was already pissed when he arrived, which I thought was a good call, and continued drinking in a committed fashion.

Aziz wasn't there yet – he'd been doing something at the university – but Astrid managed to be hospitable enough and made sure everyone had glasses and wine and nuts, although she's not exactly relaxing company.

Mum and Dad were also on decent form – another one of Mum's friends had broken a hip and Mum still hasn't broken anything which gives her a sense of superiority. And Dad has printed some flyers for his men's support group which he's planning to run in the new year, and the anticipation of showing these to Aziz was keeping him in his element. He was so cheerful he even gave me an extra £100 cash along with the £100 from Aunty Margaret and promised not to tell anyone. So, I'd be having more than a couple of drinks out with Drunk Stephen tonight after all!

Astrid and Aziz's house is spacious and calm and cool and has honey-coloured wooden floors throughout the three storeys, and white cast-iron fireplaces, and a massive modern kitchen extension at the back overlooking green lawns – you almost feel like you're not in London. Arguably, living in Chiswick, you're not. They have Daylesford soap in the bathrooms and an absence of clutter. And after the horrors of the rats and the frightful little models in Drunk Stephen's flatmate's room, it felt like stepping into another world.

So, as we all sat around the huge white table on our Philippe Starck chairs (apart from Astrid who was finding it hard to sit still), the candlelight reflecting in the vast roof light, and Roger keeping everyone's glasses fully topped, it all felt quite pleasant and I remembered why I like being with my family.

Until Astrid starting grating courgette and when I casually checked whether she was helping prep for Aziz to cook, she said she'd made the whole meal herself. Everyone exchanged surreptitious, slightly panicked looks, mentally calculating whether they'd eaten enough calories earlier to sustain them. Thank goodness I'd had a Mars bar on the way over. In a rare moment of solidarity, Roger passed Arrie the nuts. Aziz came back and then things got offbeat. Firstly, he clearly wasn't expecting the rest of us to be there. Then, rather than joining us at the table he asked Astrid if he could have a quick word with her.

But Astrid just pinged her wine glass and said she had an announcement to make and as most of us were here she was going to get on with it. Obviously she's always rude but normally Aziz seems unbothered by it. Today he looked the closest to pissed off I've ever seen. And for a second I went into a complete panic because Aziz did not have the face of someone who was about to become a father, and if they weren't announcing that, what *were* they announcing? I love Astrid but I also love Aziz and I don't even want to contemplate a life where they're not together.

Then Astrid said that she'd been doing some hard thinking and that she was stepping down as partner from the law firm.

There was a gasp round the table.

'Have they . . . let you go?'

'No, Mum,' said Astrid. 'It's my decision. I've looked at my life, and well, maybe there's more out there for me. I want to try a different career.'

There was another intake of breath. Astrid has wanted to be a lawyer since she was five.

'But, darling,' said Dad, 'you won the Chancellor's Medal! You made partner at thirty-two!'

'And now I want something new,' said Astrid. 'I'm thinking of becoming a doctor.'

'A doctor?' said Dad in astonishment. 'What about your blood phobia, darling . . . ?'

'It's good to push oneself out of one's comfort zone,' said Astrid. 'I'll have to retrain completely. But I'm volunteering at the hospital in the meantime.'

'But you'd have to *care* for others, darling,' said Dad.

Astrid's nickname as an associate was 'the onion' because she regularly reduced other lawyers to tears in court.

'I must say, Astrid,' said Mum, quickly recovering her composure. 'This seems uncharacteristic behaviour. It's verging on reckless. Why have you gone along with it, Aziz?'

Aziz swallowed. 'I haven't,' he said quietly.

'This is something I need to do on my own,' said Astrid pointedly. 'At least my partners are supporting me.'

'Your partners support you suddenly handing in your notice?' said Aziz.

Astrid rubbed her nose. 'They told me not to hand it in yet and to take some time. But they support *my* life choices.'

'I think I heard the door,' he said and left the room.

Everyone was quiet for a moment apart from Arrie drumming her fingers on the table.

'You know, Astrid, I thought you were going to say you were having a baby,' she said, 'or that you were becoming a senior partner.' Her voice was gradually rising in volume, never a good sign. 'But instead . . . you're throwing your life away! Starting from the bottom!' Arrie paused then leant forward for effect. 'You'll be like Alice!'

Er, that was uncalled for.

'I'm not throwing my life away,' said Astrid calmly.

'And Aziz's face! He clearly doesn't agree with this decision – he's your husband and you're acting like his opinion doesn't matter.'

'Be fair, Arrie,' interjected Roger. 'It's hardly like you care about my opinion either.'

'Pipe down, Roger!' snapped Arrie, throwing her napkin onto her plate. 'This is family stuff. Carver. Of course I don't care about your opinion. No one does. Aziz is totally different.'

'Thanks very much,' said Roger moodily, his neck mottling as he reached for the bottle. He topped up everyone's wine glass except Arrie's.

Astrid shrugged and fiddled with her wine glass stem.

'I want a change. I don't have to justify it. I don't really care what you think or what Aziz thinks.'

'Goodness,' said Arrie, downing her glass. 'You're sounding about as spoilt as Alice. And how's that working out for her? Forty and nothing to show for it – she barely owns the coat on her back.'

'Hey!' I said indignantly. 'I'm thirty-seven. Just. And I own plenty.'

(Although technically not the coat on my back. I actually borrowed it from Mira, Drunk Stephen's other flatmate, whose exciting wardrobe doesn't really compensate for her boringness.)

'Anyway, this is about Astrid, not me,' I said.

'Exactly,' said Astrid. 'I already have the house, the husband, the six-figure salary. I'm in a position where I have choices.'

'But if you make certain choices, who's to say you won't end up like Alice?' said Arrie.

I was anticipating that Astrid would not take this as a compliment.

'And what does that mean?' said Astrid. 'I don't think you can call retraining to become a doctor childish. It's hardly dipping my toes into marketing or publishing for children—'

'Actually, children's publishing is a sought-after profession!'

Astrid ignored me. 'Bottom line, I take my career seriously. I'm not taking selfies and handouts.'

Yep. Not flattering.

'I think you're liable to make a mess of your life like Alice has if you're not careful. Even Monty had enough eventually. Aziz is a saint but he will only put up with so much. What about what he wants? I don't want you to end up alone.' This time the 'like Alice' was just implied.

'I'll take my chances,' said Astrid. 'Roger's still putting up with you.'

'I am not alone!' I said. 'And Monty did not dump me. I dumped him.'

'Of course you did,' said Dad. 'Be nice, please, Arrie.'

Arrie sighed. 'I am being nice. I just want everyone to be happy.'

'Maybe try being less insulting then,' I muttered.

But Arrie wasn't finished. She turned to Astrid. 'Astrid, please talk to Aziz about this. You're not thinking clearly. You know it would be cheaper to buy a sports car.'

Astrid rolled her eyes.

'But you know I have faith in you, Astrid,' said Arrie, softening. Then she fixed on me. 'And Alice, I just don't like to think of you bringing in the new year all alone in some horrible industrial warehouse place at the end of the tube line, posting empty pictures of your empty life, counting out your coins for the journey home.'

God. Neither did I. What a bleak picture.

I waited for the softening bit, but Arrie just stared at me silently.

'I won't be all alone,' I said eventually. 'I'll be with Drunk Stephen and his friends and it's actually an exclusive party.' I tried to inject some enthusiasm into my voice.

'She'll be all right,' said Astrid briskly. 'Dad gave her £100.'

'Ken!' said Mum sharply. 'We've spoken about this.' She shook her head at Dad then focused on me. 'Although I agree with Arrie. I would like to see you settled, Alice. Perhaps when Astrid's volunteering she can find you a nice doctor?'

'Yes,' said Arrie. 'That would be good.'

'It would be lovely to see you happy, darling,' said Dad.

Suddenly I realised that everyone was looking at me. More to the point, everyone was looking at me with pity and it made my ribcage feel a little cramped.

'I am happy!' I retorted. 'You don't need a partner to be happy. I like being single. I'm young and I'm making the most of what London has to offer and having lots of casual sex.'

'Really?' said Astrid. 'I thought you said you hadn't had sex for months. Since that guy you met on Hinge who still lived with his mum and tried to get you to dress up like a teddy bear?'

'Oh, furries,' said Dad. 'I heard about that on *Dispatches*.'

'My little Ally-Pally!' Mum reached across the table and squeezed my hand. 'Sounds appalling!'

It was. So gross. But Mum never calls me her little Ally-Pally anymore. She must truly have been feeling sorry for me.

'Golly,' said Roger, his voice slightly croaky from being quiet so long. 'I bet you come across all sorts of things if you're single in this day and age. Depraved. I imagine.' He sounded quite admiring.

'No one asked you, Roger,' said Arrie, looking at him with disdain.

'*Really* depraved.' I gave Roger a little smile.

Roger's eyes bugged slightly. See: not everyone was feeling sorry for me.

'But luckily I'm single and I'm very open-minded sexually,' I declared, 'and tonight I'm looking forward to exploring the best that I can dredge up from London's seas of seedy desire!'

That didn't come out quite right. Never mind.

Then with the kind of timing I've come to dread, a deep voice from behind said, 'I hate to interrupt . . . but I've been standing here for a while . . .'

I closed my eyes. No way was this happening again. How long was a while? It was like the man just stood around waiting for the worst possible moments to enter a room. Please let him not have heard my last misarticulated output.

'Matthew!' exclaimed Mum and Astrid simultaneously.

'So, apart from the fact that Astrid is thinking of becoming a doctor and Alice is planning on dredging up filthy sex from London's seas of desire, what else have I missed?'

MATTHEW FUCKING LLOYD
(Saturday 31 December, 8pm)

'Honestly!' said Astrid, once everyone had stopped fawning over Matthew and he was sitting down with a glass of wine. 'I would have held off if I'd known you were going to make it this soon.'

'Traffic went my way,' said Matthew Lloyd. 'I guess I'm lucky.'

Twat.

'But you messaged less than an hour ago,' said Astrid, 'that's not possible?'

'Might have used a helicopter,' Matthew admitted sheepishly. 'It's a lot faster and you said it was important.'

'Good lord,' said Dad admiringly. 'What a way to travel, Matthew.'

Indeed. A way for a complete twat to travel.

'But I thought your company just got a B corp,' exploded Roger. 'Surely you can't be a B corp and use a helicopter? I get shit from everyone just for the Range Rover!'

'Yeah, this was personal.' Matthew rubbed his jaw. 'But you make an excellent point.'

'So where's this Ebba?' interrupted Astrid. 'Is she joining us for supper?'

'Who's Ebba?' said Mum immediately.

Yes. Who the fuck is Ebba?

'No one,' said Matthew.

'Let me guess,' mused Arrie. 'Swedish, impeccable English, only travels by private helicopter, very young, models a bit . . .'

I felt fonder of Arrie for a moment.

'Am I right?' she said.

Matthew shrugged noncommittally. 'On some counts. But I prefer to date women my age.'

'She sounds fab,' said Mum, 'rather like a young me,' and laughed. 'Obviously not the Swedish part. But how wonderful you have a girlfriend, Matthew. I hope you've explained to Ebba about Astrid's cooking?'

'Mum!' protested Astrid.

'Ebba's not coming to supper,' said Matthew. 'And she's not my girlfriend. We're just calling by a party together later.'

'Well, clearly Ebba is a special person in your life.' Mum nudged Matthew like they were conspirators. 'And I can't wait to meet her.'

'Jesus. Give it a rest, Mum,' I said. 'He said she's not his girlfriend. I don't see you asking to meet whoever I'm shagging.'

'And with good reason, Alice,' said Mum. 'Plus it's quite obvious to all you're having an extended dry patch on that front.'

'Ironic, given London's great waters,' remarked Matthew.

'Yes, well, I'll be swimming in sex later, Matthew,' I said sarcastically. 'Dripping wet.'

God. Why did I say that?

'I just can't understand why you're single, Alice,' said Matthew, his eyes glinting.

'Fuck off! You're single too.'

'Bit different though, isn't it,' said Arrie. 'When he's shagging a Swedish model.'

'Is Ebba into this furry sex business like Alice?' said Dad conversationally.

There we go – no wonder I'm unattached when I've grown up with parents like these.

'No, Ken,' said Matthew. 'Funnily enough, she's not.'

'Are we eating soon?' interrupted Roger. 'Only it's nearly eight and we've been up since the crack of dawn with the boys, and . . .'

'Yes, sorry,' said Astrid, checking in the oven. 'As soon as Aziz comes back down . . .'

'He said he wouldn't be long.' Matthew glanced at his watch. 'Do you want me to go and fetch him?'

'No,' said Astrid. 'Thanks.'

'He's probably still upset,' said Arrie. 'With Astrid . . .'

Mum shook her head. 'What do you think of Astrid throwing it all away, Matthew? Surely she can't *really* be serious about becoming a doctor?'

'Hmm,' said Matthew. 'Astrid, what kind of salary drop would you take if you retrained?'

'About eighty per cent.'

'Could you still cover the mortgage? Bills?'

'No. We'd have to downsize. Lose the holidays. But I'd barely be home anyway with the course and the hours in hospital.'

'Okay,' said Matthew. 'Well, if she's considered moving and is willing to sacrifice her house and life, then it sounds like she's pretty serious about it.'

*

By the time supper was done, I was done too. And quite pissed, as was everyone else. It was usual Astrid-style food (lean) and Astrid-sized portions (stingy): i.e., completely inadequate in terms of soaking up the alcohol. So, at half nine, having bid everyone goodbye (not that Arrie and Roger answered because they were too busy having a drunken, loud row about whose responsibility it was to have ordered an Uber in advance given that it was New Year's Eve and there was now limited availability and surge pricing), I'd weaved my way to the dimly lit front hallway and was struggling to get into my boots. I was also wondering if I was going to puke on the off-puttingly long tube journey from here to Stratford. I took a risk and bent forward properly to lever my heel into place, and it took an age, so when I stood up, my head reeled and my vision went blurry, and I felt myself stumbling. Right into a wall of warm solid muscle.

'Shit.' I put my hands against his chest in an attempt to get myself stable. 'What are you doing here? And why is your chest so hard?'

'Catching you, it seems,' said Matthew, as I swayed again. 'How pissed are you?' He frowned down at me.

'Not that pissed.' I waited for my balance to steady. His eyes were so dark in this light I couldn't tell what was iris and what was pupil.

'Alice?'

'I was just bending down. And everything went black at the edges. I feel a bit sick.'

'Well, that bodes well for all your seedy sexual activities later,' said Matthew drily.

'What have you done to your chest? I remember when you used to be all skinny. Have you had implants?'

'Yeah. So you're still extremely annoying when you're drunk.'

The doorbell chimed. Matthew moved towards the door but I forgot to let go of his chest.

'Stop feeling me up,' he said, reaching round me to open the front door.

'I'm not feeling you up! I'm just trying to work out if this muscle is real.'

There was a polite cough, and a woman's light voice answered from above me. 'Yes, it is real. Who is this, Matthew?'

'Hey, Ebba,' said Matthew, removing my hands and propping me against the wall. 'Just Alice. She's a little inebriated.'

'Oh the little sister of your friend, Astrid?' said Ebba.

I drew myself up to my full height, only swaying a smidgen, and surveyed the condescending Ebba. She was pretty. Very tall. I had to tip my head back to see her properly. And wearing a gorgeous fringed mini dress. I wondered if it was Balmain. She was also really young. Way younger than me.

'Not that little, actually,' I said pointedly. 'Is that Balmain?'

'I know.' Ebba gave me an appraising look. 'I meant little as in younger. And yes, it's a Balmain dress.'

Show-off. 'I don't think you're in a position to be calling me young, when you're younger than me,' I said. 'And Matthew – all that bullshit about dating women of your own age. I mean, hello?'

'What?' Matthew sounded confused.

'Look at her! Ebba must be about half my age!'

Matthew stifled back a laugh.

'No,' said Ebba. 'Perhaps I am four, five years younger than you at the most. How old are you?

'Thirty-seven.'

'Oh, okay. So in this case, I am five years older.'

What? Bloody models in Balmain mini dresses. I didn't need to check to know that there would be a look of pure enjoyment on Matthew's face. I needed to assert my strengths here. Regain some composure.

'Yes, well, I suppose that's the difference in our lifestyles,' I said. 'Poring over books late at night doesn't help the skin.'

'Yes, Ebba,' said Matthew. 'Alice is quite the reader. She has her very own TikTok-made-me-buy-it copy of *The Guide*.'

'I think study can affect the eyes, yes,' conceded Ebba. 'When I was writing my pure maths PHD thesis, I had a little puffiness perhaps.'

I was rescued from thinking of a response by Astrid who'd come into the hallway in time to hear the last bit. 'Wow. So you must be Ebba. Nice to meet you. I'm Astrid.'

'Hey, Astrid,' said Ebba.

'Wish you'd been around to help poor Alice here with her maths GCSE. She wanted to count everything on her fingers and toes.'

'Haha, Astrid,' I said, gathering what was left of my dignity. 'If you tall people could move out the way, I'm going to catch my tube for a fun night.'

'But you hate public transport,' said Matthew. 'Aren't you tempted to . . . I don't know . . . manifest a taxi, Alice?'

He is insufferable.

'Take these before you go.' Astrid shoved something into my hand. 'And Matthew – you forgot your jacket.'

As Matthew was putting on his jacket, I looked at my hand: there was a whole load of extra-strong condoms.

'What do you want me to do with these?'

'Use them tonight,' said Astrid. 'They give them out free at the hospital. And consider being a bit more discerning sexually.'

'Astrid! I'm super picky.'

'Please,' said Astrid. 'I swear I saw the one you shagged right after Monty on *Crimewatch* the other week.'

'Which one?'

'The one with the creepy little 'tache.'

'Freddie? The entertainment lawyer? *You* set me up with him! He works in your firm. She's being funny,' I said to Ebba.

'Not Freddie. And I didn't set you up with him. I told you all about his girlfriend and you still went there. I'm talking about the one *you* found. On Tinder. With no little finger.'

Oh Christ. I'd forgotten about him. Deliberately.

'Yes, exactly,' said Astrid, watching my reaction.

'Piss off, Astrid.' I firmly returned the condoms to her. 'Sort out your own life.' I pushed past her to the front door, careful not to look at Matthew Lloyd's chest in passing.

'Syphilis is on the rise,' warned Astrid, as I stepped out into the cold December mist. 'Could be your little finger next.'

'She'd just manifest a new one, wouldn't you, Alice?' said Matthew.

TWAT.

THE CLUB (Saturday 31 December, 11pm)

So, despite expecting it to be good, supper at Aziz and Astrid's turned out to be less than a fun start to New Year's Eve. But, while I had been dreading the tube journey to Drunk Stephen's friend's thing in Stratford, it ended up being okay. There were a bunch of kids, hoods up, playing music on their phones super loudly at one end of the carriage and so most people had consciously chosen any other carriage; this meant I had my end pretty much to myself. Just how I liked it. I scrolled through my phone. Drunk Stephen had sent me a code I had to show at the door to get into this party. He also told me to make sure I posted photos of myself outside, tagging @ LST-STP-NYE, before coming in, because the more of a story I put up, the more likely I was to get chosen the next time. He told me he was scouting the room already to find the most attractive people for us to dance near to increase our chances of social media exposure.

So I spent some time re-doing my make-up – I am bloody good at applying make-up on the tube. Never had an injury yet, unlike Annabel, who had blurry vision for a month after she accidentally jabbed herself in the eye whilst kohling on the Central line. Couldn't have happened to a nicer person. I bet they weren't doing anything as cool as going to Drunk Stephen's friend's thing tonight. They were probably at some member's club where the really fun men loosened their half-Windsor ties towards the end of the night. Thinking of Hugh and Annabel reminded me of Monty, who preferred a full Windsor himself. What would he have made of going off to an invite-only DJ set at a warehouse owned by an art collective?

It was about a ten-minute walk from the tube station and as I got closer towards the venue, it became the sort of journey that St Hilda's pupils were educated about in terms of social awareness and understanding the wider world – a cracked-concrete wasteland with broken barriers, and the odd heap of what could have been rubbish. St Hilda's were big on reminding us about why we needed to keep the perimeters in place. Anyway, I made it past the stacks of paving slabs to the warehouse alive, and dutifully took a couple of photos before posting, hoping no one would steal my iPhone because I couldn't afford to insure it. My notifications pinged. It was a new post from Charlotte. She was forever posting evidence of herself at hot places, proving she was ahead of the curve and that she was living her best life. I wondered what she'd managed tonight – probably something a lot more desirable than a dysfunctional family dinner and an hour-long tube ride. I thought about not looking, but the temptation was too great: there she was, one threaded eyebrow arched, gracing some rooftop garden, fairy lights studded through the potted tree behind her, the London skyline a black frame so perfect it seemed the city itself had chosen to be her backdrop, the moon obediently hanging above. Hang on . . . Whose hand was that on Charlotte's cut-out waist? I enlarged the second photo. Hmm, really hard to see, but definitely male and definitely hairy. There was every possibility she was well and truly dating Guy Carmichael. Charlotte was living *my* perfect life.

Still. It was banging inside and packed. The heat of so many bodies moving together was practically tropical and the atmosphere was wired – people were here to party. Drunk Stephen was already even more twatted than I was, and in full dance mode right in the centre of the floor.

'If it's like this with the warm-up,' he bellowed across the pounding bass, 'imagine what it'll be like when he comes on!'

'Yeah!' I said, moving half-heartedly and wondering if Guy Carmichael was dancing with Charlotte on the picture-perfect rooftop.

'Show me this photo Charlotte's posted,' he said, temporarily pausing his moves. 'And then get in the moment. And start dancing properly.'

We scrutinised the photos the best we could whilst we were jostled from all sides by the dancing masses. 'Meh,' he said in my ear. 'She's at Poison Rose. Totally pedestrian. Tourists go there! Probably a tourist feeling her up right now. Look at where you are!'

He grabbed my hand and raised it in the air.

'This is where it's at,' he yelled. 'This is fun. You need to get into it.'

I looked around. The entire room was pumping. People were definitely loving it.

'Dance!' he commanded. 'Go on! Dance!'

'All right. You're making me feel like Pinocchio.'

But I couldn't help it – the bass was running through the floor, through me, and soon I was dancing.

'Right,' said Drunk Stephen a little while later when I'd

danced myself into a better mood. 'You've got your glow on now. So let's show Charlotte what the cool kids are up to with some counter posts from you. Lean back with me so that we've got that logo in shot, and that unbelievably hot guy too . . .'

I did. And as Drunk Stephen held my phone aloft to capture us, the unbelievably hot guy noticed and put his intricately tattooed arms around us. Drunk Stephen looked heavenwards in thanks.

'Post it yourself actually!' instructed Drunk Stephen, shoving the phone back at me. 'Manifest. I'm busy.'

I checked the photo. Drunk Stephen was right. It did look good: the neon lights in the industrial space, the blurred movement of arms raised, and in the centre: me, Drunk Stephen and the unbelievably hot guy. To be fair, all three of us looked unbelievably hot. Maybe I could manifest the kind of life other people wanted. I clicked post.

Suddenly, the neon lights disappeared, plunging the room into darkness. A single strobe picked out fragments of smoke and the crowd roared in anticipation: the main act was starting . . .

*

Seven to ten tequilas, and one countdown to the new year later, I was having such a good time that I hadn't even checked my phone for ages, and when I did, there were not just one, but three DMs from Charlotte to me. She'd liked the photo I posted, saying, *OMG. Love. Love. LOVE!*

The next one said: *How did you get in?! Wanna be there! Can I come to next one?*

And the last message just had *LST STP* and three fire emojis.

'Stephen!' I hollered over the music. 'Stephen!'

Drunk Stephen temporarily turned away from New Steven (unbelievably hot guy). 'What?'

'Your idea – it worked. I manifested! Charlotte asked if she can come next time—'

'No,' said Drunk Stephen. 'Too little too late.'

'*And* she obviously wants to shag the band – she's put three fire emojis!'

'Again. Not a band!'

'Sorry. She wants to shag the DJ.'

'Of course she does,' said Drunk Stephen. 'He is objectively super hot. Not as gorgeous as you obviously,' he said quickly to New Steven before returning his attention to me. 'Hey, Alice, you know what you should do?'

'What?'

'Get a selfie right up next to the booth. That will make Charlotte jealous.'

Drunk Stephen resumed dancing with New Steven but I was seeking out the booth, a shadow of an island obscured by a dark sea of heaving bodies, and having a genius, tequila-worm idea. I knew what would make Charlotte properly jealous.

'Stephen!' I tugged at his arm. 'Stephen. Which one is he?'

'Who?' said Drunk Stephen, still dancing.

'L, S, T, um, S, T, P?'

'You don't spell it out, Grandma,' he hissed, checking no one had overheard. 'It's just Last Stop.'

'Oh! Okay. So which one is the vowel hater?'

'Seriously?' Drunk Stephen shook his head. 'Who do you

think he is? He's the one at the decks with the headphones! Making the floor shake?'

I peered through arms and heads in the dimly lit space and eventually the strobe momentarily highlighted the hunched figure of a guy with headphones, standing in a booth.

'That's LaST SToP? He doesn't seem all that to me?'

New Steven laughed. 'Babe, I think two million followers would disagree with you on that point!'

'No, I mean he doesn't look particularly fit,' I explained. 'From his silhouette.'

Drunk Stephen rolled his eyes. 'Alice. He turned down *Love Island* you know.'

'Fine. In that case, wish me luck: I'm going in.'

'What?!' said Drunk Stephen and New Steven together.

'I'm going in,' I repeated. 'I'm going to cop off with LaST SToP. Pretty sure he'll soon be expressing some vowel sounds. In fact, I manifest it. And I manifest Charlotte seeing the photos, and weeping.'

'Good luck getting past all the other fans who've had the same idea,' said New Steven.

LST STP (Sunday 1 January, 1am)

Turned out I didn't need good luck because the Universe, for once, was on my side: I must be getting good at this manifestation thing. I blindly (literally because I accidentally looked directly at the strobe) pushed my way through the throng (and it's not easy to orienteer when you're drunk and freshly sight-impaired) and yet somehow ended up right where I was meant to be: at the booth. I'd mouthed 'hi' to a shadowy LST STP and he took off his headphones, mopped his brow and shouted, 'You talking to me?'

And when I yelled back, 'Why, do you want me to be talking to you?'

He pulled me up to stand in front of the decks, before I could even think. 'Fuck yeah, you're fit as fuck,' he said hoarsely in my ear.

And I said, 'Thanks. So are you. Apparently.'

I couldn't make out much in the dark and the dry ice to be honest. But what did it matter? A sex symbol is a sex symbol, and actually I got it. It was incredible being up here, in the booth, with the DJ.

'All you girls like the decks. Am I right?' he said.

'Yeah we do.' Now wasn't the time to educate him on gendered norms or for a nuanced debate about fourth-wave feminism.

And then he did a bit of grinding behind me (his stomach pressed quite hard into my lower back) and I must say he was a pretty enthusiastic dancer, if extremely sexual. Essentially it was dry humping. Nothing wrong with dry humping. And there was clearly an air of star quality about it all, and him. Within a couple of minutes, revellers had noticed and a fair few photos were taken of us. That's fame for you. I swiped right, held my own phone aloft and attempted to capture us, which wasn't easy given the movement in the squashed space. LST STP took my phone for me and held it further up, immediately pressing the arrow and posting the image to my story before I'd had a chance to check it, but I imagine someone who's photographed as much as he is must be pretty adept at the angles. I danced even harder, imagining Charlotte's face when she clocked what I was up to. LST STP was panting behind me, smelling quite musky.

'Do you want a drink? I can take you somewhere private . . .' he offered.

Dirty bastard. I twisted round to give him a coy look and the light temporarily illuminated his T-shirted torso before plunging him into darkness again. The strobe lights were playing havoc with my eyes. But if he'd been asked to go on *Love Island*, he was probably ripped. Plus, Charlotte was into him. And we had similar taste in men given we both liked Guy Carmichael. 'Okay,' I said.

A few minutes later, he'd pushed us through the smoky crowds and straight out a back door into an unlit car park. He grabbed my bum and squeezed, making me jump.

'Are you sure you're comfortable with this? Touching your backside? Can't be too careful nowadays.'

Good to see even stars recognise they aren't exempt now. 'Probably best to check *before* you touch?'

'Oh yeah. You got to get consent,' he said, unlocking the back of a van. It was probably kitted out inside in some super-cool way with sofas and a bar and stuff. 'Come on into my office.' He heaved himself in. 'If you're comfortable?'

'Sure,' I said, following suit.

My sore eyes took a few seconds to adjust to the interior lighting and as LST STP had his back to me, I had the chance to have a quick look around. There were definitely no sofas – just a ladder, quite a few paint cans and a lot of mess.

'Is it better in the front?' I asked tentatively.

'Nah. Less room in there. And I dropped an egg sandwich between the seats.'

Christ, that was a fair deal of arse crack he was sharing.

'Heineken or Co-op Premium Strength Lager?' rasped LST STP, straightening up and turning round to face me.

Obviously overhead lighting is never generous and I didn't watch the last season of *Love Island*, but I've got to say I wasn't expecting LST STP to look like this. I mean, as much as I wanted to make Charlotte jealous, I was starting to feel concerned I was just too shallow to see this plan through. However famous LST STP may be, I generally favour men under sixty and with eyebrows: I guess I'm picky like that.

'Help yourself to a snack,' said LST STP magnanimously. 'Make yourself comfortable.'

'Gosh.' I riffled through the Asda bag he'd handed me. 'That's quite the array of meat-based pastry products.'

'You gotta be ready when Lady Luck calls.' He paused to tap himself on the forehead before handing me a fizzing opened can. 'It's not every day a bloke gets a beauty like you in the back of his van.'

'That can't be true,' I said, carefully blotting up the lager from my top (well, strictly speaking Drunk Stephen's house-mate Mira's top but she'd left it in the bathroom which is a shared space, so). 'You've got two million followers; you must get women literally chucking themselves at you.'

'I don't,' he said. 'There's the odd one who thinks they'll get access via me. But not many are that desperate if I'm honest.'

'What?' I said, looking up in consternation, and then imme-diately swallowing my beer the wrong way at the sight before me, and spraying it out of my nose everywhere: LST STP was naked, save for his underpants.

'Nice move.' He wiped some lager foam off his stomach. 'Got one of my own,' he said cheerfully, whipping off his pants, so he was standing there, fully naked, dick hanging limply in front of the most low-hanging testicles I've ever witnessed.

I stared.

'Sorry,' he said. 'I forgot to ask if you're comfortable with me getting naked?'

'No,' I said, 'I'm uncomfortable. Very uncomfortable.'

He exhaled noisily and bent down to pick up his underpants.

'And what do you mean – "access"?'

'Access to LST STP. The DJ.'

Oh crap. The tequila worm wriggled. My phone pinged. It was Drunk Stephen. He'd put a question mark over the photo of me and LST STP. Then he'd messaged underneath. *Who the fuck is this? Thought you were going to get a pic with LST STP?*

'You're not LST STP?'

'No.'

'So who are you?'

'I'm Dave the decorator. Fill in as roadie when LST STP can't find anyone better.'

I grabbed my phone, praying I could take down the post before Charlotte saw. Or anyone else.

A message from Charlotte: *Age is just a number!* Followed by hand-clap emoji.

Wonderful.

Dave sniffed as he zipped up his trousers. 'If this isn't happening, could you pass me a pork pie?'

THE AFTERMATH (Sunday 1 January, 4am)

We didn't get back to Drunk Stephen's until after 4am and all I wanted to do was go to bed but of course I couldn't: because Drunk Stephen's flatmate with his family 'emergency' had taken his room back.

I'd spent the last couple of hours fake laughing, as Drunk Stephen and New Steven found endless mileage in my near-miss with Decorator Dave (I just pray Astrid never finds out about the whole episode because she'd annihilate me), and watching their mutual attraction grow exponentially, and I was now feeling fatigued but wired and lonely and like I wanted someone to look at me the way they were looking at each other. But not Decorator Dave. (I can't believe his dick is the first one I've seen in the new year. It doesn't seem a good omen.) And then I had to spend another hour drinking with them in Drunk Stephen's living room, not just laughing off Decorator Dave but also the fact that in a few hours I was being evicted from Drunk Stephen's house – New Steven found the rat situation in Aunty Margaret's flat hilarious. It did feel a bit like Drunk Stephen was using my shit life to get New Steven into bed. Then the worst part was Drunk Stephen finally made the frozen pizza he'd been promising to put on (by now I could have eaten my fist) and then he and New Steven just took the entire thing and walked off to his room. Sex and food and a bed? It was plain greedy.

So finally, at 5.30, I got to go to bed on the Ikea recliner and then I couldn't sleep. Images of the night kept playing through my head. I looked through my phone at everyone's posts and messages and then I felt sad; all my friends were in couples, with sorted lives, and none of them had ended up with a random roadie in a less than satisfying sexual encounter. That's why I found myself thinking about Monty. And that's why I got my journal out and started writing about this spectacularly awful night.

And now here I am, a whole hour and a half later, still not asleep and back to wondering about whether it's worth messaging Monty again, just to see if he'd still be interested. Then I remember his wedding and how easy it would be to have him back and how that isn't really what I want, so no, I won't message. But thinking about Monty's wedding reminds me of the Lamb. And Matthew Lloyd.

Oh no, Alice. Don't think about Matthew Lloyd. Don't imagine what he'd say if he could see the state of you now; don't imagine him finding out about Decorator Dave. Definitely don't imagine his face if he could see you here, all alone, with your yellow pleather *The Guide* and your manifestations . . . Don't imagine him saying, 'So Alice. How's the "manifesting" working out for you?'

Because right now, I'd have to answer, 'Absolutely terribly.'

And then he'd smile that smug smile.

And walk off hand in hand with Ebba, doing sums or something.

And I really couldn't bear that.

Guide Post™

*Under frosty winter ground, the bulbs of spring
are awakening. You might only be able to see
earth, but green shoots are just beneath.*

*Perhaps you find yourself doubting, but there
is no place for doubt in this process. Doubt only
sows salt on the garden of your dreams.*

Do not doubt the Universe.

The Universe does not doubt you.

BELIEVE. THE UNIVERSE BELIEVES IN YOU.

Guide Post™

Take the time to revisit and reflect on your manifestations by completing the table below. Be sure to add any extra manifestations you've been working on since last time.

MANIFESTATION	PROGRESS RATING 1–10 *1 – I can see very little or no progress* *10 – I have manifested with complete success*
1. *I manifest* . . . the perfect man (specifically, Guy Carmichael) falling in love with me	*1*
2. *I manifest* . . . having a gorgeous flat to live in from 4 January (preferably central and cheap, or ideally free, and no rats)	*1*
3. *I manifest* . . . not getting fired (I may not *love* my job, but I need the money)	*1*
4. *I manifest* . . . getting a better job (more money, not boring, people bring me coffee rather than the other way round, no one gets my name wrong, etc.)	*1*

5. *I manifest* . . . respect and admiration from friends, colleagues and family (preferably with high levels of envy, veneration of my social media output, and general sense of shame for having doubted me)	1
6. *I manifest* . . . a perfect wedding (everyone whose wedding I've had to sit through can sit at mine and endure, knowing how much better mine is. Plus there will be many comments about how young and beautiful a bride I am)	1
7. *I manifest* . . . wiping that smug smile off Matthew Lloyd's face	1
7.5. I manifest having our old house and spending next Christmas in it	1

*Well done on the progress you've made! If you haven't progressed as much as you were hoping to, this could be because you are putting up **blocks**. Don't despair: we've got just the remedy for you. Try our wonderfully mindful GUIDED SUNRISE™ exercise and shift those inner blocks. We guarantee you'll feel the benefit.*

My thoughts and reflections:

So. This is weird. And wonderful. I had genuinely hit a bad place. I was seriously doubting the whole manifesting thing, but then I turned the page in my journal and that Guide Post struck a chord. As I was reading through the Guided Sunrise exercise, I noticed how it said that ideally this should take place on the first day of a new month at dawn. Hello?!

New Year's Day? 7.30am? The dawn of a whole new year.

I pulled back the blind at the tiny kitchen window and peered out at the darkness. It looked pretty black but when I pushed my face up against the glass I could see navy blue above the dark shapes of buildings. Sunrise was not far away, but it certainly didn't look inviting out in the tiny scrap of yard. I closed the blind. To be fair, it didn't look very inviting in here either.

And, at this point – how much did I have left to lose?

I let myself out the back door where all the bins are kept and pushed one out the way, so that a small patch of muddy, bald grass was showing. I stopped and questioned what I was doing, thought, *Sod it – I'd better do the exercise properly or there's no point*, and took my boots and socks off. Luckily, I was still drunk enough to ignore the potential risks of tetanus and hypothermia and fox urine and to focus instead on the slightly bizarre sensation of cold mud squishing up between my toes. Strangely enough, it wasn't entirely unpleasant. I'd brought my phone out for the torch, but actually, out here, with the daylight beginning to glow through the darkness I could make out the words on the cover of my journal. I stood there for a moment, clutching it in my hands, shivering slightly from the cold (and probably the alcohol withdrawal), wondering if I was desperate enough to continue with this Guided Sunrise thing. I really was.

So, I took out my mobile phone and downloaded a compass app, which took ages despite the supposed 5G, and worked out that I was already facing east, which seemed auspicious. I tipped my head back and inhaled deeply. I could smell the familiar: bins, petrol, a slight odour of drains, tequila. But when I inhaled deeply for the second time I noticed a note of something different, an undertone that reminded me of the country, almost peaty. After one more breath, I opened my eyes and the light had already bloomed above the rooftops of Dulwich: I looked down and the words were visible.

I read them as per instructed, and then turned the pages back until I had my manifestations in front of me. I was about to start reading them aloud and then I remembered that *The Guide* told me it was critical to visualise them too. So, as I spoke my manifestations out loud, I tried my hardest to picture my life improving. But I didn't manage it because I kept thinking about where I *actually* was and how I didn't have any of these things I wanted and smelling the bins and worrying someone was going to see me out here. So, I decided to shut my eyes for my third attempt.

I manifest the perfect man falling in love with me: it was easy to conjure up Guy Carmichael because I've spent so much time watching him in various meetings, many of which I haven't even been part of, but the glass office means I can see him most of the time. He was an officer in the army and you can tell because not only does he have strong forearms but he is always immaculately presented with perfectly pressed pastel shirts and freshly trimmed hair. And it was just as easy to visualise Guy Carmichael pushing me up against the floor-to-ceiling windows in his glass office, a look of raw hunger in his eyes, and kissing me with overwhelming sexual desire and love, etc.; it's something I've imagined loads of times. (Annoyingly, I then got a sudden flashback to yesterday evening when I stumbled into Matthew in Astrid's hallway, the solidity of his chest against my palms, the heat of his hand as he steadied me. Bloody Matthew Lloyd. Always turning up when I didn't want him to.)

I manifest having a gorgeous flat to live in from 4 January: goodness this one was urgent. Given the tenants were arriving in twenty-four hours, I had to sort out two flats. I started by trying to replace the mental image of the rats and the mess in Aunty Margaret's flat with the way it had looked when I first moved in – fresh, clean, rat-free – and imagined the new tenants wheeling their suitcases in and being pleasantly surprised. And then I tried to imagine a nice new, comfortable flat for me. It wasn't easy to create out here in the chill, damp January air. I ended up borrowing Astrid's house instead, which I can see as clearly as a photograph. Her house is like the ideal home – you could find it in a magazine spread. Every little detail has been thought through (that's Astrid for you) and it totally works and I'm totally envious. Plus it's got those luxuries I dream of having: I could almost feel the warmth of the underfloor heating beneath my chilled feet, instead of patchy grass and mud.

I manifest not getting fired: hard to imagine an absence of something. So decided to visualise placing a symbol of permanence – a pot plant – on my desk, and focus on the next manifestation which can only happen if I don't get fired.

I manifest getting a better job: this one was easy as pie because, like Guy Carmichael, it's a daily fantasy, or indeed several fantasies. My favourite one is me saying something fabulous in a meeting, outlining one of my ideas that Harry Piles has steamrollered over, and everyone else sits up and notices, including Guy, and then he says in front of everyone – *Great work, Alice* (getting my name right) and *This is what I'm looking for, people, could someone get her a coffee right now?* And then as I'm about to leave the room, he clears his throat and asks if he could *possibly borrow a minute of my time?* (In this particular fantasy we're not shagging yet but this is the moment he's realising that he finds me incredibly attractive.) So I just thought about that.

I manifest respect and admiration from friends, colleagues and family: for this one I kept vacillating between Charlotte watching me (I'm wearing a Balenciaga dress that she couldn't pull off) as I walk past with Guy and Cara who are both captivated as I talk knowledgably about a wonderful new series I've pitched at work which is why they are taking me out to lunch. To chat as fellow professionals. (And as we wait for the lift, she notices Guy's hand resting proprietarily on my bum . . .) OR a family supper where Arrie's whingeing on about getting up early for the crappy twins and Astrid's boring everyone with talk of being a lawyer or a doctor or whatever, and Mum bangs her fist on the table and says, *I'm sick of it, girls. It's all so tiresome. Why can't you be more like Alice who now makes more money than any of you due to her new important role at work, and yet remains fun?*

I manifest a perfect wedding: another easy one because I knew exactly what I want. All the same old crowd that I have had to endure time and time again at everyone else's weddings, all seated in Little Minchcombe church, facing forwards, overcome with emotion – love, but mainly jealousy – because I look so beautiful and their wedding dresses look a little bit shit now in comparison and they wish they could be me. I could easily imagine me walking down the aisle, seeing their faces react, hear the comments. Except I couldn't really imagine Guy Carmichael in a morning suit in Little Minchcombe church. I think it's because I always picture him in the office.

I manifest having our old house and spending next Christmas in it: in some ways so simple – I could call on numerous Christmases past and practically still taste them – the memories are crystal clear. But then, Matthew Lloyd kept cropping up, uninvited into every memory; walking in the orchard; sitting in the day room. And I heard him saying, 'I always win, Alice,' like he was next to me.

I manifest wiping that smug smile off Matthew Lloyd's face: this one was incredibly hard. Probably the hardest of all. I knew Matthew Lloyd's face so well. But I couldn't scrub off that smile. I kept thinking about how he looked, standing outside our old house, daring me to manifest it, and smirking. But I could imagine me, opening our old front gate, walking down the path, turning the handle and going through the front door. I could imagine it so well I could hear the creak of the second-from-bottom step, run my finger along the ledge above the oak panelling in the drawing room, see the shaft of sunlight that comes through the top pane of the sash window in the upstairs landing. And yet, Matthew Lloyd was still smiling.

I read the last part of the mindful exercise, then closed my eyes as instructed, and waited to feel the Universe holding me. Nothing happened. I opened my eyes and squinted against the watery red sun bleeding into morning.

'Please?' I said.

Nothing.

I exhaled slowly. Right, well. Clearly this exercise hadn't worked. Nothing had happened. My life was still shit.

'Alice? What on earth are you doing?'

I turned round, nearly slipping over on the mud. Drunk Stephen was standing at the back door, looking at me bleary eyed.

'Just putting some rubbish out,' I said. 'I won't be a minute.'

'Good. Because you look like a day release out there. Make sure you shut the door properly,' he said. 'It's bloody freezing.'

Once he'd gone back to bed, I looked at *The Guide* in my hands and felt a moment of pure rage towards it. What a total load of utter bollocks. It had no business promising people better lives. Time to say goodbye to *The Guide*. I heaved the wheelie bin back into place, leaving muddy footprints all over the concrete path and opened the lid.

But just then, a pigeon flapped right next to my face, startling me so much, I dropped the journal on the ground. As I bent to pick it up, I noticed a tiny green shoot with a white bud pushing up through the patch of earth. It was a snowdrop. For a moment, sunlight fell right on it, pooling on its leaves and closed petals, illuminating it as if it were lit from within.

Then my phone pinged with a message. It was Astrid. *So, I was thinking about Aunty Margaret kicking you out of her flat. Do you want to stay here for a bit?*

What? Was she for real?

I messaged back immediately to check if she was serious. She told me a room was mine if I wanted it and that I could come round later and we'd sort out details. I told her I loved her and that I wanted it very, very much and that I'd see her soon.

And then I looked at *The Guide* in my hand, and back up at the sky. Somewhere a blackbird began the opening bars of a song that was major in key; perhaps the background track of cars and buses and trucks and people was still there but all I heard was the blackbird's mellow whistle, pure, amplified, suspended. The sun briefly disappeared behind a cloud before reappearing, like it was winking at me.

I closed the wheelie bin lid, tucked my journal under my arm and went to open the back door. Just before going in, I turned back to face eastwards (well, approximately).

Thank you, I mouthed. *Thank you, Universe.*

In one word:

Believe

Guide Post™

Descartes once said, 'I manifest,* therefore I am.' If it was good enough for Descartes . . .

---

* *Translated words slightly adapted from the original in consensus with popular agreement.*

My thoughts and reflections:

I've been living at Astrid and Aziz's for over forty-eight hours and I've got to say, it feels like I've been here for ever. Aziz said the same thing. It is without doubt the best place I've lived (except our old house, obviously), and I feel such a sense of gratitude towards the Universe for having made this all happen. Because there is no doubt in my mind whatsoever that I have the Universe to thank for this. (And, if the Universe does happen to be listening at this moment, just to be crystal clear, *Doubt is for losers and you won't find any of it in me! No blocks to the manifesting here!*)

Astrid claims otherwise. She says it's her and her alone I should be thanking. In fact, she's pretty derisive about my New Year's Day manifesting episode, to the point of actively mocking it, but then that's Astrid. Relentlessly evidence-based (she was the one who sat me down and explained that both Santa and Mum used the same wrapping paper from Waitrose and that it was time I considered the empirical evidence and lived in the real world), she veers towards the dismissive and negative. And frankly, she's harsh. I mean who tells their four-year-old sister Santa isn't real on Christmas Eve? Astrid! That's who! Which, incidentally, if we're looking for 'empirical evidence', is precisely *how* I know the Universe intervened on my behalf. Because Astrid, if left to her own devices, would never have thought to let me move in, no matter what problems I was experiencing. I know many sisters would, but not Astrid. Even when I've asked for something most people wouldn't think twice about, such as staying the odd night, she's been like a Conservative Home Office Minister's immigration policy: suspicious and unrelenting. *Okay, but ONE night and you're out by midday so don't try getting round me because I know all your little tricks. Give you an inch and you'll take a mile. It'll be, 'Oh no, Astrid – it's getting late – I may as well stay again', and then before I know it, you'll have squatter's rights.*

Once, even though it was one in the morning, sub-zero and snowing – *actually* snowing in Chiswick – she still made me leave and take a two-hour-long marathon of night buses. And I told her I had a mild temperature. She just handed me a couple of paracetamol and said how she wasn't having me turn her into another 'Wet Wanda' (Wanda *was* a bit wet, which was why we're no longer friends, but it was hardly *my* fault if she wanted to keep paying rent on her Camden studio despite living with her boyfriend at his – if anything I was doing *her* a favour by staying there for that year, and watering the plant), and that she wasn't a simpleton like Monty (fair enough) and then pretty much pushed me out the door. Astrid is the harshest person I know. She genuinely had her housemate evicted *during* finals for infringing the noise-after-hours element of their shared living arrangement (which Astrid had drawn up) and according to Arrie, the noise infringement was, actually, the housemate crying in the middle of the night due to exam stress combined with her boyfriend dumping her. That's Astrid: she shows no mercy. So inviting me to live with her was significant and uncharacteristic and clearly down to a higher power.

Of course, Astrid scoffed when I told her how I'd manifested this. 'Come on, Alice. Even you can think a little more critically than that . . .'

(Just another example of how little my family know me because I'm actually an extremely critical thinker; I never do a tube journey without thinking about the surprising number of badly dressed people you can find in every carriage.)

'Did it cross your mind that I may have decided the night before to let you move in?' maintained Astrid. 'Can I just check: when you were manifesting up the perfect place to live, did you also manifest this tenancy and rent agreement?'

Astrid had drawn up an extremely detailed agreement which she showed me as soon as I turned up late afternoon on New Year's Day, utterly exhausted after fourteen hours straight of cleaning Aunty Margaret's flat. Incidentally, that's another manifesting success because that flat looked pristine by the time I'd finished and clearly the new tenants are happy, otherwise Aunty Margaret would have been kicking up a fuss. Anyway, I didn't bother reading Astrid's agreement because I knew it would be extremely dull. But I did ask the basics and essentially it was almost too good to be true. Apart from having to pay rent and having to be out the house during the day anytime Aziz was working from home, or Astrid wanted the place to herself to study, there were no restrictions. I even double-checked: 'Are you sure you don't want me to stay in my room in the evenings, to give you and Az a bit of space or whatever?'

Aziz came into the room just as I was asking this and Astrid told me I should feel free to spend as much time as I wanted with her and Aziz – and that she and Aziz didn't need any space at all. Aziz stared at Astrid for a second and then back at me and then at Astrid again. Then he asked if he'd missed something, and Astrid said, 'Alice is moving in. Problem?'

But instead of saying no like I expected him to, Aziz didn't look at Astrid; he didn't look at anyone. He just stood there for a moment and then took his glasses off and started rubbing them on his jumper.

'Az?' I said. 'Is it better if I don't stay?'

Then he put his glasses back on and said, 'Of course not, Alice; sorry, I was miles away,' and gave me one of his lovely smiles and told me to make myself at home.

'Astrid,' I said, rising to her sarcasm about the manifesting, 'maybe you need to ask yourself some questions instead of me. Like, *why* did I decide to rent this room to Alice? What *prompted* that decision?' I smiled gently at my scowling Doubting Thomas of a sister. 'I think we both know, don't we?'

'Yes, I think we do,' said Astrid. 'I need to consider how how to cover the mortgage when I leave work.'

But even Mum admitted that it was quite odd behaviour on Astrid's part. 'I'd have thought she'd prefer a stranger, Alice, to you. Not just for the rent reliability but the company.'

And Arrie went one step further, saying it was 'bloody weird', and how 'we all know that Astrid won't let us use anything that's hers, not even a bloody pen, so why is she letting you use her spare room? And you of all people, Alice.'

'There's a very simple explanation for all of this,' I told them, 'the Universe helped out!'

But, in typical Carver fashion, they ignored me.

Still, I can't help thinking, as I recline on the beautiful over-sized pale grey sofa in Astrid's second sitting room, a chilled glass of white in hand, *Made in Chelsea* about to start, that maybe it's all working in my favour – after all, the less other people ask of the Universe, the more the Universe will be able to give me.

And now I've manifested literally THE perfect place to live, it's time to crack on with my other manifestations.

Which I will do. After *MIC*.

And maybe after one more glass of wine, max, so I'm fresh as a daisy for the first day back in the office tomorrow.

I am grateful for:

Aziz and Astrid's well-stocked wine fridge – this 'lesser known yet delicious Friulano grape variety' is going down super-well. Plus it's biodiverse! So healthy. No sulphites apparently.

My thoughts and reflections:

I actually watched another episode of *Made in Chelsea* because I couldn't take the cliff-hanger.

After that, I was going to spend some time manifesting, but opened my laptop first to have a quick skim through my work inbox (as dedicated employee) and oh my god – how many emails? It's been Christmas! What these 'emailers' don't get, is that by continuing to work when they shouldn't be, they spoil it for everyone else. I initially ignored the emails out of principle – they could wait for tomorrow – and checked whether there was anything urgent on the Teams chat because that one's harder to claim you haven't seen. There wasn't much – or much that was relevant now. Cara, Non-Fiction Publisher, sent a general one to everyone in our team earlier today saying she was looking forward to welcoming us back in tomorrow. Obviously a few fawners (Yaz, Nervous Jane) immediately replied because they have no lives. And Sweaty Liam from Facilities had uploaded a fourteen-page joke of a document about health and safety in the workplace, which we've all got to read by the end of the week. There were a few moans and people saying *do we have to,* but Cara intervened saying it was *company policy.* Anyway, I can play the game with the rest of them. I scanned through the health and safety document until I found a suitable sub-heading. Then I posted on Cara's chat saying I was so looking forward to seeing everyone tomorrow and that I'd personally found the health and safety document really helpful, and had particularly enjoyed the section on 'monitor glare'.

Just as I was about to close my laptop, I scrolled up to the top email in my inbox and saw the name of the sender: Guy Carmichael. It gave me a momentary frisson of excitement that increased tenfold when I clocked the subject line: *touching in*. Had my manifesting already worked? I'd love some touching in. I opened up the email and read it. Guy Carmichael was letting me know (along with the entire division) that with the upcoming merger, it was obviously a difficult time for all, and he appreciated my (our) support and commitment to Carsons, and that his door was always open.

Well, that's not true. His door is always closed. He's just greasing me up for a firing.

'No,' I reminded myself, flicking back through *The Guide*: 'Negative talk will only take you to negative town, Alice. Come on, Alice – don't erect those mental blocks – maybe this upcoming merger is an opportunity?' I finished my glass of wine in a fortifying way, and shut my eyes.

'I believe,' I said. 'I believe like the Universe believes in me.'

Then I repeated my manifestation about having a job. And I imagined me walking into work tomorrow, bright and early, hair swinging, Lydia on security standing up straighter and beckoning me through, a look of respect in her eyes. And then me up on my floor, the team gathered round my desk, taking notes, learning from me. And then me and Guy Carmichael walking towards the lifts, going off for lunch together. And then me and Guy Carmichael in the lifts and him turning to me with unrestrained animalistic desire in his eyes and saying, *About touching in, Alice . . .*

I opened my eyes and looked at my surroundings: if I could manifest this house in Chiswick, I could manifest more.

I've got this.

I have totally got this.

I am letting go of:

Saving the rest of this bottle – it does say 'best enjoyed now' and it is important to relax and unwind and get the full bio-diverse benefits.

Date: Wednesday 4 January   **Time: 5.05pm**

My thoughts and reflections:

I booked out this privacy meeting booth so I could spend some time reflecting and thinking in peace – obviously I've got my laptop in front of my journal if anyone looks in, so it seems like I'm working. But I'm *not* working because I've been here all day and I can't be bothered now; it's not like anything important ever happens on the first day back. Frankly it's ridiculous, given they're always talking about wellbeing in the workplace, that no one more senior has suggested a staged return to work after Christmas – something sensible like ten to three would work. I've certainly been ready to go home since three.

It wasn't the ideal start to the day: I slept through my alarm and then woke up with a headache and a dry mouth. It's the biodiverse wine of course – I mean when you actually think about it, you're putting your life in someone else's (probably unwashed) hands when you go the biodynamic route as they're not subject to the same regulations you get with chemicals and stuff. In fact, the more you look into it, the more you realise you're effectively subjecting yourself to something that could be moonshine. I should have exercised greater caution with the Friulano: I'm lucky I haven't gone blind. I certainly shan't be finishing off the second bottle I opened last night, and will mention to Astrid and Aziz they may want to stick to proper sulphite-rich wine from now on.

I stood behind a woman with a huge ponytail on the tube and every time the train slowed down, she whipped her head round to peer anxiously out the window and check the station, thus flicking me right in the face. It wouldn't have been so bad but she'd evidently just had a haircut, as the ends were blunt and uniform, plus she'd used straighteners, so the whole situation was genuinely hazardous and extremely abrasive. And then when I arrived at the building, my ID card didn't swipe properly and joy of joys, it was Lydia on security, who hates me for some reason. This morning, Lydia was on her phone, texting, and she didn't even attempt to hide the fact. When I tried to ask her for help, she just held up her left hand, in my face, cutting me off mid-syllable, and said, 'Wait.' But then when the Head of Foreign Rights came in, after me, and without his card, she immediately stopped texting and used her special card to open the gate and waved him through with a 'good morning' and a smile! So I loudly said, 'Excuse me, I've been waiting for a while and I really need to get into the office but my card's not working.'

And she took it from me, without even glancing at me, and studied the card and said, 'You've got the wrong name on the card; it won't work.'

'No, it's the right name so could you swipe me through?'

And, then she did look at me. 'No, it's wrong. It says Alice. You're Alison.'

'I'm not.'

And she turned away in irritation, pursed her lips and

tapped on her computer and said, 'Yes, you're Alison – it says on my system. Can't let you through now. It's a security risk.'

'But I work here. I have done for three years. You know me?'

Lydia folded her arms and shook her head.

Just then, Drunk Stephen appeared at the lifts carrying a package which he handed to Lydia for a courier. And Lydia was all smarmy and nice to him, so I said, 'Stephen, can you tell Lydia my name is Alice, not Alison, so she'll let me in? I'm already late for work.'

And Drunk Stephen said, 'Yeah, you really are – you've missed the 9.30 team catch-up.'

Lydia stopped smiling. 'Her card says Alice. Can't let her through. Got to be the right name.'

And Drunk Stephen looked at me, and then Lydia. Then he shook his head at me like I was a proper nuisance. 'Alison, Alison, Alison,' he said. 'Always making trouble.' He turned back to Lydia and raised his eyebrows in solidarity with her. 'Lydia, any chance you'd just swipe Alison through for now, and we'll contact HR and get the typos sorted?'

Lydia drummed her fingers sullenly. 'I'm putting myself on the line for you, Stephen,' she said, before swiping me through.

I had to spend the whole stomach-lurching lift journey up to the seventeenth floor listening to Drunk Stephen giving me graphic details about sex with New Steven, whilst enduring more mocking about Decorator Dave and this latest wrong-name fiasco, with him hilariously and repeatedly calling me Alison. Okay, the lift journey is in reality only seconds but I wasn't in the mood this morning and as I said to Drunk Stephen, given the adverse effects of biodynamic wine production on my system, and the fact that the lift makes me feel a bit pukey at the best of times, he'd better be a bit more careful about stressing me. And that if he told anyone at work about Decorator Dave, I'd wear espadrilles into the office every single day. Drunk Stephen swallowed. He finds espadrilles really offensive. 'Canvas?' he checked.

'Oh no,' I said. 'Wicker.'

He gasped. 'That's so low.'

But as I said to Drunk Stephen, needs must.

So frankly, it was an ordeal even getting to my desk. And then I only had time to get my laptop out and log on, before rushing off to the bathrooms, because it was a whole division briefing with Guy Carmichael at 10.30 and I wanted to touch up my make-up first. Yaz was her usual self – 'Off already, Alice?' she called after me, 'You've just arrived! Going to do your make-up, I suppose?' She's like a prefect, with her pen pot and little disinfectant wipes and disapproval.

I turned back momentarily and leant on her desk. 'Actually, I've got a messed-up stomach.' I stared at her. 'Probably caught it from my nephews.' I saw her gaze flick to my hand on her desk and then back to me.

'So quite contagious?' she said.

I picked up a pen from her pot and bit it pensively. 'Super contagious.'

She definitely flinched. Then I put the pen back in her pot with the others and stirred it around. At least if she's busy wiping her pens, she can back off keeping tabs on me.

But things did improve: someone had left a load of doughnuts in the kitchenette, which I helped myself to, and whilst I was texting Drunk Stephen to tell him about the doughnuts, Charlotte came in. Obviously, I've been desperate to find out what's been going on between her and Guy Carmichael, but it's not like we're friends, so I couldn't text just to ask her directly. This, however, was the perfect opportunity.

'Hey, Charlotte,' I said, as she strode in and started filling her water bottle at the water station. 'You look amazing.'

She did. She was wearing that crocheted body con dress like she was about to hit Ibiza's clubs: there was a lot of skin on display. It reminded me a bit of the Balmain dress Ebba was wearing on New Year's Eve. I fleetingly imagined Matthew's hands on Ebba's skin and then immediately shoved the thought aside. Charlotte may not be a Swedish model but was still totally pulling off that dress; she's absolutely ripped because of all those hours she spends at GlowCycle. Not an obvious choice of outfit for a cold January day in the workplace but I suppose she is shagging the boss.

'Yeah, thanks.' She flipped her hair to the side. 'Just threw the first thing on really.'

Like hell she did.

'Well, I imagine Guy won't be able to keep his hands off you when he sees you!' I said, casually.

'Yeah, probably.' She turned to face away from me.

'So how's it going with you two?' I persisted.

'Oh yeah. It's not.'

She screwed her bottle lid on firmly.

'Really?' I tried not to look too excited. 'I thought you liked him?'

'It was just a bit of fun. But, like I told Guy, I'm not looking for anything serious at my age.'

Well, that's a change of heart. She told me at the summer author do that she's been on the hunt since twenty-five.

According to her mother, once Charlotte hit thirty, she'd be seeing a steep decline in her cachet as no man wants to trade in one old crone of a wife for another.

'*I'm* still in my prime,' continued Charlotte. 'No offence, Alice.'

'None taken,' I lied, standing aside to let Charlotte sashay out of the kitchenette.

Drunk Stephen arrived for doughnuts just as she left – 'Dressing to kill, Charlotte,' he said, whistling in admiration as she passed him. Perfect timing. As soon as she'd gone, I told him what she said. Drunk Stephen's eyes opened wide. He checked carefully that no one else was near. 'Yeah, so he totally dumped her.'

I gasped in delight.

'But she's his type! Young, pretty, hot body . . . ? I thought she had it in the bag?'

'Clearly so did she. Big mistake. It's one thing having a type; it's another admitting publicly that you have a type.' He leant closer. 'Word on the street is that she posted a picture of them together a couple of days in, and that was it.'

'What?' I said. 'I wonder what his problem was?'

'Er, he's married?' Drunk Stephen looked at me like I was being stupid. 'And her boss?'

'Everyone knows he and his wife are separated though.'

'If you're still married, then it's still an affair.' Drunk Stephen looked around furtively before adding, 'And Anika in PR said that apparently Charlotte asked him, like literally mid-blow-job, if she could make their relationship official on her account.'

'Oh god, I hope that's true!'

'Damn, I've eaten two of these doughnuts now,' said Drunk Stephen, 'but I'm burning calories with the anticipation – I've never been so excited for a divisional in my life! I can't wait to see her and GC in the same room.'

Up until the last ten minutes of it, divisional was, in reality, bloody boring: Amelia from HR opened the meeting by reading a statement, saying, 'We are not currently in a position to share information about the merger, but as soon as we are, you will be the first to know. For now, please operate as normal, and no questions for the time being, thank you'; then a load of department heads just talked and talked and talked – as usual. Still, it was less of a chore because I got a great seat where I could stare at Guy Carmichael listening to his droning colleagues – without anyone noticing. He's got a really sexy nod. Sort of grave, serious and powerful. I'd love him to nod at me like that. Like, *Yes, Alice* – small nod – *you can sit on my cock*. Can't believe his wife let him go. Although he's clearly slept with a number of employees over the years, which may have been an issue for her. Only attractive ones though. And very discreetly: we all pretend we know nothing about it. Can't help thinking it really should be my turn soon. Remarkably, even though Charlotte was doing a lot of hair flicking and occasional coughing (plus obviously wearing next to nothing), Guy Carmichael didn't glance her way once. Well, until the last ten minutes. Which was when things got interesting.

And, when my day started to go really quite well . . .

Guy Carmichael took the floor. He thanked all the department heads and said it was great to see us all again and he hoped we'd enjoyed our holidays. Commanding and considerate – that's Guy Carmichael. He told us that he would be keeping things brief, and that the main communication from him today was about the problems in warehouse distribution. We (Carsons) were bringing on a third-party distribution client as we needed all the profit we could get given the challenges this fiscal. Unfortunately, Glasgow weren't playing ball and were claiming it couldn't be done. So he needed to put one of his best people straight on it.

Drunk Stephen and I exchanged slightly confused glances – what did this have to do with the division? Occasionally people mentioned the warehouses, but in the same way they mentioned the mail room. Necessary, but essentially a mystery we didn't need to know too much about.

'I've had a chat with the department heads,' continued Guy, 'and we've thrown around some names and we're delighted to say, Charlotte will be our man in Scotland!'

'What?' said Charlotte, hair flicking paused. 'You're sending me to Glasgow?'

'We're giving you a fantastic opportunity to expand your portfolio.'

'But it's the warehouse,' said Charlotte. 'Isn't that Production's job?'

'I think we need fresh eyes,' said Guy.

'You can't be serious,' snapped Charlotte. 'I do PR.'

'Exactly. If you convinced Vanessa Feltz to stay at the Cheltenham Literature Festival when she was about to walk due to the smell of drains in her room, you can convince Jock Forklift and friends to pick up tools and load some bloody boxes of books.'

Charlotte stood there with her arms folded, fury barely contained, and Guy just moved on, saying he was excited about the new year, and to all work our hardest, and that we should remember he operated an open-doors policy, then promptly left the meeting room. Barely anyone else moved – we were all pretending to get our stuff together whilst actually watching Charlotte, who immediately went after him – ('She is playing this all wrong,' whispered Drunk Stephen).

Charlotte was apprehended by Amelia in HR, who said perhaps they could chat and iron out the details about Glasgow, whereupon Charlotte lost it and said, 'If you could give me a fucking moment, please,' and shoved past Amelia quite aggressively.

A collective murmur went round the room.

'She'll fit right into Glasgow with vocab like that,' said the one from Design who always wears Armani glasses. 'If she's anything like Ewan.'

'Fuck off,' said Ewan from Design. 'I'll tell you what though, she'll need a new coat. She'll freeze her tits off dressed like that.'

And for the rest of the day, the rumour mill was spinning. According to Nervous Jane who occasionally has lunch with Iris, Guy Carmichael's PA, Charlotte tried to go and speak to Guy Carmichael and Iris told her she could only speak to him with an appointment. And when Charlotte pointed out that he'd said he had an open-door policy, Iris said that it was an open-door policy with appointments. And Charlotte said, 'Can I have one then?' but Iris said he didn't have any until the end of the week. And Charlotte apparently swore under her breath and then Iris made her own appointment with HR about protected characteristics because Iris is a Christian and felt quite distressed by Charlotte's word choice and the tone behind it.

So all in all, I'm counting today as a number of mini-steps in the right direction. I may not have manifested Guy Carmichael being in love with me yet, but the key word here is 'yet'! It's pretty apparent that the Universe is paving the way for me:

a) Guy Carmichael has dumped Charlotte
b) Charlotte hasn't even mentioned my photo with Decorator Dave
c) Charlotte is being moved to a different country – talk about threat removal.

I'm certainly going to spend some time manifesting this evening.

In one word:

Glasgow

My thoughts and reflections:

So it *is* that bloody biodynamic wine. Definitely. I decided to try some more last night, as quality control, before mentioning to Aziz and Astrid they'd bought a whole case of shit wine, because I'm a considerate person. Total menace. I now have a vicious headache and am wearing yesterday's outfit which has stains on the trousers because I completely forgot about laundering clothes. Plus I left Astrid's umbrella on the tube so got soaked walking into work and had to go into Cara's meeting late, and as no one budged up, I had to walk all the way round the table, looking bedraggled, to get to the seat next to hers. Cara did that whole *going silent to wait for Alice* thing, glancing ostentatiously at her hideous Bulgari watch. I'd have preferred it if she'd just said *you're bloody late.* Then I had to listen without rolling my eyes whilst Yaz said how she had some great ideas she couldn't wait to share in Acquisitions tomorrow. Then to top it off, twenty minutes after I'd arrived late, Charlotte came in wearing pants and making every head swivel. I can't believe Guy Carmichael dumped her. Of course, people fell over themselves budging up so that Charlotte could sit down. And when Charlotte said she was sorry for being late, entirely unapologetically, Cara just brushed it aside and said, 'Who's watching clocks?'

Er, you, Cara.

To make the day extra fun, Yaz keeps wincing and clutching her stomach and spraying little puffs of Tom Ford's bitter peach. It doesn't disguise what she's doing. She's just ruined a perfectly good fragrance for me. She even said, 'I must have got it from you, so chances are you won't catch it.'

I reckon it's from those horrible fermented shot things she drinks. I wish I hadn't sucked her pen yesterday. Anyway, I'm hiding out in the little meeting booth again and will keep hoping no one comes and kicks me out for an actual meeting.

Oh, and Guy Carmichael isn't in the office today, so there's not even anything to aspire to. It all feels a little flat, and like a backwards step after yesterday.

I might find out about the GlowCycle gym Charlotte goes to and different payment options.

I am grateful for:

Private meeting rooms

My thoughts and reflections:

My overpowering thought at the moment is that Astrid is very lucky she came across Aziz at university, and got him to sign a marriage certificate, because her personality is largely repellent and has just got worse over time. She's been beastly to me this evening. She came home in a bad mood because she got a bit wet and took it all out on me. She accused me of stealing her umbrella, which I denied. I pointed out that I, too, was wet, and that if I'd stolen her umbrella, surely I'd be using it. Then when I tried to strike up a conversation with her about GlowCycle and spending some quality time together as sisters, she said there's no way she's joining GlowCycle and that I need to stop trying to manipulate her to get things I want and start paying for myself. Then she opened the wine fridge to get a glass of the Friulano wine, made a big fuss about the bottle being nearly finished, went to get another bottle and seemed aghast that there were only two left. I pointed out that it's horrible wine and has given me nasty headaches. Astrid was rude and said that it was more likely the after-effects of drinking nearly four bottles of wine by myself over two days and that I owed her £80.

I said, 'What the fuck, that's insanely expensive,' and that

I'd never buy toxic wine at that price and that if anything she should be asking for a refund. She said I was welcome to get her a refund or pay her, and to stop stealing her wine if I wanted to stay here.

Upon reflection, I can't help thinking how many people there are in my life – friends, family, colleagues – who would benefit from doing the kind of thing I am doing right now, reflecting, thinking, becoming a better person. Astrid could certainly do with being less of a twat. So could Cara. And Charlotte. Lydia won't manage it, but she should at least try. The more I think about it, the more I realise I am surrounded by twats. I might message Drunk Stephen so we can talk about twats in the workplace. (Although he himself is also guilty of being a twat on occasion – I had to invoke wicker again today.)

God. No wonder it's hard for me to get my life in order.

I ask the Universe:

To help other people be less awful.

Guide Post™

Are you tuned into the right frequency or could you take the time to re-tune? If you're seeing some results with manifesting, but progress is slower than you'd like it to be, it could be that you've fallen into 'negative energy spaces'.

*As Albert Einstein said, 'Manifesting** is energy.' But ask yourself: am I manifesting the **right** energy?*

* *Words slightly adapted from the original but the sense remains identical.*

Guide Post™

Answer the following questions:

1. *Do you surround yourself with
    negative people and let them steal your
    positive energy? How to notice negative
    people: slumped posture, negative
    talk, whiny, sad, critical, rude . . .*

I mean, hello?! Yet again, the Universe has responded to my
need. Thank you, Universe. But when you read this . . . scary!
How on the nose can you get? Literally describing Astrid here.
Apart from the slumped posture, but that's only because she
does shitloads of Pilates. Her true self is slumped. And Yaz who
sits next to me – really whiny and negative. Cara – so critical.
Lydia – rude. And all the rest of the team – where do I start?
No wonder I'm having problems! I knew they were all twats,
but to find out they're also blocking me from having my perfect
life . . . of course I can't manifest when I'm surrounded by such
negative people. At least I know now it's everyone else's fault!

2. *Do you allow negative talk airtime? It's
    your station – control what goes out there!*

How to notice negative talk: you may use
words like 'can't', or find you're making
judgements or blaming. Blasphemy and
swearing can be prevalent. Negative
words breed negative thoughts . . .

Doesn't really apply to me. I'm quite supportive of others.

3. *Do you allow negative air into your*
   lungs? When you breathe negative you
   live negative. How to notice negative air:
   often the air doesn't smell as pleasant
   as it should. Sulphur, burning, bitter,
   acrid smells can be a sign your air is
   negative. You can also feel negative
   air: feeling hot or cold, headaches,
   tiredness are all symptoms.

Well, this is a real eye-opener. I'm dealing with negative air
literally all the bloody time! Constantly breathing it in. It's
remarkable I do as well as I do.

If you recognise your life in any of the above,
re-tune your life using simple tips from
WAVEGUIDES: TUNING INTO POSITIVE ENERGY™

My thoughts and reflections:

I am taking this opportunity to reflect on how amazing *The Guide* is and to be grateful. That Guide Post yesterday found its way to me at the perfect time.

I woke up sprightly and alert and before my alarm this morning, the tube arrived as I did, and I got to work twenty minutes early! I took a second outside the building to arm myself against Lydia's toxic energy, and entered reciting my affirmations: *'I surround myself with positive energy. I am living my best life. My heart is pure.'* And it worked, because she wasn't even there yet. It was still Clyde, who does like me, and he gave me a wink and called me 'ma'am'. (He's very flirty as well as very fit. We had a little snog at the summer do, but turns out he is also very young, so we left it there.)

I'd nipped into the Tesco Metro by the tube station and bought some basil (they didn't have sage or eucalyptus) and some matches ready to clear the negative air near Yaz, but the Universe threw me another line – Yaz was off work. So I drank my matcha tea, said a casual hi to a couple of people who arrived after me and flicked through the post. And yes, I will admit that maybe a tiny grain of doubt did momentarily enter my mind when I tore open the large cream envelope and saw the stiff, heavy gold-rimmed christening invitation.

> **Mr and Mrs Tristan Cavendish request the pleasure of your company at Little Minchcombe church, and afterwards at the Lamb, on Saturday, 24 June, to celebrate the joyful arrival of Edgar Austen William Augustus Cavendish.**

A handwritten note from Mrs Tristan Cavendish herself tumbled out along with the rigid, grandiose invitation.

> *Darling, your mother mentioned you were between digs so I thought I'd send this to your work – if you're still there, LOL. Such a shame not to catch up at the wedding but I could see you were finding it hard, poor thing. Have you heard the wonderful news? Minty's expecting! Do RSVP this time – what are you like! – and we completely understand if it's too much for you. Lots and lots of love, Penelope x*

She's ghastly. How can one envelope contain so many knives? Astrid's always said Penelope is insufferable and she's right. Now Penelope really *is* a twat, unlike Astrid, and I feel I should state, for the record, that I didn't really mean what I wrote about Astrid last night. (In fact I got her a bottle of wine when I was at the Tesco Metro earlier, just as a little apology; it was only £5 in the bargain bin because it didn't have a label.) Whereas Penelope – she invokes long-lasting feelings of dislike. And Minty! Well, that explains the 24th December wedding. And why she didn't touch the blue cheese.

I propped the invitation up on Yaz's desk so it wouldn't gloat quite so directly in my face, but I was feeling sort of hot and uncomfortable so I knew it had affected the air. I took action by saying a couple of affirmations, and got the basil out of the bag and was fumbling around with the matches, when Cara caught me, mid–'I breathe in peace; I breathe out peace'. And here's my next lucky-girl moment because instead of Cara being her usual disagreeable self, she just put her hand on my arm and said that she personally found the affirmation 'I am a beacon of love and joy' really helpful. She recommended not lighting a match because it would set off the automatic fire sprinklers, plus basil wouldn't work as it's too damp. Then she told me she believed in me and so did the Goddess and that my day would be filled with abundance and harmony.

Who would have thought it?!

Even better, when I bumped into her again later, in the loos, and quickly put my make-up away because it was nearly time for the 11.45 catch-up and we both knew it, she scanned my face and said, 'I don't really need to see you today.' She told me to go to Selfridges and get my make-up done and remind myself that self-love starts with self-care.

I didn't need telling twice.

And now, here's the second best bit. After an amazing hour spent eating sushi and having my make-up done by the Chanel girl at Selfridges, I was so buoyant that waiting to get swiped in by Lydia didn't faze me at all. I just watched her eat her massive baguette, and slowly repeated affirmations in my head. *I surround myself with positive energy. I surround myself with positive energy.* And I did. Because then . . . Then, Guy Carmichael appeared behind me. Can't get much more positive than that!

'What's the hold-up?' he asked.

Even his voice was magnetic: I could feel the underwires in my bra vibrate in response.

I said, 'My card's playing up today.'

Lydia put down her baguette and swallowed her mouthful.

'Damned pain these new cards,' he said. 'Come through on mine. Lydia can sort it out on her computer later.'

And he stood back and ushered me through – it's probably the closest I've come to him and his scent was intoxicating, sort of musk and cedar and a hint of citrus and power, and like he'd be commanding and unrelenting in bed.

'Thanks,' I said to Guy, pleased to notice that a fair bit of filling had dropped out of Lydia's baguette when she set it down. Serves her right.

'Pleasure's mine,' he said, then he looked at me again. 'Nice lipstick.'

'It's Chanel.'

He nodded. 'Have a good afternoon, Alison.'

I didn't care that he called me Alison, or that Lydia gave me a triumphant glare because I could sense that the Universe was working hard for me. And I was right. I've saved the best bit for last . . .

That afternoon, whilst I was sitting at my desk drumming my fingers and putting off replying to emails, Guy Carmichael walked by and . . . paused. I nearly stopped breathing. He was staring at something on Yaz's desk. Then he picked up my invitation and started reading it. I panicked.

'Er, sorry,' I said. 'I'm between addresses so it got sent here to work. I'll take it home tonight.'

Guy Carmichael looked back at me.

'This is yours?' he said, his attention turned fully towards me.

'Yes,' I babbled on, trying not to salivate at his proximity. 'There's always someone back home getting married or producing babies.'

'You're from Little Minchcombe, are you?'

'For my sins!' I joked. 'Not inbred though.'

Oh god. *Why* did I say that?

'Interesting,' he said, perching on my desk. 'I've just been reading about it.'

Fuck. Guy Carmichael was sitting on my desk.

'Small place, is it?' he asked. 'Everyone know everybody else?'

'Pretty much. Most of us all went to the same schools.'

'Hang on, is St Hilda's there?'

'Yes. So most of us went there. Apart from a couple who went to Eton.' And of course Matthew who went to the comprehensive (apart from sixth form). I'm guessing Guy Carmichael doesn't deal in comprehensive schools.

'Well, well, well. Aren't you turning out to be an interesting one.' He paused for a moment. 'Why is it addressed to Alice, Alison?'

'Um, because I'm called Alice?'

'For goodness sake, Alison, you should have said.'

'Alice.'

Guy Carmichael squinted at me for a second. 'I prefer Alice,' he said.

'So do I.'

'Hmm.' Guy Carmichael leant forward, his attention fully on me.

I watched his gaze drop to my lips.

'What shade is that lipstick you're wearing, Alice?'

'Rouge Allure,' I said, my voice emerging a little croaky.

'It's working.'

Just then, Cool Jason from Design wandered by and Guy sat back slightly. He handed me my invitation and stood up. 'I'll see you on Monday, Alice,' he said.

Yes you will, Guy Carmichael.

My intention is:

- To sacrifice going out tonight and instead use the money to go and buy some Chanel Rouge Allure.
- To get Guy Carmichael to think about my lips and me in a non-work-colleague way.

Date: Sunday 8 January   **Time: 8.30pm**

My thoughts and reflections:

Normally I love a weekend, but I've been wishing this one away. I can't wait until tomorrow. I'm setting my alarm for 5.30 so I can wash and dry my hair properly, and apply make-up before leaving, just in case I meet him at the entrance. Charlotte sent me a DM yesterday asking if I wanted to go to Scotland in her place and that there was a really good scene in Glasgow I might enjoy. I said no. I felt bad but then Drunk Stephen said she's been asking everyone. Apparently, she got really pissed at The Green Room after work on Friday and revealed that even though she wasn't meant to tell anyone, Guy Carmichael had dumped her literally ten minutes after they'd had sex and that he was a complete bastard.

I am letting go of:

Trying to be more like Charlotte.

Date: Monday 9 January   **Time: 12.30am**

My thoughts and reflections:

Pulled all the stops out – arrived early and looking as good as I'm going to get. But no Guy Carmichael at work today. What a waste of effort. Drunk Stephen and I went for compensatory Monday Margaritas – Blakes does happy hour six to eight, which is actually happy *hours* if we're being accurate. Then we had non-happy-hours margaritas which were still really happy. And then kebabs. (It wasn't strictly a break-out day, but as I said to Drunk Stephen – what could be more Stone Age than effectively hunting for food on the way home?)

I ask the Universe:

To wake me up in the morning as I'm having trouble with alarm-setting.

Date: Tuesday 10 January   **Time: 8.30pm**

My thoughts and reflections:

Got to work forty-five minutes late this morning, hair in a crazy bun, wearing yesterday's make-up and work outfit, carrying a residual whiff of lime and tequila and lamb, and experiencing more than just a touch of nausea. I was just waiting for the lift, sipping Lucozade, and rifling through my bag on the floor for more Nurofen when I sensed someone behind me. I could smell the cedar and musk. *Oh no*, I thought, slowly standing up, *please don't let it be him. Not until I've got to the loos and done my make-up.* I looked over my shoulder. Fuck.

'Ah,' said Guy Carmichael, his eyes narrowing as he gave me a rapid once-over. 'Good morning, Alice. Or should I say good afternoon?'

'Er, yes. Sorry I'm late.' I wondered how rough I looked and whether he was going to go annoyed-employer on me or whether he was going to continue where we left off last week.

'Doing something special last night, Alice? With the boyfriend?'

'Just a couple of drinks after work.' I swallowed my pills and screwed the lid back on my Lucozade. 'No boyfriend.'

'Interesting,' he said, staring at the lift doors.

We both stood there for a moment, waiting, and then he reached across for the call button.

'Excuse me,' he said, leaning just past me so that the sleeve of his navy blue cashmere overcoat slightly brushed my breast.

I swear it was deliberate. There was plenty of room.

'Of course,' I said, not moving, to see if he'd brush against me again.

He did.

The doors pinged open, interrupting my lascivious thoughts.

'After you,' said Guy Carmichael.

Oh my goodness. This was like a fantasy come true: we were going to be in the lift together. Alone. My skin went on high alert. I could feel him come in, closely behind me – that man certainly knew how to fill a space. It boded well.

'Um, so do you want the seventeenth floor?' I checked, keeping my voice steady.

'I do.' Guy Carmichael watched me as I pressed the button. As the doors closed I was intensely aware that it was just him and me in the lift. He didn't say anything and neither did I, but it felt like he was looking at me the way I looked at that kebab last night, voracious and ready to go to town. However, just in case he wasn't, and was in fact wondering about the slight smell of doner special sauce coming from me, I didn't launch myself across and snog him. Instead, I stood there, mirroring him. Silent. Staring back. Hypnotised by his sheer charisma and power. Then, just when I thought I couldn't take it any longer and I was going to involuntarily make a move and risk both rejection and unemployment, he took a step towards me, a predatory look in his eyes. 'So, Alice,' he said, his voice low. 'Alice, Alice, Alice . . .'

A prickle of excitement danced up my thighs. He was coming on to me. 'Yes?' I moved towards him.

'I've been thinking . . . ' he said.

But the bloody lift doors pinged open on the ninth floor, and so we both took steps back, and Sweater-vest Gareth from Accounts stepped in, and said hello to us both, then immediately looked uncomfortable because Guy Carmichael is the kind of man who makes most other men feel uncomfortable at the best of times.

Guy tutted with irritation. 'Garth. Can't you afford sleeves?'

Gareth looked at his sweater vest and his short-sleeved shirt and then back at Guy and said, 'It's just how they come.'

And Guy said, 'It looks fucking awful, Garth.' Guy constantly says things that would have anyone else hauled into HR for a chat. His audacity is part of his armour.

'It's Gareth,' said Gareth quietly.

'That's what I said. Get someone to take you shopping and buy something with sleeves.'

'I get hot,' explained Gareth.

'Show some respect to the ladies. Cover it up. Lovely Alice here doesn't need to see your little forearms. No one needs that in January.'

He'd called me lovely, but it didn't really register, because Gareth's ears were going red and whilst Guy was pure sexual magnetism, he needed to back off. Gareth's got the air of an asthmatic to me, and besides, he's demonstrably a committed sweater-vest man. I was just about to interject, but the lift pinged again on twelfth and Verni from the exec team entered and immediately pounced on Guy, asking, 'Can I have a few minutes?'

And Guy said, 'We'll have to walk and talk.'

And so I didn't get to hear what he'd been thinking . . .

. . . until later that day, when he came past my desk. Yaz had gone upstairs to talk to the design team and Nervous Jane and Karim were at a meeting with an agent, so it was just me on my own, and I could see Guy register that. He paused and retraced his steps.

'You've put that lipstick on again.'

'I have.' I tried not to look too pleased that he'd noticed.

He had a quick look around and then sat on the edge of my desk. Oh my golly. One of my favourite fantasies about Guy starts like that. I could feel my temperature rise in response. He stared at my mouth and then leant towards me and inhaled.

'And you smell less like a bar,' he said. 'But still quite intoxicating.'

My heart rate picked up. I needed to make a move. Now was my chance. I cleared my throat. 'So, erm, Guy, earlier in the lift, you said you were—'

'Ah Guy,' interrupted Cara, 'there you are!'

Guy leant back and faced Cara, and I tried not to jump away guiltily and instead acted like it was completely normal that Guy Carmichael was sitting on my desk.

Cara glanced briefly at me and then returned her attention to Guy. 'Charlotte's looking for you,' she said meaningfully.

'I take it she's still not happy about Glasgow?' said Guy.

I bent my head and started opening various documents on my laptop in a bid to pretend I wasn't there. Yaz told me earlier today that Amelia said that Charlotte was getting used to the idea of a week in Scotland until yesterday evening, when she apparently found out she'd be going for one to two months.

'No,' said Cara. 'That's an understatement. She'd like to talk it through with you.'

'I'm afraid I can't,' said Guy Carmichael, brusquely standing up. 'You'll have to manage it, Cara.'

I could sense Cara bristle, even staring down at my keyboard. 'But Guy,' said Cara stiffly, 'Charlotte's not even on my team—'

Guy cut her off. 'You're on the *management* team, Cara. I'm sure you can handle it. I've every confidence in you.'

He strode off manfully, all commander-in-chief vibes. As Cara swung in the opposite direction, I could just hear her muttering under her breath, 'I am power, beauty and love. I manifest respect.' It's quite gratifying to realise that even people as successful, together and professional as Cara still need a little help from the Universe.

Guy was in meetings all afternoon so I still haven't found out what he was thinking. Will rectify this as a matter of urgency tomorrow.

I am grateful for:

Lucozade, lifts, lipstick

Date: Wednesday 11 January   **Time: 3.45pm**

My thoughts and reflections:

So today, I was in bright and early and feeling hopeful. I was wearing full make-up before I even got on the tube, in my Zara trousers that are indistinguishable from Tom Ford's, and smelling of Astrid's Marc Jacobs Daisy perfume. Of course I didn't get so much as a glimpse of Guy, but that didn't bother me, because given what she's already done for me this week, I had complete faith in the Universe.

Even my worst meeting of the week – Creative Review with the heinous Harry Piles – couldn't dampen my gratitude. He is probably my least favourite person at Carsons and is even worse than Security Lydia. He's not deliberately mean like Lydia but he is impervious – he just doesn't really care about anyone else. I think you could burst into flames in front of him and he'd just use it as an opportunity to warm his slippers. According to Drunk Stephen, Harry only got in because his father was second cousin twice removed to the CEO at the time. He certainly didn't get in based on aptitude, because he doesn't have a creative bone in his body. He's lazy (so am I) but he doesn't even try to hide it and he doesn't get anything done (I do get stuff done, and my particular form of laziness means I'm good at making things more efficient).

And all of this would be less bad if it weren't for the fact that someone promoted him to Deputy MD, which means it directly impacts all the people under him or junior to him, including me. He's at the same members' club as Guy Carmichael so good luck complaining about Harry. The worst thing about him is he fundamentally believes he's better than everyone and that he alone has his finger on the social pulse. So meetings consist of Harry asking people for their opinions and then telling those people why their opinions are wrong. Of course he takes all the credit for other people's work (I swear he got promoted to Deputy MD on the back of stealing my idea for repackaging the One World series) whilst blaming others for his own awful ideas.

Today's meeting wasn't going well. Harry had just told Drunk Stephen that his cover was too retro and that he needed to understand that young people today were a bit cooler than that; I thought Drunk Stephen was going to punch him – he's not a fan of Harry's signature cravat and white trainer look. But then the door opened and Guy Carmichael put his head round it.

I sat up straighter (along with everybody else because he's that authoritative) and took a sip of my raw juice, hoping he'd notice that I'm usually a healthy, dynamic woman, rather than a hungover pill-popper.

'Harry,' he said, looking serious. 'I need a quick word with Editorial. Let's see . . . Alice – could you come?'

Yes, I could, Guy. Probably very fast.

'Alice?' Harry frowned. 'Are you sure? Don't you want Yaz? She's more senior.'

'Happy to help,' said Yaz.

I sat there trying not to look desperate and hoping that Guy Carmichael was consciously picking me, rather than someone who was genuinely good at their job.

Guy Carmichael gave Harry a look and Harry immediately realised his error; Guy is not the sort of man you question.

'Of course,' said Harry quickly. 'Sorry, Guy.'

Guy turned on his heel, and Harry gestured at me to follow him out of the meeting room.

I studiously avoided eye contact with Drunk Stephen (he'd know full well this little power-play would have aroused me) as I meekly made my way after Guy Carmichael. Guy waited until we'd passed by the glass windows and then checked no one was nearby before speaking.

'Alice, I'm going to level with you. Okay?'

'Okay.'

'You don't get to my position in life unless you've taken a few risks.'

'Nor mine,' I said, thinking about the time I took a risk and guessed some of the figures for market research when developing new products at Carlsberg. It didn't go down well. Neither did the new blueberry Carlsberg.

Guy Carmichael's brow furrowed. 'Not sure I follow, Alice,' he said. 'Bottom line: employer-employee relationships are a big no at Carsons. I need you to understand that.'

'I do,' I said, slightly concerned as to where this was going.

'Good. Nothing could happen between us, Alice.'

Okay, I wasn't loving this. I nodded politely.

Guy Carmichael looked in both directions and then leant closer to me so that we were both against the wall, his body angled towards me. He spoke with a low voice.

'I hope you understand that I couldn't have thoughts about what those alluring lips of yours could do, Alice. Because HR don't like that kind of thing.'

Oh. My. Goodness. It was happening . . . I was manifesting Guy Carmichael. He was definitely going there.

'Understood,' I said, biting my bottom lip just a smidgen.

'So if I ask you to lunch, Alice,' he continued, staring at my mouth. 'You understand that it would be strictly above board?'

'Of course.'

'And that whilst you could therefore tell anyone you wished to about it, including HR . . .'

'Best not to mention it? At all?'

'Good girl, Alice,' he said, his eyes glinting. 'Very good indeed. Hard to understand why someone as sharp as you is still only Editor.'

'Like I said, Guy, I'm a risk taker too. It just hasn't always paid off.'

'I believe in risk, Alice,' said Guy Carmichael, leaning so close that I could hear him breathe. I could feel the faint scratch of the expensive made-to-measure woollen suit sleeve on my neck. Then he trailed a finger down my throat and along my collar bone. My stomach tightened in anticipation.

'It's a cliché for a reason,' he said under his breath. 'You've got to speculate to accumulate.' Then I felt his tongue trail where his finger had. Good bloody gracious, he was going to accumulate me. My knees almost gave way, and I had to bite back a small moan. My boss, Guy Carmichael, was licking my neck in the corridor at 11am-ish on a Wednesday morning – this was even better than my fantasies. I leant back against the wall, willing him to continue.

A sudden burst of talk and a slight draft as the meeting room doors opened, and Guy Carmichael didn't even falter – the man is brazen – he knows his potency. He nipped my earlobe lightly with his teeth and then said smoothly, 'Thank you, Alice,' before standing to one side just as Yaz and Adeola walked past, followed by Cool Jason from Design. Guy did a double-take.

'What's with the new little moustache, John?' said Guy. 'You look like a fucking Liverpudlian.'

'The name's Jason,' said Cool Jason. 'And I am a Liverpudlian.'

'Are you?' said Guy, frowning.

'Yes,' said Cool Jason.

'Well, why the fuck haven't you said?' exploded Guy. 'Go and tell HR right now. I keep getting it in the fucking ear about inclusivity and diversity and look – there you are – and I bloody hired you. Get them to take a photo of you and your moustache or something, stick it on the web, and put a bloody large tick against my name.'

'Are you serious?' said Cool Jason.

But Guy Carmichael had already walked off.

'Is he for real?' Cool Jason asked me.

'I'm not sure,' I said, watching Guy Carmichael go. Gosh he wore that bespoke suit well. I bet it was from Savile Row. He wore power well. I realised my mouth was hanging open slightly, and that Jason was looking at me with an expression of consternation.

'Er, Alice,' said Cool Jason, his brow furrowing. 'It may not be my place to say this, but, you know, watch out for him.'

'What do you mean?' I said, breezily.

'I'm just saying, it doesn't tend to work out well long term for the women in Guy Carmichael's life.'

'What!' I laughed self-consciously. 'I'm not a woman in his life!'

'Okay,' said Cool Jason. 'Forget I said anything.'

As if I'm going to forget that compliment! Cool Jason called me a woman in Guy Carmichael's life! Not only have I attracted the man of my dreams, but I have successfully commanded the respect of my colleague, Jason from Design, who's frankly always intimidated me with his achingly cool ahead-of-trend trendiness, and who has barely spoken to me before. He speaks to Drunk Stephen, obviously, because everyone does, but not me usually. Times are a-changing!

I ask the Universe:

To keep me on the path towards my perfect life.

My thoughts and reflections:

Caught a few glimpses of Guy Carmichael today, but nothing more. That's okay. The Universe presumably has other things to take care of too. I went shopping after work and bought a beautiful limited-edition H&M scarf which looks just like the Gucci one and is worth every penny. I know Guy Carmichael has said that we'll have to keep it under wraps when we go out, but I can imagine a photo of me, in this scarf (and ideally the silver trousers and boots the model in the campaign is wearing) at the Blue Bar (*Tatler* favourite), as my profile pic. (At the moment I've got a picture of me in Astrid and Aziz's kitchen, standing at the island, looking like I'm cooking. I'm not, as Astrid, Arrie and Mum have all been quick to identify. But to non-family members who don't know I can't cook, it certainly gives off a smug vibe of which I'm quite proud. But the Blue Bar selfie would top that.)

I didn't get home until late and when I let myself in, I heard raised voices from the kitchen.

'If you keep avoiding it,' Aziz was saying, 'we're going to have a problem.'

'And if you keep pushing, it, Aziz, we're going to have a far bigger one,' shouted Astrid.

Aziz said something too quiet for me to hear. So interesting hearing people who aren't Carvers argue – they don't all get louder and louder and louder. I hung up my coat and went upstairs to put my new scarf away. Astrid keeps mentioning contributions to the electricity and gas and I've said I don't have any money until I'm paid, which is true, but she would be bitchy about my buying the scarf if she knew. By the time I'd been to the loo, it sounded a lot calmer downstairs and safe to venture into the main living area so I thought it would be a good time to chat to Aziz about borrowing a pair of his glasses for work tomorrow. I feel like Guy Carmichael would be all over that look – sort of a classic hot-secretary Chanel thing. But when I got into the kitchen, it was only Astrid, her back turned to me, rummaging in their behemoth of a fridge which they keep really quite disappointing food in. Still, it's all been useful in the Paleo diet – look at me instantly turning obstacles into opportunities!

'Hey, Astrid,' I said. 'Where's Az?'

'Still at work,' she said shortly.

I was about to tell her that I'd heard him in the kitchen so he couldn't be, but when Astrid turned round, her eyes looked a bit pink and piggy, like they do when she's upset.

'You okay, Astrid?'

'Of course I'm not okay, Alice,' snapped Astrid, aggressively peeling an edamame, and tugging up her trouser waistband, which seemed to be too loose. 'I've been working all day and then volunteering at the hospital – oldest work experience they've had ever and no one treats me with any respect – and I'm exhausted. Plus I've just spent a fortune on textbooks.'

I settled myself on a bar stool and took a bean. 'How did it go at the hospital?' I asked. 'Any fun stuff?'

'Couple of broken bones, a heart attack, one DOA, and a man who'd blended his thumb.'

'Shit,' I said, thinking about the thumb. That had to involve blood. 'Sounds gross. Were you sick?'

'A couple of times,' said Astrid grimly. 'And fainted once.'

We both ate beans in silence.

'Hmm,' I said tentatively. 'And you're sure you really want to go through—'

'Don't say it!' said Astrid shrilly. 'Do not ask me if I'm sure I want to do medicine. Not if you want somewhere to sleep tonight.'

'Woah, Astrid. Take a chill pill. I was only going to ask if you were sure you really wanted to go through hot yoga tonight after all that vomming? Can't be healthy.'

'What?' Astrid looked momentarily confused.

'Thursday night? Your yoga class?'

Astrid pushed back her hair from her forehead and shut her eyes. 'I completely forgot. And I'm not sure I am in the mood.'

We both looked at each other for a second. Astrid lives for hot yoga. And power yoga. And vinyasa. She's a fanatic. A tall, bendy, freakishly strong obsessive yogi. She's always in the mood for yoga.

'Do you want a glass of wine or something?' I said hopefully.

Astrid sighed. 'I should do work. I've got so much work. I've got cases to review and I'm trying to study basic anatomy.'

'Yeah. Or you could get into your PJs, order pizza, drink wine, and catch up on *Newsnight* with me. Sister time.'

'You've never watched *Newsnight* in your life,' said Astrid.

'Okay, well, if you insist, we could watch *Below Deck*.'

Astrid harrumphed. I could tell she was considering it.

'Everyone needs a break,' I said. 'Even you. And you really need to eat something proper if you've been sick. I'll pay.'

Astrid looked down at herself, and brushed ineffectively at stains on her top and trousers. Then she stopped and examined her hands and gave a small dry heave. 'Okay,' she said, suddenly making a move. 'I'm going to get changed out of these clothes because they are pretty saturated with bodily fluids – most of them mine. If you're paying, I'll have the capricciosa – make sure it's from Little Italy. And you need to pour the wine.'

I didn't need telling twice. I selected a nice frosty bottle of Pinot gris, and was just pouring a couple of generous glasses when Aziz came in. Perfect timing. 'Az!' I beamed at him. 'Wine?'

'Not for me, Alice,' he said. He looked at the second glass. 'Do you have someone coming over?'

'It's for Astrid.'

Aziz paused. 'Really?'

'Yeah. I thought she looked a bit tired, so I suggested wine and takeaway pizza.'

'Good,' said Aziz. 'Good. Well done, Alice.'

'For someone who's praising me, Az, you look a bit sad?'

'No, no, all good, Alice.'

'What pizza do you want? Astrid said it had to be Little Italy. My treat. Hope Deliveroo do it.'

Aziz gave a little laugh but it didn't sound super cheerful. 'Yeah. Deliveroo do Little Italy.'

'Super!' I said. 'What do you want?'

I took a sip of the wine. I am a huge fan of the wine-fridge way of life. Honestly, Aziz and Astrid have a better set-up here than a bar. Their wine is so nice (except for the Friulano). I checked Little Italy pizzas on Deliveroo. Bloody hell. They weren't exactly kebab prices.

'Um, Aziz,' I began. 'Is there anywhere else a bit cheaper I could get pizza from?'

Aziz sighed. 'If you get her to eat pizza from Little Italy, I'll not only pay for it, but I'll give you £50.'

I nearly choked on my wine with delight. Today was shaping up well. 'Er . . . done!'

'But don't tell her. Okay?'

Aziz looked dejected. And tired. Kind of like Astrid.

'Aren't you going to have pizza with us?'

He shook his head. 'I've transferred you £100. That should cover it.'

My phone pinged with the notification that my account had received £100. Normally that would bring me unprecedented joy.

'Are you at least going to hang out with us?' I asked Aziz. 'Watch a bit of *Below Deck*? It's amazing seeing them vacuum, and cock-up drink orders . . .'

Aziz gave me one of his trademark grins. Sweet and very loveable. 'Nah. I'm going to get an early one, Alice. You can fill me in tomorrow.'

I am letting go of:

Asking Aziz if I can borrow his glasses – the man needs a break.

Guide Post™

Manifesting through visioning

A visioning board is a great reminder of your intentions and a manifestation of your manifestations! It's a tangible, visible projection of your perfect life.

1. *Use photos, images, drawings, key words, text and anything else that visions your future.*
2. *Put your visioning board somewhere you will see it frequently.*
3. *Place your most desired manifestation at the centre of the board.*

My thoughts and reflections:

Friday the thirteenth: an inauspicious day for some, but not for me. I've just spent the entire night on my own, visioning. (Astrid's been working in the office and has made it clear that tonight she is not having wine, or TV, or anything fun, and that she is slightly annoyed with me for having derailed her from her mission of misery last night. Aziz has gone to see his family in Coventry. Astrid said he was staying the night but I swear I just heard the front door and a male voice, so he must have come back early.) And not only has it turned out to be a cheap evening, it has also been entertaining. I love my board. I've cut out loads of amazing designer outfits from *Vogue* and put them round the edges, alongside a few celebrities and influencers I'd be happy to be compared to.

I've downloaded a picture of Guy from the publishing awards last year, cut off the other people and stuck him in the Blue Bar along with me! I've also stuck us over the words 'The Mandrake Hotel' because it's one of my fantasies – ever since Charlotte posted a photo of the public bathrooms there on Instagram and told me it is even more super atmospheric in reality and she'd actually had one of the best sexual encounters of her life in there with the lesser-known fifth Jonas brother,

I've thought about me and Guy doing the same. And I've even found my ideal wedding dress, which I've put next to some photos of the old school crowd from various weddings I've endured over the last decade, and the part I enjoyed most was adding little speech bubbles of them saying things like, *fuck me, Alice is stunning* and *did you hear she's practically running Carsons* and *golly, don't you wish you could garner just half as much admiration and respect as Alice does.*

And then I've found an old family photo from a few Christmases ago and I've made them all say *thank you, Alice* because they've borrowed money from me because I'm rich and I've added a few tears of joy and pride to Mum's face as a nice little touch.

And then right in the middle of the board is our old house – I downloaded a photo from the Savills website and I nearly cried because it was taken in spring and the wisteria is on the cusp of exploding and smothering the stones with purple blooms, but right now, it's no idea of just how beautiful it's about to be. And then next to the house, I've cut out the face of Matthew Lloyd. Well, quite a few faces of Matthew actually. I ended up taking my time trawling through old photos and looking online, and it's weird how many photos there are. He keeps cropping up. And in almost every one, there he is smiling that stupid self-satisfied smirk, like he knew even when he was a gawky sixteen-year-old with too much wax in his hair that he'd end up being rich and successful. I was desperate to find just one photo where he wasn't smiling so I could focus properly on visioning his face when I wipe that smile off it.

I did manage to find one in the end. I knew instantly when it was taken; it was at the end of that summer in Little

Minchcombe, late August, maybe early September, at the party we decided needed to happen because Matthew's then best friend from Cambridge, Ollie, was visiting – we used any excuse for impromptu parties.

That summer had felt like everything and nothing. In one way, it was like being in the centre of the Universe, coming home to Little Minchcombe after three years of travelling around, back to my family and friends. For once, Arrie, Astrid, Matthew and I had aligned, and for the first time in years, we were all together for two whole months, and took every opportunity to hang out. Arrie was doing some advisory work for a nearby farm, Astrid was on rotation at a relatively local law firm, and I got a job behind the bar at the Lamb. And Matthew, who was midway through his second MA, also ended up working for the summer at the Lamb, which meant that he and I spent practically every minute together. There was a heatwave and the sun shone the entire time. I'd spent time in some amazing places but that summer in Little Minchcombe was a slice of privileged paradise. We didn't even argue much. Just enjoyed cricket and boating on the river and lying in the sun, talking, drinking, laughing.

In another way though, it felt like a bubble that would inevitably burst. And indeed, not long after that summer, everything changed. I started university, Mum and Dad sold the house, Arrie met Roger, and Matthew left for America. And that party was the start of it.

You can see from the photo that we're all on the paddock behind our old house and next to the village green. The apple trees are heavy with fruit and the long grass verges are stooped and thick and yellowed, the occasional late blooming wildflower a minority splash of colour on parchment. You can tell it'd been a scorcher, and not just from the patches of parched grass. Although the shadows are long and the sun is about to give way, shirtsleeves are still rolled, feet are bare, and hands are raised to shade eyes. You can see the wrought iron gates leading to our garden and, in the distance, roses climbing up the pergola. Shafts of sunlight are coming through the canopy of the apple tree, the sky is paint strokes of lilac and peach, and our friends are everywhere – mine, Astrid's and Arrie's.

Loads of the boys are in cricket whites, including Matthew, but he clearly didn't know he was being photographed. Everyone else is laughing or smiling – Astrid's whole face is screwed up with mirth – but Matthew isn't. He's standing there amidst his friends and he isn't smiling, he looks . . . thoughtful, and sort of wistful, his eyes elsewhere.

It feels a bit weird looking at him, like I was intruding on something private that he wouldn't want me to see. If he'd known that camera was capturing him, I think there would have been the usual smile in place.

Still. You've got to be ruthless if you want results, and I do. Plus I can still remember exactly what Matthew said that night. So I cut out the photo of him without his smile, reminding myself *this* was precisely what I was aiming for, and no less than Matthew deserved, and added it right next to the house which is in the centre of my visioning board – because it's the thing I want most.

The annoying thing is, now I've hung the board up on the wall, I can see I was slightly skewed in my sticking – had to go for farewell drinks with Charlotte after work and felt a bit icky sobering up on the journey home so I bought a dented can of Desperado at half price from the twenty-four-hour food and wine shop near Highbury and Islington station (broke after shopping and farewell drinks) which may have affected my hand-eye coordination.

It's ended up with Matthew Lloyd's face smack bang in the middle of my visioning board.

In other news, I went back to H&M during my lunch hour and got the silver sequinned trousers and the boots (courtesy of the money left over from pizza). Guy was only in the office for an hour this morning so I didn't get to see him, although he got to see Charlotte. We all did. It was her last day before leaving for Glasgow and she pulled out all the stops to make sure we remembered her. She turned up in gym gear – sports bra, abs on full display, tiny shorts, etc., waited until Guy was facing the right direction, and proceeded to pack up her desk (couple of Post-its and a lipstick) in the sort of protracted and choreographed way that could have provided a decent opening to a soft porno. Even Drunk Stephen said he felt quite turned on by the whole show, so unless Guy Carmichael is impervious, he'll have surely thought about what he's missing. Everyone was talking about how he put his blinds down before she'd finished packing and how much that must have stung, but I noticed how long he kept his blinds open for. And I noticed that he still hasn't made good on asking me out for lunch.

But then I quickly replaced the self-limiting negative talk with some positive actions, like a bona fide manifester. Hence the H&M purchases.

Ready for when Guy Carmichael asks me on my date.

Which he will do.

I ask the Universe:

To make Astrid's mood a bit less shit tomorrow because it's Saturday and I can't really afford to go out, so I'm stuck here.

My thoughts and reflections:

So, not one to complain and obviously I have every confidence in the Universe's decisions as well as unstinting gratitude and this is not me in any way, shape or form questioning her infinite wisdom, but I have to confess I was slightly surprised this morning when, after being confronted with Matthew Lloyd's face in the centre of my visioning board upon waking, I went downstairs only to find the real Matthew Lloyd actually in the kitchen.

Looking very pleased with himself.

To be completely clear, that was *not* what I was trying to manifest.

He and Astrid were sitting opposite one another, drinking coffee companionably, the papers spread out in front of them, deep in conversation; he looked totally at home and, frankly, they could have passed for some kind of advert-perfect couple. There was a swordblade of sunlight slanting straight through the enormous roof light and illuminating the side of Matthew's face, making his skin dazzle like he had been chosen. When he bent his dark head closer to hers to see whatever she was pointing out in the newspaper, I felt a stab of something sharp lodge in my side. Astrid noticed me first.

'Hey, Alice,' she said. 'Do you want a croissant? Matthew went out and bought them from Laurents.'

Of course I wanted a croissant. They looked like buttery, flaky deliciousness. But it seemed wrong to take one. Clearly it was him I had heard late last night, not Aziz. So I said crossly, 'No, I don't. You know I'm Paleo.'

Astrid squinted at me through her hair, which had fallen over her eye. 'You had pizza the other night. And doughnuts?'

'It was a break-out day. Why is your hair down? You never have it down.' She always wears her hair back unless she's going out. Was this some kind of bid for sexy?

'I don't know,' said Astrid. 'And why are you asking like that? You're being weird.'

'*You're* being weird actually. Sitting here with your hair down, having breakfast with him. What's he even doing here?'

'*He* is staying here.' Astrid tucked her hair behind her ear. 'Not that it's any of your business.'

'Morning, Alice,' said Matthew, without looking up. 'Lovely to see you too.'

I didn't look at him either. Self-satisfied giant. 'Staying here?' I said, appalled. 'Why?'

'Because I said he could,' said Astrid. 'He's got loads of meetings in London this week.'

'This *week*?!'

'Yes. Problem?'

She gave me a cold stare, indicating that there had better not be a problem and that I was starting to piss her off.

'No, no,' I said, going over to switch on the Fisher & Paykel bean-to-cup coffee machine (absolutely gorgeous and I got loads of likes when I shared some photos of my morning coffee routine last week, not that I'll ever be able to afford my own one). 'I just thought Matthew would have preferred a hotel, what with his hotel hobby, that's all. And everyone loves a hotel breakfast.'

'Yeah, well, we've got croissants here,' said Astrid, defensively. 'And coffee. You don't mind, do you, Matthew?'

Matthew shook his head. 'Great service so far. Croissants are good. I'm happy.'

I set my cereal bowl on the side a little too loudly. 'Shouldn't you be eating croissants with Etta instead of Astrid?'

'What is up with you this morning, Alice?' said Astrid, frowning. 'Let's not descend to retrograde misogyny – you know her name.'

But Matthew Lloyd didn't even look up from the paper. 'Nah,' he said. 'Ebba doesn't eat croissants.'

'Well, who doesn't eat croissants,' I huffed under my breath, fetching the milk from the fridge.

'People following a Paleo diet,' said Matthew calmly. 'Like you.'

'Well, yes, of course. If she's Paleo like me, that makes sense.'

'Not *that* like you,' said Matthew. 'She actually does follow a Paleo diet.'

Astrid laughed.

I retrieved a spoon and slammed the drawer shut, but because it's soft-close it didn't make a sound. Normally I love the soft-close. 'Actually, I do follow it quite strictly,' I said, carefully measuring a level teaspoon sugar into my coffee. 'I tend to stick to grains, nuts and berries for my breakfast.'

Matthew looked briefly up, stared at me so intently that my hand wobbled and I spilled my coffee, then returned to his paper. 'You're absolutely right, Alice,' he said. 'What self-respecting caveperson didn't sit down to Jordans Country Crisp and a flat white on a Saturday morning? By the way, you've got coffee all down your top.'

God, that man makes my blood boil.

Astrid's phone started buzzing. I glanced over surreptitiously from where I was stationed by the coffee machine, and saw Aziz's name flash up on the screen. I also saw Astrid look at her phone, pause and then turn it over.

'Aren't you going to answer that?' I said pointedly. 'Might be important? What if it's Aziz?'

'It's not,' lied Astrid, pulling back her chair, decisively. 'So, Matthew,' she said. 'What shall we do today?'

I felt so bothered by the whole situation that I ended up taking my breakfast back up here to my room. What is Astrid playing at? I have no idea why she's ignoring Aziz, and as much as I know that Aziz and Matthew are friends too, it doesn't feel right Matthew being here on his own with Astrid, when Astrid's treating Aziz like this.

Maybe the solution is to make sure that Matthew *isn't* on his own with Astrid . . . ?

Action: I shall spend this weekend selflessly protecting my sister's virtue, by being a 'chaperone' in the vein of *Little Women*. (Or, as we'd say today, a 'cockblock'.)

I am letting go of:

Matthew's childish attempts to rile me. Jordans Country Crisp is wholegrain and it really clearly says on the package 'tasty by Nature'. Plus I had it with soya milk.

Guide Post™

The tiny grass seed manifests a green blade,
The humble acorn manifests the great oak tree,
The young stream manifests a river,
which manifests a sea,
Look to Mother Nature and
manifest all you want to be.

My thoughts and reflections:

I spent most of the rest of the morning downstairs in the sitting room, bored, whilst Astrid and Matthew worked. She had her nose in a textbook entitled *An Introduction to Pathology*, and he was pacing, and occasionally scribbling on bits of paper, and looking generally pensive. I put on some music and Astrid told me to turn it off; I tried chatting and Astrid told me to be quiet; I had a go at that new dance move on TikTok that everyone's recording themselves doing – the Cossack one – and Astrid said, 'For goodness sake,' and left to go and work in the office.

Matthew said, 'Just me and you now, Alice. Why don't you show me some more of that lovely dancing?' And raised his eyebrows suggestively. But before I could ask what he meant, he put on these massive noise-cancelling over-the-ear Bang & Olufsen headphones (which I assume Ebba bought him because they hardly go with his messy look) and opened his laptop: he didn't even blink when I told him to piss off. As Astrid wasn't in the room anymore, I decided it was safe for me to go back up to my room and have some Me Time.

I had a look at my visualisation board (I think you can really tell I got an A in GCSE Art) and did a bit of manifesting. *Guy Carmichael will ask me out on a date. Guy Carmichael will ask me out on a date*. And then, because I'm an initiative-taker, I decided to try on my new limited-edition H&M Guy-Carmichael-date outfit, and felt really glad that I'd stretched to the boots as well as the sequinned trousers because it all went together so well, and when you added it up, was only a fraction of the cost I'd have spent at Gucci. Sorry. Correction. A fraction of the cost I *will* be spending at Gucci because I'm inviting abundance into my life. I experimented with a bit of silver eyeshadow and frosted lipstick, looked in the mirror and really visualised myself getting very lucky.

And I was visioning me, in the Mandrake bathrooms, with their black walls and designer sinks, and hearing the door swing open and footsteps behind me, and then Guy's clipped husk in my ear saying, *Christ alive, I can't contain myself, Alice – you exude raw sexuality and make models like Ebba look quite frumpy, truth be told.* And then me saying, *We don't need to put down other women to make me feel better, Guy. Even smug ones like Ebba.* And he'd say, *God, you're not only stunning but principled too. Fuck I respect you.* And—

'Alice,' bellowed Astrid, interrupting my manifesting. 'We're going out. See you later.'

Shit. I was meant to be chaperoning.

'Hang on,' I shouted, running down the stairs, which wasn't easy in the new boots. 'Wait for me, I'm coming too.'

Astrid was in the hallway, tying up her shoelaces.

'Where are we going?' I said.

'Matthew and I are going for a walk in the park,' said Astrid. 'So you won't want to come. Besides, we're leaving now, and you're not ready. I'm not waiting for you to get changed.'

'I don't need to change. I'm ready to go.'

Astrid looked up at me. 'You're wearing that to the park?'

'Yes,' I said. I looked down at myself in the sequinned trousers and silver boots. And then I remembered that post of Charlotte's I saw earlier this morning, of her by some miserable drab water in Scotland. But the dreary background made her new highlights and lipstick stand out and she'd entitled it 'an injection of colour' and I also remembered what I read in *Vogue* about the Gucci collection my outfit was mimicking, and worked with what I had. 'It's my "communing with nature in winter" outfit, actually,' I said. 'The cool silver palette matches the January skies and bare branches of deciduous trees, and then the multicoloured scarf is inspired by the richness of evergreen foliage, the sun's red and gold rays – nature's jewels. The whole outfit is at one with the natural world.'

Of course, Matthew chose that moment to come into the hallway, pulling on a black Canada Goose expedition parka. He did a double-take as he saw me. 'Yes,' he said. 'That outfit does scream nature's jewels.'

Astrid took a breath. 'You're going to be cold.'

'Actually I'm pleasantly warm.'

'That'll be the synthetic trousers,' said Matthew.

'Negative energy spreads like wildfire, Matthew,' I said coldly.

'Yep.' Astrid reached for her coat. 'So, apparently, does gonorrhoea amongst the under thirties. That was some hard reading this morning.'

I shuddered. 'You really need to surround yourself with more positivity, Astrid,' I said. 'I mean, what's it got to do with you anyway? You're definitely the wrong side of thirty.'

'Because most people expect their doctors to have knowledge, Alice.'

'You should stick with law. Less gross, and it pays better.' I thought back to my bank balance.

'There's more to life than money,' said Astrid.

'Of course,' I agreed, following her out the front door of the house she owns in Chiswick. 'But it does help with paying the bills.'

Astrid zipped up her hideous thick parka. 'In that case, I'll have the £50 back you owe me from the Friuli wine.'

*

A lesser being might have complained that it was bloody freezing, but I was grateful. Grateful for the opportunity to be in nature. Grateful for the beautiful January lack of light and absence of warmth. Grateful to be able to repay Aziz for his kindness through proactive chaperoning. Grateful to not be as tedious as Astrid and Matthew, who were now wittering on about corporation taxation and justice, having just exhausted the scintillating subject of the ethics of psychometric testing. But I was also on the brink of hypothermia.

'Christ, it's absolutely freezing,' I said, interrupting them at last, having trudged across wild, frigid terrain just as stoically as Laura Ingalls Wilder did in *The Long Winter*. 'And it's been way longer than you said it would be.'

'I told you not to come,' said Astrid crossly. 'Anyway, we're nearly there now. It's just taken longer than usual because of your silly boots.'

'My boots aren't silly.'

'Of course not,' said Matthew. 'They're perfect for rotavating the park.'

Astrid smiled and I imagined the heel of my boot accidentally making contact with the back of one of Matthew's long legs.

'Yes. Well, we left the park miles ago,' I reminded him. We were walking in the sort of open countryside you see on the train ride home to the Cotswolds.

'No, we didn't. We're still in Richmond Park,' said Astrid.

'What?' I said. 'No way this is a park. How come I never knew about it?'

'Because you hate going outside?' said Astrid.

'I love the outdoors.'

We came through the last of the trees, into a clearing. 'There we go,' said Astrid, 'See? Worth it?'

'Oh, wow.' I stopped in my tracks. It really was absolutely stunning. A broad gentle slope of grass and bracken led down to a lake, which melted at its edges into mist. An actual stag stood just by a stand of trees, the shadows of a herd of deer visible in the woods. And also my left boot was rubbing my heel.

'And as you can see, we're very much still in London.' Astrid turned to point to a white building behind us. 'That's the Royal Ballet White Lodge. So you should be right at home. With your dance background.'

I gave Astrid a hard stare. That ballet incident is very much a family joke and whilst Mum always makes out like Matthew is family, he jolly well isn't.

'Well, yeah, but dance doesn't preclude an enjoyment of the great outdoors, Astrid. Since I started manifesting I'm much more in tune with the natural world and all it has to give. Oh my goodness – look at the size of that duck!'

'It's a swan,' said Matthew.

Obviously, I could see that now it had got closer, but I ignored him, and focused on the view before me. Muted tones of grey sky and river somehow made the russet and moss and purple of the bracken and heather pop like a Gucci label on a plain blazer. I watched the swan sail majestically towards the bank. The fine mist rendered everything in soft focus: the world was truly beautiful. We walked down closer to the lake, almost as if dreaming. I was completely and utterly in the moment, at one with Mother Nature. Then I realised that whilst I'd been looking at the view, Matthew and Astrid had started talking again – he had his arm round her shoulders. God, these two were impossible to keep apart.

'Can you take a photo of me, Astrid?' I asked loudly, holding out my phone.

'Why?'

'Because this would beat Charlotte's bleak Scottish post hands-down.'

Astrid sighed. 'Is Charlotte the one who's shagging your boss you fancy?'

Matthew looked up.

'Not anymore,' I said.

'Okay.' Astrid took my phone. 'One photo.'

'Hang on a second,' I said, getting closer to the bank. 'Try and get the swan in.' I did a pose, very similar to the H&M model one, sort of one leg back like I was mid-skip, with the scarf flowing over my shoulder, but my heel caught in the grass, and Astrid watched with irritation as I struggled to free it.

Eventually, she just yanked me out, with her freakishly strong yoga arm.

'I told you to stay at home. And you'd better not even think about putting those' – she eyed up my mud-spattered trousers – 'in my washing machine.'

'Of course not,' I said stiffly. 'They're dry-clean only.'

'Well, this has been lots of fun,' said Matthew. 'Inspiring to see Alice really getting to grips with the great outdoors.'

*

If it was a miserable trek to the park, it was even worse getting back home. My heel was rubbed raw, my trousers were sticking uncomfortably, and my scarf was so saturated with cold drizzle that it was in danger of asphyxiating me. But at least I'd annoyed Astrid to the extent that she and Matthew didn't do much chatting. And then when we got in, Aziz was there. I was so relieved to see him that I nearly cried. It had been quite the pressure, feeling like I had to look out for him – and now there he was, back in the kitchen, a pot of soup simmering on the hob, the whirr of the extractor fan a soothing background of ordinary. Aziz gave Astrid a brief kiss like everything was normal and she hadn't been ignoring his calls and when he hugged me, he smelled of cooking and comfort. He was his lovely, easy self with Matthew, and I felt like I could stop being responsible and leave him in charge of making sure weird dynamics didn't play out. To be fair, Matthew genuinely looked like he was pleased to see Aziz and said how he insisted on taking them both out for supper tonight all the way over at The Clove Club in Shoreditch. Astrid said

Aziz probably couldn't, because he had work to get on with, and besides, couldn't they go somewhere that wouldn't take so long to get to, but Matthew and Aziz pretty much ignored her and started talking about Michelin stars and truffle puree.

So, confident all was safe, I left them to it, heading upstairs to take a bath. I helped myself liberally to Astrid's Neal's Yard bath oil (she shouldn't have made that comment about my dancing career in front of ML) and as I sank back into the scented warmth, the blurred murmur of the others' voices downstairs and the lazy occasional drip of the hot tap, the stress of the morning faded away and I gradually thawed out. From this angle, I could mostly see treetops and sky, and only the edges of other houses. I watched a lone robin land on a branch, its orange chest a flash of colour in a chiaroscuro; after the last couple of hours of outright unpleasantness spent trudging round Richmond Park, I couldn't help thinking it was actually more meaningful to connect with Mother Nature at this spiritual level, from inside. It was certainly moving me a lot more effectively now I was warm and comfortable. I wouldn't be surprised if it emerged the Romantic poets took my approach too – artistic licence and all that. Wordsworth pretty much owns the daffodil, but for all we know, he never got closer to one than the bunch Dorothy popped on his desk as an incest-y come-on.

My phone pinged, with a message from my old friend Louise from St Hilda's whom I bumped into at the wedding. She said sorry for being last minute about it, but could we meet at Turners instead of Soma and she'd forgotten if we were meeting at three or four, so she was arriving at half three and she hoped that was okay.

Shit.

*

On my way now (love the Piccadilly line – so fast, and I've noticed a few people eyeing up my copy of *The Guide* with envy) but I can't say I'm relishing the prospect of seeing Louise. In fact, I've been putting off meeting for ages, ever since she reproduced if I'm honest, but when I saw her at Monty's wedding I couldn't think of an excuse fast enough. It'll be the usual new mum shit – bearing false testament to alcohol and fun, and then being trashed after a glass and a half of Chardonnay and rushing off to the loos to stare at photos of the progeny before making an excuse and bailing. Still, she's an old school-friend, and at least if it's a short one it will be a cheap one. Might message Drunk Stephen in case he's around later . . .

I am grateful for:

- Nature
- Piccadilly line
- Aziz

My thoughts and reflections:

Well, I was wrong about Louise. Really quite wrong. I mean I was right as in it wasn't fun, but it was me who bailed rather than her. Turns out she was on a mission to get absolutely trashed. I got the impression she'd been drinking before I got there because when I squeezed myself onto the velvet banquette opposite her, even though it was dimly lit, I could clearly tell:

a) there were three empty espresso martini glasses on the table
b) she was wired and slurry and smelt of coffee.

I love getting trashed with the best of them, but being in Soho mid-afternoon with a couple of proper drunks shouting at the bar, and sitting knee to knee with Louise, was a sobering experience. She kept asking me to describe what it felt like waking up in bed alone and calling me a *lucky bitch* and saying things like *of course you probably don't leak urine when* you *do that, you jammy cow* (about mundane things like walking, or laughing, or chewing, or watching TV) and it freaked me out a bit. And then, after a couple more drinks, she leant forward and held on to my forearm a little bit too grippily, her eyes frankly a touch wild, and asked me whether I'd consider running her over, just lightly maybe, at fifteen miles per hour, so she could have a week in hospital, or a mild coma, for some *me time*. And then when I asked if she was okay, she said *just joking* and laughed too loudly.

She said Annabel and Fizz were coming here for a quick drink and then we were all going to supper at the Pavilion Club because Fizz had just joined, and wasn't that fab, and with any luck Penelope might make pudding. And as Annabel is totally awful, and I detest Penelope, and there is no way I can afford supper at the Pavilion Club, I had no qualms about inventing an urgent request from Astrid to get back home and let her in because she'd forgotten her key.

'Do give them my love, won't you?' I said. 'And let them know I can't wait to see you all at the christening.' And then just as I was leaving I felt bad and told Louise that Arrie had found it a nightmare when she first had kids and that I may not have them myself, but I did know it was perfectly normal to find it hard and she could call me anytime.

And Louise went all snotty and gaspy and clung on to me and said, 'It's killing me. No one said it was this bad. Why didn't they say? It's a conspiracy.'

But another espresso martini arrived and she cheered up and I scarpered.

Drunk Stephen messaged saying he was going to a show in town but could meet later for drinks. But having duly considered the state of my finances and the fact it was only six o'clock, I decided that rather than wait around and stay out, I may as well make the most of having Astrid's house all to myself. Hence being back on the Piccadilly line, heading home, on a Saturday night, at half six. Unheard of but semi-exciting in its novelty.

I'm planning to sort out my visioning board and move Matthew's face because I'm a little concerned I accidentally manifested him today. Also, given some of the crapness of my day (not that I'm doubting the Universe, I'm simply experiencing understandable feelings of uncertainty), I think I should try some other approaches to manifesting – maybe candle gazing. I've just seen a TikTok video where that famous YouTuber says how she manifested a baby through candle gazing. Then I accidentally clicked on a link where a woman from Texas warns about the side effects of candle gazing; apparently she gazed too long and now has permanent retinal damage resulting in everything appearing green.

Hopefully inspiration will strike, and I will feel more assured that I am making progress towards manifesting my perfect life.

Will write again before bed.

My intention is:

To investigate candle gazing without retinal damage.

***Guide Post*™**

Moon Manifesting

Taking your manifestations to the moon can be extremely powerful. The moon and her cycles are nature's own Guide™ and gifting yourself the time to align yourself with the Moon Goddess can help you to achieve your perfect life.

A new moon provides a particularly powerful time to manifest: it is a time of beginnings, of energy, of potential, and it is all yours to tap into. All new moons are conducive to positive realisations but the most potent new moon of all is January's Capricorn. This is the ideal time to set intentions and manifest your desires. Use GUIDED MOON MANIFESTING™ to help guide you.

My thoughts and reflections:

Oh my gosh. Not in bed yet – obviously – I'm still on the tube. But I had to take a second to thank the Universe for, once again, reaching out and helping me. I can't believe I ever doubted *The Guide*. To literally ask for inspiration, then turn the page and find it there? That's beyond coincidence. *Moon Manifesting*. Even writing the words gives me a tingle – it sounds so powerful and significant. And then to google and discover today is the third day of Capricorn's new moon?! Wow. Again, thank you, Universe! Can't wait to get home and try this one.

In one word:

Inspired

My thoughts and reflections:

It's late Monday morning, and the last time I wrote in here was only Saturday evening, and yet it was centuries ago. I'm at the BFI café, and it's noisy and familiar and anonymous and I've come here quite a few times because it's close to work, usually with Drunk Stephen, but this time I'm on my own, so that I can write this. I want this pocket of time to relive the weekend – the crazy, amazing weekend, which already feels like a shining bright fever dream.

*

Less than an hour after I'd left Louise in Soho, I arrived at Stamford Bridge, and walked back from the tube station along Chiswick's leafy streets where you could barely tell it was a Saturday night. Even though it was dark with a faint drizzle, and January, I felt a sense of anticipation and excitement. I had manifested living in Astrid's beyond-beautiful residence; I'd manifested Guy Carmichael finding me attractive and now, just when I'd been feeling low, an opportunity to harness the power of a Capricorn new moon had fallen into my lap.

What if I really could manifest the perfect life?

The walk home hadn't yet afforded me a glimpse of this new Capricorn moon, but it was barely seven o'clock. I let myself into Astrid and Aziz's house and luxuriated in its emptiness: for one evening it was all mine. If I felt like that, borrowing a house, imagine what it must feel like to actually *own* somewhere like this – somewhere with an entrance hall the size of a bedroom, elegant period features like high ceilings and wooden bannisters, and slick modern conveniences like underfloor heating. I went upstairs, changed into my Lululemon dupe tracksuit bottoms (thank you, TikTok) and Astrid's Nike hoody, and piled my hair up. As I padded through to the kitchen to make a sandwich, my thick socks sliding satisfyingly on the polished oak floors, I peered up out of the skylight, but all I could see was darkness. Never mind – still plenty of night left for some moon-spotting. I put some music on and was halfway through an incredible sandwich I'd compiled when I heard the unmistakable sound of rain clattering against the glass ceiling. Hmmm. I finished my sandwich slowly, hoping the rain would abate, but it didn't: moon manifesting in Astrid's back garden was rapidly becoming less appealing.

Although, I reminded myself, every obstacle is an opportunity . . . I decided to go the Wordsworth / warm bath route (no incest obviously) and moon-manifest from the comfort of indoors. I checked *The Guide* again and had a hunt through the fridge, but I couldn't find any sage. Then I had a brainwave and looked in the spice cupboard: one already opened and another brand-new jar of sage. I tipped the contents of the opened one into a small blue bowl. It looked rather sparse, so I added a bit more from the new jar. I fetched Astrid's Baobab

Black Pearl candle from the downstairs loo (where it seems to be used for general decorative purposes as it's never been lit) and set it on the coffee table in the living area along with the sage, my copy of *The Guide* and a box of Cook's Matches (only ones I could find and they did somewhat spoil the effect).

I turned off all the lights, which was harder than it sounds because Astrid and Aziz have set some up on timers and others are linked to ring circuits which should be simple, but seem to involve a number of light switches that do nothing at all. Eventually, the house was in complete darkness (well, not complete because there are quite a few electrical appliances as well as far more street lights outside than I previously realised and the neighbours have effectively illuminated their garden like it's a brothel in Amsterdam, which I might mention to Astrid because surely that's got to affect house prices, solar powered or not).

Next, by the light of my phone, I lit the revered Baobab Black Pearl candle, then attempted to ignite the sage. This proved tricky. It involved a fair amount of smoke, a couple of insignificant burns to my fingers, and some prolonged coughing, and eventually I made the kind of executive decision that would have impressed even Guy Carmichael himself, and decreed the room cleansed and sacred. So, I focused on the candle and stared at the flame. I waited until at least a minute had passed and the flame flickered and swayed and dipped and sprung in a way that I think I may have found surprisingly and utterly captivating, but I'm not entirely sure. Because there's a chance it was as underwhelming and candle-y as anticipated.

Or it may have been quite the transcendental moment.

Either way, after a minute or so had elapsed, I took the bull by the horns and began manifesting.

> *By the light of you*
> *I make myself new*
> *Shed this old skin*
> *And unfurl wings*
> *Bathed in your glow*
> *Ready to grow*
> *Released, renewed,*
> *Ready, imbued,*
> *Cleansed, reborn*
> *I am yours, Capricorn.*

(If I'm honest, at this point, it did feel a bit surreal talking to a candle. But it wasn't like there was anyone here to witness it, so I pushed ahead, through the misgivings, and followed the path of *The Guide*.)

I articulated carefully in a kind of churchy voice because it seemed right to do so.

By the light of Capricorn, I manifest the perfect man falling in love with me. That's Guy Carmichael, to be clear, and thank you for all you've done already on that front. If you could also stretch to making him as fantastic in the sack as I imagine him to be, I'd be super grateful. And maybe one post on Instagram just for Charlotte's benefit.

By the light of Capricorn, I'd like to manifest continuing to live in Astrid's house until I get my own flat and it would be great if she'd maybe go easy on the utilities and be a bit more generous with the wine sharing.

By the light of Capricorn, please do not let me get sacked from work. Sack some of the other fuckers who are useless. Please keep my job secure, and add in a pay rise whilst you're at it. And could everyone get my name right?

By the light of Capricorn, I manifest garnering respect and admiration from friends, colleagues and family. I don't want to get too specific, but I'd like Cool Jason from Design to do one of those little nose laughs when I speak, as if I've said something genius. And I want Charlotte to ask me how I always put together such amazing looks and Arrie to ask me for some advice and Astrid to say, You make me feel like a complete dunderhead, Alice – how do you know so much *and Mum to say,* Who would have thought Alice would be the highest earner of the—

And then, like a needle scratch in the Moonlight Sonata, a deep voice said, 'Alice, can we manifest making it less dark in here? Would the light of Capricorn stretch to that?'

Seriously?

'What the actual fuck, Matthew?' I said in disbelief, turning round to see a shadowy outline in the doorway. I mean, what was he? Some kind of stealth ninja? 'You're meant to be in Shoreditch.'

'Yeah, I took a rain check,' said Matthew.

I fumbled frantically around in the blackness and managed to get a side lamp on.

'What do you know,' said Matthew, dripping onto the oak floor. 'Manifesting really works! We have light. You've won me over, Alice.'

'Where are Aziz and Astrid?'

'They've gone to dinner at The Clove Club,' said Matthew,

picking his way over to the kitchen and grabbing a tea towel. He started roughly drying his hair.

'They agreed to go without you?' I said in surprise.

'No,' said Matthew. 'I said I'd catch them up. But by now, they'll be at least one course into the ten-course tasting menu, so you don't need to worry: they can't leave even when they realise I'm not coming. They'll be stuck there together for hours.'

'Why didn't you go? Astrid's going to kill you. And what makes you think I'm worried?'

'Because you've been chaperoning me and Astrid all day.'

'I haven't!' I lied.

Matthew pulled off his sodden jumper, stretched lazily and yawned; his T-shirt rose up at the side, exposing part of his abdomen. I tried not to dribble. For an arsehole, he was aggravatingly built.

'Look, I know your sister will be mad at me. But I figured they could use a little space. She's shutting out Aziz at the time she most needs him. So I bailed.'

'Hmm,' I said, trying to keep focused. That was thoughtful of him. I could see the start of a tattoo on his upper arm. When did he get that? 'So, you, erm, want them to be together, then?'

Matthew stopped and gave me a seriously pissed-off look. 'No, I'm just patiently waiting for things to go wrong so I can cop off with Astrid. Problem?'

I don't know how he gets to be so arsey. It's a perfectly reasonable concern given how attractive Astrid is and the fact she and Matthew are as thick as thieves. 'No problem here,' I said stiffly.

'Anyway,' said Matthew. 'Things are definitely going to go wrong for you when Astrid gets back and finds out you've been doing a bong in her house.'

'I haven't!' I said indignantly. 'I've been burning sage.'

Matthew scoffed. 'Did your journal tell you to?'

'Yes. Problem?'

'No,' said Matthew. 'No problem here. I mean if *The Guide* franchise are comfortable exploiting vulnerable females with mental health issues, it makes complete sense to cash in via the cultural appropriation route too.'

'Again, I am not a vulnerable female with mental health issues.' I grabbed the box of Cook's Matches and took aim at his head. But the glib twat caught them.

He raised his eyebrows at me. 'No, definitely no anger issues here.'

'Only where you're concerned. I get on super-well with other people. In fact I—'

'—*Garner the respect and admiration of friends, family and colleagues*?' said Matthew, his eyes glinting.

'You shouldn't have been listening to that!'

'Quite private is it then, manifesting?' said Matthew conversationally. 'Just seems like it crops up a lot on social media.'

'Why don't you piss off back to your hotel and go arrange face towels or something,' I hissed at him.

'No need.' Matthew took a large crunch of an apple. He had very even white teeth. Like the devil. 'I've got people who do that kind of work for me. How's *your* job going by the way? Secure? Pay rise? People know your name?'

I gasped in horror. Matthew Lloyd was insufferable.

I looked at his smug, grinning face, his messy damp hair and his horrible tatty torn jeans and his wrist as he took another bite of apple. Hang on—

'Is that a Rolex?' I asked him, eyeing his wrist.

'Well . . . yes. An old one.'

'You are such a hypocrite!' I exploded. After briefly dating Smarmy Sebastian the auctioneer a few years ago (he barked 'going, going, GONE!' before he came so that had to end), I happen to know that vintage Rolexes are exclusive and expensive, usually more so than new ones, and should not be worn by people who have holes in their jeans. 'You're all sanctimonious and dismissive and you've got a *Rolex*, a model girlfriend, your own hotel, and you travel in helicopters – how much more obvious can you get in terms of status symbols? How dare you mock me for trying to get somewhere myself when you're so privileged? Has it crossed your mind that some of us *need* manifesting?'

Matthew drummed his fingers on the island for a second. 'I told you, Ebba isn't my girlfriend. And yes, I may have a hotel, but I earned it. Nothing I've got has been handed to me on a plate, Alice.'

I couldn't tell if he emphasised the 'me' when he said that. Was this him making a point again? 'How come it bothers you that I grew up well off and yet you're happy to be besties with Astrid and hang out with my family? It's not my fault that I grew up like that any more than it's yours you didn't. What *is* your problem with me?'

'I never said I had a problem with you, Alice.'

'Not directly to me. But what was it you said about me? Hmm. Let me remember. I think your precise words were,

Alice is the quintessential spoilt, lazy youngest child who'll probably read English because her mother went to school with the Head of Faculty so can get her in. She's frivolous.'

'When did I say that?' asked Matthew, looking confused.

'That summer you were doing your master's. You were telling Ollie all the reasons why you found me unappealing.'

I waited for Matthew to call me out on the fact that this was all more than a decade ago and he didn't remember any of it. But he just nodded once, then leant back on the counter and folded his arms. 'Okay. So what else did you hear?'

'Nothing,' I lied.

'I wasn't telling Ollie why I found you unappealing. I was telling him why he shouldn't hit on you.'

'Same difference,' I said, ignoring the way his biceps flexed.

'It's not,' said Matthew. 'If you actually think about it.'

Was that another insult about my intelligence?

'And if I remember correctly,' he continued, 'that was on the same evening you kept telling other people that my presence was a classic example of one of your parents' pet-charity projects, rather like the lame incontinent donkey your dad rescued, that you'd all lived to regret.'

'I don't remember that,' I said. I remembered it perfectly well. And it wasn't 'people', it was only Monotonous Margot because she was standing near enough to Matthew that I knew he'd overhear. And it was right after I'd heard Ollie say to Matthew, *Come on, mate, be fair, Alice is fit as fuck, and I reckon she's giving me the eye*, and Matthew had shrugged and said, *Yeah. She gives everyone the eye. Don't go there. You should go for Astrid. Seriously, Ollie. If you make a move, I'll lose all respect.* It had stung so much, I still remember it now. Plus Monotonous Margot had ruined my efforts to pay Matthew back by saying she'd take him as a pet project in a heartbeat and then she'd droned on for ages as usual. Actually, on reflection I might have also slagged Matthew off to Crispin, but he's always doing charity work, so another bad choice.

And German Gunther, but he didn't even have a British passport so it hardly counted.

'Well, I remember it,' said Matthew shortly.

'I was drunk. People say things when they're drunk that they don't mean. All the time.'

'Then I must have been drunk too.'

'No, you weren't, because you were driving really early next morning to see your granny. So stop lying.'

Matthew gave me a curious look. 'You remember that, and you don't remember what you said about me?'

'I remember that you were right. I have turned out unsuccessful. But I'd rather be unsuccessful than end up like you.'

'How have I ended up?'

'Rich and prejudiced.'

'I'm not prejudiced.' Matthew frowned. 'You're the one who judges others instantly. You even give people adjectives – you literally label them.'

I needed to overlook the criticism (accurate if I'm fair) in favour of finding a way to win this argument. 'Yes, but you are rich and privileged.'

'Says Alice Carver.'

'Fine. I'm privileged too. But *I* am female.'

'Clutching at straws here, Alice.'

'No I'm not!' I said. 'Because, actually, if you think about it, manifesting is predominantly a female market. And maybe, Matthew Lloyd, that is your problem. Maybe *you* are a misogynist.'

Matthew stared at me for a moment, and then said, 'Very good, Alice. Fine. You win. Let's get on with it.'

'What?'

'Manifesting. I'll join in with you.'

'No, you won't.'

'I kind of have to. Can't have you besmirching me with accusations of misogyny.'

'But you think manifesting is bullshit.'

'I do. But I haven't tried it, so I'll give it a go. What do we do? Sounded like I have to address Capricorn directly?'

'No way. You'll ruin it for me. I'm not doing anything with you.'

'Come on,' said Matthew, raising his eyebrows. 'You can't hate me *that* much. I promise I'll do whatever you tell me to.' He scratched his jaw, revealing the edge of his tattoo again.

'Do *whatever* I tell you to?'

He gave me a slow smile.

Bloody great. Now he thought I fancied him and was thinking about him servicing me sexually. Which I wasn't. And now I also wasn't thinking about whether he smiled like that when he was— Fuck. No.

'Not like that!' I said, crossly.

'I didn't say anything,' he replied, grinning. 'Your face did though.'

Self-satisfied, overly confident, unfairly good-looking prick. I was starting to feel uncomfortably hot and a little bit on the brink, like I did at my eighth birthday party, right before I cried

234

because I came second in musical chairs. I busied myself by getting a glass of water from the fridge, brushing past Matthew crossly, and then making sure my back was towards him and he couldn't see my face.

But clearly my back is communicative too because I could tell from his voice that Matthew had stopped grinning. 'Alice?' he said, coming closer to me.

'Piss off. I wasn't thinking about you like that. I'm seeing someone actually. Someone really eligible, FYI.'

'Yeah, Astrid mentioned,' said Matthew. 'Your boss with hairy knuckles that was shagging your friend?'

'Well, I'm glad Astrid filled you in,' I said quietly, wondering just how much more humiliation one person could take. Plainly I was just a joke to my entire family.

'Alice?' he said.

I didn't answer.

'Don't go all silent on me.'

I still didn't answer. I just stared ahead and listened to the raindrops drumming on the roof light and the ticking of the refrigerator and tried not to focus on his physical proximity. He waited a second and then gently jostled me. 'Alice. Can we just get on? Even if only for tonight? Look, if you've got something else on, I'll back off. But if we're both here, we could hang out together. I genuinely want to hear about manifesting if it's important to you.'

Oh golly. Was Matthew Lloyd trying to be nice? Now I really felt on the brink. I gulped my glass of water and tried to regain some self-control.

'Fine.' I set my glass on the island, putting some distance between me and Matthew. 'But I'm not spending any time with you unless you give me wine and tell Astrid you took it. And you'll have to take the blame for burning the sage.'

'Okay,' said Matthew, going over to the wine fridge and selecting a bottle. It was the shit one without the label I'd picked up from the bargain bin at the Tesco Metro. 'How about this?'

'Er, maybe not that one?'

'Why not?'

'I bought it as a thank-you gift for Astrid. It's, erm, special. Why don't we try one of those Petit Chablis?' I've been desperate to try those but Astrid said they were a corporate gift and they were to be appreciated, not necked by someone like me.

'Oh no. I think you deserve something special yourself. That Petit Chablis is decent, but you've certainly pushed the boat out here. It looks like a really wonderful vintage. Can't I unscrew it and serve you a lovely glass?'

'No, seriously, Matthew,' I said, panicking he was going to make me drink the shit I'd bought. 'I'd rather have the Petit Chablis.'

'Yeah, I know.' Matthew grinned at me. 'Astrid warned me it would be paint stripper and not to open it because she was saving it to make you drink as payback. Do you want me to pour it down the sink?'

Sneaky Astrid. She acted like she was really pleased when I gave it to her. 'Er no,' I said, taking the bottle from him. 'No need to waste wine. Might need it sometime.' Clearly Matthew, with his hotel bar, had forgotten how normal people are obliged to keep shit wine, cooking sherry and gross holiday spirits on hand for emergencies.

Matthew looked quizzical then turned back to the wine fridge.

'But thanks for the heads-up,' I said.

'You're welcome,' said Matthew, opening a bottle of Petit Chablis.

*

About half an hour later and nearly one bottle of Petit Chablis down (really nice, by the way, a bit like those sour peach Haribos, so Astrid's wrong, as patently I can and do appreciate fine wine), I was feeling relatively relaxed even though I was hanging out with Matthew. Maybe it was the wine, or the background lullaby of raindrops on the roof, or the gentle undulating flame of the posh candle, but it all felt quite spiritual and womb-like. I was barely bothered by the pins and needles from sitting on the floor for so long. Or the ache in my back.

'Ow,' said Matthew, suddenly standing up and stretching. 'I've got cramp in my leg.' He looked down at me, still sitting crossed-legged. 'How come you're so comfortable sitting on the floor?'

'I guess I'm just naturally quite good at physical stuff,' I said, deciding that as he'd failed first, it was fine for me to stand and move to the sofa. But as I tried to get up, I found my foot had gone to sleep, and stumbled and banged into the coffee table, knocking the candle; I just managed to save it, before my foot went numb again and I collapsed back on the floor.

'Gosh, yeah,' said Matthew. 'And so graceful. Probably the dancer in you.'

'It's actually recommended to lie on your back like this,' I said casually. 'Helps to connect with the ground.'

Matthew didn't answer. He was still stretching his leg, but facing away from me, so I could have a quick stare unwatched. I swear, even in the dark, I could see the muscles on his back and shoulders ripple as he moved. No wonder Ebba had that irritatingly gratified look on her face.

'Stop staring at me,' said Matthew.

'I'm not. I'm focusing on the candle. Like you should be.'

'I'm not sure I should be,' said Matthew. 'I can see green flame imprints everywhere.'

He turned round to face me.

'You have a green flame instead of a face.'

'That's probably your third eye. It just means you're connecting well,' I said.

'No, it probably means I've given myself retinal fatigue,' said Matthew.

I remembered that woman from YouTube who claimed to have permanent eye damage. I hoped I hadn't burned Matthew's retinas. I felt pretty sure Astrid would be really pissed off with me if I had. And Mum would go mental. I sat up quickly, and blew out the candle.

'There we go then. Problem solved. Can you see properly now?'

'No,' said Matthew. 'Maybe turn some lights on?'

We both blinked in the soft glow of the side lamp, our eyes adjusting. Matthew picked up the candle and looked at the label. I felt oddly disappointed that the manifesting was done.

'Alice, why were we calling this candle Capricorn? It says Baobab on the side.'

'Because it's raining,' I explained.

'Yeah,' said Matthew. 'I still don't understand. And how is the candle granting wishes? Is it like a candle on a kid's birthday cake?'

'The candle doesn't grant wishes. We were meant to be using Capricorn to manifest and so the candle served as a representation.'

'Sorry, who is Capricorn?'

'It's the new moon tonight – it's called the Capricorn moon.'

'Why didn't we just use the moon then?' asked Matthew.

'Because it's *raining*!' For someone with two masters and his own successful business he seemed pretty slow to me.

'I reckon it would feel marginally less ridiculous to speak to the actual moon,' said Matthew. 'As opposed to Astrid's bathroom candle.'

'Well, yes,' I said authoritatively. 'Manifesting works much better outdoors. Effectively it's tapping into our longstanding relationship with nature, to ancient ways. That's why I have an affinity with nature. Something I have in common with Romantic poets and ancient philosophers. And, of course, you'll find they truly understood manifesting. Aristotle, Descartes. Big fans.'

Matthew gave me a puzzled look and opened his mouth to speak, then paused. 'Aristotle?'

'We are what we repeatedly do. Excellence then is not an act but a habit,' I quoted from *The Guide*, which was proving to be educational as well as helpful. 'Arguably he was talking about moon manifesting.'

'Arguably.' Matthew seemed to grapple with something for a moment. Probably how impressed he was by my philosophical awareness. He walked over to the glass doors and raked his eyes over the garden. 'It's a shame. So much light pollution here. You struggle to see the night sky properly.'

'The weather's terrible anyway,' I sighed. 'You wouldn't be able to see the Capricorn moon even if we weren't in London.'

Matthew stared at me for a second, frowning, and then pulled out his phone. 'I like your thinking, Alice,' he said, without looking up from his screen.

'What?'

But he didn't answer straightaway. I listened to the beat of the rain and waited.

'Have you got plans later tonight?' he asked.

I couldn't tell if he was just making conversation or whether he was asking because he was planning to spend more time with me. I thought about lying, but then took the risk and didn't. 'No. None.'

'Anything pressing early tomorrow morning . . . ? Work stuff that can't wait?'

It was Sunday tomorrow. The only pressing commitment I had was to a long lie-in. 'I know I come across as quite the career-woman, but my diary is pretty clear.'

Matthew glossed over my sarcasm. 'And you're still up for more manifesting with me?'

'Er, of course I am,' I said, trying to sound casual. 'It's more a question of your suitability and commitment.'

'I said I was committed to trying manifesting tonight. And I am. But are you happy for us to try talking to Capricorn more directly?'

'How directly?' I looked nervously at the miserable weather outside. I may have overemphasised my affinity to nature. 'I don't want to get wet.'

'Fair enough,' said Matthew, picking up his phone and making a call. I could vaguely hear the sound of a female voice answering. 'Hey. Tall order I know, but can you organise a helicopter within the hour? And a car to collect me? I'm still in Chiswick.'

What?

He looked over at me, 'Sorry,' he whispered, 'I forgot to check if you were comfortable with me using my privilege and obvious status symbols to fix a meeting with Capricorn . . . ? I don't want you to have to sacrifice any principles, so we can use public transport if you prefer?'

I stared at him, momentarily lost for words. 'No, no,' I said at last. 'I could probably manage to push through. Helicopter's fine.'

*

A couple of hours later, and as we hurtled round bendy single-track lanes that did not seem road-worthy, narrowly avoiding the dense overhanging woodland on all sides, I was starting to think Matthew's ideas of privilege and status were not the same as mine; or at least, he certainly used his differently to how I would. Not only was I now sober and feeling car sick, but I was frankly freaked out by the direction this journey had taken.

It had all started incredibly promisingly: as Matthew made brief arrangements, I'd tried to contain my excitement whilst planning what to wear. But as soon as he'd finished on the phone, Matthew told me I didn't have time to change and that what I was wearing was fine, all I needed was a thick coat, and handed me another glass of wine. And then the car arrived (big step up from your average Uber) and we drove the short distance to Ham Polo Club where our own private helicopter was waiting, and someone gave me a glass of champagne and welcomed me on board, and then within minutes, we were in the air, flying over London.

It was even better than I imagined it would be. Matthew said he needed to do a bit of work, so I looked out the window, through the raindrops, and watched the city pass by below, and took some selfies that will beat the shit out of anyone else's, even if my hair was a bit damp. And then it started to get darker and even though it was no longer raining outside, I couldn't really see anything below apart from uninteresting shapes, and I'd finished my champagne a while back, and then the helicopter started to slow. It took me a while to realise we were descending in the middle of this uninteresting nowhere, and for the first time I fully apprehended that our Saturday night out was going to be more than just a helicopter ride, so I said, 'Are we meant to be landing here? Or are we having an accident?'

Matthew looked up briefly from his phone. 'Yeah. There's a car coming. Don't worry.'

So I relaxed and hoped this car was as luxurious as the last one, which had had cream leather seats and Fiji water (free). But it *really* wasn't. It was one of those old-fashioned Land Rovers, which was:

a) Hard to get into, unless you're of Astrid / Matthew / Ebba unreasonably tall stature, or capable of doing the splits.

 b) Hard on the hips / thighs / arms / head when you're
   repeatedly flung against its sides.

The uncomfortable car was driven by a surly-looking chap who was clearly not going to serve any refreshments, and there was zero conversation because of the overriding sound of a vehicle attempting to navigate terrain that did not want to be navigated. I was becoming increasingly concerned when the car slowed down and then turned left, into even thicker trees, and onto what can only be described as hostile territory. The branches were cracking against the windows in a distinctly aggressive manner, and at one point the car pretty much drove vertically and I cast a sideways glance at Matthew who was still glued to his phone screen and I had the horrible thought that he may have planned something awful for me. Deliberately.

Suddenly we came to a stop.

'You're taking it from here?' said the man.

Matthew put his phone in his pocket and nodded at the man. 'Yeah.'

'All the arrangements have been made. Any problems, you know how to contact us.'

What arrangements? This whole trip was becoming decidedly sinister.

'Yep,' said Matthew, swinging his long legs out of the car. 'Coming, Alice?'

I really didn't want to get out of the car and that's saying something because I didn't like the car at all. 'It's very woody,' I called.

'Is that a problem?' asked Matthew, scaring me by suddenly appearing at my door.

'I just can't see anything. At all. Definitely not a moon. And where actually are we? My phone's stopped working.'

'Dartmoor,' said the man. 'You're off grid. Won't get a signal anywhere here.'

'Dartmoor?' I said. 'As in prison?'

The man said something quietly to Matthew that I couldn't hear. Probably along the lines of 'it won't be long before they notice I've escaped'.

'Come on, Alice,' said Matthew. 'I'm getting cold out here.'

'You're not selling it, Matthew. And if our phones won't work, how are we meant to know what direction to go in?'

'I know where I'm going.'

Both of the men were staring at me, frankly a little impatiently. So, after weighing up my options – prison man or Matthew Lloyd – I opened the car door and tried to step down but it was too far, so I sort of slid out, getting mud and other gross stuff all over my nicest tracksuit bottoms.

I looked up and Matthew was already off, trekking through the woods.

*

I managed at least five minutes in the manner of full-on *SAS: Who Dares Wins*, slogging, tripping and stumbling behind Matthew, panting – and, if I'm honest, terrified – before I caved.

'Please,' I said. 'Just tell me where we're going.'

'It's through these last few trees,' called Matthew. 'Come on!' He marched ahead and I started rushing again, worried he was going to leave me completely behind.

'Where?'

'You'll like it.'

'Matthew?' I called, pushing ahead through the dense trees. 'I can't see you.'

'Follow my voice. You're nearly there. Trust me.'

I didn't trust him. And that was before the trees suddenly gave way and I saw him standing, encircled by mist, next to a stone cross with an iron ring on it. And that was before I realised he was surrounded by gleaming eyes. It was like a billboard for a horror film.

I squealed, 'What the FUCK?'

'Stone cross,' said Matthew, smiling. 'They're everywhere. It's seriously old here. Ley lines everywhere.'

'No.' I took a few steps backwards, my heart beating a rapid patter that rivalled Phil Collins. 'What are *they*?'

More and more eyes were emerging from the mist. And then I saw the horns.

'Sheep. How can you not recognise sheep? You grew up in the Cotswolds.'

'They've got horns! I'm not going near them. We'll have to turn around.'

Matthew sighed. 'Alice, you're fine. Come on.'

Then something screeched and flapped, literally right next to my face, and I screamed again, sprinting towards Matthew, and dived into his solid chest, my arms up shielding my head.

'Help me,' I gasped. 'I'm being attacked by an eagle.'

'It's a bat.' His calm voice vibrated through his body and into my ear, sounding even deeper than usual. 'You don't need help.'

He put his hands on my arms and moved them down to my

sides, but he didn't push me away; he stood there, letting me press my face into him, taking my weight.

'When you said you had an affinity with nature,' Matthew said drily, 'I had no idea just how much.'

'I do have an affinity with nature.' My voice was muffled against his coat. 'I just have it from a safe distance.'

We stood there not moving for a second, then Matthew wrapped his arms around me and gave me a brief, hard hug, before stepping back, leaving me momentarily with a strange and unexpected empty feeling. Then he reached for my hand and took it in his. 'I know,' he said, striding off and bringing me with him, past the creepy horned creatures, which did, admittedly, scuttle away in a sheep-like fashion.

'How do you know? I've always hidden it well.' I've had to. My sisters absolutely love nature. Especially Arrie.

'Hmm,' said Matthew. 'You used to make me piggyback you through the field down to the boat house in case you stepped in cow pats.'

That's true.

'And you cried when Arrie and Roger bought the farm.'

'If you bloody know I don't have a hands-on thing for nature, then why have you brought me to these moors? It's horrible. And you promised it would be privileged. I don't see how it's privileged at all. It's worse than Guide-camp.'

'Cheer up,' said Matthew, 'Once you're doing some whit-tling and digging an earth toilet, it'll all feel much more homey.'

This is why Astrid and Matthew are best friends: they're both sadists.

Just then, the curtains of cloud opened and a sliver of new moon momentarily peeked through, centre-sky, fleetingly transforming the landscape of rolling hills and gorse into a luminescent sea of silver, stopping me in my tracks, before disappearing again.

'Oh,' I said. 'That was . . . incredible.'

Matthew tugged me forward. 'Dark skies. Perfect for moon gazing. It'll be more incredible from up here.'

And I realised we had come to the base of some kind of wooden staircase. I tipped my head back to follow its progression and saw that it stretched up to a massive wooden platform and a bridge that extended all the way to the trees beyond. 'What . . . is that?'

'That,' said Matthew, 'is our treehouse.'

*

I lounged on the oversized curved sofa, my head resting against a fur throw, luxuriating in the warmth cast out by the blazing wood-burning stove in the middle of the room. I took another sip of the ice-cold champagne, and noticed how the rich, polished grain of the wooden floor, walls and ceiling gleamed in the fire-light. Treetops stretched beyond the window and above them a smattering of stars were perfect pinpricks in a black sky. For a second I closed my eyes and basked in the gentle hiss from the stove, the whisper of wind in the branches outside and the sound of my breath.

'Hey,' said Matthew, coming back from the kitchen area. 'Don't go to sleep. We haven't done the manifesting yet.'

'Mmm,' I said.

'Wake up, Alice,' said Matthew. 'We need to get out there and do what we came to do.'

'I'm not asleep.' I opened one eye lazily to prove it.

Matthew loomed above me, his arms folded across his chest, looking even broader than usual against the glow of the fire. His skin was burnished and shimmering, like the wood, the contours of his face and body sculpted by the flickering shadows, and for a second he appeared almost otherworldly.

'Come and sit down with me.' I patted the sofa, and squinted up at him. 'It's so comfortable here. We can have more champagne. And then do the manifesting in a bit.'

He gave me a slow smile and something in my stomach snapped and went free-falling into a bottomless crater.

'If I didn't know you better,' he said, looking down at me, 'I'd think you were trying to get out of manifesting with Capricorn. I'd think you just wanted to hang out in a treehouse and enjoy the trappings of wealth. With me.'

'No, no,' I said, looking up at him and not moving. 'You know I love the outdoors. I'm only here for the manifesting.'

Matthew chuckled. 'You really don't want to go outside at all, do you?'

'This is the nicest place I've ever been,' I admitted. It really was. And even more amazing after that horrific approach. 'Don't make me leave it.'

'Get up,' said Matthew, shaking his head. 'Time to go out to the deck.'

*

So, it emerged that whilst I thought the inside of the treehouse was the best place I'd ever been, the outside deck might have beaten it by a hair's breadth.

It was just as beautifully put-together as inside, with lavish sofas, sumptuous fur throws piled everywhere, and perfectly placed fire pits, which spat and sizzled and warmed, seamlessly designed for intimacy, luxury and comfort, and maximum enjoyment of location. There was even a free-standing copper bath with heated towels awaiting. But unlike inside, here you could reach out and touch the neighbouring trees, and see for miles.

Matthew and I were lying, side by side, on the enormous day bed, and despite being outside in January, I wasn't freezing.

'See?' He turned to face me and gave me a quick grin. 'Worth leaving inside for?'

I looked up at the night sky, which stretched in every direction above us, forever and beyond, and felt dizzy.

I turned my face back to his. 'I love it. It really is a wonderland. Thank you so much for bringing me here.'

His grin softened. 'Well, every Wonderland needs an Alice.'

It felt like a small explosion in my heart.

If I could have pressed pause, I would have.

'Okay.' Matthew drew his gaze away and glanced at his watch. 'Let's do the manifesting. It's after one, so even if we set off by two I'm afraid I'm not going to have you back to Astrid's much before half three . . . '

'Oh.' The buzz from the champagne and the setting flattened a little, like I'd drunk a shrinking potion, giving me a slight ache in my ribs. 'I didn't realise we had to go back tonight. Sorry. Okay. Yeah.'

'We don't *have* to.'

'No, I get it.' I tried to sound upbeat but suddenly I could feel how cold it was out here, despite the fires; there was a chill that was creeping in. 'This has been amazing, but you need to get back. Totally.'

'I don't need to get back,' said Matthew. 'If you don't. I mean, in some ways, it would probably be more practical to fly back tomorrow morning, get to Chiswick for a late breakfast.'

'Much more sensible. In so many ways!'

'Except,' said Matthew, 'this whole place is set up for a couple. In terms of sleeping arrangements.'

I shifted so that I was facing him properly. 'Matthew,' I said, my breath clouding in the air. 'If the bed inside is anything like this day bed, it'll be full-on enormous. We can just share it.'

Matthew looked down at me. 'Hmm. Would your hairy-knuckled boyfriend be okay with that?'

I could feel my face getting hotter, despite the cold. I hope he didn't think I was coming on to him by wanting to stay here. 'Guy is not my boyfriend. And I don't see it's a problem. You and I are family friends. Unless it's a problem for you. Or Ebba.'

Great. Now I was thinking of Matthew and Ebba. Together. I wondered if he'd brought her here before. Maybe they bathed together in that copper tub; two flawless specimens in an idyllic setting.

He said nothing.

I rolled awkwardly onto my back again putting distance between us. 'Look, I'll sleep on the sofa. Or out here. Problem solved.'

Matthew laughed quietly. 'How have you managed to offend yourself, Alice?' he said. 'Neither of us is sleeping out here. It's freezing. If you're okay to share a bed with me, it's all good.'

I swallowed. 'I am. It's no big deal.'

'Cool.' He extricated himself from the covers. 'Give me a minute to sort the travel arrangements for tomorrow, and then manifesting begins.'

Not going to detail the manifesting; suffice to say it was mostly going through the actions. We used champagne for moon water and spoke directly to Capricorn this time, and the moon was definitely more mesmerising than a candle. Obviously, however, I couldn't do my real manifestations in front of Matthew, so just kept them work-related, and did a vague one about being a happy and fulfilled person. He did an equally bland one about finding a better work-life balance and being in the moment, as if there is any alternative. Then he insouciantly asked me why I hadn't manifested my old house, and I said, carelessly, 'Actually I was just getting to it,' and then had to do so out loud, whilst he pretended he was open-minded and tried to keep a straight face, and I pretended I believed it would work.

He suggested we write down our manifestations. I agreed but neither of us had any proper paper. Or a pen. So we had to improvise with what I could find in my bag.

'We'll each write one manifestation,' said Matthew. 'But let's keep them private.'

We turned away from each other and Matthew went first.

'You should sign and date it,' I said.

'Exceedingly hard with eyeliner,' said Matthew.

I wrote, 'I manifest the perfect man falling in love with me' on a train ticket but before I could write Guy's name, the eyeliner broke. Honestly, I was more interested in what Matthew had written. I did try (unsuccessfully) to find out but he distracted me by giving me another glass of champagne.

And actually, when you're with Matthew Lloyd in a fantasy treehouse drinking champagne under a canopy of stars, it's hard in the moment to think of what else to ask for.

'No way!' I said in disbelief an hour or two later, sitting up in bed and looking at the ceiling and walls of the round bedroom, which had peeled themselves away, like a noisy orange, revealing a glass dome. As I slowly turned around, all I could see were the night skies spread out, surrounding us, as if we were suspended in space. 'It makes Swiss Family Robinson's efforts look like toddler time.'

'Yeah, it's awesome,' agreed Matthew.

'It's breathtaking.' And it was. It almost hurt to be somewhere like this. I put a hand to my abdomen and rubbed it. 'Sort of overwhelming.'

'I can shut it again?'

'No! No. Definitely not.'

'Okay, sleep well, Alice,' said Matthew.

As we carefully lay down, on our respective sides of the bed, gazing up at the canopy, that ache inside seemed to inflate with every breath I took. I'd been punctilious about not looking over whilst Matthew stripped down to his boxers and T-shirt before getting into bed, but this whole set-up was designed to throw reflections around, and I saw. And now I couldn't unsee. All those muscles. My mind kept flicking back over the evening: images of Matthew imprinted in my mind's eye like flames in the black. He was lying there now – somehow taking up more room in the silence – centimetres away from me. Suddenly I felt uncomfortably overheated. I sat up again.

'You okay?' he asked, sleepily.

'Mmm. Just a bit hot.'

'Did you watch me get undressed?'

How the fuck did he know?

'No!' My voice sounded shrill even to me. 'Why do you always have to make me sound like such a pervert!'

'I know you have a healthy appreciation of the male form. Didn't you nip off on New Year's Eve for seedy sex after feeling me up? Hope I'm safe here next to you.'

'Why would you bring me here if you thought I was going to jump you!' I drew back the covers huffily, ready to stalk off to the sitting room.

'Hey, I was joking.' Matthew reached out and circled my wrist with his hand, stilling me instantly. A treacherous tingle went up my arm. 'Don't get offended again. I know perfectly well I'm not your type.'

'You do?'

'Yeah. You're into stuffy, traditional, pompous suits. Like Hugh. Or Monty. Your boss at work. Plus Ollie . . .'

'Hey, Ollie is *your* friend.'

'Was. Anyway. Relax. You're not going to jump *me* because you've got terrible taste in men.'

Then he pulled me back down, slightly too hard, so I ended up over on his side of the bed, partially on top of him, our bodies pressed together, our faces nearly aligned.

I could feel the faint coolness of his breath on my forehead, the heat and hardness of him underneath.

For a second, or maybe a day, neither of us moved. I don't think I even breathed.

Matthew cleared his throat. 'Alice,' he said, wincing slightly. 'Yes?'

'If you wouldn't mind getting off? You're going to give me a boner . . .'

'Shit, sorry!' I skirted back over to my side quickly, my heart pounding. 'I'm really sorry,' I gabbled. 'I didn't think.'

There was a moment. Then Matthew yawned.

'I'll cope, Alice. I guess it's a common hazard where you're concerned.' I could hear him grinning in the darkness.

What did that mean? That he thought I went around trying to induce boners, or that he actually found me attractive? I was just about to ask him when he yawned again.

'Sleep well,' said Matthew. 'We've got an early start tomorrow.'

And before I could even answer, Matthew was asleep, his breathing a gentle rhythm, accompanied by the movement of the trees in the breeze. I, however, was nowhere near to falling asleep. And the longer I lay there, the worse it got. My body felt awake and alert and taut; I was excruciatingly aware of *his* body, so close, yet oceans away. I started to feel a bit annoyed with him. He did this. Bringing me here. Turning me on. Going to sleep. The longer I lay there, the crosser I felt. How did he always screw me over? Now, instead of enjoying being here, I was focused on what I didn't have, what I couldn't have.

I stared at the skies and then at his face, bathed in the silver glow of the reclining Capricorn moon; both looked touchable in this light, but neither was in my reach.

Having spent most of the night not sleeping, predictably I had to be woken up by Matthew when it was time to leave. When we arrived at the helicopter, we were greeted with steaming coffee by a properly hot (and diminutive) pilot, and despite being knackered, I stayed awake for the whole journey, determined not to waste a second of travelling the way the rich and famous do. Imagine if that were my daily commute:

What temperature would you like your helicopter cabin set at, Ms Carver, and can I offer you a coffee?

Yes, you flipping-well can, Captain Helicopter. And maybe pilot with your shirt off, today.

Right away, ma'am.

Matthew worked for some of the journey, his brow furrowed as he concentrated, but when I pointed out it was actually Sunday morning, he did play I-spy over London. For a bit. Until someone called him again. I guess that's the problem with being in a line of work where you travel by helicopter: people keep expecting you to do work even whilst you're on said helicopter. Matthew seemed preoccupied and told me sometimes the worst part of his work was making big decisions. I assumed he was talking about the other part of his business, rather than hotel napkins, or cocktail menu choices. A town car – similarly deluxe to the one that brought us – was waiting to collect us in Ham; and as the houses rapidly passed us by, I began to long for a traffic jam or two, just to prolong the experience.

'What's up, Alice?' said Matthew, without taking his attention from his phone.

'Nothing! Why do you think there would be?'

He looked up then, raised his eyebrows at me and waited.

'Okay,' I admitted. 'I'm kind of not ready for this to be over.'

I knew that would make the grin appear. 'Is that right? What are you going to miss most: my fantastic body, or my privilege of being chauffeured around?'

He is possibly the most irritating man I've ever met. But you can't miss what you've never had. 'The chauffeuring thing,' I said. 'I've got to take the tube to work tomorrow.'

I saw his grin get wider. 'But then, at the end of the tube journey, you get the reward of seeing your lecherous, hirsute love interest.'

'What makes you think he's lecherous? And he's actually very attractive. FYI.'

'He's your boss. He shouldn't go there.'

'Okay.' I folded my arms. 'Well, *some* people find me attractive. FYI.'

'Stop saying FYI. And I'm not saying you're unattractive. I'm saying he shouldn't be abusing his position of power.'

'Yeah, well, he's not. I want it.'

'Sure you do,' said Matthew, patronisingly. 'It makes complete sense that a beautiful woman like you would want old hairy knuckles. With any luck, he'll have a hairy back too. You'll be able to cling on to it in bed . . .'

Despite trying to stay cross, I could feel my mouth twitching into a smile. Matthew Lloyd just called me beautiful.

'Do you often do this kind of thing?' I asked.

'What? Discuss other men's body hair?'

'Take, um . . . people . . . off to treehouses on a Saturday night.'

Matthew scratched his jaw. 'Er, no. Not often.'

I turned and looked out of the window in case my face looked too pleased.

Matthew's phone buzzed. The screen was reflected in the blacked-out glass. Ebba. He answered. I shamelessly listened to his side of the conversation, which went:

Hey.

No, I had no signal.

Dartmoor.

Yes, the whole night.

Because it's a good place to see the moon.

No, not on my own.

With friends.

Alice.

No, not Astrid.

Just Alice.

Okay. Friend. Singular.

Yes.

What exactly do you want me to say?

Hello?

'Who was that?' I asked nonchalantly, turning round to him.

'You know it was Ebba.'

'Ebba, your girlfriend?'

Matthew sighed. 'Again. Ebba is not my girlfriend.'

'She clearly thinks she is,' I said, my face breaking out into a grin. 'And she totally freaked out about last night, didn't she? Admit it.'

'You're really annoying, Alice,' he said. 'But yes. She was not happy about last night.' He looked straight at me. 'Specifically, you.'

'Well, I'm sure you set her straight.' I stared right back, hoping he couldn't hear the sound of my heart pounding. 'I'm just Astrid's younger sister. Right?'

'Astrid's interminably annoying younger sister,' said Matthew Lloyd, looking at me with an expression I couldn't quite fathom, before answering another call.

Even when we were back at Astrid's, there was still that feeling of possibility, of adventure, like Matthew and I had shared something. I was half worried about Astrid being weird about the fact we'd been off on our own together, but she didn't even ask; she was curled up on the sofa, next to Aziz, with a hangover from hell, but a look of contentment on her face that I hadn't seen in weeks. Months. Longer, maybe. She was faux pissed-off with Matthew for bailing last night, and for paying for everyone's meals in advance (imagine being at the point where you're rich enough to tell people off for paying for you), but essentially she was too tired and sick to be her usual acerbic self.

'It paid off,' I said to Matthew quietly, when we ended up in the kitchen together, and we both looked over at Aziz and Astrid, entwined and dozing on the sofa. 'Your ten-course tasting menu romantic evening worked.'

'I definitely paid over the odds to get your sister laid,' said Matthew.

I sniggered. 'She obviously needed it. You've solved everything.'

'Yeah. I doubt that.'

Whilst they were sleeping, Matthew and I went for a walk and he asked why I was worried people didn't value me at work, and he was so genuinely interested I found myself opening up to him. I told him it was difficult to be motivated with Harry Piles as Deputy MD, and how much it annoyed me that he has such shit ideas, doesn't understand the market, and was only employed because of his family connections and that any good ideas he had were in fact stolen from other people, viz., largely, me.

He raised an eyebrow when I told him that the whole company, in fact, was founded on a bunch of old family connections. (Guy went to Eton with half the shareholders; Edward Puesdon's brother runs a TV channel that is effectively owned by the same parent company; Harry Piles' father is second cousin twice removed to the CEO.)

Matthew said, 'Because of course you've never used your family connections to get ahead.'

I said he sounded like Drunk Stephen and Matthew said Stephen was patently 'a highly perceptive and intelligent individual'. So I explained that Drunk Stephen was also pissed off at work because he'd been overlooked for a promotion at least once and he'd basically done all the covers for our bestselling books as well as the new logo for the company AND the new non-fiction list, which wasn't even his job.

I even took him through a few of my own ideas and why I thought they would work, including the one for a series of light non-fiction books for teens about mindfulness and mental health and consent and so on, authored by popular TikTok creators, which luckily I hadn't mentioned in front of Harry Piles and thus he had not yet been able to steal.

Matthew said that for someone who claimed not to care about my job, I'd certainly put a lot of thought into it. He suggested I work up some of my ideas into a document, rather than wait for manifesting to deliver, and that my publishing company sounded like it had a fairly toxic work environment and a culture shift evidently needed to happen. His phone rang and I saw it was Ebba again before he muted it and returned it to his pocket. He explained he had a tough week ahead, work-wise, and he needed a bit of head space. I said, 'I guess your job is often challenging,' hoping he might remind me of what he actually did without me having to admit I'd never really listened to him before, but we passed a wine shop and Matthew decided to buy a bottle for supper.

On the way back, and after a couple of samples at the wine shop, I told him about Lazy Veronica who does shit-all work, and how stressed Cara is, and amused him with stories about Drunk Stephen and Charlotte and Yaz, and Matthew wanted a detailed description of Gareth's arms and why Guy took against them.

In fact, it was all like some alternate universe, where Astrid and Aziz were happy again, and where Matthew and I got on. Right up until we were about to sit down to eat. Aziz was cooking at the stove, and Matthew and I were sitting next to each other at the table. He was on his laptop and I was scrolling through my phone when Astrid pushed something over to me.

'What's this?' I asked.

'Your work security card. You put it through the washing machine. Again.'

'Sorry, Astrid,' I said meekly, taking the card. She's a real pain about that machine.

'It's ruined. Not only has the security code been washed off, but your photo's practically invisible.'

'Well, at least you can still see Carsons on it,' I said, trying to be positive. 'Just about.'

'Also,' continued Astrid, 'I happened to catch up with an old friend when we were out last night, and that boss of yours you're planning to shag . . .'

'Yes . . .' I said, checking to see if Matthew was listening. He wasn't. He was now absent-mindedly playing with my security card.

'You know he's very much still married.'

'Only in name. They're separated.'

'Separated or separating? Don't be gullible, Alice,' countered Astrid. 'You're not going to hear the real story whilst you're working there. Remember all the stuff you heard after you left Bloomsbury?'

Matthew looked up from his computer. 'You left Bloomsbury?'

'Er, yes,' I said. 'A couple of years ago.'

'Did you seriously think Alice had kept the same job for five years, Matthew?' said Astrid. 'How would that work for her? She'd be complete— Matthew?'

But Matthew had abruptly walked off.

'Matthew?' she called after him. 'It's nearly supper.'

'Sorry, Astrid,' he said, without a backwards glance. 'I don't think I'm going to be able to join you.'

And then he *didn't* join us for the rest of the evening. At all.

This morning, when I came down to the kitchen, Astrid was scowling over a cup of coffee and practically bit my head off when I asked about Matthew. 'He's gone to stay in a hotel,' she said.

'Gone?' I repeated. I put down my full cup of coffee.

'Gone,' she said.

'What? Why? I thought he was staying here?'

'Well, now he's not. So you've got what you wanted.'

It certainly didn't feel like I had. It felt like the opposite. 'Is he coming back . . . ?'

'No. He's taken all his stuff. And now I'm stuck here. On my own.'

When I automatically pointed out she wasn't on her *own*, because I was there, and so was Aziz, her husband, she said that was as good as being on her own. That Matthew had let her down. And suddenly, I felt dangerously close to tears, so I left without having a coffee or anything.

The tube was so full I didn't even have to hold on because I was buttressed on either side, and thus shoved right into the armpit of a very tall teenager with a penchant for Lynx Africa, which I found oddly comforting. And as we lurched from side to side and I stared unseeingly at the reflections in the windows, it felt almost impossible that only twenty-four hours ago I'd been in a helicopter with Matthew Lloyd.

In my mind's eye, I could see his face bathed in the silvery light of Capricorn as clearly as midnight. But then when I tried to look closer, it drifted away from me, dissolved, and was gone – like rain on a window.

I couldn't settle to anything at work, and it was only when Yaz asked me if I knew whether Guy Carmichael was coming back this afternoon that I registered he wasn't in his glass office. But what's really weird is that I didn't tell Drunk Stephen anything about my weekend. Normally I'd be desperate to give him a blow-by-blow account of everything, and that's just your average weekend, not one where I've gone in a helicopter to Dartmoor. Not today, though. When Drunk Stephen suggested lunch, I said I couldn't and later I told Cara I had a headache and was going to work from home for the rest of the day, because I knew I wanted to escape and write in this journal.

But I didn't go back to Astrid and Aziz's. I couldn't face its emptiness. Instead I've come here, to the busy, anonymous BFI café and sat. Alone. And I've written for hours, got it all out. The longest journal entry in the world. Problem is, now I've finished, I don't feel much better.

In fact, if anything, putting it all on paper has made it worse. The weekend has gone, all the trees and moon and sky have melted into air, as if they were never there. And so has Matthew. If it weren't for the faintest trace of wood smoke in my hair I'd wonder if I imagined the whole thing. And honestly, I have no ideas for how to improve my life other than this journal – and even that I messed up – I had a great opportunity to manifest by the Capricorn moon, which I wasted.

But mostly, I feel like a complete idiot for getting caught up in the moment with Matthew Lloyd, and for allowing myself to be happy with him. If anyone should know better, it's me.

I am letting go of:

Moonlight and treehouses

Guide Post™

*If you miss the wave, don't worry: there's
another one coming right behind.*

My thoughts and reflections:

Hump-day today . . .

Worked from home again yesterday as genuinely did have a headache. This time I actually was at home and actually did do work. Had to join Harry Piles' Product Development meeting on Teams. Marginally better than being there in person because I could put a chicken face on him. But still the usual bullshit:

Harry Piles: Come on, people. We need to pull it out the bag here. Revenue is down by thirteen per cent on last year. I'm getting it in the ear and we panned over Christmas. Fucking S&S stole all the seasonal with that Hunt the Christmas Cracker shit they pulled and we are starting to look like complete donkeys here. What's going wrong, people?

Silence. Everyone knew what was going wrong – him.

Harry Piles: Seriously. I want answers. Now. Yaz – why did the Christmas Traditions Around the World flunk?

Yaz: *(panicked inhale)* Well, if you remember, the consumer group did clearly say it didn't appeal at the time. I think, in terms of concept—

Harry Piles: No thanks, Yaz. Concept was solid; execution was lacking. So, Cara, lessons for Editorial?

Cara: Lessons for all, Harry. Poor concept and text heavy.

Harry Piles: Thanks, Cara. Embarrassing, for Editorial really.

Cara: Harry, I distinctly remember saying at the time that the concept *you* came up with was—

Harry Piles: So blue-sky thinking. What can we do?

Me: How about we bring our non-fiction list into the twenty-first century and think about more relevant titles for today's readers? Make the layouts more appealing and actively target the TikTok market. We could even use TikTok creators to—

Harry Piles: Not your usual dumb-dumb for dumb-dumbs, please, Alison. Blue sky.

Me: We need to exploit new markets if we want to increase our sales.

Cara: She's right, Harry.

Harry Piles: Readers want traditional from Carsons. Anyone else? Blue sky. Mark?

Mark: Backlist?

Harry Piles: Thank you. Sensible idea at last. Which backlist?

Drunk Stephen: Yes, which one haven't we exhausted? Love this blue sky.

Mark: The Discovery one?

Harry Piles: Discovery series . . . Remind me.

Mark: Very successful in the Eighties. Fell off the radar.

Drunk Stephen: Don't they all have intros by JJ?

Mark: Obviously you'd lose the intros. Or is it still too much of a risk post Operation Yew Tree?

Cara: Yes. What if someone posts an old one on social?

Harry Piles: That's your job and PR's. We're not re-writing history for the wokes. Pull up some old titles, Mark.

Mark: Um, *Discover Shooting for Boys*, *Discover Sewing for Girls*, *Discover Hunting for Boys*, *Discover Baby Animals for Girls*.

Drunk Stephen: Those titles hardly scream 'now'.

Harry Piles: People want traditional. Think how many copies *The Dangerous Book for Boys* sold. People like security, especially in times like these. Couple of tweaks is all we need; hide the rest under the umbrella of 'retro'.

Drunk Stephen: We'd need to re-shoot at the least.

Harry Piles: Expensive. Use the umbrella. Let's get creative, Stephen.

Drunk Stephen: *(shares his screen)* All the kids are white. The books are exclusively either for girls or for boys. JJ is literally in photos with children. How creative can we get?

Harry Piles: Fucking shame we didn't think of this pre-Christmas. Could have stuck a cracker over his face, like Simon and Schuster. What did Hachette do with Enid Blyton – goblins, was it?

Me: *(sarcastically)* Well, it's coming up to Easter. You could always use eggs. Combine *Discover Hunting for Boys* and *Discover Baby Animals for Girls* in one handy volume perfect for Gen Alpha. Cover up the paedophile's face with eggs. Add some colour. But . . . will it solve the fundamental issue that the topics are dated and won't sell?

Harry Piles: Fucking great idea, Alison; look into it. And aren't you marketing?

Me: It's Alice. And no. I'm an editor.

Harry Piles: Okay. Great. It's your job to make lemonade out of this shit. The idea's top drawer. See, Cara? Someone in your team gets it. Stephen – can you stick eggs on the kids' faces? And JJ's? Then it might as well be diverse 'cos no one can tell. You'll have to colour in the hands.

Drunk Stephen: . . . Um. Yes. That's just the kind of representation I dreamed of as a child.

Harry Piles: I love it. Deep backlist, no advances. Creative adaptation. Let's bring the Discovery series back in a big way. That's what I call blue-sky thinking.

So that was the headline from yesterday.

Back in the office today, and it was super-boring. Guy Carmichael out again, so nothing to distract me. Plus I broke my headset by sitting on it. Everyone gave me space, assuming I still wasn't feeling great, and I wallowed in it. Same at home. I've barely seen Astrid and Aziz since Sunday (and I don't think they've seen each other at all – they're both working crazy hours) and it's suited me well.

But . . . enough is enough. That Guide Post resonated. It's already the middle of the week. Haven't heard from Matthew and in a couple of days it will be the weekend again. Getting on was clearly a one-night thing for him. Time to move past last weekend.

I'm going to wait for that next wave, and get on with the manifesting.

I am grateful for:

- Guide Posts
- Yaz, who let me borrow her headset (she doesn't like lending her stuff)

My thoughts and reflections:

I'm going to feel rough tomorrow . . .

Yaz invited me and Drunk Stephen along to meet her parents at the members' club at the Royal Festival Hall for happy hour (well, we kind of invited ourselves when we heard she was going) and her parents insisted we join them for supper – they're really nice despite the fact that their idea of a good night out is a 'smorgasbord of song and poetry and spoken word', followed by 'dramatised readings by NHS heroes of excerpts from six Booker Prize longlists'. I never had Yaz down for having parents like that (Yaz sounds decidedly *EastEnders*) but it does explain how she got into Carsons. I'm fairly sure her mum was wearing a genuine Hermès scarf.

Once Yaz and her parents had nipped off for a fun evening of intellectual pursuits, Drunk Stephen did not hold back on his feelings and said that whilst he liked Yaz's parents, he always knew she was a fake, and why would she affect a downwardly converged accent whilst working in an industry that was so elitist. I joked, 'Maybe that was the only way she managed to get into Carsons, on the diversity quota.'

Then Drunk Stephen got really arsey and said there was no diversity quota and she would have got through the same way every other person did, because her parents knew someone or knew someone who knew someone, and definitely because her parents could afford to subsidise her existence.

And I said, 'That isn't true because my parents don't know anyone at Carsons. I did it all on my own.'

And he said, 'Alice, don't be a twat. How did you first get into publishing?'

'I can't really remember, that was years ago when I was in my mid-twenties and I was desperate and so I got that assistant job at Granta.'

But Drunk Stephen wasn't letting it go. 'How did you get that job?'

'Well, through Mum's old school-friend, Worthy Glenda – I did an internship, but—'

Drunk Stephen cut me down with a hand gesture. 'No buts. Not everyone, Alice, can afford to take on an unpaid internship. I'm literally the only person at Carsons who came in through the front door, and who isn't privileged or fucking awful. And you can pretty much count the non-hetero and non-white employees on one hand.'

It wasn't like Drunk Stephen to get this worked up, and it was reminding me uncomfortably of the time Astrid and Matthew fell out. She'd dragged an unwilling Matthew along to a dinner in the summer when everyone was back from uni, and there were a ton of old St Hilda's people there. It was quite an expensive restaurant, and everyone went to town, getting increasingly drunk and then Hugh or someone had insisted on ordering a bottle of vintage champagne to end the meal. Matthew hadn't been drinking, and had been unusually quiet all evening; Astrid kept jostling his elbow and telling him to cheer up. When the bill came, someone suggested we split it equally. Astrid could see Matthew was looking uncomfortable and pulled him aside. And he told her that this was why he hadn't wanted to come in the first place and that he deliberately hadn't drunk, and had chosen his meal carefully, so he would have enough money to buy the set textbooks for next term. And Astrid, who was pretty drunk, got defensive and made out that he should have just said earlier, and she would pay for his meal tonight and that it didn't need to be a big deal. But Matthew shook his head and said in this really quiet voice that it wasn't for Astrid to decide whether it was a big deal or not.

Drunk Stephen said he didn't know how much longer he could sit through meetings listening to people who were fundamentally out of touch talk authoritatively about the current market. 'The irony of the ivory-towered deciding what diversity in publishing looks like no longer amuses me.'

I said, 'But what about me? I'm not like that.'

'Alice, you went to St Hilda's. You're entirely privileged.'

'Well, what about Clyde? He went to a school with cages in Hillingdon.'

'Clyde's on security.'

'Yes. But technically, that means you're not the only one.'

'And that, Alice, is why you're fucking awful.'

And because I was a bit pissed by then, I said, 'I know. But at least I own it. I hadn't really thought about the internship thing. Sorry.'

'It's not your fault,' said Drunk Stephen. 'It's like the sea and you're a fish, you know?'

And then we both laughed because I did know but also it sounded like nonsense.

Then we did a few tequilas like we usually do, and Drunk Stephen stopped being so annoyed. I told him in full detail what had happened last week with Guy Carmichael and how I'd been on edge this week, wondering if he was going to make good and ask me on a date or not. And Drunk Stephen said, 'Seriously, Alice, you saw what happened to Charlotte. Do you want to go there? It will all be on his terms.'

So I said, 'But Charlotte kind of sucks and I don't. Plus I haven't had sex since last year and Guy Carmichael is consummate seduction,' and Drunk Stephen couldn't really argue with that.

'If you sleep with him, check the grey herringbone suit label. I'm sure it's Dege & Skinner.'

Drunk Stephen is obsessed with Guy Carmichael's fierce suit collection.

I promised Drunk Stephen that when I was shagging Guy Carmichael, I'd not only check all his suit labels, but get him to give Drunk Stephen a raise. Drunk Stephen told me that if I successfully managed to shag Guy Carmichael and keep my job, then he had every confidence I could also get him a raise.

I was more than a little bit pissed by then, so I said, watch me, and then manifested it. (I got quite into the cheersing in between manifestations and broke a couple of glasses, and so did Drunk Stephen because he thought it was part of the manifestation process. I hope Yaz's parents aren't charged for it. We also got into an argument with a real jobsworth when Drunk Stephen and I found out that happy hour was in fact happy 'hour' and it had ended ages ago and we therefore had a much larger bill than anticipated. Eventually, we were asked, in an unnecessarily aggressive way, to leave.)

Still. All in all, it was a fun night out.

I ask the Universe:

- To do something about inequality in publishing.
- To help Drunk Stephen get his raise (and I wouldn't be averse to one myself).

My thoughts and reflections:

Manifesting works! It genuinely works.
    Just received the following email:

    To: alice.carver@carsons.com
    From: guy.carmichael@carsons.com
    Re: touching in

    Lunch next Thursday, 12.00. Confirm with Iris.

I am letting go of:

Any misgivings I ever had about manifesting – I am in touching
distance of Guy 'touching in'.

My thoughts and reflections:

Have spent a dynamic and productive weekend (largely on my own as Astrid was working and Aziz had gone to his parents' for his mum's birthday) maximising my new status as an authentic manifester. I finally sat down and worked up some of my ideas for non-fiction into a proper document so that they're ready for me to start to build on my manifesting successes in the workplace. Okay, it was smug Matthew Lloyd's suggestion which means I should be ignoring it on principle, but once I'd finished and included my evidence-based research, I did actually feel quite smug myself. These were good ideas that stood to be profitable and popular. And they were now ready for me to share, thus proving my worth, should Guy Carmichael ask me intelligent and probing questions over lunch. It did, however, take a massive chunk of time.

When Arrie FaceTimed this morning to show me Maud's new puppies and complain about the twins' school and the way that they'd treated her (one of the twins had apparently given a haircut to another child and there was some discussion about consent and Arrie had felt slighted as a parent and dog breeder), she wouldn't believe I was in the middle of work until I showed my laptop. Then she went weirdly emotional and said, 'God, how has Astrid managed that? Alice working on a Sunday?' And made a big show of shouting out to tell Roger how fab Astrid was and look what she'd achieved with Alice, and when Astrid had children there probably wouldn't be difficult conversations with schools, and got a tear in her eye and tried to pretend it was pride that I'd come so far but we both knew she was secretly upset at the idea that Astrid had managed something Arrie never had. Arrie is so competitive.

So eventually I put her out her misery and told Arrie that my working had nothing to do with Astrid, and that if I were honest, watching Astrid puke and faint and lose her marriage over deciding she needed a dramatic career change was enough to make me want to opt out of life altogether and join the circus. I explained how Harry Piles was such a dick at work and that when the cuts started happening, I didn't want to lose my job on the back of his incompetence. Arrie said it was an indication of poor leadership when someone like Harry Piles took root. 'Who does he report to?'

'Guy Carmichael's divisional leader,' I said. 'But it's not his fault.'

'Oh Christ,' said Arrie. 'Please tell me that's not the one you're hoping to shag? If you're crushing on your boss, Alice, at least he should be an effective boss.'

'More than crushing actually, Arrie. I've got a date on Thursday.'

At least that cheered Arrie up. She said that Astrid was undoubtedly doing a way worse job with me than Arrie would, and why would Astrid stand by while I went and proffered myself to sub-standard executive leaders? She wouldn't listen when I told her that Guy was authority itself and has won loads of awards so is indisputably good at his job. She just told me that I needed to have a good hard think about exactly what it was I hoped to achieve and that judging by this latest mess with me, Astrid was the sort of person who'd probably end up with the type of child who ended up receiving haircuts at school then crying about it later. And now, on reflection, when she really thought about it, Arrie would prefer to be the mother of haircutters.

I mean that says it all. Arrie is verging on a psychopath. That's why she made all that money when she was young.

I took a few screenshots of the puppies snuggling together (they were cute, despite their belligerent mother) to mollify Arrie and to show Astrid later.

But Astrid was typically derisive about the puppies when she eventually got home later that evening. 'They're not snuggling together, Alice. That one's plainly trying to hump his brother. Animals don't always respect boundaries. Neither do you, by the sound of it.'

Like Arrie, Astrid wasn't impressed by my manifesting date success with Guy Carmichael: neither of my sisters is good at being happy for other people.

'Going for lunch with Guy,' I said, 'is not the same as incest.'

'He's married,' said Astrid. 'And he's your boss. You're crossing boundaries.'

'He's getting a divorce! Besides, you're crossing boundaries too with your new career.' I was thinking of Aziz at his parents', on his own.

'At least I know it's what I want. And I take responsibility for it.'

'I do know what I want: Guy.'

'Really? So do you want a date with Guy because Charlotte had one and you want to beat her? Or because you want him to notice you, get your name right and respect you at work? Or just because you always want hairy-knuckled men in their fifties?'

'I'm a complex woman, Astrid. It's possible to want many things. Plus you haven't seen him; Guy is in his prime.'

'Congratulations, Alice. Glad you're perpetuating the patriarchy by continuing to participate in gender ideology where the older male form is revered, and the older female form despised.'

Christ. Someone was stressing about hitting middle age. 'I'm not,' I said quickly. 'I'm always telling Cara at work that in a couple more years, when she hits fifty, she'll be at her zenith, and that her skin is just getting better as she ages.'

'Really?'

'Yes!' I said, trying not to feel guilty about the fact that last week I'd told Cara she might want to try a light-therapy mask for her crêpe-y neck. But only because she was saying the Charlotte Tilbury Magic cream she'd just bought didn't seem to do a lot and that she hasn't had any matches on eHarmony in the last fourteen months since she updated her profile pic.

'Have you thought about what's going to happen after this date with Guy?' asked Astrid.

'Sex.'

'After that!'

'More sex.'

'What do you actually want from Guy?' said Astrid. 'A relationship?'

'I prefer to live for today, Astrid,' I said coldly. 'It's not healthy to plan too far ahead. We don't all have control issues.'

'Oh right. Well, that's entirely consistent with your manifestation fixation.' She looked at me like I was a major irritation in her life. 'I don't think you really have a clue what you want, Alice.'

I chose not to point out that maybe she didn't know what she wanted either, unless of course she was actively wanting to screw up her marriage. I chose not to, because I want to stay living in Astrid's house, thus proving that I am very much a woman who knows what she wants. Actually. Many people would hail me as 'clued-up'. Well, I would.

I am grateful for:

Having the good fortune to be me, rather than Arrie or Astrid. Or worse still, Roger or Aziz who have to be married to my sisters – so grateful not to be them!

Guide Post™

Manifesting is a team effort – tell her what you want, what you really, really want . . .

The first step to getting what you want, is to know what you want. And you need to really know what you want. Vague ideas lead to vague outcomes. This is why it's so important to be as clear and precise about your desires: the devil is in the detail.

Take this example: Nancy from Ohio really wanted a boyfriend. She had some vague ideas of what it could be like – someone who brought her things, didn't give up on her, and who loved her. So she went ahead and manifested. 'Please Universe, I want a boyfriend.' A week later, the mailman started sending her extra parcels so he could ask her out and keep asking her out. He said he loved her. Eventually Nancy took out a restraining order because he wouldn't leave her alone and she thought he was a creep.

So . . . did the Universe get it wrong? No!
Nancy got her manifesting process wrong
– she didn't go into enough detail.

Fact: The more you are able to give to the
Universe, the more she will be able to give you.

*Choose a manifestation and write it out below
as if you are living it RIGHT NOW! Be as specific
and descriptive as you can be to make it easy for
you both: collaboration is the name of the game.*

see it, feel it, make it

What is the manifestation?

I am on a date with Guy Carmichael

Where is it taking place?

At the Mandrake so that we can have sex in the bathrooms
when he's overcome with lust

When?

Thursday lunchtime!

What happens?

The maître d' knows my name and gives me an undisguised look of appreciation because I look so hot in my H&M Gucci knock-offs, and leads me straight over to the best table in the house where Guy's already waiting. Despite his commanding nature to which everyone in the room instinctively responds, when he sees me, Guy experiences a rare moment of nervousness and doubt as to whether he's worthy of me. But Guy quickly pulls himself together and we sit opposite one another, sexual tension sizzling. He asks me all about myself and finds himself intrigued and amused and fascinated. He quickly realises I'm an intellect to be reckoned with, and starts seeking my opinion about work-related matters but I gently redirect him to enjoy the date. The food is delicious and I eat it daintily and sexily, without spilling anything down myself. Near the end of the meal, I stand up and excuse myself and sashay away. Guy Carmichael cannot contain himself. He follows me to the bathrooms which are mercifully empty; he catches me mid-selfie and we have mind-blowing sex in one of the stalls. During sex he is hard and urgent and masterful and confesses, at the end, that he's catching feelings already. I laugh. We travel back in the car together, holding hands and at the end he asks, hopefully, when he can see me again. I post my selfie on Insta and get a lot of likes. Charlotte notices Guy's hairy knuckle, just in shot, and feels extremely jealous.

How are you feeling?

Amazing. Sexy, smart and dynamic. Like I'm going places. I wish everyone could see me right now.

Let's revisit your manifestation in a while and see how well you and the Universe collaborated.

Remember: see it, feel it, make it

My thoughts and reflections:

Tomorrow is the day!!!!

Iris, Guy's PA, confirmed that the booking is for noon at Bacchanalia in Mayfair. I've looked it up. Very sexual. Bodes well. Have outfit ready for tomorrow; I managed to shake off most of the mud from Richmond Park incident once it had dried. I've read through my manifestation from yesterday.

Going to bed in a minute because trying to look fresh-faced for tomorrow. Sorry. Correction. Because I *will* look fresh-faced tomorrow! Because I manifest it. And I manifest everything going smoothly.

In one word:

Anticipation

My thoughts and reflections:

So . . . thus far, nothing has gone my way.

Some twat who insisted on eating his doughnut on the tube squirted chocolate sauce and it went on my top and my trousers. I unsuccessfully tried to get it out in the loos at work and now have brown stains on my outfit as well as some little bits of paper towel caught in the sequins. Drunk Stephen called me a dirty stop-out and said I looked like I'd had a rough night, which is hardly the 'fresh-faced' look I was going for.

My desk chair has got stuck on a ludicrously low setting, so my desk is effectively at breast height and when Harry Piles walked past he said, 'I hope you've got something bloody useful to show me on the Discovery series next meeting, Alison.'

I was just coming up with a professional reply when he added, 'By the way, I think you've got a bit of shit on your top.'

At 9.30 precisely we all got this email. And whilst it's not a surprise, since Guy Carmichael warned us all before Christmas, it's not exactly a cheerful communication.

Dear Colleague,

With the merger of Carsons and Montague Place, I have some difficult news to share. Given that many roles are doubled across the two companies, we will be reducing the combined workforce by 20% before the end of the fiscal year in April.

Where roles are identical across companies, they may be pooled, and those affected will be encouraged to apply for their own roles. Assessments, interviews and 360 reviews will form part of the process. Please know that this is not a decision we take lightly and the welfare of our employees is paramount.

As such, we have voluntarily invited a trusted and industry-leading third party to quality assure. They will be working alongside both companies, at all levels.

It is hard to say goodbye to colleagues. It is also hard to live with uncertainty, so we will be moving through this process as swiftly as we possibly can.

Sincerely,
Alistair Fridman
CEO Carsons

If I'd had to apply for this role in the first place, I'd never have got it – I was just lucky that my predecessor defected the same month as Yaz had gone off on compassionate leave when her tortoise died (it was like a sibling) so they didn't follow normal protocol. I'd taken a temping job at Carsons because I wanted to move into children's publishing. And then, suddenly, they lost their Children's Editor and Senior Editor in the same month. So I stepped up and covered both roles. To be honest, it was like a dream come true, but of course Yaz eventually came back and resumed her role. As thanks, they gave me the editor position without an interview or anything, which I was grateful for, although it's hard stepping back. Shortly after, Harry Piles was promoted to Deputy MD and everything changed. I've just googled Montague Place, I can see I very much have an 'identical' there. I recognised her headshot immediately – she was featured in *The Bookseller* as a Rising Star. (Obviously I don't read *The Bookseller* – it was left open on Yaz's desk and it was marginally more interesting than listening to her story about the three varieties of falafels she'd fashioned over the weekend.)

I am so losing my job.

Clearly I'm not the only one freaking out: editorial assistant Nervous Jane just burst into tears so of course everyone's comforting her and telling her how good she is at her job which should have been enough to pacify her but Yaz magnanimously gave Nervous Jane her last muffin. I'd had my eye on that muffin. Yaz said, 'Oh sorry, Alice, I didn't think you'd want it because of the Paleo thing?'

It was an *oat* muffin. Totally Paleo. To be honest, I can think of a fair few colleagues I'd be happy to say goodbye to, starting with Yaz and Nervous Jane.

I ask the Universe:

To be a bit more on my side, please.

Guide Post™

As William Blake famously said:

'Joys impregnate. Sorrows bring forth . . .

The thankful manifester* bears a plentiful harvest.'

Pause. Reflect. Give thanks. Use the
GUIDED AFFIRMATIONS™ *to help you.*

* *Words slightly adapted from the original.*

My thoughts and reflections:

Just taking a moment to thank *The Guide* and the Universe.

I was going through those (wonderful) affirmations and Cara heard me saying how grateful I was for gratitude, and she said, 'You are enough, Alice. You'll make it through. One step at a time. Hour by hour.' Then we had a good chat about manifesting, and about what a twat Harry Piles is and she told me not to stress about the Discovery series and to think laterally and in terms of damage control. She also told me if I needed anything, anything at all, I was just to tell her, and that I wasn't alone. So I confessed I was a bit worried about not looking fresh-faced today, and she said, 'Say no more; the perimenopause is a bitch,' and literally gave me her Charlotte Tilbury Magic cream! To keep! So grateful. (Obviously I'm not perimenopausal and Cara is a lot older than me – she's on eHarmony – but what a gift.)

And I would like to make it clear that I am totally on board, and indeed grateful for the 'challenges' that came up today because, well, they've come from the Universe! And she's the Boss!

Anyway, in the face of adversity I offer serenity and thanks. I exude positivity and I attract positivity and I'm super grateful for all these experiences – I welcome the twenty per cent workforce reductions and am sure it will be a valuable and affirmative process and a super opportunity for personal growth.

So, I'm really up for – and very much deserving of – that plentiful harvest!

My intention is:

To reap a really plentiful harvest of sex in Bacchanalia!

Guide Post™

A poor worker blames their tools;

A Guided manifester values their jewels.

*If you are not having the results you hoped
to, don't make the mistake of looking to
find fault in the Universe – it isn't there.
Instead, review the way you manifest.*

*And remember, it's better to do something,
than nothing, as William Blake says:
'Manifesting* is an eternal delight, and he who
desires, but acts not, breeds pestilence.'*

* *Words slightly adapted from the original in keeping with author's intention.*

Guide Post™

*A couple of days ago you completed
a manifestation exercise. Review and reflect.*

What was the outcome of the manifestation?

I went on a date with Guy Carmichael

Where did it take place?

At Bacchanalia in Mayfair. Super trendy.

When?

Thursday lunchtime!

What happened?

The tube sat in a tunnel for ages, and a journey that should
have taken twenty minutes ended up taking nearly twice as
long so I had to run to get there so probably wasn't looking
'smart and elegant', and the maître d' couldn't find my name
on the reservation list – it turned out I was 'plus guest Alison'
but eventually a very pretty woman in an insubstantial toga

took me through to the restaurant – I was nervous in case I accidentally trod on her outfit and disrobed her. We had to squeeze past an influencer who'd set up her camera in the walkway and was talking incessantly, but at least I could look at the sculptures until she'd finished. It possibly wasn't the best table in the house, being as close to the door as it was, and I did find it a bit distracting being right next to the influencer, but no complaints from me.

Guy was on his phone when I got there, being all executive and impressive. He looked at me without smiling, which really does it for me, and nodded at the waiter to fill my glass. The waiter waited for me to try the wine, so I did, obediently. It was flinty and dry and a bit salty for my taste. I wondered if Guy was going to order food for me too – but he pushed the menu over to me and then walked off to continue his conversation. When he got off the phone he checked that I hadn't told anyone else at work I was coming here and said, 'So what do you think of this place?'

I had another look around. 'Loads of boobs. What's not to like?'

'Indeed. You can never have too many breasts in my opinion.'

I felt his gaze roam; he eyed mine up appreciatively. He also appreciated the gravity-defying breasts of the woman serving us, but in a way, he was showing me respect by not hiding the fact he was looking at them. He asked me briefly about my family and what it was like growing up in Little Minchcombe. Then he dealt with an email whilst I finished my wine and watched him and revelled in the situation. He wanted to hear about the Lamb and whether we knew the owner. To be completely honest, I didn't want to ruin the vibe talking about Matthew Lloyd so I hedged it and asked him about the merger at work, but he told me that words like 'merger' didn't mix with lunch, and went back to his phone for another email. I was relieved when the food arrived.

I quickly realised that ordering tagliatelle was an amateur move for a date. I had to attempt to eat it without splattering my outfit and chin. I thought I was doing a pretty good job of it until Guy said, unsmiling, 'You eat like a savage, Alice.' When he told me the fact I didn't give a fuck about having sauce all over me was giving him ideas, his eyes flashed and I self-consciously wiped my wet chin.

I swallowed and said that I hoped he was the sort to act on his ideas. I even quoted Blake at him (again – thank you, *The Guide*). 'He who desires, but acts not, breeds pestilence, Guy,' I said. 'Maybe this would be a good time for a bathroom break?'

Guy surveyed me. 'For a millennial you're unusually forwards. So let's be clear, Alice. I'm not fucking in a public bathroom. Look how it turned out for George Michael.'

'No, of course not.' I backpedalled quickly. 'I wasn't suggesting that we— I mean . . . Sorry if I gave the wrong idea.'

He called the waiter over for the bill, whilst I sweated and worried I'd blown it even faster than Charlotte had, and tried not to get too turned on by the way he straightened his cufflinks. Then, with the timing of a man who has honed power play, he leant closer. 'I have a perfectly good bathroom back at the Carsons serviced apartment,' he said softly, 'so I'm going to fuck you there. Alice. If you want.'

It wasn't a question. But then it didn't need to be.

I didn't even know Carsons had a serviced apartment. And I couldn't tell you where it was. I was caught up on the journey. Guy may be anti-fucking-in-public, but he was certainly pro fingering on the back seat of the car – pro in both senses. At one point he even took a call. 'What?' he sounded irritable. Then he looked directly at me as he said, to them, 'You'll have to deal with it yourself. I've got my hands full right now.' It was seriously erotic. As we drew up at the apartment, Guy pulled down his cuffs and straightened his cufflinks, and my stomach tightened with lust. I don't know how I'm going to cope with seeing those hands at work now – it was hard enough before. Guy led me straight through the principal bedroom and into the bathroom. I fleetingly thought about suggesting to him that we make use of the perfectly decent bed we'd just passed, but he clearly thought I was fixated on the bathroom idea and within seconds I wasn't thinking about anything much other than what my boss was doing to me. (Apart from one annoying moment when I ran my hand down Guy's back, feeling relieved at its smoothness and Matthew Lloyd's smug grinning face appeared in my mind.)

How did it make you feel?

Successful, powerful, satiated, sexy – I got what I wanted – I shagged Guy Carmichael. (Physically I feel a little bit itchy – think I may have slight reaction to his stubble or his cologne or something, but at least it's a reminder that it all really happened.)

How did your real-life experience
compare to your manifestation?

So, so close. In fact, the sex was even better than I'd manifested. The taxi ride ranks top ten, and the actual sex was really hard and urgent, and he totally took charge, and although I've got a bruise on my hip from the sink, it was thrilling to see us in the bathroom mirror. Literally fantasy coming to fruition. It was a bit awkward afterwards when he called a car to take me back to the office whilst I was still doing up my bra, but you don't get to his position in life by letting the grass grow, and essentially, I'd got what I wanted. Mostly. He didn't ask me on another date but he did explain he had an important call and when I asked casually, just as I was leaving, if he'd be back at work later, he called me 'greedy Alice' in an appreciative way, before shutting the door.

Out of ten, rate how well you and
the Universe collaborated?

In terms of the reality matching my manifestation, I would say 9 out of 10. (And the missing point is down to me – not the Universe!)

Are there any lessons to learn for next time?

I totally understand the story about Nancy from Ohio now. The devil really is in is the clarity of detail. I think the Universe thought I was fixated on the idea of sex in the bathroom which I really wasn't. I'll be more careful about that sort of thing from now on. Also, because I've spent so much time thinking about the sex, that's what I got, and I should probably have focused a bit more on the fact I'd like the sex to happen again. Along with a bit more conversation. But also, I trust in the Universe. (And that the sex was good enough that he's likely to want more.)

Take a moment to appreciate the journey you are on and to feel gratitude in your heart for all that has been gifted to you already.

Date: Sunday 29 January   **Time: 5.45pm**

My thoughts and reflections:

I am so annoyed with Astrid. Yesterday, she made me come back early from drinks with my old Bloomsbury colleagues by sending pathetic needy text messages (so not Astrid's usual style) saying she was feeling a bit lonely and could I join her for supper and spend some sister time with her because she didn't want to be on her own? *Please, please?* I was meant to be out all night with Gabriella and Suzanne, but this neediness from Astrid was so out of character that I felt a rush of protective concern and left early. I did feel bad about bailing, but not that guilty, because Gabriella and Suzanna were wittering on about their honeymoon at length, and if I'd stayed they would probably have made me sit and look at photos. Besides, they understood that I owed Astrid big time for allowing me to stay at hers, and let me off the hook. In fact, Gabriella even said I was 'such a good sister' which made me walk a little taller. No one has ever called me a good sister before. So I put myself out for Astrid because I am a 'good sister', and bought a bottle of Lambrini on the way home and a bag of Haribo (a lot of which I ate on the tube, but it was nervous eating because I was worried about Astrid), and came into the kitchen singing to cheer her up, and was she on her own? No she bloody wasn't.

Aziz had obviously gone to a huge effort to make a lovely meal and the table was set for two, and there was soft lighting and romantic music, and Aziz looked at me in what can only be described as dismay, and said, 'Alice . . . I thought you were out for the night?'

'I was,' I said, giving Astrid a pointed look.

She completely ignored my look. 'Well, the important thing is you're here now and you look starving. Join us.'

'No, you're clearly having a meal for two.'

'No, we're not.' Astrid grabbed my arm and forced me to sit down.

'Yes, you are. I'm going to leave you two to it.'

'Sit down,' said Astrid. 'Please?' And she genuinely looked slightly desperate.

And then Aziz, because he's the nicest human ever, went and got me a plate and smiled at me. 'Join us, Alice.'

For once, I didn't enjoy Aziz's cooking: it was just plain sad, sitting there with the two of them, making conversation, and not talking about what really needed to be talked about.

I spoke to Arrie this afternoon and she said that it was dummy-gate all over again and that I wasn't the only spoilt one and that frankly, Astrid was acting up.

'What do you mean?'

'Astrid was horrific when you were born,' Arrie told me. 'Mum and Dad seriously thought about having her board in Switzerland.'

'Can you send a toddler to a foreign country?'

'She was nearly three. Old enough to know better; old enough to board.

Mum and Dad weren't always the incompetent soft-touch

parents you're used to, Alice. When I was little, they were much tougher. Why do you think Astrid and I have the mettle we do?'

'So what was dummy-gate?'

'She wanted a dummy when you had one and Mum and Dad refused. So Astrid started protest-shitting behind the sofa.'

'What? Why would you share that with me?'

'The point is,' continued Arrie, 'eventually Mum and Dad caved and bought her a dummy. Normal toileting resumed.'

'Not sure this is the same,' I said, trying to push away the mental images.

'It's absolutely the same,' scoffed Arrie. 'Poor Aziz.'

I suppose that was one thing we agreed on.

Poor Aziz.

I am grateful for:

- Being single.
- Being a babe in arms whilst Astrid was a psycho protest shitter – thank the Universe I wasn't crawling.

My thoughts and reflections:

Guy Carmichael has just emailed asking me if I want drink after work. Yes, I do. Guy's wearing a charcoal suit with a pale pinstripe that makes him look particularly masterful today. Anika in PR (never remembers my name and makes it clear she's not going to) had a meeting with him in his office and we could hear her laughing flirtatiously; everyone knows she has a crush on Guy. Shame I can't mention that I've acquired a second date in under a week. Bet she'd remember my name then. Still. Good work, Alice.

In one word:

Congratulations

My thoughts and reflections:

Yesterday's Business Development meeting was short and shouty. Harry Piles keeping saying, 'It's my job on the line, people. Let's pull it out of the fucking bag.'

I really tried, because, having looked up my equivalent at Montague, I knew I was going to be needing a really good reference soon. 'Harry, completely appreciate why you love the branding and history and kudos associated with the Discover series' – I don't – 'and obviously you know what sells' – he doesn't – 'so I had the thought that we could maybe come up with some new content?'

'What do you mean?'

'Well, we could use this as an opportunity to expand, refine, include some new titles. Like, Discover Mindfulness? Or—'

'Horrible idea, Alison. What about Discover My Cock. Come on. This isn't some leaflet series for the doctor's surgery.'

Gentle Jadan from Design visibly shook his head and Harry asked him what the problem was. Gentle Jadan said he wasn't comfortable with aggressive sexualised language in the workplace. There was a moment of silence and then Harry told everyone he'd been asked to fill in 360s by the end of the month and so it was time for our best work.

I was going to say thank you to Gentle Jadan afterwards, but he disappeared quite quickly, so I asked Drunk Stephen to pass it on. I pointed out that Harry Piles was so dense he didn't seem to understand the concept of a 360 and he had better hope no one from this outside company coming in to 'quality assure' decided to conduct an interview with Gentle Jadan. But Drunk Stephen didn't seem as convinced. 'They all know each other, these people,' he said. 'What's the bet Harry Piles somehow makes the grade, despite everything?'

I am grateful for:

- Gentle Jadan from Design
- Sex with GC on Tuesday – and he didn't call me a car for a full half an hour afterwards this time so that's progress.

My thoughts and reflections:

Saw Guy again after work – that's the third time, so I've already beaten Charlotte. He sent me an email telling me to come straight to the serviced apartment and that the concierge staff would let me through. I could happily live in a serviced apartment. (I stupidly mentioned this to Astrid last night and she said in effect I always have lived in serviced accommodation, and that if I didn't start replacing the loo rolls when they ran out, she'd tell Arrie I would babysit the weekend after next. Arrie's been trying to rope one of us into childcare whilst she and Roger go to some farming convention: apparently Mum and Dad can't help – and both Astrid and I have covered each other's excuses because neither of us want to be saddled with our nephews. *You wouldn't*, I said. *Try me*, she said.)

Anyway, the serviced apartment is quality, if box-like. If you want a glass of wine, or ice, or crisps, you just ring concierge, and someone in a fawn uniform brings it to the door. And they'll do laundry. (I'm thinking of getting them to do my sequinned trousers but may wait until week three of relationship – tactics and all that.) So, whilst I was waiting for my Diet Coke to arrive, Guy spoke to me about work a bit (another success story for my manifesting). He didn't say much, mainly that he'd had to start handing over loads of paperwork to these third-party business consultants that Alistair had bloody invited in, and that whilst he was absolutely confident Carsons couldn't operate without him, he'd be under real pressure during his divorce if anything were to happen.

'You're not really worried, are you?' I checked.

'Worry gets you killed,' said Guy. 'I don't worry.'

His army background is quite hot. 'What's the timeline?' I asked.

Apparently the top people had meetings off-site the next couple of weeks and then the consultants would begin to meet staff.

'None of this is to be repeated, Alice,' said Guy.

He's particularly sexy when he orders me about.

'Of course not,' I agreed, thinking how I'd probably only tell Drunk Stephen.

'I don't trust them,' said Guy. 'It's one of these new, woke companies. They're looking to catch people out.'

That didn't bode well. There was a lot I could be caught out on. 'So they're not coming in to the building yet?'

'End of the month soonest,' said Guy. 'No one's coming in yet.'

Then he gave me a lascivious look and started grazing his knuckles up my thigh which I do find as erotic in reality as I did in my fantasies – the hair makes it simultaneously tickly and a smidgen disturbing – and told me that it was high time he was coming. In me. 'Or, better still, on you, Alice.'

I tried not to imagine Arrie's reaction if she heard this. What she doesn't acknowledge is that I'm not Tess of the d'Urbervilles. Personally, I like a bit of jism. We don't all have

OCD, frigid tendencies, like Mum and Arrie. Besides, Arrie objectifies Roger all the time. She calls him a 'fun vacuum'. And when you think about it, she's pretty much his boss too, so equally troubling.

I am letting go of:

Sisterly ideals of feminism

My thoughts and reflections:

This Easter Discover book is making my job bloody hard. I'd been putting it off and getting on with the other projects, but Cara just emailed, chasing, so I couldn't delay any longer. I spent a couple of hours this morning looking through the back issues of the Discover series – standout titles included *Discover Needlework for Girls* and *Discover Maths for Boys* – and then made the mistake of looking up JJ on the internet. Honestly, I still feel slightly nauseated and sullied from the combination. Add Easter into the mix and it was enough to make me consider voluntary redundancy.

However, that may well involve moving back into Mum and Dad's which would in turn involve being closer (location-wise) to Arrie. I've just received another text from her saying how the twins are desperate to see their Aunty Alice soon (bullshit) and suggesting I come and see the puppies whilst they're tiny. If those puppies are anything like their mother, then I don't like them. But they do look pretty cute in all the photos she sent.

So I steeled myself and got on with thinking creatively, and finally sent the following to Cara:

From: alice.carver@carsons.com
To: cara.durante@carsons.com
Re: Discover Hunting and Baby Animals Easter version

Hi Cara,

Firstly, apologies for the delay on this.

Have given this a lot of thought, and the only way I can think of to make an Easter version is to get Design to border the pages and hide eggs on every page. There is not a huge amount we can take from Discover Hunting – some generic farm and countryside pursuits – unless we are going full-on Blood of Christ? A title would really help to move this forward IMO. Baby Animals has more usable content. We would, however, definitely need to generate new puppy images to replace those that are unusable (lots with JJ and also a surprising number of pit bull puppies – now banned).

We could add a Q and A, word search and a link to an online game – if Design and Digital can turn around in time? Could potentially look at an interview with a dog breeder and a farmer to make marginally more informative.

We do need to move the 'which dog are you' quiz which contains several racist references, and all photos of JJ as well as his commentary – I'm surprised they got through the first time – even in the Eighties.

Please let me know where you want me to go from here,

Ax

But then Yaz and Lazy Veronica from Production paused by my desk on their way out and oohed and aahed over the photos of Arrie's puppies which gave me another idea.

From: alice.carver@carsons.com
To: cara.durante@carsons.com
Re: Discover Hunting and Baby Animals Easter version
– thought

Cara,
Just had a thought . . . my sister is a dog breeder. Puppies born last week (attached images). If Harry is agreeable to some new content, she'd let us shoot for a donation to her dog charity.
   Hope you have a good evening and thanks again for the Charlotte Tilbury cream – it is AMAZING!

A x

My intention is:

To repay Cara (at some point) for her kindness.

My thoughts and reflections:

Both Astrid and Aziz are out again (separately of course) at work events this evening and Guy is coming round soon for a midweek speedy supper (if, by supper, you mean an hour of sex). He was impressed by Astrid's address when I told him where I lived (after he called me into his office for a 'quick question please, Alice') and said that his wife had been at him to move to Chiswick for years and that if she ever found out about tonight, she'd probably be even more upset at the idea of him being in Chiswick than sleeping with me.

I felt an itch of disquiet. If Guy and his wife were separated, why would she be 'upset' at the idea of him having sex? Obviously I didn't want to come across as clingy like Charlotte but Astrid had got in my head with her 'separated or separating?' Bloody Astrid. I needed some clarification here. 'I thought you and your wife weren't together?'

Guy didn't hide his annoyance. He pushed his desk chair back and stood up. After checking no one was looking over from the floor, and that Iris was busy on the phone, he closed the door. 'We're not,' he said, his voice clipped. 'We still share a house – it's a delicate situation. Until the divorce comes through, I have to be careful. At home, at work. I thought you understood, Alice,' he said, fixing me with that distant stare he gives in meetings just before he tells someone something they don't want to hear.

'I do,' I said quickly. 'I haven't told anyone about . . . this . . . fun we're having.'

Guy's eyes flicked behind me. 'Not Cara?' he said, impassively.

I shook my head. 'No.'

'Are you sure?' said Guy, his eyes narrowing. 'These 360s are on my mind. Alistair's being cagey, but looks like I'm finally meeting the LL Group tomorrow.'

'Who?' I said.

'The merger, Alice. I'm meeting the consultants. The job snippers.'

'Oh.'

'I can't afford mistakes, Alice.'

Gosh, he was even more sexy when he was rattled (even if I didn't understand why he was worried about his job) – sort of extra cold and ruthless. And we were in his office. I was feeling more and more turned on.

'Look,' I said, biting my bottom lip which I know he likes. 'I haven't told anyone. And I don't intend to. But it's your call . . .'

Guy's gaze raked down over my body.

'And that, Alice, is what makes you particularly attractive,' said Guy Carmichael, taking a step towards me.

There was a polite knock, and then the door opened, and Iris poked her head round.

'Oh,' she said, 'I thought you'd finished.'

'Sorry,' I said, 'I just took the opportunity to quickly ask Guy about my 360.'

'Come in, Iris,' said Guy, without missing a beat. He stood back so I had to walk past him and he whispered to me, 'I'll give you a full 360 whilst you're sitting on my face later.' Then he said, at normal volume, as my neck burned, 'Good work, Alice. Thanks.'

Filthy fucker.

In one word:

360

My thoughts and reflections:

From: cara.durante@carsons.com
To: harry.piles@carsons.com
cc: alice.carver@carsons.com, stephen.banks@carsons.
com
Re: Discover Hunting and Baby Animals Easter version

Hi Harry,

Ahead of Monday's Product Development, can I just check that you are still absolutely set on the Easter Discover publication? In our conversation yesterday, you mentioned wanting to solely use material from Hunting for Boys and Baby Animals for Girls and turn this into a generic Easter animals book for boys and girls with a focus on baby animals – namely puppies, countryside (no religion) and an emphasis on fun and chocolate. I mentioned that this could be tricky. Have you had a chance to think about this further?

KR,
Cara
Cara Durante
Non-Fiction Publisher, Carsons

From: harry.piles@carsons.com
To: cara.durante@carsons.com
cc: alice.carver@carsons.com, stephen.banks@carsons.com

No need to think further. Just pull out the pictures of baby animals and remove the dead animals, JJ and old-fashioned kids. Why haven't your team done anything? Update please.

H
Harry Piles
Deputy MD

From: cara.durante@carsons.com
To: harry.piles@carsons.com
cc: alice.carver@carsons.com, stephen.banks@carsons.com
Re: Discover Hunting and Baby Animals Easter version

Dear Harry,
All the team have been working super hard.

Key point is that there is **limited material** we are able to pull from the original publications. Most images are dated and feature children in 70s outfits and hairstyles, and I'm afraid it's very hard to remove unwanted parts of photos as these are pre-digital images.

If this is definitely the direction you are pursuing, I urge you to factor in a photo shoot.

Attached are some mock-ups from Design. Also, Alice has put together a flat plan of the content.

KR,
Cara

From: harry.piles@carsons.com
To: cara.durante@carsons.com
cc: alice.carver@carsons.com, stephen.banks@ carsons.com

Let's use stock images.

Thanks

From: cara.durante@carsons.com
To: harry.piles@carsons.com
cc: alice.carver@carsons.com, stephen.banks@carsons. com
Re: Discover Hunting and Baby Animals Easter version

Dear Harry,
There are very few stock images for Easter dogs – see attached from Stephen (copying in Stephen and Alice).

However, Alice has access to puppies so we can produce at cost (plus travel which is minimal) – again see attached.

To be clear, have met with the team several times over last couple of days and exhausted all options; this is very

much our best route. Strongly suggest we exploit this exciting opportunity kindly offered by Alice.

KR,

Cara.

From: harry.piles@carsons.com
To: cara.durante@carsons.com
cc: alice.carver@carsons.com, stephen.banks@
carsons.com

Look Cara, I don't know what you're missing here: jazz
up the originals. Think of the profits.

From: cara.durante@carsons.com
To: harry.piles@carsons.com
cc: alice.carver@carsons.com, stephen.banks@carsons.
com

Harry

I am thinking of the profits. End results would be poor,
plus we need to distance the product from the JJ scandal.
Multiple images need replacing, and generating our own is
an easy win with clear profit margins, if the Discover series
is the way you are set on going.

Can you please take to Guy and get us the go-ahead?

KR

Cara

From: harry.piles@carsons.com

To: cara.durante@carsons.com
Cc: alice.carver@carsons.com, stephen.banks@
carsons.com

No.

In good news, Guy Carmichael says his wife is away next weekend so we may be able to meet up . . . At least that's something to look forward to in the wettest February ever.

I am grateful for:

- Cara (and actually, I'm coming to realise that the Bulgari watch quite suits her. Apparently she bought it as a present to herself on her fortieth)
- Ex-wives going away

My thoughts and reflections:

Was just running myself a nice bath – so important to look after yourself – when I noticed a little note in Astrid's writing stuck to the empty loo roll. It said, **I warned you. Enjoy some special time with the boys. Sort the loo rolls.**

I rushed back into the bedroom to check my phone, ignoring Matthew's face staring at me from my visioning board, and she'd actually done it. There was a voice message from Arrie saying that I was a trooper and that the boys were already planning lots of fun things to do with their aunty next Saturday and could I please be there for 10am sharp? If my plans with Astrid changed, it would be fab if I could do Friday night too.

Bloody Astrid. Well, no point doing the loo rolls now. She'd completely screwed me over. And the one weekend where Guy's wife is potentially away. My phone buzzed with a message from Astrid: *if you don't keep on top of the loo rolls from now on, I'll volunteer you for Friday night too. Next step: half-term aunty.*

Oh my god, Astrid is brutal: the punishment far outweighs the transgression. Thank goodness she's planning to stop practising law; imagine all the innocent people now languishing in prison because of her.

Also, haven't heard from Guy since Thursday. Hope that doesn't mean his meeting with the job snippers went badly . . .

My intention is:

To have a bath and to double-check the wifi is working properly and that I haven't accidentally missed a message.

My thoughts and reflections:

Just as I'd admitted defeat, concluded he had moved on and, therefore, stopped checking phone every ten minutes, I finally heard from Guy Carmichael.

We had an hour of messaging back and forth. He said sorry for being incommunicado and that his meeting with the consultants last week had not gone well. Apparently, he'd been saddled with some jobsworth who was clearly an oik and therefore had it in for Guy on principle. I sympathised and said he should try living with Astrid. *He wanted me to sit tests and justify my job, Alice. For fuck's sake. I made more for the company last quarter than that little shit could ever make.* There was a gap, whilst I thought about how I could barely justify my job to myself, let alone an independent third party, and whether Guy Carmichael would still be fit if he were fired. Then he messaged again saying that his wife was away next weekend and maybe I could come over on Saturday night. Had to tell him about going home to the Cotswolds for babysitting.

Haven't heard back and so now back to checking phone every ten seconds and wondering if I've blown it . . .

I ask the Universe:

- To teach Astrid the consequences of her teaching me lessons.
- To give me another chance with Guy Carmichael.

My thoughts and reflections:

Still haven't heard from Guy Carmichael or seen him (he wasn't in the office today). And it's Valentine's Day tomorrow. . . Suddenly TikTok is flooded with 'How to Manifest your Perfect Partner' and 'Make This Valentine Make YOU' and women talking about how they manifested true love by using the zodiacal energy of 14 February. I know that Valentine's Day is over-commercialised, but it would have been nice, just for once, to not have a shit one.

In one word:

Worried

Guide Post™

*Does the faithful dog worry about its
next meal? Or does it trust its owner
will take care of it, and feed it?*

Write down a recent worry:

I worry . . . Guy has lost interest in me and I will have a rubbish
Valentine's Day

Replace that worry with trust:

I trust . . . Guy is still interested in me and I will have a nice
Valentine's Day

*The hungry dog that trusts its owner
shall be fed. The hungry manifester that
trusts the Universe shall be fed.*

My thoughts and reflections:

Happy Valentine's Day! I've been fed! I **love** the Universe!

Just had creative review with Harry Piles and when I walked in, there was the man who'd been on my mind all weekend, Guy Carmichael himself, looking all powerful and masculine in a mid-grey suit with navy pinstripes and a pale blue shirt. He didn't even say good morning to me, just nodded briefly, all business-like, and barely looked at me, and whilst that totally turned me on in one way, my stomach also dropped slightly because he hadn't been in contact as much as usual, so I couldn't tell if he was being discreet or genuinely uninterested.

First of all, I had to sit through Harry Piles welcoming Guy to the meeting and being an arse-licky git. Then, I had to endure an agonising first half of the meeting surreptitiously watching Guy who didn't glance my way once; he basically sat there looking disdainful and bored. Although he did do that thing where he straightens his shirt cuffs exposing his hairy wrists and watch a couple of times, and he knows what that does to me. We both do. So I was both aroused and anxious.

When we got to the Discover series, Guy looked confused. 'Back up, Harry, you're really reintroducing the Discover series?'

And Harry said, 'Yes, I mentioned it to you last week, Guy. If you remember. Puppies and shit.'

Guy nodded slowly. 'I do remember now. Everyone likes puppies.'

I squirmed in my seat remembering last Wednesday's speedy supper when I'd tried to tell Guy about the Discovery series but Guy had turned the direction towards how much he liked my puppies.

Harry made Cara update everyone for Guy's benefit, but when Cara got to the bit about the puppies at my sister's farm and how, unfortunately, that photo shoot wasn't able to happen and how she had serious concerns about 'drawing on' stock images, Guy interrupted.

'Where's the farm?'

'Alice?' said Cara.

Guy knew where Arrie's farm was. I told him the other week. I tried not to blink. 'Little Minchcombe. Cotswolds.'

'That's barely an hour away. Why aren't you using this opportunity to get some fresh images?'

Harry began confidently, 'I want the fullest profit margins, there's no plant cost to spare here—'

'Who would need to go on the shoot?'

The way he interrupted Harry Piles, and the way Harry Piles just shut the fuck up, had me squeezing my knees together.

'Well, obviously a couple of Design,' said Cara, 'Stephen and Jadan, and Alice, but it wouldn't—'

'Do the shoot,' said Guy. 'Thanks.'

Then he stood up abruptly and left the room.

I zoned out for the meeting, fantasising about various scenarios of telling Harry Piles I was shagging his boss.

Minutes later an email pinged up on my screen from Guy.

Ask your sister if we can shoot next Monday. You babysit on Saturday. I'll come up and see you on Sunday.

I emailed him straight back. *But you could bump into the others?*

Leave that to me, Alice. Maybe it's time we move things forward anyway. I've got an extremely busy week and I'd like to see you next weekend.

Possibly the sexiest experience without having sex ever. Guy Carmichael has commandeered me and the work environment and I love it.

My intention is:

To ask Guy if he's still got his army uniform to hand.

My thoughts and reflections:

Guy's booked the Lamb for Sunday night. I explained it would be awkward staying at the Lamb because of my family's connection with the owner, but Guy just said, 'Well, Alice, you just keep on getting better. In that case we're definitely staying at the Lamb. I'm starting to think that for someone who moves in all the right circles, it's remarkable you haven't made more of it.'

I told Astrid that I thought it was a lovely way of putting it and that Guy clearly respected me and acknowledged that I'd built my successes independently. 'Or,' said Astrid, 'he can't believe how you've managed to mess up all the opportunities you've been handed in life. I mean, it is remarkable.'

That stung. Especially with all the manifesting I've been doing. I've taken every opportunity I could. In fact, earlier this week, I gave Guy a very quick hand job in his office whilst everyone else was out for the fire alarm, plus we fitted in half an hour together on Wednesday evening in his serviced apartment. So, in total, two sexual encounters in a week that he explicitly said was 'extremely busy': if that's not maximising opportunities, I don't know what is.

Astrid said that servicing my married boss in secret, for free, was hardly 'résumé material'.

'It's not all about my career,' I said. 'I also manifested a proper relationship and I would say that's working out pretty well so far. He's booked a night in a hotel for us both. A whole night together. That's significant.'

I've bought some La Perla knickers and matching bra (on offer because of Valentine's) in a shade of dark red that totally does it for men of a certain age who went to single-sex public school. It's the kind of underwear that Monty would have gone full-on puce-eared for. I can't really afford the spend, but it's an investment. And it's all paying off – I'm almost slightly taken back by how fast it's moving with Guy. A night away is the kind of commitment I wasn't expecting for another few months at least. Apart from the author he had the affair with that triggered the separation from his wife, word on the floor was that when he did hook up with someone, it was a handful of times at most, and then he moved on. He made it clear he was not up for commitment and got spooked if anyone even hinted at wanting more. If I'm completely honest, I'm a tiny bit spooked myself. I've not really seen Guy in nonwork clothes. What if he's wearing Vans or something frightful? Obviously dream come true that we're having this night together, but it feels like quite a big step and is really not ideal to take such a step at a hotel owned by Matthew Lloyd. Would be awful to bump into him.

The problem with that visioning board I made is that Matthew Lloyd is always there. In my room.

At some point I'm going to have to work on manifesting that house. I've been putting it off. But for now, given I'm doing so well on the relationship front, I'm going to focus my manifesting on the work aspect more. And on getting more respect from friends, colleagues and family. Mind you, now Cara's on board, Yaz *has* been a lot more respectful. Drunk Stephen has also been more grateful since I secured us this trip to Arrie's. Previously, he hasn't exactly been supportive about the Guy thing; he's gone on a lot about the power dynamic, saying that my love language 'took acts of service to new depths of sadness'. But now he's benefiting vicariously, he's stopped reminding me to write everything down ready for HR when Guy tries to send me to Scotland. In fact, he helpfully suggested that I tell Guy that my love language was receiving gifts, and that a new coffee machine in the kitchen would definitely merit a blow job.

Oh my goodness – I almost forgot – Lydia called me Alice the other day! I don't know how Guy's managed it: suffice to say he's not just pure filth in the sack, he's evidently a master manipulator of people too. That's power for you. And it's sexy as fuck. On reflection, I am absolutely ready for Sunday.

I am letting go of:

The fact I can't tell Harry Piles I'm shagging his boss.

Date: Saturday 18 February   **Time: 11.30pm**

My thoughts and reflections:

Roger has just dropped me back at Mum and Dad's after one of the most horrific days of my life, babysitting the twins. Honestly, I feel like I've aged years in a day. Arrie was trying to press me to stay and drink with her, saying, *I've still got it in me, Alice, I'm more than just a wife and a mother*, but luckily she fell asleep after just one double vodka because as Roger pointed out, she'd been up since the crack of dawn. Of course she's exhausted. Honestly, I'm surprised Arrie hasn't turned to drugs – the cleaning, the children, the animals, the constant stress and responsibility – it made my day doing Aunty Margaret's rat-infested flat seem like a holiday.

I'll list the worst bits in an attempt to avoid PTSD and then I'm going to try my best to forget the whole episode.

a) Drew, who was meant to be helping with the animals, had some kind of cow emergency on his own farm so I was left to feed horses and hens in the frigid February rain. All the food was disgusting and smelly: I hate farms.

b) I also had to pick up the faeces of seven puppies (whilst a hostile Maud watched my every move) because otherwise they apparently eat them. Why do people like puppies? What kind of animals shag their siblings and eat their own crap? All the while, I was meant to prevent the twins from breaking windows, toys and their own bones.

c) When the boys had finally expelled enough energy to stay in one room for more than a minute, Ernie wanted to know about my thighs and elephants and whether I had any more body parts that were animal and whether you could create hybrid animals and aunts using DNA like in *Jurassic World*. And then he made me recite the plot of *Jurassic Park* about five times until I said, 'Why don't we just watch it?'

'The Lego one?' asked Ernie.

'There's no Lego in it,' I said. 'But someone gets eaten on the toilet.'

The boys got really excited so we watched it, and I felt like a cool aunty and like I had this childcare thing down pat. Ernie wanted to cuddle up to me, not because 'he' was scared, he said, 'but because you might be, Aunty Alice,' and it was actually rather sweet. Until he suddenly bent forward and threw up all over the rug.

I literally nearly had a heart attack and Edwin burst into tears because he was worried about his twin and I phoned Astrid in a blind panic, whilst frantically cleaning up the mess, and she said, 'Is there any chance he's seen blood because that sounds vasovagal – you know he's got a blood phobia like me?'

Clearly I didn't.

I looked over at the paused screen where Ellie Sattler had

a dismembered arm on her shoulder. 'He may have seen a little bit of blood.'

'Give him chocolate and lie him down – distract him and he should recover quickly.'

I put Edwin on my knee and stroked Ernie's sweaty, silky hair and invented endless types of silly hybrid animals to make them giggle. I ended up giving both boys all the chocolate I could find. 'Aunty Alice,' said Edwin in delight, 'we're not allowed any food or drink in the sitting room because of Mummy's new sofa.'

'I tried to be sick only on the rug,' whispered Ernie weakly.

'Ah! Good call, Ernie,' I said, feeling a wave of love for him. 'I'm sure a little bit of chocolate's fine – we'll be super careful.' And when Ernie was back to normal and I could breathe again I promised them I'd send more chocolate in the post if they didn't tell Arrie about the *Jurassic Park* viewing.

d) Just before bed, when I'd finally cleared up and the boys were bathed and in their pyjamas, and I was so close to the end, Edwin asked if we could play a quick game of Monopoly; against my better judgement I agreed, thinking it couldn't get as bad as our Carver games of Monopoly. It did. When Ernie landed on Edwin's Park Lane Hotel and was bankrupted he threw the board, knocking my tea all over Arrie's new cream sofa. 'Oh dear, Aunty Alice,' said Edwin. 'That's why we're not allowed food or drink in the sitting room.'

I am grateful for:

- It being over
- Chocolate
- That I don't live on a farm
- That when I flipped the sofa cushions, the other side was clean – Arrie will never know
- That Arrie and Roger asked Astrid and Aziz to be legal guardians for Edwin and Ernie; both my sisters and both their husbands have to die before there's a risk I'm saddled with the twins (even if they're quite nice to cuddle)

My thoughts and reflections:

Still at Mum and Dad's but they're not coming back from Aunty Margaret's in Scotland until late this evening, so I've got the whole house to myself: a bit of a step up from last time when I was relegated to the camp bed in the garage. I've had to lie to Arrie about having a migraine today as she wanted me to come to lunch and she said the twins were desperate to see me again and I'd been a real hit with them but did I have any idea about why Ernie was suddenly afraid of the toilet? I also had to lie about this evening because otherwise she'd try and meet Guy; I told her a couple of colleagues are coming down early so we can do prep work ahead of tomorrow's shoot and, unfortunately, I'll be tied up until late. I've used Astrid's own technique against her and warned her that if she tells anyone in the family I'm meeting Guy tonight, I'll tell Arrie that as a surprise Mother's Day treat, Astrid wants to babysit the boys to give Arrie a break, *and* spend the day with Mum.

Mum's just texted and told me to make sure I put on the *Archers* omnibus because Mitzy likes to listen to it with her lunch and she heard I had a migraine and *did I have visual disturbances?*

I asked if Mitzy had been in touch with her directly, and she said, *Don't be ridiculous, Alice. Arrie told me*. Mum also said that Dad was worrying about my migraine because he didn't warn me not to touch the home-made whisky that Alan from down the road gave us at Christmas; apparently Alan's gone temporarily blind from it.

Even when they're not in the house, they still manage to suffuse the environment with stress.

Only a couple of hours until I'm meant to be meeting Guy Carmichael at the Lamb. Can't quite get my head around the idea. Last time I was here, I was fantasising about Guy and scrutinising Charlotte's posts for evidence they were still shagging. Fast forward six weeks and I'm about to check into the Lamb to spend a night with him. That is clearly more than shagging – it's moving towards relationship territory. I have beaten Charlotte hands-down here. *The Guide* has transformed my life. (Just wish I'd been clear about manifesting this success somewhere, anywhere, other than at Matthew Lloyd's hotel. And also can't imagine what we would talk about when it's not rushed. Usually we have time limits and he's working . . .)

Not sure whether to bath here and be in my new underwear already (in which case I've got nothing else to pull out the bag), or whether it would be better to lay the underwear out on the hotel bed like a kind of enticing preview and then bath there? Think will do proper, useful bathing here (and the necessary hair maintenance – Guy has mentioned how grateful he is for the millennial approach to pubic hair and said that if he wanted to meet with an untamed bush, he'd still be servicing his wife) and then I can do seductive bathing and (unnecessary) underwear change there.

God, I'm nervous. Almost tempted to have some of Alan's home-made whisky – bet it's awesome.

I ask the Universe:

- To please make sure Guy doesn't turn up looking weird or wear one of those sleep mask things or decide tonight is the time to reveal he likes a gimp costume
- To please, please help me out re Matthew . . .

My thoughts and reflections:

Thank you, Universe!

Everything has gone way better than I could have hoped for.

Guy doesn't look that different out of work clothes; he is still smart, sexy and with that sort of European Armani model vibe (albeit a little shorter and a little more hirsute than an actual Armani model). But he's got the cashmere scarf, woollen jumper, three-quarter-length coat etc. No Vans in sight. He was duly appreciative of the beauty of Little Minchcombe, and downright grateful as soon as he'd entered the Lamb with its expansive reception and curved velvet sofas. 'It's fucking decent, Alice, for the countryside. What's the wifi code?'

We were in the middle of checking in at the island desk when he got a call which he had to deal with, so I used the opportunity and casually leant round the vast bunch of flowers to ask the intimidatingly immaculate woman behind them whether Matthew was about and was told, 'I'm sorry, but unfortunately Matthew's away and won't be here until Tuesday.'

'Are you sure?' I said. 'Any chance he'll be popping in? How do you know he won't be here?'

'Erm, well, Mr Lloyd is currently out of the country,' she said.

'What time is his flight back on Tuesday?'

'I'm afraid I'm not at liberty to give out personal details. But our manager will be very happy to help you today if—'

'No, that won't be necessary,' I said quickly, trying to hide my relief. I had a sudden flashback to Matthew's grin as he walked in on New Year's Eve whilst I was talking about procuring seedy sex. 'Are you absolutely confident he won't just turn up suddenly?' I double-checked. 'I mean the man uses helicopters. Can you ever *truly* relax? Can *I* relax? That's what I need to know really.'

There was a moment where she looked bemused and where I had to hold my nerve, because when you're paying this much (or when Guy Carmichael is, in this case) you expect good service.

She blinked a couple of times. 'If Mr Lloyd does arrive unexpectedly, I can notify you . . . ?'

'That sounds reasonable,' I agreed.

So now, I finally get to enjoy the Lamb properly – and my first full night with Guy! The room we're staying in is gorgeous – all pared-back luxe, cool linens and warm oak, gunmetal grey roughly plastered walls and exposed beams, natural rugs and flattering lighting. Guy gave it the once-over and said his wife would bust her Botoxed brow if she saw this – apparently they have the same cream boucle mid-century armchair. Still, at least he feels at home. We've already sunk one bottle of champagne and had sex (he was a bit louder than usual but nothing disturbing), and now we're companionably working. Well, I'm writing this and Guy's working (and occasionally running his hand up my thigh in a decidedly proprietary fashion which is doing it for me), but it all looks the same to the casual observer. I only wish I could capture it and put it online for the casual (or not-so-casual) observer, but I've been careful to only take shots where Guy is definitely not in them – no way I'm doing a Charlotte. Am about to have a bath in the ascetic yet excessively generous tub and then I imagine it will be more sex before we go down for dinner, especially as Guy has just said, 'The way you're sucking that pen, Alice, is giving me ideas.'

Manifesting is the business.

In one word:

Winning

My thoughts and reflections:

So, I'm curled up over here on the boucle armchair that Mrs Carmichael also owns, entirely awake, and wondering if I'll ever be able to sleep again. Guy is snoring, contentedly. Something seems to have gone a little awry manifestation-wise. I'm in no way criticising the Universe (a poor workman blames tools, etc.) but I'm going to have to review my approach after this.

To recap, the bath was up there with the best baths I've ever had, and the La Perla underwear stayed on for all of two minutes and therefore can be deemed successful, and we were still only fifteen minutes late for our dinner reservation. All going well, so far, and I was looking forward to the opportunity to impress Guy with my dazzling conversation over supper as we'd done very little talking since we arrived. The ambience of the restaurant was intimate yet convivial, with its warm wood-panelled walls, medieval arched doorways and double-sided stone fireplace, and whilst it was busy, it was very much geared towards seclusion, with tables carefully placed to give the sense of discretion and separation. Maybe it was the result of sex and champagne, or maybe it was because Guy was looking particularly saturnine tonight – from a certain angle, the candles were giving him horn shadows – but I felt simultaneously relaxed and on edge.

Like any well-brought-up woman of my generation, I committedly drank and ate my way through my feelings, and we were therefore midway through dessert before I realised that the conversation wasn't going as I'd imagined. I was enjoying a spoonful of my caramel miso, bergamot and buttermilk sorbet when Guy said, 'Christ, Alice, the way you're sucking that sorbet is giving me ideas.' And as sexy as I found that, I was slightly tempted to point out that I'd given him ideas several times this evening, and all of these ideas were quite similar in nature. Then Guy tried the dessert wine which was paired with his chocolate marquise, and pretty much orgasmed on the spot. 'Notes of honey and apricot with the chocolate, Alice. Riesling icewine in the fucking Cotswolds? The man is a bloody genius.'

This was on the back of Guy admiring the décor and the menu and even the service (admittedly good) and quizzing me about Matthew Lloyd – how long had we known each other? (Too long.) Had he always intended to turn his hand to hospitality? (I'd kind of assumed he was set on turning his hand to being an asshole, so no.) And he really hadn't asked me anything about me.

'I hardly think he's a genius,' I said, feeling a little prickly. 'Anyone can choose wine.'

'Alice, that kind of statement reminds me of just how young you are. Not that I'm complaining. Not with those thighs. But choosing the right wine is an art.'

'Well, Matthew is certainly into his art.'

'Indeed,' said Guy, nodding. 'A man with a finger in many

pies. How much do you know about his other business ventures?'

'Nothing, really. Why?'

'I'm interested.'

'I'm more interested in you. You still haven't told me how your meeting went last week.'

'Alice,' said Guy, 'if I wanted to be quizzed about work, I'd have brought my wife here.'

'Well, probably not here,' I pointed out, 'to the village I grew up in.' But I laughed, if a trifle shrilly, because I didn't want to piss him off.

'As did Matthew Lloyd?'

'Yes.'

'He's certainly done well for himself,' said Guy, 'I feel like we'd have a lot in common. And he seems to be a good-looking bastard too, judging by his photo.'

I fleetingly recalled that night in the treehouse and Matthew's face in the moonlight, almost supernatural in its perfection.

'He's okay-looking if you like that kind of obvious thing,' I said. 'I personally don't think he's good-looking in the flesh.' I watched Guy across the table and tried not to compare him to Matthew. 'He's overdone the muscles. Probably on steroids for all we know, and got a dysfunctional cock.' Great. Now I was remembering the feel of Matthew's body beneath mine, before he told me to get off him. It definitely wasn't dysfunctional. Then I remembered him falling asleep, leaving me lying there awake.

'Definitely not a hit as far as I'm concerned,' I continued. 'My advice is try to avoid him. He's really fucking annoying. Trust me, Matthew Lloyd is not all that.'

And of course it was precisely then that I felt a little prickle of unease, and even before I heard him, I knew – that yet again, despite drilling his receptionist to ensure that this *didn't* happen, he'd somehow managed to come in to overhear me at *the* worst moment possible.

'So,' his familiar voice was deep and grave, 'is this the charming customer who was "extremely" keen to talk to me?'

The woman from reception desk faltered. 'Yes,' she said, nervously. 'I promised I'd let her know straight away if you arrived back early.'

Then she spoke to me directly, just in case I wasn't aware of the shit situation I was in. 'Madam, Mr Lloyd has returned early.'

'Great,' I said. 'Thank you so much.'

I could hear blood whooshing in my ears but there was no way out of this one. I turned round slowly in my seat.

There he was, his height and strength emphasised by the shadows. He looked like he hadn't shaved in a couple of days, his hair was even more rumpled than usual and his expression was inscrutable. We stared at each other whilst the sound of my heart pounding probably reached the nearby customers.

'Just a thought,' he said, at last. 'If you're trying to avoid me, wouldn't it be better to *not* come to my hotel?'

He sounded genuinely irritated.

'Look, I didn't mean it like that. You caught me at the end of—'

'Assassinating me?'

'Maybe I went a little far . . . '

Matthew shrugged indifferently. 'I thought, after Dartmoor,

that maybe we were friends. I was even going to share my steroids with you.'

Now he'd brought up Dartmoor, the guilt faded and the resentment resurfaced; it was galling that he had such a physical effect on me, especially considering he clearly didn't give a shit. 'Friends don't walk out without saying goodbye. Or saying anything at all.'

Matthew scratched his jaw. 'Yeah, okay. That was unfortunate.'

'Unfortunate?' My voice was getting louder. 'How about trying "sorry"? I mean, you managed to speak to Astrid several times since then. You could have sent a text. How rude can you—'

'Speaking of rudeness,' said Guy, silencing me with a squeeze of my waist, 'I'm going to cut in, and verify that you are, indeed, the Mr Lloyd who owns the place?'

'I am.'

'Which uni did you go to?' asked Guy.

'Er, Cambridge,' answered Matthew, looking slightly perplexed.

'College?'

'Oriel.'

'Fucking knew it,' said Guy, almost to himself. 'I take it you were in the wine society?'

Matthew nodded.

'Oriel's is the only one to rival ours. I was in Durham's wine society. Superb wine list you've put together here. I'm impressed.'

'Sorry,' said Matthew, 'have we met? Do you work in wine?'

'No, no,' said Guy. 'But I believe our paths are crossing work-wise. I've been wanting to meet you. Well, if you're who I think you are!'

Matthew gave me a sideways look, but I didn't know any more than he did.

'You'll have to forgive me.' Guy did not look remotely sorry. 'But as soon as they told us, I looked up the LL Group. I'm sure people do that all the time. Probably why your website is so sparse.'

Matthew said nothing.

LL Group . . . Why was that name familiar?

'And then when Alice mentioned a Matthew Lloyd who owned a hotel in the same village, I thought, what are the odds?'

'So,' said Matthew. 'You're at Carsons.'

Why were they talking about Carsons?

'Indeed,' said Guy.

Just then Guy's phone started buzzing. 'Sorry.' He looked at the screen. 'The wife keeps on bloody calling.' He pocketed his phone and put his hand on my lower back, proprietorially.

'The wife?' Matthew raised his eyebrows. 'Alice? Aren't you going to introduce us?'

'No,' I said. It didn't work.

Guy smiled but told me 'not to be fucking rude' and waited for me to introduce him.

'Guy, Matthew,' I mumbled eventually, hoping Matthew wouldn't remember our conversations about Guy. That didn't work either.

'Guy Carmichael?' Matthew looked at me pointedly. 'How interesting.'

My palms were clammy with stress – was Matthew about to tell Guy what I'd said about him?

Guy extended a hand. 'A pleasure to meet *the* Matthew Lloyd – we're delighted to have the LL Group on board at Carsons.'

'Good for you,' said Mathew, insincerely. 'A lot of people in your position find it all rather stressful. Especially as we're independent rather than *on board*.'

'Sorry, what exactly are you doing at Carsons?' I asked.

Guy ignored me and smoothly continued. 'Of course no one wants a merger, but it's crucial it's done the right way: your reputation precedes you. I note you won a Hunter award for social justice.'

Oh my god. The 'reputable third party' overseeing the merger at Carsons. The LL Group. It was Matthew!

'You really have been reading up,' said Matthew.

'Absolutely,' said Guy. I could see little wavering flames burning in his pupils. 'And I'd like to buy you a drink, Matthew. Have a good talk. Alice says you're practically family. It couldn't be more felicitous.'

'I see,' said Matthew dispassionately.

Guy's phone rang again. 'My wife is relentless. Let's park this for five minutes whilst I answer her. Keep hold of him, Alice,' he ordered. ' Matthew and I have a lot to discuss.'

I smiled obediently but as soon as he'd moved out of earshot, I turned to Matthew. 'Why the fuck didn't you tell me? That it's *your* company reviewing our merger?'

But Matthew seemed pretty frustrated himself, which was remarkable considering what I'd just heard. 'Why, Alice? Just why?'

'Why what? How do you get to sound pissed off? I didn't even know your company did stuff like this! You're always boring us with talks of ethics.'

'My company *is* ethical, Alice,' said Matthew, his voice clipped. 'Unlike your boyfriend.'

'But I thought you did coaching and training? All that psychology stuff?'

'Yes. We do multiple things.'

I was barely listening because I was trying to remember exactly what I'd said to Matthew. 'Oh no, and I told you about the taxi expenses loophole.' I actually felt like crying. 'Drunk Stephen . . . I feel like a traitor. You can't use what I told you to sack my friends! You can't!' I could feel my eyes starting to well, and I was finding it hard to catch my breath.

'Get a grip, Alice.' Matthew glanced over at the other customers, some of whom were looking our way. 'And stop shouting in my restaurant.' He indicated the door curtly, and I followed him out of one of the arched doorways and along a corridor to the cellars. 'You're being entirely unreasonable,' he said bluntly, as soon as the cellar door had closed behind us.

I rested my back against the cool wall, looking up at the vaulted ceiling and the stacks of wine, and tried to regain a sense of control. But the thought of Drunk Stephen being fired by Matthew, because of me, triggered it off again.

'How can you live with yourself?' I said. 'How can you fire people and ruin lives?'

'I'm not firing anyone. My company literally protects the rights of innocent people in the corporate world.'

'Then why is everyone terrified of you? Huh? Guy's been panicking.'

'I think you'll find it's the company directors and leaders who have an ambivalent relationship with me,' said Matthew irritably. 'Not everyone.'

'Yeah, right. So why would they invite you to be involved in the merger then? I'm not totally naïve, you know.'

'Because I'm preferable to multiple employment lawsuits.'

'I trusted you, Matthew. I thought we were friends. How could you let me babble on about everyone, knowing you'd be deciding their fates? I even told you about Guy. He'll kill me. Oh my god, Matthew.' I looked at him appalled. 'Is that why you took me away for the night? Was it part of the process of finding out and digging deep?'

The thought made me feel slightly sick.

Matthew shook his head at me and sighed. 'Thanks, Alice. Good to know what you think of me, although I suppose you have made it perfectly clear over the years.'

'You lied to me.' I poked him in his stupidly unyielding chest.

'No, Alice, I've told you what I do before: *you* weren't interested.'

'I mean you lied about this!' I shouted. 'Coming into my place of work.'

'I didn't know,' he said, his voice measured. 'I thought you were at Bloomsbury, otherwise of course I wouldn't have discussed your work with you. It was only when I saw your ID card that I realised.'

'So why didn't you say something to me when you did know? This is worse than cheating at Scrabble.'

'I'd only had initial meetings at that point. All confidential. And I don't cheat at Scrabble. I don't need to.'

'So why haven't you warned me since?'

'I'd have potentially compromised you,' he said. 'It's better for you that I minimise contact with you until it's done. You deserve the same protection as the others.'

'But all that inside information I've given you.' My voice broke slightly.

'It's largely irrelevant, Alice,' he said patronisingly. 'Most employee information is anonymised; I take all the steps I can to ensure I reach fair and independent conclusions. Anything where there's a conflict of interest, I'll recuse myself.'

'You're putting my career at risk, for yours.'

'Oh come on, Alice.' Matthew was losing patience. 'The only person putting your "career" at risk is you.'

I could hear the air quotes, condescending prick. 'How am I putting it at risk?'

'Having sex with your married boss.'

'It's none of your business who I sleep with,' I reminded him sharply. 'And for your information, I like him.'

'Actually, it *is* my business. And, for *your* information that kind of exploitative relationship shouldn't be taking place at Carsons.'

'So you're firing me for hooking up with Guy? *That's* exploitative!'

'Again, I'm not firing anyone,' he said calmly. 'I'm pointing out the implications of sexual relationships in the workplace.'

'My relationship is out of work. And it is not exploitative. I'm the one that fancies him.'

'And if the relationship ends . . . ?'

I thought about Charlotte, in Glasgow, but I'm not her.

'It's hardly ending – we've come away for the night together. The only problem I can see is you.'

'Alice, he's talking to his wife *right now.*'

'He has to because she's a nightmare.'

I could see Matthew's jaw clenching. 'Fine,' he snapped. 'Have it your own way. He's here because he's committed to you. Not because it's an easy lay, or because he's using you for your connection to someone who could influence whether he keeps his job. And definitely not because if it all goes wrong, at your level, you're straightforward to replace in the workplace.'

I've disliked Matthew Lloyd for a long time, but I don't think I really, truly hated him until that moment.

I could feel my eyes smarting.

Matthew bit his lip and then exhaled. 'Alice,' he said. 'Don't get upset. I'm sorry, I didn't mean it like that. I just think you could do so much better.'

Somehow his pity was even worse than his stupid smile; I could feel my fists curling.

'Don't think about trying to kick me,' he warned. 'You'll miss and hurt yourself – the walls are stone.'

'Where do you get off on trying to ruin my life?'

'I'm trying to help you.'

'I don't need your help. And I don't want it. I know exactly what I'm doing.'

'Sure,' said Matthew. 'I suppose if you lose your job, you can always manifest a new one. Or move back in with your parents. Or just keep on living with Astrid and Aziz and ruining their relationship.'

That did it. I lashed out. I may have never succeeded in

kicking him, but I had a good idea of how to wound him. 'So this is what it's all about? You're fucking *jealous*?'

'Jealous?' Matthew stalled.

'I've got the family you want. And even if they bitch about me, I don't have to prove myself. If I fall, they'll catch me. Whereas you? Well, you may have the hotel and the company, but you'll spend the rest of your life continuing to try and prove yourself. And if you fall, well . . .'

There was a silence. Matthew's face was motionless. He didn't speak.

I had that unpleasant sensation in the pit of my stomach that I may have gone too far, like when I told Mum she was a terrible mother and that the only reason we all stuck around was because Dad overcompensated for her unkindness and maybe she should stop being such a bitch to him. It's the only time Dad has ever shouted at me.

Then Matthew took a step towards me, his face hard. If anything he was even more offensively attractive when he lost his characteristic insouciance – he looked older and tougher, slightly menacing, like he'd lived a life, and like you wouldn't want to piss him off. And right now, I was extremely aware that I had, indeed, pissed him off. I took a step backwards, and met with the wall. There was nowhere to go. He took another step closer, so we were inches apart and then he leant down to me. I involuntarily swallowed. His physical nearness was intoxicating and unfair: I could feel my muscles weakening in response.

'For a second, Alice,' he said, his voice dangerously quiet, 'I thought you might be on to something, when you called me jealous. But I should have known that someone as inherently selfish as you only sees half the world.'

But then there was a sudden change in temperature as the cellar door opened.

'Oh, I'm sorry for interrupting,' began the waitress.

'You're not interrupting anything.' Matthew's voice was cold as he smoothly stepped away from me. 'I'm done here.'

And then he turned and left, without a backwards glance.

Guy was irked when I found him in the library and rejoined him, without Matthew. 'You've been bloody ages *and* you let him go, Alice?' He set his brandy down a little too vigorously on the wooden table. 'This was my opportunity to do some networking.'

'I don't get it,' I said. 'I thought we were meant to be keeping this all secret. Why would you want Matthew Lloyd to know you're seeing me?'

'Because you two are family friends – it's a connection.'

'Yes, but it's still literally one step away from screwing your secretary, sleeping with me!'

'Alice,' said Guy, exhaling. 'It's entirely different. Look at you – he'll understand. Matthew Lloyd is a man of the world. Anyone who understands how to pair an Eiswein Riesling correctly understands the ways of the world. Sex in the workplace happens.'

'Hmm,' I said, thinking that Guy had really misjudged this one. 'I'm not convinced. Matthew's almost as boring as my sister when it comes to the law and ethics.'

'Maybe. But the man is also serious business. He's not some "i dotter" Brenda in HR who wants to sack her boss because she's grown up with a sense of inferiority. Or a pencil-pushing Paul who's vindictive because he has to be grateful for a bit of vintage vagina from his wife twice a year. Matthew Lloyd is a success story. And I'm bloody successful at my job. Now you've connected us, I've got the chance to ensure he knows that.'

'Right.' I thought back to what Matthew said about Guy using me. 'It would have been useful for me to know you had this in mind when you suggested this night away.'

'Alice, Alice.' Guy reached under the table and squeezed my knee. 'I had other ideas in mind. Meeting Matthew was a useful adjunct to spending time with you.'

'I still wish you'd told me. You didn't even mention that Matthew was the LL Group.'

'I wasn't sure it was the same person. I did tell you that my meeting last week didn't go well, and that I'd prefer to deal with the main man. Now I am. Thanks to you.' His eyes lingered on my breasts. 'There's something else I'd like to deal with too. Shall we go upstairs?'

As much as I was usually up for having sex, I didn't feel like it right at that moment. 'I need a brandy myself.'

We had a couple more drinks and he suggested that I organise breakfast with Matthew Lloyd tomorrow and he would head back to London later than planned. Rather than tell him now that Matthew and I were no longer speaking, I gave a noncommittal response, as the chances are, some pressing work issue will mean Guy won't be able to hang around anyway. I was relieved when he changed the subject and started quizzing me about Arrie and whether she and Astrid and I looked alike. He said he might come along to the shoot for a bit so he could meet Arrie. He then told me that the thought of my sisters was 'giving him ideas' and he bet Matthew Lloyd spent half his teenage years cranking out a fair few over us. I said that was gross and Guy shrugged and said it was a mark of appreciation and if I were really honest with myself I wouldn't want to be like Iris because he doubted anyone had ever whacked off to her.

Despite his many ideas, indigestion is a bitch and Guy and I ended up not having sex. He said he'd have a good night's rest and promised to wake me up rudely in the morning. I, however, have not been afforded a good night's rest. I can't sleep. Maybe it's because I drank too much. Or maybe it's because it's weird being here with my boss. My boss, who technically still has a wife, and going by this chair, a wife with good taste. If I could afford it, I'd buy one of these chairs myself; it's beautiful and comfortable. What's not so comfortable is the resulting itching from the combination of overzealous hair removal and lacy underwear. Guy's wife allegedly hasn't trimmed her pubes since 2015 when she told Guy she wasn't a fucking box hedge and if he were so keen on topiary he could take out a RHS membership and leave off pestering her for sex. One of the many reasons they're getting a divorce, according to Guy. I squash the recollection of Matthew saying, 'Alice, he's talking to his wife *right now*.' Just because Guy's expedient doesn't mean he's a liar. I don't need to worry about Guy's wife. In fact, she's probably sleeping soundly now, free from itching and snoring. Unlike me.

I wish I hadn't thought of Matthew again. I'd rather think about Guy's wife. Every time I close my eyes, I picture how Matthew looked, hear how cold and final he sounded when he said he was done with me. And despite the fact that I'm in

a hotel, surrounded by people, and sharing a room with Guy,
I feel totally alone.

I ask the Universe:

To make sure we **don't see** Matthew Lloyd tomorrow.

Guide Post™

Are you feeling tired? Stressed? Worried that your manifesting is going awry? You may have 'Energy Drain'. Energy Drain blocks the flow of vibrations and inhibits manifesting success. Take steps to redress your Energy Drain:

1. *Say no to unnecessary obligations*
2. *Stay away from energy vampires*
3. *Eat well and avoid meat*
4. *Enjoy solitude and sleep*
5. *Practise yoga and meditation*

My thoughts and reflections:

Again, *The Guide* has come through for me. At least this seems like a simple fix. I've cancelled all my evening plans for the rest of this week and told Drunk Stephen I won't be going for lunches with him because I have to rebalance. He assumed it's because I'm tired from a sex marathon with Guy Carmichael. Well, it's less of an assumption and more that I pretty much told him that on the train yesterday, but it was an excuse for not talking to him much. I was still feeling angry with Matthew and I couldn't share it with Drunk Stephen without telling him why and I doubted I'd get much sympathy from him when he realised I'd effectively compromised his job. Guy texted last night to say sorry he'd had to rush off without breakfast and that he had a crazy week, but that works to my advantage in terms of 'enjoying solitude'.

Now I've looked up energy vampires, it explains a lot about why the manifesting hasn't gone smoothly. Must stay out of the way of Astrid (critical), the twins (innocent), Yaz (talker), Lydia (dominating), Cara (victim), Drunk Stephen (dramatiser), all the design team (manipulators) and obviously won't have anything further to do with Matthew Lloyd (narcissist). It's actually extremely alarming how prevalent energy vampires are – they're literally everywhere. I'm hard pushed to think of an interaction where someone hasn't been stealing my energy. Mum's been robbing it since birth.

I've already said no several times this morning – *Alice, can we have that cover brief? No. Alice, would you be happy to take us through how the shoot went? No. Is it okay if I sit here? No.* And whilst people have looked a bit surprised, I've had a great time. I probably need to learn to say no a lot more. Haven't tried it on Astrid yet though.

I haven't even had any meat today and it's already nearly lunchtime, so easy win. I've booked myself a meeting room this afternoon and will put down the blinds and have a sleep, and possibly start a TikTok yoga challenge. Hopefully in a few days I'll be vibrating with positivity all over the shop!

In one word:

Focused

Date: Saturday 25 February   **Time: 11.40pm**

My thoughts and reflections:

Just made the mistake of filling Astrid in about last weekend and ending up in the middle of another marital cold-war. Well, I didn't tell her the Matthew bits but as I'd already told her I was going with Guy, it was too late to lie about that. I should have said no to her, or at least *let's talk when you're in a better mood* but Astrid isn't an easy person to put off, especially as she'd decided I was deliberately avoiding her. 'I've barely seen you all week, Alice. Normally you're always on the scavenge for something.' (Plus she'd opened a bottle of white wine and still hadn't poured me a glass, so it was blackmail, effectively.)

Astrid didn't mince her words about Guy. 'Alice, he's the type of man who tells you he's treating you with respect by watching porn in front of you and not hiding the fact he's sleeping with other women. Plus he's nearly twenty years older than you and he's your boss. This is one of your most stupid moves yet. And that's in a long history of dating lackwits. How do you think this is going to turn out?'

It was uncomfortably similar to the conversation I'd had with Matthew (don't argue with lawyers) although at least I was getting snacks during this one.

Me: Plenty of successful relationships begin in the workplace.

Astrid: You're planning on this being a long-term thing?

Me: Yes (*more confident than I felt, especially given he's left me on read since yesterday*).

Astrid: So the fact he's married doesn't present an issue?

Me: I keep telling you they're getting divorced.

Astrid: (*chopping carrots with the kind of precision that bodes well for her career change*) If you're genuinely into it, how come you didn't want Mum and Dad or Arrie to know?

Me: I'm totally into it.

Astrid: He's old and he's got hairy knuckles. He's probably got hairy shoulders. And I bet he's made it clear he appreciates a full Hollywood.

Me: (*impressively not rising to bait about pubes but intelligently using her own lawyerish approach against her. Hopefully correctly*) That's rather ad hominem, Astrid. Surely we don't need to resort to shaming others' appearances?

Astrid: (*pausing her chopping and blinking rapidly, probably feeling a little in awe of my judicious use of Latin*) You're right. Sorry. But I don't see how you're into him.

Me: (*deciding to end this conversation by pushing her own frigid buttons*) Well, he's a highly proficient lover. In fact he does this thing where—

Astrid: Fine. You're into the sex. Spare me. Apart from that, what have you even got in common?

Me: Loads. He's fascinating. He knows lots about wine.

Astrid: (*over-confidence resumed despite my Latin*) Oh my god, Alice. He's one of those. You have to listen to him and I bet he doesn't know anything about you.

Me: He does! He knows what I like in bed and . . . We've got loads in common.

Astrid: Yes. An interest in him.

In a rare moment of functional relationship-ship, she even drew Aziz, who was reading a journal over on the sofa, into the lambasting. 'Tell her she's a complete idiot, Aziz. In your professional opinion.'

'As a therapist,' I said, 'I'm sure Aziz knows people fall in love at work all the time.'

Aziz was characteristically restrained; he didn't look up

from his journal. 'It may be helpful to consider this relationship in the context of previous relationships,' he answered.

'As far as I remember,' said Astrid, 'she hasn't had a decent relationship since Ollie.'

Aziz ignored her. 'If you've experienced love in previous relationships and you're seeking that in this one then there is a chance you'll find it. However, if this is a pattern of relationships that don't work out, that don't make you happy, you may want to consider if you're seeking out partners that aren't really available. And indeed why that might be.'

'There you go, Alice,' said Astrid. 'Aziz thinks you're an idiot.'

But then Aziz did something I wasn't expecting. He stood up and looked at Astrid. 'She's no more of an idiot than I am, Astrid.' Then he turned to me. 'Maybe just think things through before you dive into marriage, Alice,' he said, closing his journal and leaving the room.

I am letting go of:

The idea that there is such a thing as a happy ever after.

My thoughts and reflections:

We received another of those merger emails from Alistair Fridman, CEO of Carsons, this morning. He said that the senior leadership at Carsons have now had their initial meetings and outlined their plans for workforce direction with the LL Group, and that the same is currently happening over at Montague Place. He said we could look forward to welcoming the LL Group at the Carsons' offices from next Monday for up to three weeks. Although they will be dividing their time between here and Montague Place, we should be prepared for them to be on-site at any time, and prioritise making ourselves available when we are called upon.

Nervous Jane wasn't in today so I didn't have to listen to her ostentatious crying again but Cara left her desk quite abruptly a few minutes after the email came through and when she returned, she looked a bit red-eyed. Everyone noticed. Yaz whispered to me that apparently Cara and Harry Piles had an argument last week where Cara had lost her cool and said, 'No, Harry, Editorial wouldn't do it that way in any publishing company, which is why we need to do it this way.' And then Harry had said that she might want to fact-check that, because he was confident Montague Place would be keen to do it his way. So Cara did some 'fact-checking' and discovered that her counterpart at Montague Place, James Harrison, was at school with Harry Piles. Yaz reckons Cara must be terrified about getting fired now.

I know it's not my problem and I should be worrying about my own role, but I feel for Cara. Thing is though, Cara's my line manager so I don't really feel I can just go up to her and try and reassure her about her job. It would be easier if it happened organically, like over a glass of wine. I was going to keep tonight free in case Guy Carmichael invites me over, but I haven't heard from him since I messaged on Friday asking if we could talk, and I know he's seen me because he's in his office. I should never have used the word 'talk'. Cara's not the only one worrying that her job is in danger . . . Keep thinking about Charlotte and hoping there are no important editorial issues arising in Scotland that Guy decides I'm perfect for. Anyway, I might suggest Monday Margaritas to Drunk Stephen and see if Cara wants to come along. Might even invite Yaz too. I need to make the most of still having friends, because at some point, I'm going to have to tell them I know the CEO of the LL Group.

I ask the Universe:

- To make sure I don't have to see Matthew Lloyd.
- To help Cara keep her job.
- To get Guy Carmichael to message me back.

Date: Tuesday 28 February   **Time: 11.05am**

My thoughts and reflections:

Still too hungover to write much. Suffice to say Margarita Monday was a success in a number of ways. Cara loosened up after a few drinks and had a proper cry – snot and all. Apparently, she's just remortgaged her place so she can pay for her mum's nursing home, and is worried sick about what will happen to her mum if she loses her job. Cara has been caring for her mum ever since she was thirteen, and financially supporting her for years. No wonder she's so serious and stressed. The care home has transformed Cara's life – her mum is happy and, for the first time ever, Cara has some freedom. We were all a bit pissed by then and told Cara we'd give her money if she lost her job so she could keep her mum in the home. Well, if we keep ours.

Drunk Stephen also said he was angsting over his job. Cara told him that he was one of the best designers she had ever worked with in nearly thirty years of publishing and that he had it in the bag. Then they started talking about the consultants coming in next week and how tense it was all going to be. Cara said she'd googled the LL Group earlier; this felt like the time I should mention the fact I knew Matthew. But I bottled it. More drinks arrived and Yaz started talking about how she's worried her flatmate is wanking in her bed. The moment had gone.

We must have been about four rounds in when I got a message from Guy Carmichael asking if I wanted to come over. I was pissed and bold and I've lost loads of jobs anyway so what's one more: I took the risk and told him *No, I want to see you for a drink first. Can we meet at the Mulberry Bush?* Then I felt less bold for about half an hour whilst I heard nothing. At last he texted *American Bar at the Savoy – I want a proper drink.* So even though it was a bit more of a trek from here, I went to the loos and redid my make-up and made excuses about leaving – Drunk Stephen said, 'She's got her about-to-get-shagged face on,' and I kicked him but I knew he wouldn't give anything away, but Yaz, who was also drunk, kept asking who I was going off to see and really wouldn't let it go.

And eventually, I said, 'Just a friend.'

And then Yaz turned into a bit of a nightmare and said, 'Oh my god, it's someone from work, isn't it?' And then, 'It is so totally someone from work, look at her face! Who is it? Cara do you know who she's shagging at work?'

And I was actually getting a bit stressed until Drunk Stephen distracted Yaz by saying he thought Timothée Chalamet had just walked in.

*

Guy was already there when I arrived (he was wearing the same clothes he had at work and his navy coat which I think is my favourite) and for the first time since we'd gone for lunch, I think both of us were aware that this could go either way.

He ordered a negroni and I ordered another margarita, but before I drank it, I came right out and just said, 'So, Guy, is your interest in me primarily an interest in Matthew Lloyd? I would appreciate your being straight up with me.'

And as the pianist played smooth jazz, Guy blinked for a second and seemed a little taken aback. But then he reached across the table and took my hand and said, 'Look, Alice. It certainly doesn't hurt your appeal, that you have the connections you do. But I like you.'

I must have looked uncertain at that point because he reiterated, 'I do. I've got to admit, you're rather unexpected. I'm not going to do you the disrespect of pretending this is something it isn't. But, I will say there's something refreshing about you, Alice. As well as extremely fuckable.'

'You mean I'm an easy lay,' I echoed Matthew's words in the wine cellar.

'More like the perfect-level-of-challenge fuckable.'

Well, there you go, Matthew Lloyd, I thought. *Maybe I'm refreshing and unexpected and the perfect-level-of-challenge fuckable.* Doesn't sound like I'm off to Scotland any time soon.

I drank my margarita, and did not think about Matthew, or what Drunk Stephen would say if he knew I were having drinks here (he's very derisive about the sort of people that listen to jazz) and then we went back to the serviced apartment and had a lot of slightly slapdash and enthusiastic sex. It had been a week since we'd last had any and you could tell. Well, it had been a week for me, at least. I ended up staying the night there.

Guy woke me up before he left and told me to wait a while before I came to work.

I did a finger and toothpaste job, ordered a coffee from

concierge (and tried to order painkillers to no avail), squirted a bit of Guy's Acqua di Parma cologne to cover up the smell of sex and alcohol, and then went into the office. Yaz, Cara and Drunk Stephen all commented that I was wearing the same clothes as yesterday, but they were too hungover themselves to care. It was only when Yaz was at my desk just now, that I got slightly nervous. She went all nose detective and kept saying that I smelt different to usual but strangely familiar. 'Have you switched fragrance?' she said, sniffing me. 'I swear someone in the office wears exactly the same scent. It's kind of woody and leathery and lemony, almost like aftershave. I know who it is, it's on the tip of my tongue.'

'Probably just residue of margarita from yesterday.' I backed away from her. 'I get a bit sloshy when I'm pissed. Have you got any decent painkillers?'

I am grateful for:

- Yaz's fibroids. (Well, obviously I don't want her to have them but the naproxen she's been prescribed for it really does sort out a hangover and I am grateful for that.)
- Not having a parent in a nursing home. Thank you.

My thoughts and reflections:

It's kind of amazing how responsive the Universe is . . . in many ways. Just received this email:

From: Clare@MLG.com
To: alice.carver@carsons.com

Dear Alice,
I am contacting you because it has become apparent that you are in some way known to / have had prior involvement with a member of LL Group. In keeping with our company policy, and to preserve the impartiality of the process, I will be your point of liaison and all responsibility is devolved to me.

I would ask, at this time, that you do not share any information with me regarding your involvement with LL Group, or attempt to make contact with your known person until further notice, otherwise the process may be compromised. Please be aware that you should similarly expect no communication from LL Group, other than from me.

We thank you for your cooperation and understanding;

should you have any questions, please do not hesitate to get in contact.

I look forward to meeting you next week.

Clare Atkins
Managing Director
LL Group

I emailed her straight back, asking whether I should let my colleagues know the situation or not mention it. She told me that, as she was unaware of the precise nature of my prior involvement with LL Group, it was my decision, although she suggested I carefully consider any possible ramifications of sharing information and think with regard to professionalism and 'need to know'. She said based on the information she did have, she could tell me the connection had been deemed 'personal and insignificant' in terms of any potential conflict of interest.

So, manifesting works again: I don't have to see Matthew Lloyd. Which is really good. And it sounds like it's best if I don't mention I know him to my colleagues, which is, again, what I wanted. Thank goodness I didn't get a chance on Monday night! My 'insignificant' connection to him. I don't quite know where he gets off deciding that though. I would say turning up at my family home every bloody Christmas is pretty *significant*. I wouldn't say that summer we spent together working at the Lamb was insignificant. I wouldn't say that going away to Dartmoor for the night was insignificant. But, you know, whatever. Obviously I won't attempt to make contact with the complete twat. Not now I've been instructed not to. I've got half a mind to tell my mum though. About the insignificant. She'd make contact. Or maybe I should just track him down myself. Tell him what he can do with his instructions.

In one word:

Rude

My thoughts and reflections:

Just got off family FaceTime. Mum and Dad have booked
flights to Majorca for the May bank holiday weekend to stay
with Aunty Margaret in her flat. I felt extremely envious and
like I should have thought of this myself, given that Aunty
Margaret said I could stay there. But Mum pointed out that
the flights are upwards of £350 return; I couldn't afford that.
Mum and Dad were going on about how the *Sunday Times*
had come to do a piece on the Lamb and how Dad was going
to be quoted as saying that Matthew was 'like a son'.

That did it; I decided to tell Mum what Matthew had said
and get him into trouble. But as soon as I started, Mum cut
me off.

'Now, now, Alice.'

'Erm, what?'

'Matthew did warn us,' said Mum.

Sneaky fucker. 'About what?'

'Well, darling,' Dad chipped in, 'you know Matthew can't
talk about the merger with us. And we'd prefer it if you didn't
either. We want to be fair and support you both.'

'How's that fair? I'm your daughter. Why shouldn't I talk
about the situation at work *with my own parents*?'

'I'm disappointed, Alice,' said Mum sternly. 'There's Matthew, insisting he shouldn't see us at all until all this is over – such a thoughtful boy and we told him "nonsense" – and you're not willing to give an inch. Mind you, Matthew warned us you'd find it tricky.'

'Find it tricky?'

'My love, you're hardly one for keeping things to yourself,' said Dad gently.

'Yes, indeed,' agreed Mum. 'I, for one, Alice, could have done without knowing that Monty has a right-leaning curvature to his erect penis which he inherited from his father. I find it hard to look his mother straight in the eye.'

'I can be discreet. I haven't told you anything about . . .' I was going to say Guy Carmichael, but realised I'd be shooting myself in the foot.

'It would be wonderful if you could be, just for a couple of weeks,' said Dad. 'I knew you'd understand that this is Matthew's career. Not something to compromise.'

'It's my career too!' I muttered.

'Career?' said Arrie. 'That's a bit of a stretch, surely.'

'He's got to protect the interests of these poor people who are helpless in the stranglehold of big business,' continued Dad sadly. 'What a pressure to oversee something as serious as a merger; people's entire lives depend on those jobs.'

'I'm one of those poor people!' I pointed out. 'And he's a big bloody business himself. I'm not convinced he's about helping others.'

'You're living practically rent-free in Chiswick,' said Astrid sharply. 'If you lose your job, the worst it's going to do is affect your social life. And, for clarity, Matthew does more to help others in one day than you'll do in a lifetime.'

There was Astrid's bedside manner coming through again. I didn't mention it but I suspected she'd make a shit doctor. 'Thanks for your feedback,' I said instead.

'Decision made,' said Mum. 'We shall erect a Chinese wall and continue to see both Alice and Matthew.'

And then Edwin came in and asked what World Book Day costume he'd be wearing tomorrow and Arrie said, 'But that was last Thursday? I assumed the school weren't doing it this year?'

And Edwin explained it had been moved to Monday because Mrs Kemp was at a conference last Thursday, and it had to be a home-made costume – you weren't allowed a bought one. Understandably, Arrie started swearing and saying how much she hated fucking books and that bloody Roger was utterly useless and how was she meant to do everything?

And Mum said, 'Well, don't you have a tea towel? Surely he could go as a nun, or an Arab?'

I left Astrid to explain to Mum why he couldn't.

I ask the Universe:

To one day, get my family to respect my career.

Date: Monday 6 March   **Time: 7.10pm**

My thoughts and reflections:

Weird coming in to work today. Everything is, essentially, the same but very slightly different. Lydia was on security but instead of her suit jacket being on the back of the seat, she was wearing it buttoned up, and instead of a scowl, she was wearing a smile – well, at least until she saw it was just me. Yaz's desk was pristine and devoid of food and there was a fruit selection in the kitchen. Even Drunk Stephen had sharpened up his skin fades, which shouldn't be possible considering they're always immaculate. His trainers were a dazzling white that would rival the brightest Turkish veneers. 'Wow,' I said, 'someone's made an effort.'

'I always look good, Alice,' he said. 'Nothing out of the ordinary here.'

Except, of course, for the notice which had been stuck to the meeting room door: Clare Atkins, LL Group.

Guy's assistant, Iris, was wearing lipstick and had put a bunch of battered fake flowers on the desk. 'Nice flowers,' I said.

'They're dusty,' she said. 'I took them from the bathroom at home but every little helps, doesn't it?' I noticed her hands were shaking as she tidied papers on her desk.

'Iris,' I said, 'I don't think you've got anything to worry about. You're a lynchpin round here.'

'It's hard not to worry, Alice,' she said, 'when you've got cats to feed. I don't want to let them down. They need me.'

'I'm sure you won't let them down, Iris.'

I didn't mention that she had lipstick on her teeth because she seemed quite wobbly as it was.

Guy strode past without pausing at my desk and went straight to his office. 'Christ, Iris,' I heard him drawl, 'did you do your make-up in the dark? You're going to scare the consultants.'

Cara called a quick meeting in one of the side rooms and told us we all had this and to carry on as we normally would. She said we'd been clearly told that that the LL Group were an independent third party and that we needed to accept this at face value and feel confident.

Nervous Jane said, 'But they're firing us.'

'No,' said Cara patiently. 'Carsons are.' Then as Nervous Jane's face crumpled, Cara hastily added, 'Some of us! Only some of us.'

'Is this Clare Atkins in the main meeting room already?' whispered Yaz.

Cara didn't know. No one seemed to know. 'Just get on as normal,' Cara repeated, her voice only slightly strained.

So we got on as 'normal', and there was a sort of hive of activity and industry, but the door stayed shut, and I felt like I'd been on the Red Bull.

Just before lunch, Guy came out of his office, knocked on the meeting door room, waited and then opened it. There was a sudden hush as everyone watched. 'For fuck's sake,' he said.

'She isn't even in there,' and then he told Iris to keep a fucking eye whilst he took an early lunch.

'Someone's stressed,' said Yaz under her breath.

A moment later, my phone buzzed with a message from Guy, saying this whole merger process was making him hungry, and asking if I had plans this lunchtime or if he could eat me out. I didn't know if it was a typo, but said yes.

FYI: Clare Atkins from LL Group didn't turn up all day.

FYI 2: It wasn't a typo.

I ask the Universe:

To let me get my meeting with Clare Atkins over and done with quickly.

My thoughts and reflections:

So it's only lunchtime and I've already got my meeting with Clare Atkins over and done with. Maybe I should start my own TikTok: manifest work meetings at your convenience! Honestly, I only asked the Universe yesterday and the very next day my meeting with Clare Atkins was booked for 9.30am! I don't know if it would pull the views but I mean there is no getting round the fact that I am manifesting successfully.

Clare Atkins was not what I was expecting. She was probably in her late fifties and small and smiley. I didn't expect to cry, either. She did the whole thing about this being a confidential process, and reiterated that same stuff Matthew had said about how the LL Group were actually here serving the interests of Carsons' employees. Then came the normal questions about strengths and weaknesses, teamwork, achievements, etc., after which she quizzed me about my colleagues. And then she asked me what I thought other people at work would say about me. All fine, until she asked if she could read me one piece of feedback she'd been given about me from the 360s. I shat myself whilst smiling and saying, 'Of course, I welcome feedback' but I clearly didn't fool her because her eyes twinkled and she said, 'I think you'll enjoy this,' and then I panicked

387

thinking what if this is a trap and she's going to read out a dirty message from Guy Carmichael and then HR will come and escort me and I'll have to leave the building with a cardboard box and I don't even have a plant to put in it.

But then she read, 'I'm always glad when I get to work with Alice because I know that not only will the work get done, but it will get done quickly and expertly, and that everyone ends up giving more than they usually do yet without feeling like they have – she brings an energy that's kind of special and makes everyone feel valued.'

'Oh,' I said.

'Here's another,' she said. 'Alice is a born leader when it comes to her projects, and a creative and dynamic and, as of yet, untapped asset to the wider team; I have no doubt that when she chooses to do so, she will rapidly rise in her career and deservedly so.' Clare stopped at this point and surveyed me over her glasses. 'There are more comments like these,' she said, 'and they were a pleasure to read. I think what surprises me then, is the fact that you've mentioned several times that you are in your late thirties—'

'Well, mid,' I corrected.

'And that you are an Editor. And then I looked back through your form and saw that when you started here, you spent six months covering as Senior Editor. Why the backwards move when the fixed term ended? Something doesn't add up here, Alice. Why are you settling for a position that doesn't match your potential? Are Carsons failing to recognise the worth of certain employees? Or is it because, for some reason, you don't recognise your own worth?'

And I don't know if it's because she looked a tiny bit like

Granny Carver (not that I could see her thighs because she was wearing a skirt) or whether it was PMT, but I ended up snivelling and snuffling and explaining to her that my older sisters were horrifically successful and that Astrid regularly worked seventy hours a week, and that Arrie had her own business with a million pound turnover by the time she was twenty-five, and that I was quite different to them and that I'd had some awful school reports from St Hilda's, which was probably why I always ended up having to sleep in the garage when I went home.

She said she'd often had to sleep in the shed when she went home. Then she asked me what I felt were my greatest weaknesses, and because I was emotional, I forgot to lie and say something that made me sound good like 'my flaw is I give too much and work too hard', and just answered, 'I like having a laugh and I'm lazy,' and then I clapped my hand over my mouth, because I shouldn't have said that.

And Clare Atkins adjusted her half-moon glasses and said, 'Interesting. What you see as laziness, these people you work with' – she held up the 360 reviews – 'seem to view as efficiency, and finding effective solutions. And what you call having a laugh, they appear to consider good-humoured and personable leadership. Which is a quality much in need in any business.'

I swallowed.

'Just something to think about, Alice. You have a lot of influence here. It might be time to adjust your perspective.' Then she handed me a tissue, said that we'd leave it for today and told me to go and get myself a nice cup of tea.

When I came out, Sales Chloe was walking past and she

took one look at me and trotted off, at twice her normal pace. Yaz told me that it had gone all round the building that I'd been reduced to tears and that Clare Atkins was brutal and that Chloe was having to breathe into a paper bag because she was so nervous. Another day, I might have left Chloe to her paper bag, but after those nice 360s, which almost suggest I have manifested the respect of some colleagues, I think I'm going to take a trip to Sales and put her out of her misery . . .

My intention is:

To manifest a free holiday (after I'd calmed Chloe down she was quite sweet and showed me her snaps from skiing in Verbier this Christmas, as well as a new charm she'd got for her bracelet. There are, it transpires, stories behind all her charms, and it's actually rather touching).

To consider my perspective and maybe get myself some of those half-moon spectacles – I rather like the Alice who Clare Atkins saw.

My thoughts and reflections:

I'm actually going to take a little break from writing in here because I think I may be inadvertently manifesting incorrectly. Sometimes I get what I want and it's easy, but sometimes, I get what I want and it turns out I don't want it after all, or at least not quite like that.

You know how I wanted a free holiday? Well, this evening, I went into the kitchen and Aziz and Astrid were mid-argument, and Aziz said, 'No, it's not an ultimatum but I think I have reached my threshold – we need time together, *on our own*.'

And Astrid, said, 'Fine,' in the same way someone might say 'fuck you', so I turned straight around to get out of there but then Astrid saw me and said, 'I've got an idea. Alice?'

I halted and said, 'Yes?'

And Astrid said, 'Do you still fancy a holiday?'

'Why . . . ?'

Then Aziz said, in a low voice, 'Astrid, are you really going to do this?'

And Astrid said, 'What? See if my younger sister fancies a holiday? Surely you can't have a problem with that?'

'I have a problem with your avoidance, Astrid.'

And Astrid ignored him. 'Guess what, Alice?! Aziz has

booked us a little trip and we'd love for you to come too. Have a look!'

Then she turned round the iPad and it was the ski resort that Chloe had been to. *The exact same one in Verbier.*

'We're paying of course,' said Astrid. 'In fact all expenses paid. Isn't that right, Aziz?'

I didn't even dare to look at Aziz. I just said, 'Erm, sounds amazing, but I think I'm busy actually . . .'

'Don't go,' called Astrid, as I hastily backed out. 'See what you've done, Aziz?'

And then I spent the rest of the night in my room listening to the muffled sound of Astrid's raised voice, and then the front door slamming, and then silence. I think the silence was worse.

I am letting go of:

- Thinking about the fact that technically I've just turned down the free holiday I manifested.
- Trying to understand Astrid.

My thoughts and reflections:

I was going to have a longer break but I need somewhere to let off steam because I'm starting to find work a real nightmare. It's not even that I'm so worried about losing my job anymore; it's more that I'm at risk of losing it full stop. It started on Monday when I was in the lift with my earbuds in and I overheard Natasha (Head of Sales) say to Anika (PR) really quietly, 'Did you see him yet?'

And Anika said, 'Yes.'

And Natasha said, 'And?'

And Anika said, 'It's unbelievable. Genuinely. I mean . . . yeah.'

I didn't think that much more of it until mid-morning when Yaz leant over her desk and whispered, 'Have you heard the rumours?'

So I said, 'Which rumours?' hoping they were nothing to do with whom Guy was shagging, because only last week Drunk Stephen had warned me that Gentle Jadan who knows Paul in HR said they were pretty certain he was using the Carsons serviced apartment as a fuck-pad and it was likely someone from work. (Er yes, and yes. And thank you.)

But Yaz said, 'The rumours about the nineteenth floor?'

And I said, 'No?' feeling relieved because it's adult fiction on eighteen and nineteen.

And she said, 'Apparently they've got an unbelievably hot one.'

'Hot one what?'

She nodded over towards the meeting room. 'Consultant.' She lent forwards. 'He's so hot that people keep offering themselves up for extra interviews.'

Then Drunk Stephen walked towards us looking dazed. 'Oh my god,' he said.

'Are you okay?' I asked.

'I've just seen him,' said Drunk Stephen. 'And it's all true.'

'Seen who?'

'Nineteenth floor?' checked Yaz.

Drunk Stephen nodded. 'He's so good-looking I didn't even check his shoes.'

'What?' I said. I mean, that's unheard of.

'I have no idea what was on his feet. I think I've actually broken out into a sweat.' Drunk Stephen looked at me in panic.

Drunk Stephen hasn't sweated since 2006. Everyone knows. Yaz inhaled.

'Oh come on,' I said at last. 'He can't be that fit.'

'The man on nineteen?' asked Nervous Jane, stopping at my desk. 'So, so fit. I could see the muscles move under his T-shirt. It was hypnotising. And the messy sex hair.'

'It's the smile,' Drunk Stephen added. 'Beautiful and sweet, and yet sort of so cocky you just know he's an incredible fuck. And that he knows you know he knows it.'

Was there any point even asking?

'So, who exactly is this man on nineteen?'

'I don't know what he does for the LL Group,' said Drunk Stephen. 'I just saw his name on the door. Matthew Lloyd.'

My intention is:

To stay away from the nineteenth floor.

Date: Wednesday 22 March   **Time: 9.45pm**

My thoughts and reflections:

Stayed over with Guy again last night, and at the weekend too. His wife's therapist thinks it's important for his wife's self-actualisation that she should have the house to herself, at the weekend as well as during the week, to get used to life alone. He's not, it transpires, a fan of the therapist. 'I'm paying her, Alice. So I've effectively handed over thousands of pounds for her to kick me out of my own home. She's a bloody shark in a cardigan.' The upside is he's been at the serviced apartment more than usual; we spent half of Sunday together. When I mentioned the situation between Aziz and Astrid to him, Guy was surprisingly thoughtful and said I may as well just stay with him and give them some space.

'I hate it,' I said. 'Watching two people who were so close grow so far apart.'

'That's marriage for you,' said Guy. 'People change. They'll either grow back together and be even stronger for it, or they won't.'

'Do you think you and your wife could grow back together?' I asked casually. 'With space?'

'Christ, no,' said Guy. 'Those shoots have been well and truly cauterised. And I get enough ball-aches at work.'

He's been increasingly stressed by the LL Group. He said the barrage of questions about his personal life was taking fucking liberties and that little shit Paul in HR had clearly shopped him in. 'No, I haven't gone on the Menopause Matters training. Why do I have to learn to manage my menopausal colleagues with respect and compassion? Why can't my menopausal colleagues learn to be less fucking shouty and emotional?'

He said he was convinced someone had also mentioned that he'd slept with a 'couple' of women from work over the years. 'The sad thing, Alice, is it makes you doubt people you thought were friends. I feel like I've got to watch my back all the time, now. At least I can trust you.'

My stomach shifted uncomfortably at that; I remembered everything I'd prattled on about to Matthew Lloyd when we went away, and hoped that it wasn't me who'd inadvertently screwed over Guy.

He got quite drunk and maudlin and said that the tide had turned, just like his father had warned him it would. 'I've got a horrible suspicion that being a white male who can speak properly and has a healthy sexual appetite puts me at a disadvantage in this day and age.' He didn't like Clare Atkins, either. 'She's got it in for me,' he said. 'Acts like I'm some kind of predator.'

'You're not going to lose your job, though, are you?' I said. 'Didn't you go to school with half the shareholders?'

'A couple. But a couple of others went to school with my wife, and she doesn't just want the house – she's made it clear she's going to take me for everything I've got.'

'Ah.'

'Thing is, Alice,' he said, 'I beat budget by miles every year. Regardless of who I know or don't know on the bloody board.'

Just as I was falling asleep, Guy said, 'Alice, can you ask him?'

'Who?'

'Matthew.'

'I'm not allowed to.'

'At the end of the week when they've wrapped up. I'd like to know before everyone else knows. It will affect my divorce.'

'Okay,' I said. 'If I see him.'

I doubt I will see Matthew Lloyd. He has managed to make sure our paths haven't crossed for this entire time and they're out of the offices on Friday. I'm looking forward to no longer having to listen to my colleagues losing it over how fit he is; they seem to have forgotten exactly why he's in the building. I haven't.

I just really hope Guy hasn't been fired.

I am grateful for:

Guy letting me stay over more.

My thoughts and reflections:

When I sauntered into Astrid and Aziz's kitchen at half past three this afternoon, I really did not expect to see Matthew Lloyd, or, to be fair, Astrid either. I didn't expect to see anyone – in fact, I'd counted on it. But there they both were, sitting at the island.

'What are you doing here?' said Astrid.

Clearly, I wasn't the only one who'd banked on having the house to myself.

'Working-from-home-Friday-afternoon,' I said. Then added for Matthew's benefit, given the good-looking fucker could get me fired, whatever he claims: 'Working-*hard*-from-home. Like always. Work, work, work.'

'Looks like you've been shopping. And had your nails done,' said Astrid.

'Anyway, more importantly, what's he doing here?' I said.

'He's drinking coffee,' said Matthew. 'Do you want a cup?'

'No,' I said.

Matthew shrugged nonchalantly. 'Sure,' he said. 'I guess you'd better get on with your work. So, is it a Carsons-wide initiative? I can't think why Alistair Fridman failed to mention it.'

399

Astrid sniggered and held out her cup for more coffee.

I felt a surge of indignation about the two of them laughing in the kitchen and name-dropping CEOs, whilst some of us had been under extreme stress. 'Hey. You can't send letters like that telling me to keep away from you, and stay on the nineteenth floor all month, and erect Chinese walls with Mum and Dad, and then just appear where I *live* like it's normal!'

'Yeah, well, the merger is pretty much done,' said Matthew, 'so I'm not worried at this point.' He pushed back his hair which was even more dishevelled than usual. 'Messy sex hair' Nervous Jane called it.

'Well, what about me? What if I'm worried?'

He surveyed me over his mug. 'Are you worried? We asked Carsons to ensure all employees had access to counsellors.'

Ah. Well, that would explain that email telling us about support services available to Carsons' workforce. We'd all assumed it was a joke at first, given it contained the phrase 'your wellbeing is our priority' and was sent from Harry Piles, who couldn't give less of a crap about anyone. So: it actually came from Matthew. I stared back at him. He looked more tired than he usually did, and serious. Maybe overseeing people's fates wasn't as much fun as it sounded. 'That's not the point,' I said.

'If I'm making you worried, I'll leave,' he said.

'I'm not worried. But you can fuck off.'

Matthew gave me a slight smile, but as slight as it was, it still had that glimmer of total smugness. I immediately remembered Drunk Stephen saying 'so cocky you know he's an incredible fuck'. Then rapidly wished I hadn't remembered that.

'He's not going anywhere,' said Astrid. 'I want to check if you've kept your job.'

'You can't ask that!' I said. 'Can she?' I checked with Matthew.

'Both of you can ask anything you want.' Mathew yawned, looking bored. 'Whether I'll answer . . .'

'You won't let them fire Alice,' said Astrid confidently. 'But what about Harry Piles? You know he told Alice's line manager to calm down in a meeting and asked if she had her period or something. Surely you have to make sure he's out?'

Matthew yawned again.

'Obviously, the LL Group can't effectively condone sex-related discrimination in the workplace,' said Astrid, 'or ignore gross misconduct. Presumably it's more of a question of whether they've gone for individuals or used it to target at structural level, and whether that leaves it open to a counter.'

Golly, I'd forgotten how intimidating Astrid is when she gets into her legal stride.

'Luckily,' said Matthew, 'we're on it.'

'Are you sure?' said Astrid, doubtfully.

'Aren't you scared you'll cave and accidentally tell her?' I asked Matthew.

'No.'

'What about Guy Carmichael?' said Astrid.

'Alice's charming lover?' said Matthew lightly.

'Aha! That sounds like he's been fired!' said Astrid in delight.

'Guy's fate is down to Alice,' said Matthew.

'What?' I panicked. That didn't sound good.

'Well, presumably you've manifested the outcome already,' said Matthew.

Astrid laughed.

I didn't.

'It's not funny. These are people's lives were talking about.'

'Not really people,' said Astrid dismissively.

'Guy is a person and he's really worried—'

'Guy should be worried,' said Astrid. 'He's a disgrace. You're his employee. And he tried to manipulate you to get to Matthew. You could do better. And you should know better—'

'So should you,' I snapped. 'It's my life, my relationship and it's up to me who I sleep with. So Guy made a mistake or two. He's no more manipulative than you are, Astrid. Has it even occurred to you that I might care about him?'

'Has it ever occurred to you,' she said, looking over her coffee at me, 'that I might care about *you*, Alice?'

I was in my room folding clothes when there was a gentle knock on the half-open door.

'Not right now, Astrid,' I said.

'It isn't Astrid,' said a deep voice.

I whipped round and there he was, leaning against the door frame, arms folded, waiting. No wonder my heart was beating faster – it was probably just the shock. I wondered if he'd practised standing like that in front of the mirror: *hmm, what's the ideal pose to look sexy, insouciant, and yet patently powerful. Okay. Perfected.* Maybe Ebba helped him. I thought about trying to close the door on him, but in a fight, he'd definitely win against the door. I realised I was staring and turned away again.

'The email I received from your LL Group didn't explicitly state that we shouldn't meet in my bedroom, but I'm thinking it may not be *best* practice,' I said.

'Yeah. About all of this. I am sorry,' said Matthew.

I could hear he'd come further into the room. I waited for the sarcastic follow-up. 'And . . . ?'

'That's it,' said Matthew. 'I wanted to say I'm sorry. And whilst it's genuinely not up to me what happens to Guy Carmichael, I have heard what you've said.'

'What does that even mean? Hearing what I've said doesn't count for anything. Presumably, if I've said it, it actually works against me, given what you think of me.'

'What do I think of you?'

'Well, to quote from our recent conversation at your hotel, you think that I'm inherently selfish, that I only see half the world, that—'

'Yeah,' said Matthew. 'I did say that.'

'So you're not saying sorry for that?'

'I'm saying sorry for putting you in this position with your work and Guy,' said Matthew. 'And yes, I am sorry for what I said to you at the Lamb too.'

'But you still think it . . .'

'I think plenty of other things about you too, Alice,' he said, his voice low. 'Always have.'

I turned round again to face him, but his attention was caught elsewhere, staring ahead at the wall. I followed the trajectory of his gaze and realised he'd clocked my visioning board. I knew there was a reason I should have at least tried to shut the bedroom door on him. I quickly moved to get in between him and the board but I was too slow.

'That's private,' I said.

He ignored me and continued to examine the photos in silence. It was excruciating, waiting for comment. He'd have plenty to say about the photos of him, I reckoned. He'd assume I had a crush on him and that fucking annoying smile would emerge and nothing I said would remove it and—

'Jesus, that photo. . .' said Matthew, staring at the photo on the paddock where he isn't smiling. The one in the centre of my board.

'Yes?' I felt impatient, wanting to get the humiliation done with.

'I had no idea someone took it. Strange seeing it after all these years.'

Okay, well so far, no smug smile. If anything, he looked slightly discomposed.

'Yeah,' I said. 'It was a long time ago.'

'Probably the best summer I ever had,' said Matthew.

'What – the one we spent being completely shit bar staff at the Lamb?' I said, imagining he had confused it with a different summer.

Matthew shrugged.

'I guess you really liked the Lamb. Even then.'

'I guess so,' said Matthew, giving me a brief look.

He scrutinised the photo again. 'That was the night you and Ollie got together.'

'Yeah.'

I saw that muscle in Matthew's jaw twitch slightly. Surely, he still couldn't hold a grudge over that? He may not have thought I was good enough for his friend, but the fact we'd ended up staying together for such a long time said something. Besides, Ollie was happily married now and had a daughter – it was all water under the bridge.

'How long were you two together for?' he said.

'I don't know. Four, five years, on and off. So you were wrong.'

'Wrong about what?' Matthew looked puzzled.

'Me not being good enough for Ollie.'

'I never thought that.'

'Well, you told him he should go for Astrid instead of me, and if he went for me, you'd lose all respect for him.'

Matthew looked at me, appalled. I looked right back at him. It felt good to finally challenge him on it, after all these years. Well, if good means uncomfortably close to tears.

'Did Ollie tell you I said that?' he asked at last.

'I overheard you. At the party.'

'But the other week, you said you only overheard . . .'

'I lied. I overheard everything you said.'

'Everything?'

'Yes.' I remembered him saying that I gave everyone the eye. Remembered how it felt to hear him speak the way he did about me when I felt the way I did about him.

Matthew nodded. He looked at me and then looked away again. 'And what did you think?'

Well, that was a weird question. What I'd really thought was, *So, Alice. Evidently Matthew doesn't feel the same way you feel. It's never going to happen. You're never going to be happy.* But I couldn't say that. 'I guess I thought it's probably better I know how Matthew really feels,' I said. 'It explained a lot. And I was glad that Ollie went there anyway. He was my type.'

There was a pause.

'Yeah,' said Matthew. 'Ollie plainly knew what he was doing. He was your type. I can't blame him for that. And at least I had America.'

'Er, okay,' I said, not really following the train of thought.

'I shouldn't have interfered then,' said Matthew. 'And I shouldn't have interfered again, with Guy.'

'It's not quite the same.' Unless he's been slagging me off to Guy on a 'don't go there' WhatsApp group?

Matthew gave me a small smile. 'Well, you made it pretty apparent last time we saw each other that I should back off. And it turns out you had the whole picture all along. I think this time I finally got the message.'

He leant towards me, and for a fleeting second I smelled ocean and fires and home, and then his lips brushed briefly against my cheek.

'See you around, Alice,' he said.

And then he was gone, and it was just me and my visioning board.

In one word:

Confused

My thoughts and reflections:

The culling has started at work. It's like *The Hunger Games*. Everyone is furtive and on edge and the rumour mill is rife. And now that Matthew Lloyd is no longer distracting everyone with his beauty, people are seeing this for what it is: sudden death. Matthew was never going to be able to save them all. And we're scared. There are a lot of dark circles that no amount of Touch Éclat will fix, Yaz has got a break-out on her chin and I saw her eat a bag of Walkers, and Chloe has got a stress-stye. It's far-reaching – the fear: it's even got to Scotland. Charlotte posted a clip of herself, all shadowed, saying how as much as she loved social media, sometimes she felt a lot of pressure to impress others with her life. Right now she was dealing with a lot of uncertainty. She needed to focus on making sure she felt good enough, for herself, so she was taking a little break. I initially assumed it was just a stunt to get more traffic but she genuinely hasn't posted anything since then.

Every single time Outlook pings with an email, Cara visibly flinches and she's not the only one. We're all waiting for the invitation no one wants: the meeting with HR. So far, I've only directly witnessed one recipient of the firing process; Lazy Veronica who works – well, worked – in Production but often hot-desks up on our floor. She sat for an hour with her head in her hands and then stood up and walked out, leaving her coat and bag. Amelia from HR came and fetched them mid-afternoon and said Lazy Veronica was going home with a headache. She's not been back in. Yaz, who's friends with Amelia said that HR told Veronica she doesn't need to come in to the office before her proper meeting tomorrow. 'Oh my god,' I said. 'It's brutal, the way they string it out.'

Yaz says they have to. Apparently you get warned you're going to get fired and then in forty-eight hours you actually get fired. Sorry, *made redundant*. Guy's been in a foul mood and yet had the audacity to shout at poor Iris for being depressing.

My intention is:

- To start up some kind of GoFundMe for Lazy Veronica.
- To DM Charlotte just to say hi.

My thoughts and reflections:

I'm starting to realise just how serious things are between Aziz and Astrid: it comes to something when you look forward to getting to work for a potential firing because it's a break from the tension at home. I almost want to go back to last week when Astrid asked me whether Aziz had any plans for the weekend, even though he was in the room at the time. At least she still cared enough to be horrible. Now she's being polite, and Astrid isn't polite. She apologised yesterday for coming into the kitchen when Aziz was in there.

And, worst of all, Aziz isn't being himself. Aziz is the most patient, kind, calm person ever. But last night, when he was helping me with the modem because the internet didn't seem to be working again (you have to unplug it, and restart it, and re-enter the code which I keep forgetting), he suddenly threw the modem on the floor and stamped on it until it snapped.

'Er, Aziz, what are you doing?' I said. 'I don't think that's going to fix it!'

'That modem *keeps* going wrong, Alice,' said Aziz. 'I've tried everything with it. I've given it my best shot. I really have. Over and over again. Maybe it's time to accept it's broken. I don't want to waste another decade restarting the modem only to have it screw me over once more.'

In one word:

Heartbreaking

My thoughts and reflections:

I've not been fired. It's official. I got the email today saying that all colleagues affected by the merger rationalisations had now been notified and had met with HR, and that therefore anyone receiving this email should take this as confirmation that their existing contract with Carsons remained unaltered. Drunk Stephen's kept his job. Charlotte has too: she posted a picture of the sun coming through the clouds. Cara and Yaz and Cool Jason and Gentle Jadan and Karim and Nervous Jane have all kept their jobs too. Cara cried and we hugged her. I honestly don't know how Cara doesn't spend ninety per cent of her time crying.

I had a moment of abject panic though, when Guy flung open his office door and yelled across the entire floor, 'Alice Carver! A word, please. In my office. Now!'

I could feel Yaz's concerned gaze as I walked over to his office; all the blinds were down which was usually an ominous sign. But as soon as I was in there, Guy shut the door, pushed me up against it and gave me a hard kiss on the mouth.

'I'm safe,' said Guy. 'Well, for now anyway.'

'That is such good news!'

'Yes. But I've had to agree to undertake management

coaching. Plus sign some new piece of shit HR policy for managers in influential positions about disclosing any co-worker romantic or sexual relationships.' He shook his head.

'Right . . . But you've been clear this isn't a relationship, so you don't need to disclose anything!'

'You really are a good girl, Alice,' said Guy appreciatively. 'But depending on what they already know, if we have to go official, this could really fuck up my divorce.'

I tried not to let my face betray the jolt that gave me. Go official? He was talking about potentially making our relationship official?

'Still,' continued Guy. 'I've had a better deal than many of us.'

'Us?' I asked, only half paying attention.

'A lot of the old boys are gone. Brutal cut at senior level. James. Wilson. Harry . . .'

'Harry Piles?'

'Gone. Edward Puesdon. Archie Kavanagh. Gone.'

'Gosh.' Those were some big names. And big tossers. I was warned on my first day not to end up alone in a room with Edward Puesdon. How he's lasted this long is the real surprise. And Harry Piles . . . couldn't happen to a nicer person.

'Archie Kavanagh went to Oriel, Cambridge,' said Guy. 'He thought he was safe when he heard Matthew was a fellow graduate. I'm guessing Matthew Lloyd isn't a rugby player?'

'More into football,' I confirmed.

I ask the Universe:

- To help me out with the Guy relationship thing. I'm aware I manifested my getting married to Guy and obviously before that can happen we need to go official so that's super exciting, but I'm wondering if we can slow it down just slightly?

- Also please help Astrid and Aziz to be happy again – please do something, or show me what I can do to help . . .

My thoughts and reflections:

I'm moving in with Yaz. Even though she's like a prefect.

I saw her writing the advert, asked her, and she said, 'Why would you move when you get to lord it up in Chiswick?'

'My sister and her husband need space.'

'So they've asked you to move out?'

'No,' I said.

'Then . . . why?'

'So long as I'm there, Astrid's going to keep using me as a buffer to avoid having difficult conversations. And I don't know, I don't want to be responsible for her screwing up her life. She's my sister.'

'Look, Alice,' said Yaz, scratching her nose and wriggling slightly. 'I'm going to have to be honest with you.'

'Okay. ' I braced myself for what was about to come. No one ever tells you they're going to have to be honest and then says something good.

'It's a really shit house,' said Yaz. 'And not in a cool way.'

'Okay.'

'So, if you're thinking that my parents bought me a nice place and you're going to get some good deal, you'd be wrong.

They take me on nice holidays and out to dinner and stuff but they believe in making your own way.'

'It had never crossed my mind,' I lied.

'I live in,' she leant in closer so no one else could hear, 'Sidcup.'

'Isn't that Kent?' I asked.

'Pretty much.'

Fuck. 'How long does it take you to get into work?'

'Over an hour each way.'

Once she'd shown me photos and told me the rent, the whole thing was even more unappealing. I mean, it's shit. Totally shit. But I can afford it on my salary. Just.

Drunk Stephen told me I was mad.

'You're not going to be less posh just by living somewhere hideous, Alice,' he said. 'You're just going to be less happy. Don't do it.'

Astrid told me I was mad.

'You won't cope, Alice. And even with that amount of rent, you'll struggle. You know you still have to spend money on bills, and food, and loo roll, right? I don't think you realise what a good arrangement you've got here . . .'

Guy told me I was mad.

'Looks like a fucking halfway house,' he said.

'It does,' I agreed.

'Stay here more,' he said. 'I can probably get you a key card. Especially if we have to disclose to HR . . .'

*

I'm moving in with Yaz on Sunday.

I am grateful for:

- Yaz organising the rent agreement for me.
- The time I spent living in Astrid's beautiful house – it's been a dream come true. I will always, always be grateful that my first manifestation came into fruition on New Year's Day (even if I've paid in other ways).

My thoughts and reflections:

I've been living in Sidcup for one full week. It's actually perfectly pleasant. I don't have a Land Rover for anyone to steal, so that's an advantage. It has a restaurant that was shortlisted in the British Kebab Awards. And a reliable train connection to London Bridge. Don't, however, make the mistake of catching one of the supposedly late trains: if you miss the 23.35 you end up in a walking, busing, train-less nightmare.

Harry Piles' replacement from Montague Place turned out to be a friend of my ex Bloomsbury colleague Gabriella, and she is amazing. Genuinely inspirational. Kelly believes in growing people and creating opportunities and listens to what you say. And she thinks big too; she says that diverse publishing starts at ground level and that actions speak louder than words and that until we make visible the invisible nothing will change. She's already roped Drunk Stephen into giving a talk at a local secondary school about publishing and has loads more schools lined up. She's keen to start a scheme with City University where graduates can apply for a year in publishing as part of their course. Plus she wears limited-edition Adidas trainers so she's cool too.

I've made an appointment with Kelly for Thursday and

I've decided I'm going to do what Clare Atkins recommended – tell her some of my ideas and show that I'm interested in career progression – I'm literally going to manifest a better job.

I'm staying over with Guy tonight – haven't seen him since Friday when he again mentioned talking to HR about our 'relationship'. I'm going to suggest to him that we don't. Not yet. Don't get me wrong, I'm still into Guy and it would be amazing, in one way, to be dating him publicly. Amazing. Charlotte would be completely jealous. And I can think of a few other people too (Amelia and Anika) but also, it would change things. Yaz would watch what she said. And Cara, well, Cara wouldn't be super impressed. She was cross about the way Guy treated Charlotte. And whilst that's not my problem, I think it would be best for Guy to finalise his divorce before we declare an interest in each other. Plus it's not like we're going to hang out with my friends anyway, so what's the point in a way?

It's weird, but I didn't get a response from Matthew Lloyd after I emailed to say thank you about my job and Guy's. What's even weirder is that Mum says he's probably not coming for lunch on Sunday. Mum was upset. 'I kept the Chinese wall, Alice, so I know it's not my fault. And Matthew says it's nothing to do with that and he's got a lot of work but it's Easter! He should be here. When are you arriving?'

'Sunday morning.'

'I don't know why you're not coming for the whole weekend.'

'I told you, Mum. I've got plans.'

And I did. Me, Yaz, Drunk Stephen and Cara were going for spa treatments on Friday. And on Saturday, finally having heard back from him, I was meeting Ollie for morning coffee.

I am letting go of:

The past – it's a different country. Now I live in Sidcup.

My thoughts and reflections:

I met Ollie at Sam's Café in Primrose Hill and it was gorgeous with its painted tables and vases of fresh daffodils and windows overlooking the pastel front doors and roomy streets. It was one of those unseasonably warm spring days where the world feels suddenly transformed. Ollie looked pretty much the same, though, if a little grey and slightly softer around the edges. He showed me photos of his daughter, who was adorable – a mass of curls and a suspicious expression – and told me the latest honour his wife had been nominated for. And I filled him in about Astrid and Arrie, and, being Ollie, he didn't harangue me about whether I was married or had children. Eventually, however, he did say, 'So what's prompted this, Alice?'

'Matthew,' I said.

'Ah,' said Ollie. 'How is he?'

'Good. Successful.'

'Yeah,' said Ollie. 'I follow him. He always said he was going to earn more, by himself, than any of the rest of us stood to inherit, and I believed him. But it's sort of crazy how well he's done.'

'Yeah. I know. So you're not in touch directly at all?'

Ollie shook his head.

'Since when?' I asked.

'Last time I saw him was probably shortly after you and I split up.'

'You haven't seen him for over a decade?'

Ollie shook his head again.

'That's such a shame,' I said.

'Hmm,' said Ollie. 'You've changed your tune since we were together.'

'I know he wasn't my favourite person at the time . . .' (After that night when I'd overheard Matthew warning Ollie off me and all the other things he'd said, I'd covered up the humiliation and hurt of rejection by going all out in slating Matthew every opportunity I got.)

'That's an understatement,' said Ollie.

'And I do realise that made it hard for you to hang out with him whilst I was around.' Ironically, despite claiming Matthew was the last person I wanted to see, I was always hoping I'd bump into him when I visited Ollie. 'But you and Matthew used to be so close that I assumed once I was out of the picture, even if you didn't pick up where you left off, you'd certainly pick up again.'

'I assumed the same thing.'

'So how come you haven't?'

'I tried. About four years ago when Taylor was pregnant,' said Ollie. 'He totally shut it down. That is one grudge he's not going to let go.'

We sipped coffee amid the hum of neighbouring conversations. I felt like I should ask him about Taylor, and work: move onto safer territory and let the past stay in the past.

But I couldn't. I couldn't stop thinking about Matthew. Fair enough that he felt that Ollie could have done better than me, and I could even understand if it bothered him enough not to hang out with Ollie for the duration of our relationship, but why would Matthew throw away his friendship with Ollie beyond that? Especially now Ollie had visibly learnt his lesson and was with Taylor, who must be a great choice of partner in Matthew's eyes – she runs a bloody charity. No way he could accuse her of being spoilt and selfish.

'It doesn't even make sense,' I said at last. 'I mean what is he even holding a grudge about now? How can he have a problem with Taylor?'

'He doesn't have a problem with Taylor,' said Ollie. 'It's because of you.'

'I wish he'd just get over it.'

'You're a hard woman to get over, Alice.'

'Sorry?' I said.

'And it's not easy when your best mate screws you over,' said Ollie.

'Say what?'

I looked at Ollie in confusion. He stared back, similarly confused.

'You know Matthew had a thing about you when we got together?' he said. 'So—'

'Matthew?' The sounds of the café disappeared. 'He didn't have a thing about me! He told you not to go there and that he'd lose all respect for you if you did.'

'Ye-es,' said Ollie slowly, like I was being obtuse. 'Not to go there because he liked you.'

'Matthew did?'

'Yes.'

'Sorry, are we talking about the same person? Matthew Lloyd?'

'Matthew Lloyd liked you,' said Ollie. 'A lot. And he asked me to leave you alone.'

'Seriously?'

'Yeah. But I liked you too. So I went there anyway.'

'Oh my god,' I said, falling through empty space, running it over in my mind. 'That night we got together, Matthew was warning you off? Because . . . he . . . liked . . . me?'

'Yeah. I didn't listen though. I assumed he'd get over it. Bros before hos, and all that. I was seriously mistaken.'

'Why didn't you tell me?'

'Tell you what?' said Ollie.

'How Matthew felt about me?'

'It was pretty obvious.'

'Not to me,' I said.

'I thought you knew.' Ollie shrugged. 'And it seemed like you didn't feel the same way about him. You kept going on about how I was your type – Eton boy, rugby bod, play before work, likes to party, etc.'

I momentarily shut my eyes. The irony. The efforts I expended to conceal how I felt . . .

Ollie looked slightly perturbed by my undoubtedly weird reaction. 'I was hardly going to try and get you two together, was I?' he said reasonably. 'And it's not like Matthew needed my help – he's never been short of offers.'

'Yeah, sure.' I tried to process. I felt a little bit sick. My hand shook embarrassingly as I lifted up my beautiful, pointlessly beautiful, green enamel mug.

Ollie shifted his chair back. 'Look, Alice, I've got to go and meet my girls at the park. You can come if you want?'

'Maybe another time.'

'It's not my place to say this,' said Ollie, standing up and pushing his chair under the table. 'And I don't know whether either of you is even single. But if he's still this bothered, and if you are as bothered as you seem to be, that's kind of amazing. And maybe you need to do something about it . . .'

All I could think about was the White Rabbit in *Alice's Adventures in Wonderland* saying, ' Oh dear! Oh dear! I shall be too late! . . .'

In one word:

Blindsided

My thoughts and reflections:

Mum was rearranging one of the multiple posies of primroses, forget-me-nots and grape hyacinths dotted around the house. 'I'm just saying it's not like Alice to turn down chocolate on Easter Sunday.' Mum sounded offended, as though I'd just rejected her and Easter itself rather than a mini egg.

'And she didn't want my bacon either,' said Dad, drying his hands on the red-and-white checked tea towel whilst the kettle whistled boisterously and the pips on Radio 4 signalled the hour. 'I think the stress of the merger got to her, Nell. I really do.'

'I'm fine,' I repeated, fiddling with a forget-me-not. 'Honestly. Just excited. About Easter.'

'Yes, and normally that's because you're excited about chocolate,' Mum said, pulling the vase away, and sliding the basket of mini eggs across the table towards me.

'And bacon,' added Dad, sadly.

Edwin came running into the kitchen, red-cheeked and asking for water, and Arrie sighed with irritation. 'Roger, get him water.'

Roger stood up and dropped his newspaper on the floor. 'Totally incompetent,' Arrie muttered, watching him with undisguised disgust. 'I told you to stay in the garden, Edwin,' continued Arrie. 'You'd better not be after more chocolate. You've got the manic look in your eye of someone who's already exceeded their fair share.'

'He's just excited,' I said, palming him extra chocolate as agreed. 'Like his aunty.' The twins never did tell their mum about *Jurassic Park* and I like to think we've reached a position of mutual respect.

'Out!' Arrie took his empty glass and shooed her progeny away.

I checked my watch again. Any minute now, Matthew would be here. I texted him yesterday to ask if we could talk. And, despite having spent near enough every minute since then planning what I'm going to say, I am still unprepared. I don't think I've ever felt so unhungry in my life. I zoned in and out of Arrie's conversation with Mum and Dad. They were talking about Astrid and Aziz and what the announcement could be. Dad was lugubrious and trying to prepare himself for bad news. He was midway through a four-part special on Radio 4: *Grounds for Divorce*.

'The sad fact is,' he said, 'forty-two per cent of marriages in the UK end in divorce, and seven years is particularly high risk. The odds are stacked against them. Add to that the other life changes and you're looking at a cataclysm.'

'Astrid and Aziz are fine,' snapped Arrie. 'Their life is a bloody picnic. They don't even have kids. Let's face it, that's the real problem. For fuck's sake, Roger, could you sniff any louder?'

Roger looked affronted. 'It's all the flowers. They're every-where.'

'Allergic to spring,' said Arrie. 'That's what I've married . . .'

And then the doorbell went.

'I'll get it,' I said in a shrill voice, jumping up, and dashing out the kitchen.

I could hear vague snippets of my family's concern, 'very odd' from Dad, 'I didn't think she understood what a doorbell was' from Mum, and 'she's done full make-up and got dressed and it's not even noon' from Arrie, but I wasn't really listening. I was on a mission. All I could think about was the person waiting for me on the other side of the front door. Matthew. Matthew. Matthew.

I took a second to prepare myself in the hallway; I don't know if I'd ever felt this nervous before. It was even worse than the time I realised Belinda Howard had overheard me bragging that I'd shagged her stepdad.

'Please,' I asked the Universe. 'Help me.'

I took a deep breath and opened the door.

'Take your time, why don't you?' said Astrid, hopping from one foot to the other, then pushing past me rudely and rushing into the house.

'She's needed the loo since the flyover,' said Aziz by way of apology, and giving me a quick squeeze hello.

*

'But what about the house?' said Mum. 'How will you pay the mortgage? And you won't have jobs to come home to!'

'My partners are classing it as a sabbatical,' said Astrid, looking a little embarrassed. 'And being very generous in

428

terms of extending my salary. So the mortgage will tick over. I've told them not to but . . .'

'They don't want to lose her,' said Aziz.

'And Aziz is just taking one month's extra leave on top of the crazy long summer holiday he gets, plus he can do some remote teaching and therapy.'

'Advantages to working at a university,' agreed Aziz. 'And being a therapist.'

'Besides, it's only four months,' said Astrid.

'For now,' added Aziz.

I watched as Astrid reached across for Aziz's hand, their fingers entwining whilst they both glanced at Mum and Dad.

'Well, I think it's fantastic.' Dad wiped a tear from his eye. 'What a marvellous thing to do.'

'Are you serious?' said Arrie. 'It's fucking mental.'

'I'm a bit uncomfortable with using "mental" pejoratively, Arrie,' said Aziz.

'Well said, Aziz,' said Dad, reaching across for Aziz's other hand.

'Oh come on,' said Arrie. 'Mum, you'll back me up? I mean it's one thing having a mid-life crisis because you've got a big birthday coming up . . .'

'And quite another to go travelling,' agreed Mum. 'To Indonesia of all places. God, darling, haven't you seen *Bangkok Hilton*?'

'Wrong country,' said Astrid.

'But she makes a bloody good point, Astrid,' said Arrie. 'Tell her, Roger.'

'I loved Nicole Kidman in that,' said Roger. 'Pre the surgery. And I've always wanted to go to Bali.'

'Fucking useless,' said Arrie.

'They'll do bottom searches,' said Mum, 'mark my words. And they love the death penalty.'

'I think we'll be okay,' said Astrid, meeting Aziz's eye and smiling.

'It's so nice to see you two happy again,' I said. 'You'll love Bali. When are you off, Astrid?'

'Thirtieth of June.'

Mum looked panicked at the imminent reality and tried again. 'Look, wouldn't it be more sensible to have a couple of weeks in Spain, maybe even three?'

'Not the same,' said Astrid.

'What about Verbier? Weren't you planning a holiday there?'

'We were. But we're not now. We're doing this.'

'So presumably you'll forget this whole medicine thing at least?' said Mum.

'I'm not sure,' said Astrid. 'Maybe I was a bit hasty looking to change my career. Maybe I just need a break. I guess I'll, we'll, reassess when I get home.'

Mum elbowed Dad. 'Aren't you worried Astrid's going to destroy everything she's worked so hard for?'

Aziz stroked the back of Astrid's hand with his thumb.

'She's not destroying anything, Nell,' said Aziz. 'She's exploring her options.'

'Quite right,' agreed Dad. 'You only get one life.'

'Bollocks,' said Arrie. 'You explore your options when you're nineteen. And Bali! It's bad enough that Alice thought it was acceptable to have gap years into her twenties but you're forty next birthday, Astrid! Who has a gap year at forty?'

'Us,' said Aziz, calmly. 'And strictly speaking, it's a gap

four months. At the moment, our return flights are booked for 30 November.'

'Maybe Alice had the right idea all along,' said Astrid. 'She made the most of her twenties. I spent my time working. And then my thirties doing the same. And what's it all for? All the seventy-hour weeks, all the earning, all the stress. Do I just barrel on up the ladder until I retire?'

Arrie rolled her eyes. 'Yes!'

'I'm serious,' Astrid insisted. 'I've been so busy trying to succeed that I've never really had that time. For me.'

'Yes, darling, and that's why you're successful. I mean, look at Alice.' Mum inclined her head.

Everyone looked at me.

'What can I say?' said Mum. 'I remember the day the head of St Hilda's told me that Alice had the lowest maths score she'd ever seen in a child, but that with hard work anything was possible. Then she told me that Alice was also the laziest child she'd ever encountered. So obviously, given that, we're proud of anything you've achieved, darling Alice.'

'So proud,' murmured Dad.

'But honestly, Astrid,' continued Mum. 'Don't start thinking Alice had the right idea. Just look at her.'

'She looks all right to me,' said a deep voice from the kitchen door.

'Matthew!' Mum and I responded simultaneously.

I swivelled round, and for a second our gazes collided, and it may have been an aneurism or it may have been the after-effects of last night's chilli, but the force of seeing Matthew Lloyd, really seeing him, did something irrevocable to me.

'What a wonderful surprise!' interrupted Mum.

'The front door was wide open,' said Matthew, 'do you want it open, Nell?'

'Oh dear,' said Mum, 'it's that latch. No.'

'I'll shut it,' said Matthew, leaving.

'No, no, I'll shut it,' I said, jumping up, and following him out. 'It was my fault.'

'Coffee?' shouted Mum to Matthew.

'Yes please,' called back Matthew.

And then Edwin and Ernie ran past us, slamming the kitchen door shut behind them and suddenly it was just me and Matthew, alone in the hallway.

He closed the front door, securing the latch and then started walking back towards the kitchen.

'Matthew!' I stopped him in his tracks. 'I was hoping we could talk?'

'I know,' he said easily. 'I got your messages. Shall we go in the kitchen?'

'Um, can we go in the sitting room actually? It's kind of private.'

'Sure . . .' He sounded uncertain.

We walked through to the sitting room in silence and sat down on the faded sofas facing each other, the April sun forming windows of pure light on the rugs. The clock ticked softly. I stood up and went to shut the door, and then sat back down again.

He looked at me, his eyes unreadable. I waited for him to smile. He didn't. He just waited and suddenly I didn't know if I could do this.

'So,' he said. 'What's up, Alice? Work?'

'No, not work.' I swallowed nervously. My palms were

clammy, my stomach gurgled, and I was genuinely concerned I might be about to shit myself. I would never ever want to do a job interview with Matthew Lloyd.

'Some time today would help,' he said.

'I saw Ollie,' I began, and then faltered.

'Right,' said Matthew, slightly impatiently. 'And you're telling me this because?'

'I saw Ollie,' I tried again, 'because I wanted to find out why you two were no longer friends. And because I kept thinking about what you said in my room, about that night the photo was taken, when Ollie and I got together. You asked me if I overheard everything. And I said I did. But it turns out I didn't.'

'I don't think there's much point raking over this, Alice,' said Matthew, sighing.

'But there is. There really is.'

I took a deep breath and hoped my voice wouldn't crack. 'The thing is, I only heard you tell Ollie that I wasn't worth it and not to go for me and that if he did you'd lose all respect for him. So I assumed that was the way you felt about me: that I wasn't worth anything and that I wasn't good enough for your best mate. That's what I've thought for well over a decade.'

Matthew didn't say a word.

'And yesterday,' I continued, 'Ollie told me that you didn't think that. And I never knew, Matthew.'

There was a silence.

'Okay,' said Matthew. 'Well, thanks for sharing that.'

He sounded pissed off. This wasn't going how I'd hoped.

I tried again. I'm trying to say that I had no idea. Otherwise—'

'Otherwise what? You wouldn't have got with Ollie?'

'You're not getting it,' I said, my voice rising. 'I thought you didn't like me.'

'I am getting it,' he said. 'And my point is, what difference would it have made? Your interests lay elsewhere.'

'My interest lay entirely with you,' I said. 'I was coming over that night to tell you how I felt about you. That I really liked you.'

I could barely breathe, waiting. Days, weeks, years passed. Someone knocked at the front door. Then knocked again. Did they have no idea that a life-changing conversation was happening in here?

Finally, Matthew spoke. 'But then you got with Ollie. As I said, your interests lay elsewhere.'

'What?! I told you I only did that because I heard you say you didn't want me!'

Matthew looked at me and then shook his head. 'And you'd have been interested in someone like me beyond a summer fling? I don't think so.'

'What is that even supposed to mean? Someone like you?'

'You'd always have ended up with an Ollie, Alice. Ollie, Monty, Guy – that's your type. Someone who can afford to have fun and not take work seriously. Someone from the right family going the right places. Like you said.'

'That's unfair. And you're deliberately choosing not to hear what I'm saying.' I could feel my eyes stinging. This conversation was not going the way I'd imagined it would. I looked down at the ground and tried to compose myself. I could hear the front door opening and muffled voices in the hallway.

'Well, what does it matter now?' Matthew stood up. 'It's

in the past. It took me a long time, but we've both moved on.' He started walking away, but I grabbed his hand.

'Matthew,' I said, and my voice sounded weird. The White Rabbit from *Alice's Adventures in Wonderland* saying *Oh dear! Oh dear! I shall be too late!* kept repeating in my head, mocking me. Please don't let me be too late.

We both looked down at our hands. I didn't let go.

I cleared my throat. 'But what if I haven't moved on?'

The sitting room door handle turned and Matthew pulled his hand away just as Mum came in.

'There you are!' she said. 'Hiding away from the rest of us. Your coffee's getting cold. And Ebba's arrived.'

'Hey, darling,' said Ebba, peeking round the doorway.

'Hey,' said Matthew, smiling at her.

'Are you staying for lunch, Ebba?' asked Mum.

'Of course,' said Ebba, 'if you're happy.'

'Well, this is marvellous,' said Mum. 'Matthew's never brought a girlfriend for Easter before.'

I waited for Matthew to say, 'Ebba's not my girlfriend.'

But he didn't.

And then Ebba said, 'Ah, that's sweet,' and walked over to Matthew (it only took two strides because of her modelly long legs) and used her modelly hands to pull his face towards hers, and then she kissed him. Full on the mouth. Lingeringly. She even slightly bit his bottom lip at the end.

My insides churned.

I was too late.

'Excuse me,' I said, pushing past them.

Easter lunch was the worst I've ever endured. And that includes the one where Mum cooked Easter Soups from Around the World and we had to struggle through her borscht and fanesca. But this one was torturous. Ebba sat unnecessarily close to Matthew and every time I saw her hand resting possessively on his thigh, my hands itched to slap them off, the way Arrie did Ernie's when he tried to help himself to pudding. My stomach was a complete mess, fizzing, gurgling and wriggling like I'd eaten a bag of snakes.

Dad was making a fuss about the fact I wasn't eating much, and as I could hardly give the real reason why, I had to blame it on the chilli and then that reminded Dad of the time I had food poisoning on the ferry over to France and he decided to regale everyone with that tale. I know Matthew had heard the story before, but I was raw, and sitting through Dad saying how Astrid had to buy me new trousers in the duty free shop but the only thing she could find were swimming trunks and everyone finding it all quite hilarious, was not fun.

'You must have smelled as bad as Jesus, Aunty Alice,' said Ernie, impressed.

'Yes,' agreed Edwin. 'We learnt all about how Jesus farted for forty days in the wilderness.'

Ebba looked at Matthew in confusion.

'It's the English public school system,' said Matthew.

Then Astrid asked if I was still seeing Guy, and Arrie interjected and said, 'Is that the old one with the hairy back? Married?'

And Astrid said, 'Oh yes.'

'He doesn't have a hairy back,' I said, quietly.

And Arrie ignored me and shuddered and said, 'God. I bet his ball hair is horrific.'

'Ah,' said Dad, 'now there was a fascinating programme about this on Channel 4 the other night, *Extreme Groomers*; I learnt so much. These young people, Nell, take it all off. All of it. We're talking every bit. Right to the anus.'

Roger coughed on his parsnips.

'Jesus, Dad,' I said.

'Surely they must end up cutting themselves? And the angles?' continued Dad. 'Think of the angles?'

'Ask Alice,' said Astrid, her eyes gleaming. 'I'm sure she manages the angles. Didn't you say Guy liked his women clean-shaven?'

'Ghastly idea,' said Mum. 'Why, Alice?'

'Do you really take it off . . . everywhere . . . Alice?' said Roger, sounding a bit strangled.

'Shut up, Roger,' said Arrie. 'This doesn't concern you.'

If I hadn't already lost Matthew, maybe this would have felt fractionally more painful knowing I'd certainly lost him now, but it's hard to imagine how it could have felt worse. I closed my eyes momentarily and tried to think about kittens and snowdrops and sunlight.

'Your mother has always had a substantial amount of pubic hair,' said Dad, 'and I'm a big fan.'

437

No. It wasn't working. Just humiliation followed by a whole series of awful mental images.

'I'm very lucky to still have it,' said Mum. 'At my age.'

'Oh yes,' said Dad. 'They had a whole thing about post-menopausal pubic hair loss on *Woman's Hour* just last week.'

'Nice,' said Astrid. 'Clearly Guy Carmichael is essentially turned on by females at both ends of the age range.'

'So, who is this Guy Carmichael?' asked Ebba.

'Alice's boss,' said Arrie.

'Alice's lover,' said Astrid.

'And you've met him?' she asked Matthew.

Matthew nodded and we caught each other's eye before Ebba's fingertips on his thigh distracted him.

'I am looking forward to meeting him at this christening next month,' said Ebba.

Mum clapped her hands. 'Oh Alice, are you bringing some-one? Is this Guy a boyfriend?'

'Very much not a boy,' said Astrid acidly.

Mum ignored her. 'Imagine it. Matthew with Ebba, Alice with Guy – all of you happy and settled. That would really show Barbara Cavendish with her ridiculously over-named grandson.'

'And that's what it's all about,' said Aziz, making Astrid laugh.

'Matthew, you're almost as quiet as Alice today,' said Dad. 'What do you think of Alice's boyfriend? We've not had the pleasure yet!'

That's the amazing thing about my family. You think things can't possibly deteriorate further. And yet they do.

'I think he's exactly Alice's type,' said Matthew. 'In fact, I wouldn't be surprised if she manifested him.'

I ask the Universe:

Why?

Guide Post™

Are you feeling frustrated with the manifestation process, or sensing a resistance to getting where you want to be? If so, that's the Universe telling you to stop trying to control, to take a step back and let her lead.

Sometimes we can get so caught up in our own plans, controlling and specifying what we want that we forget the most important thing of all: **the Universe has her own plans.** *Of course, the Universe will help you to manifest what you think you want, but please remember that sometimes,* **the Universe knows better than you do what is best for you and what you** truly **want.**

Try this manifestation:

I surrender myself to the greater power of the Universe. I am ready to receive all that she gives.

My thoughts and reflections:

I know I haven't written in here for a while but, I haven't really felt like it. Honestly, I've felt like complete shit. The high of realising how Matthew felt about me once, followed by the crushing reality of how he feels about me now is like watching the dream house you've just bought disappearing into a sink hole.

Oh yeah. Dream houses. That reminds me of another manifesting failure on my part. Our old family house. On a whim, I called up the agent – I don't know why because obviously I was never going to manifest our old home but a small, desperate guttering flame of hope in me associates it with Matthew and clearly the Universe hadn't already battered me enough yet. So I called up and enquired and was told that the house was under offer and due to exchange shortly.

It felt even harder when I realised that the usual distractions no longer cut it . . . Guy told me he'd decided I could come away with him this weekend to Rutland and said we would take his daughter to lunch. Together. I didn't even know he had a daughter, probably because he hadn't mentioned it. I asked how old she was, imagining a cute little girl, and he said she was eighteen. 'Eighteen?!' I repeated.

'Yes,' he said shortly. 'We had a gap between them.'

'You've got two children?'

'Victoria's hardly a child – she's twenty-five.'

My gasp may have been audible. I've never been the best at maths but suddenly the age gap between us felt quite relevant.

'I don't know,' I said. 'It sounds like a big step. Are you sure?'

Guy stared at me, shrewdly. 'Well, Alice, judging by your reaction, it seems more like a case of are *you* sure?'

I stared back at Guy, hoping it would trigger some kind of emotional release from Matthew, put the genie back in the bottle, make me recognise what I had right here in front of me. Guy Carmichael. My perfect man, exactly as I'd manifested. Pretty much offering me a part in his life – the chance to meet his daughter.

It didn't work.

Instead, it made me realise that things needed to come to a conclusion with Guy, even if it meant me losing my job.

He was understandably pissed off when I said so to him. 'I don't get it, Alice. I thought this was what you wanted.'

'As did I.'

'Unbelievable,' said Guy, shaking his head. 'Most girls bloody go on and on about wanting more from me.'

'I know. I'm so sorry.'

Then the worst bit was when Guy changed tack and told me that we were good together and had I really thought this through. 'I like you, Alice. Beyond the sex. You understand me. This works.' He looked almost deflated and it didn't suit him. Guy's most sexy when he's inflated.

'I like you too,' I said. 'But I'm not sure you understand me or that it would keep working. What if I wanted kids myself?'

'Do you?'

'No. But I might. In the future.'

'You wouldn't,' said Guy. 'Certainly not after you'd met mine.'

'But what if I did? Would you want that?'

Guy looked irritated.

'Exactly,' I said. 'You like things how they are now. But I'm not sure we'd work in real life. If I'm completely honest with you, I didn't actually like the mouthfeel of that wine last night.'

Guy told me that he'd be more careful about sharing his Château Margaux 2010 in future, that all women were a fucking nightmare, and that I'd messed up his plans for the weekend.

I said sorry and that I felt bad.

He said, 'As you should. Sucking my dick might help you to feel better about yourself.'

I told him to fuck off.

And he said, 'No, I think you need to fuck off.'

It was unclear all round whether either of us was being humorous; he's not a big smiler at the best of times.

I guess I'll be off to Scotland to join Charlotte next week . . .

My intention is:

To 'surrender' myself and accept that the Universe knows better than me what I really want. (But it does all sound remarkably similar to the argument Mum used to justify buying Arrie those NHS prescription glasses that Christmas.)

My thoughts and reflections:

So, I've had a pretty significant day today; the kind of day that prompts you to write and record (even if you're not actually manifesting) and acknowledge that maybe it's not the worst idea to surrender to the Universe . . .

I met with Kelly (Harry Piles' replacement) last week and shared some of my ideas with her. She was super-excited about my 'Break Into and Break Out Of' non-fiction pitch for a fast, responsive, trend-driven series giving teens insider / expert information and tips about how to break into things like publishing, TV, football, exam success, dating, etc., and how to break out of things like toxic relationships, negative thoughts. I showed her trending clips on TikTok and the market research I'd done and the potential for us to create social media content and package existing content. So excited that she called in Drunk Stephen and started talking about design straight away and if he thought this was the type of project he could add value to. And obviously he did, because I'd already bored him senseless with it and he'd not only helped me (in fact, he kind of inspired the idea in the first place with the Break Into Publishing talk he did at the local secondary school) but got pretty enthusiastic himself. So she set me and Stephen the task of putting everything together, in a wish-list sort of way, and to think big. Which we did. We consumed a lot of margaritas along the way but we came up with a fucking solid plan even if I do say so myself.

Anyway, today, Drunk Stephen and I were invited to a meeting with Kelly and Guy to catch up. Drunk Stephen thought it was hilarious. 'What if you forget yourself and accidentally fellate Guy?' he said.

'Ha,' I said. 'So funny. I think you should be more scared that he's found out you know about us and is going to send me – and you – to Scotland.'

It was, of course, as awkward as you'd expect it to be. Guy was polite and formal with me (because he's still a bit annoyed that I wasn't more grateful for his offer to keep shagging him and also have lunch with his adult child), and I was so careful to give the impression that Guy was only a scary boss to me that I practically called him guvnor and curtsied. However, then Kelly said, 'Guy and I have some news we'd like to share with you. Cara is leaving.'

'What?' I said, genuinely taken aback.

'It won't be until the summer,' continued Kelly, 'but she's very kindly let us know now so we can think about succession planning. In fact Cara has been instrumental in the succession planning.'

'But, why?' She'd been so worried about losing her job during the merger. Plus, I'd become quite good friends with Cara and she hadn't mentioned leaving to me.

'It's the right time for Cara. Now her mother is doing so well in the care home, Cara's planning to rent out her house, and take the gap year she never had.'

'Oh.' It made sense now, all the questions about Astrid and her gap year. 'Good on Cara.'

'Fucking ridiculous,' said Guy Carmichael.

'So she's coming back after a year?' said Drunk Stephen.

'Well no,' said Kelly.

'And we offered to keep her job open,' said Guy.

'Cara's moving in a different direction,' said Kelly. 'I think she'll do superbly. The point is, we find ourselves with a vacancy. A senior role.'

'Okay . . .' said Drunk Stephen, looking over at me uncertainly.

'We've decided not to seek a replacement for Cara,' said Kelly. 'Instead, Cara, Guy and I have spent quite some discussing and planning, and we're all agreed that the best way forward is to grow what we have here. Including the design department, which we need to bolster if we're going to create the kind of rapid publishing ideas you're coming up with, which Guy and I genuinely believe could be transformative for the overall P&L.'

'That's where you two come in,' said Guy. 'Providing you don't piss off on gap years.'

'We'd like to create two new flexible roles,' said Kelly. 'Editorial Director and Art Director, and we'd like you both to take these. You'll each have responsibility for a small, discrete team, probably only of one or two to start with, but that can grow. You will work together to ensure continuity and effectiveness and to lead a brand-new imprint. You can come up with the name and logo – I'm sure you'll create something amazing.'

'You want us to be . . . directors?' said Drunk Stephen. 'With our own list?'

'We do,' said Kelly. 'Guy is keen to expand and I'm going

to have a lot on so I'd quite like to hand this fast, responsive, TikTok-style imprint over to you. You've both raised your heads above the parapet and we think you can do this.'

'Um. What about Yaz?' I asked.

'Don't worry,' said Kelly, 'she's being promoted too. But she'll stay in the main non-fiction team – you guys will have your own stream.'

'There'd be more money of course,' said Guy.

'It's a once-in-a-career opportunity,' said Kelly.

'You're drooling, Alice,' said Guy.

'Sorry,' I said. 'You're going to promote us?'

'Yes,' said Guy. 'If you're not having a stroke.'

'Can I just check,' said Drunk Stephen, 'is the job based here, in London?'

'Where else would it fucking be?' said Guy. 'Of course it's here.'

I am letting go of:

Feeling bad for Cara. She looks like a weight has been lifted. She's told me that so long as her flat stays rented out, it not only pays for the mortgage, but the nursing home and the letting agency fee. Plus Carsons are paying her notice period and letting her leave next week. She said this is the first time she's had the freedom to do this because she knows her mum is being cared for properly, and is healthy enough to safely leave. 'If I don't do it now, Alice,' she said, 'I never will. As Mum gets older it will only be harder to leave her.' She said she's been inspired by hearing about my sister, that manifesting is about the here and now, and she wouldn't be surprised if gap years for women in their forties take off. And when she comes back, she's going to become an agent. She's decided she wants to grow and invest in individuals, and manifest success for people. I told her I think she'll be brilliant. Look at all she's done for me.

My thoughts and reflections:

It's six weeks today since I last saw Matthew. You'd think it would get easier. I'm not sure it has.

Even Astrid has noticed something's up but she assumes it's because I'm missing Cara at work, and because Guy and I have broken up; I'm not going to disabuse her of that. She keeps asking me over for supper, and I keep finding excuses; I don't think I can risk sitting through another meal with Matthew and Ebba. I've pretty much given up social media (apart from the TikTok content for teens) because coming across photos of them together feels about as pleasant as norovirus and recovery is slow.

The only person I've confessed all to is Drunk Stephen – I have to if we're working together – and he was surprisingly kind about it, even the fact I didn't tell him about Matthew Lloyd and the merger. He just made me tell him everything, right from the beginning, and hugged me and said, *Knowing you've missed out on Matthew Lloyd must be like realising you've given away your winning lottery ticket*. And that on reflection, Matthew Lloyd should really have stretched to a shirt and tie when he was working here, and even if you did look that indecently good in a T-shirt, there was such a thing as an iron. The fact that that was Drunk Stephen's best effort to be bitchy says a lot.

The worst thing is Ebba went to some film premiere a couple of weeks back and Matthew accompanied her and their photos are everywhere, and everyone at work has been poring over them and commenting and talking about how gorgeous he is and how weird it was that he was working on the nineteenth floor and how of course he'd be with a model like Ebba. The media picked up on Matthew's background and how he's self-made, so everyone's even more in love. And it snowballed further when the media got hold of a recent Turner prize short-lister who credited their success to Matthew's art foundation charity for disadvantaged youth. The other day, in our team meeting, Yaz suggested that we use Matthew Lloyd for our Break Into series. That was a particularly low moment.

Drunk Stephen has tried to protect me from the worst of it, or compensate for it with margaritas, but we can't drink quite as much tequila now we're running an imprint – there's too much to do.

At least Charlotte's back from Scotland now, and it seems like it all turned out well for her, so I can stop feeling guilty. She not only got everyone on board with the third-party distribution and increased overall productivity in the warehouse by fifteen per cent, but was behind Forklift Stewart winning the Forklift Championship finals in Canada, which resulted in loads of publicity and cash prizes. Plus, bizarrely, she's started dating Sweater-vest Gareth from Accounts; whilst she was in Scotland, there was a lot of emailing between them about distribution finances, and one thing led to another. According to Drunk Stephen, Charlotte's constantly posting clips of them doing couples trapeze skill classes. Apparently Gareth's arms have really filled out.

I am grateful for:

- The fact there are still four weeks to go until the christening back home. Something might still happen in the meantime to save me from it.
- All the positives. Like being alive. Etc.

Date: Tuesday 13 June   **Time: 8.15pm**

My thoughts and reflections:

Last night's Margarita Monday was devoted to Matthew Lloyd and the issue of the christening. Have also told Yaz now because she was getting concerned about my misery. Yaz and Drunk Stephen decided it was too much for me to see Matthew Lloyd and Ebba, especially in that context, and helped me compose apologetic email to Tristan and Penelope saying that something had cropped up at work and I would now be unable to join them.

I should feel relieved . . .

My intention is:

To send Cara an email letting her know her mum was doing really well when I visited on Sunday.

Date: Wednesday 14 June   **Time: 6.00pm**

My thoughts and reflections:

Have spent the day fielding messages and calls from Mum and Arrie.

> Arrie: WTF? You can't cancel last minute. It's not a pot luck, it's a christening, Alice.

> Mum: Darling, have just had horrific run-in with Barbara Cavendish in the co-op and she says you're pulling out of the christening for work! Absolutely not, Alice. You'll ruin her seating plan. Penelope's your old school-friend. Also I've told everyone you're bringing someone?

> Arrie: If you're coming for Astrid and Aziz's leaving party the very next day it looks even ruder.

I'd completely forgotten about that leaving party. Fuck . . .

> Me: I may not be able to make that either, unfortunately.

> Arrie: Don't be so bloody selfish, Alice.

Mum: You are not missing your own sister's farewell do, Alice Carver. Think of how Astrid will feel. Not an option.

'So, you have to see Matthew Lloyd either way?' checked Drunk Stephen.

'Pretty much. If I want to keep my family.'

'Well then,' said Drunk Stephen, 'the only thing I can suggest is that you do both events in style, and that I come with you.'

I am letting go of:

The fact that Drunk Stephen looked at me and said ten days wasn't a lot to work with.

Guide Post™

Sometimes, the hardest gift of all to accept is defeat.

Guide Post™

*Getting gifts that you are not ready to receive can be uncomfortable, especially if you're resisting. Take a moment now, to consider some recent experiences and reframe: each of these may have hurt, but **only because you were resisting the Universe**. Remember: 'Never look a gift horse in the mouth*.'*

Let's take the time to say thank you for the gifts.

Date of gift	Nature of gift (describe what happened)	Symptom of gift-resistance	Re-framed and re-evaluated (your chance to thank the Universe)
23 June	The eyebrow technician saying, *So I've done the second one a little bit more than what you wanted but as you can see, it does match what I did with the first one* . . .	Panicked	They did indeed both look equally horrific – thanks.
23 June	Drunk Stephen saying, *I told you to go somewhere reputable* and me saying, *And I told you that no good could come of it.*	Resentful	Always good to be right – thank you.

* *Widely accredited to St Jerome AD 400, but should be accredited to his lesser-known mother.*

23 June	Mezcal shots to overcome the trauma of the eyebrows. More mezcal shots to overcome trauma of seeing Matthew tomorrow. More mezcal shots because they're hangover free.	Headachey	Now I know that sufficient Mezcal does create a hangover – cheers for the learning.
24 June	Rail replacement bus between Oxford and Charlbury when we were already cutting it fine, and then train carriage with standing room only and no air conditioning for the rest of the journey to Little Minchcombe.	Stressed	Nice to know my sweat glands work effectively and to receive compliment from Drunk Stephen about *earthy scent* – appreciated.
24 June	Being so late that we couldn't get any lunch apart from chocolate bars from the train station and then having to hang my head out of the taxi to avoid being sick, thus ruining my hair.	Nauseous	At least my bad hair now worked with my bad eyebrows – grateful for that.
24 June	Walking into the church and the vicar saying, *We'll just wait for our latecomers,* and having everybody turn and look at us, Tristan and Penelope smiling through gritted teeth, as we made our way to the only free seats, which were – of course – near the front of the church. And then hearing Annabel say to Joyless Julian, *Always has to make an entrance. Who is* that *with her?*	Disgraced	Well, at least Drunk Stephen enjoyed himself – he loves an entrance and said if he spent that much on his threads, they may as well be enjoyed from all angles.

24 June	Trying not to burp mezcal and chocolate through the horrifically long christening ceremony whilst scanning the church to both catch a glimpse of, and avoid seeing, Matthew and Ebba.	Tense	It's probably better that they weren't in the church – thank you.
24 June	Having to walk into the Lamb and endure not only Monty and a pregnant Minty, but Monty's mother too, who told Drunk Stephen that she wished him luck with me, and by golly he'd need it.	Insulted	I am appreciative that Monty's mother is no longer a part of my life.
24 June	Dutifully minding three different babies in prams whilst Louise went to the loo and then when Lucy who was still heavily pregnant came over, I said, *Let's hope your one doesn't turn out to have a head like that*, pointing to a newborn / traffic cone. *Can't be long for you now: you look like you're about to pop!* Turned out the traffic-cone newborn was Lucy's baby, and she was no longer pregnant, just still carrying the baby weight.	Ashamed	**It's always good to have a reminder to think before you speak.** And Lucy and I have never been particularly close anyway so I guess I'll cope.
24 June	Endless small talk, cake, sandwiches, fielding questions, being introduced to people by Mum as if Drunk Stephen were my partner; congratulating Penelope and Tristan; Penelope clocking my eyebrows and asking if they were stress-related; and everyone speculating whether Matthew and Ebba were going to materialise – they're obsessed with him since he's been in the media.	On edge	At least if everyone else is obsessed with Matthew they're not noticing that I am. That's a bonus.

24 June	Being cornered by Monty in the library (again) who confessed he thinks Minty might like his mother more than him, and that I was the only woman who ever really got him. All I kept thinking was how much I wished I could turn back time to Christmas Eve when Matthew walked through that very door.	Sad	It could be worse – I could be miserably married, like Monty, rather than miserably unmarried.
24 June	Realising that Matthew was not coming to this christening and deciding to sample from the Lamb's new cocktail menu.	Desperate	It turns out that gin, vetiver and violet can dull the desperation. Grateful for that . . .
24 June	Insisting to the really fit barman that I used to work in the Lamb, and that I knew the owner and that I should therefore be allowed to mix cocktails myself, offering to sleep with the fit barman if he let me behind the bar, and being ushered out of the Lamb by Drunk Stephen (not before he exchanged numbers with the fit barman).	Rejected	Well, Drunk Stephen has got lucky . . . every cloud and all that.

Guide Post™

Which moment of all these hurt the most?

Knowing I'm never going to be with Matthew.

The reason it hurts so much is because you want it so much. At the beginning of your journey we talked about writing as action; writing as change.

Write a letter to the thing you most want.
(Use **GUIDED MANIFESTATION LETTERS™** *to guide you.)*

Dear Matthew,

I remember the first time I ever saw you. It was on the green, on a Saturday, and you were playing football with other kids from the local school and I was riding my pony in Miss Brown's pony club and I was so busy staring at you that I rode straight into the fence and tipped off the pony. And then the next Saturday you were there again, so I pretended there was a problem with the stirrup and paused to sort it so I could look at you. Usually, I hated that bit, riding past the footy boys who shouted 'posh girl alert' whilst pretending to cough; in fact, I used to hate riding full stop – you know how I feel about large animals, especially ones you can fall off – and Mum had finally agreed I could give up pony club. But after seeing you, I got Mum to sign me up for another term. Just so I had an excuse.

And then the next year you got the scholarship to St Hilda's for sixth form and I was so excited that I'd get to see you every day that I drove Mum mad, singing all the time. It was like my prayers had been answered. I kept preparing these amazing, clever, funny things I was going to say (I even wrote some down in my diary) so you'd instantly fall in love with me. Then Astrid brought

461

you home for the first time, and introduced us, and I was so overcome to see you up close that I couldn't do anything but stare. I literally couldn't speak. And you grinned at me and said, 'Hey, Alice, you're a lot more verbal when you're falling off ponies.' Astrid laughed and said, 'That's because she's always eyeing up the footballers', and I felt so stupid because I knew it was obvious how I felt about you and you were laughing at me, and why would you be interested in me when I had an older sister like Astrid. So I just said, 'Yeah. But no. I prefer rugby players.'

Then I got to watch you hang out with Astrid and admire her and like her throughout sixth form; I hoped I'd grow as tall and model-like as her. Mum told me I never would because I took after Granny Carver. Sometimes it was hard to like Astrid. And Mum.

That first Christmas you came back from university, I'd planned it all to show you I was grown up enough for you and that whilst maybe I was no Astrid, I got plenty of attention; I left 'sexy' underwear that I'd bought from Tammy Girl lying about and made a couple of jaded comments about politicians. I even did my make-up differently. Honestly, it still makes my insides curl up now when I remember it. Then Astrid told us you were seeing one of your tutors and asked me why I'd done my make-up like Pat Butcher, and you laughed.

And yet I didn't give up. I literally had no shame and there were no limits in my efforts. There was the Christmas I dated that single dad in a bid to show you I was mature. And then the summer I learnt Italian because you said you admired people who could speak different languages. I even volunteered at Young Farmers (and you know I hate farms) because I overheard you telling Astrid how you could never end up with someone who was selfish. And still you didn't see me as anything other than Astrid's little sister.

And then I remember that summer I came back from my gap travelling year (okay, gap-multiple-years, and less travelling and more lying on the beach), and we hadn't seen each other for ages, and I was in that frayed denim mini, and I saw you looking at me, and, for the first time, I thought I was in with a chance. And my luck was in, because you were midway through your second master's, in business administration, and we both ended up working in the Lamb together for the entire summer. And even though Astrid and Arrie were around too, because you and I worked together, we ended up spending almost all our time together. And it was like I'd stepped into Wonderland – you used to joke about it, how I'd taken so many recreational drugs on my travels that I was on a permanent high, but it was getting to be with you – you were my Wonderland. And, as that summer progressed, I thought maybe you liked me too. But you never made a move. So, that party on the paddock, I decided I would make a move.

And we both know how that went. Now.

Back then, I overheard what you said to Ollie. Or part of what you said to Ollie. But I didn't know that at the time. I just knew that not only did you not like me back, but you didn't think I was even good enough for your friend. The higher you're flying, the further you fall, and honestly, Matthew, after the summer we'd had, that fall hurt. And after spending all that time with you, for it just to stop like that . . . it was brutal. That entire first year with Ollie, as awful as it sounds, I was with him hoping that I'd see you – you were best mates after all. But every time I came to visit in Cambridge, you somehow weren't there. I guess I should have got the message, but I didn't. I think I only really got it when you left for America without saying goodbye. Well, you said goodbye to Astrid and Mum and Dad. But not to me.

After that, it was only weddings, funerals and Christmases I saw you. Every time you'd turn up looking more gorgeous than the next – more confident, more charming, more you. And every year I hoped this would be the year I didn't want you. And you'd smile that cocky smile and I'd think, 'He knows. And I still can't get over him.' In fact, even though everyone thinks I'm lazy, I've actually worked extremely hard for many years convincing myself – and trying to convince everyone else – that you're everything I don't want. Because what's more pitiful than constantly wanting someone who doesn't want you back? Someone who thinks you're selfish and spoilt and frivolous?

It takes its toll. I think Astrid's wedding was the worst one when you turned up with that German underwear model, Frieda, and not only was she nice, she was fun, and Mum kept saying how wonderful it was to see you that happy after all you'd been through *after your dad. And I hated myself for not being happier that you were happy. I guess you're right: I am selfish. That was the night I ended up with Monty. Poor old Monty. Never stood a chance.*

I can tell you still think you have something to prove, but the truth is, you were always the best person I knew. The best thing in my life.

Every man I've dated I've chosen because they're not you.

Problem is, they're not you.

And all I've ever wanted is you.

I love you, Matthew Lloyd. I think I always have.

Alice Carver

My thoughts and reflections:

I made it downstairs for painkillers sometime this morning but after nearly throwing up in the kitchen sink, was deemed more hindrance than help in terms of party preparation, and was sent back upstairs with instructions to stay there – along with admonitions about wasting such a stunning day, and unfavourable comparisons to Drunk Stephen who'd been up since the crack of dawn, like Arrie. (More like Drunk Stephen had come in at the crack of dawn after shagging Fit Barman all night.) Despite the incessant noise of everyone crashing about and party prepping, the sun aggressively poking through the curtains, and Mum shouting because someone had spilled Earl Grey all over the counter and left the back door wide open all night and the neighbour's cat had come in and sprayed on the door mat, I slept again, fitfully, dreaming of the christening and the past and woke up late afternoon, dehydrated, overheated and miserable, with the kind of dull, persistent hangover that only a shag or more alcohol can cure. After showering on the coldest setting, dressing and going heavy on the make-up, I made it downstairs for the second time that day, and walked straight into Mum who said, 'Alice, you look horrific. At your age you need concealer.'

'I'm wearing concealer,' I said flatly.

'Oh dear. Well, put some lipstick on and smile, darling. It will detract from the puffy eyes.'

'I don't feel like smiling.'

'That's precisely when you need to,' said Mum briskly. 'Now pull yourself together, grab those bottles and load up Roger's car.'

'Where are the others?'

'Drunk Stephen's been at the paddock for the last hour with Dad, getting it ready. He's a treasure. Worked like a Trojan all day. Unlike you, Alice. Arrie's fed the boys and they've just set off on foot with Astrid and Aziz. So, all we need to do is load up the last few things and drive down with Roger.'

'I need water.' I went over to the sink. As soon as my back was safely turned towards her I asked, 'What about Matthew?'

'I don't know if Astrid's managed to persuade him to come. We've barely seen him recently.'

I closed my eyes, and tried to block out the dull pain.

'Right,' said Roger, 'the Landy's nearly full. How much more, Nell?'

'Just these bottles, Roger darling,' said Mum. 'And the pink napkins. And ice! We need more ice. Thank goodness we went for an early evening party – hottest day of the year so far. Did you know that, Alice?'

'I suspected,' I said, sweat blooming already.

We'd just pulled out of the driveway when Mum remembered her mobile phone. 'It's charging in the sitting room. On the bureau. I left it when I picked up the cards.'

'I'll get it,' I said, climbing out the back, 'and catch you up.'

'Be quick,' said Mum. 'The other guests are coming from six.'

And it was only when I was reaching behind the bureau to retrieve Mum's phone, which had fallen behind, that I started remembering little snippets from the night before . . .

Last night, whilst everyone was sleeping (not Drunk Stephen) I'd crept down and sat at the bureau, swaying slightly from my cocktails, and hunted through the cubbyholes for paper. I was set on cream paper. Because *The Guide* told me it was best. I couldn't find cream paper – only white A4. Oh god, with the bent genius of the thoroughly inebriated, I'd decided to craft cream paper myself: I'd gone to the kitchen, brewed some Earl Grey and daubed the paper like I did at school for my pirate project in Year 5. And then I'd had to dry the paper so I'd put it in the oven. I put my hands to my eyes in shame. Me in the state I was, dicking around with combustibles; it was like the start of a *What's Your Emergency*? Then what did I do? I looked at my hands; there were blotches of purple on the palms. Purple ink. I used purple ink because that was all we had although I wanted blue to symbolise the 'endless bounty of the Universe'. I'd wanted cream paper and ink because I was totally and utterly set on writing a letter.

Oh fuck, fuck, fuck. Suddenly I remembered everything with horrific clarity: I was totally and utterly set on writing an entire letter. To Matthew Lloyd.

And then, once I'd written it, I let myself out the back door. Oh shit on a brick. I'd folded the letter and stuffed it into an envelope out on the lawn, trying to stare up at the moon, which was weirdly big and pink and because *The Guide* said to. I was so pissed I'd fallen over and then I'd lain there, on the grass, trying to focus on the moon and talking to it about Matthew until the dew had chilled me, and then I'd finally stumbled indoors, not shutting the door behind me and put the letter back in the bureau, ready to give to him.

. . . I opened the bureau, my heart tripping over itself in panic. There was the bottle of ink and the ink pen. And envelopes. I sifted through them frantically. Where was my letter? I checked again and then through all the little cubbyholes, pulling everything out and searching. I checked behind the actual bureau. And under it. And under the sofas and the sofa cushions and in the drawers and under the drawers. I yanked everything out and checked everywhere.

Then, I stood, staring at the bureau, amidst the chaos I'd created, a cold trickle of realisation running down through my spine. The letter was no longer here. If it was no longer here, logically it must be somewhere else. What if, though, it was with some*one* else? Mum said she picked up the cards from the bureau; what if my envelope had been taken to the paddock by accident? What if Mum was there, right now, handing my drunken, desperate letter to Matthew?

I've not really run full speed since Year 11 and the 200 metre on sports day, but despite a horrific hangover and the searingly hot June temperature, I got to the paddock in under seven minutes. It was a cavalcade of sprinting, limping and weeping, a distillation of sports relief. I nearly collapsed before the paddock gate but managed to collapse onto it, feeling the relief as it took my weight for a moment, whilst I tried to catch my breath. In between rasps, I noticed the bunting strung between tree branches and the trestle table, slightly bowed under the weight of pitchers and bottles and glasses, the hay bales, the floral cushions, jam jars with tea lights. The hedgerows were verdant; cornflowers joined the poppies and clouds of cow parsley, gently rolling hills of yellow and green beyond the paddock giving way to clear blue sky. There was a hive of activity and they were all there, Dad and Mum, Roger and Arrie and the twins, Astrid, Aziz, Drunk Stephen and . . . oh.

Matthew Lloyd.

My breathing hitched up a notch again.

Ernie saw me first. 'She's here, Aunty Alice is here.'

'Get a wriggle on,' shouted Arrie, from by the table. 'As soon as Matthew and Aziz have done the last lanterns we're having a family toast before all the guests arrive.'

I tried to speak but it came out as a wheeze, and then I got an excruciating pain in my side. So I held up an arm and stayed there, bent double.

Dad came over to me, full of concern. 'What's wrong, darling? You look dreadful. Astrid! Is Alice having a heart attack? Darling?'

Astrid took one look at me. 'Did you run, Alice?'

I managed to nod through the agony.

'Stitch?'

I nodded again.

'Yeah,' said Astrid. 'She's just incredibly unfit, Dad. And hungover. You could do with some make-up, Alice.'

'Grandpa! Aunty Astrid!' called Edwin. 'Mummy needs help.'

Astrid went off again to help Arrie who was laying out blankets near the hay bales and after patting me gently on the back, Dad followed. Twenty metres or so away, I saw Mum reach into a bag underneath the table and pull out a bunch of envelopes which she started arranging, before moving to stir the punch. You know how mothers have lifted trucks when their babies have been trapped beneath? Well, somehow, I found the strength to get across that paddock, despite the agonising stabbing in my side.

'Mum,' I wheezed, grabbing her arm.

'Christ,' said Mum. 'You look even worse that you did before. Where's my phone?'

'Mum, are these the cards?'

'What cards?'

'The ones from the bureau. I need them. Now!'

'Darling,' she said, 'you're gripping my arm like Granny Carver did when she was dying. It's quite unpleasant.'

'Mum, the cards!'

'They're just there, darling, next to the lemonade.'

I dragged myself along the table and with sweating, trembling hands fumbled through them. There was no envelope addressed to Matthew. No envelope.

'Have you seen an envelope with my handwriting on it?' I said, still catching my breath.

'What does it say on it?'

'Matthew.'

'Matthew?' said Mum. 'Why would I bring an envelope for Matthew to Astrid and Aziz's leaving party?'

'You wouldn't,' I said, feeling a little of my panic evaporate. Then I panicked again. 'Unless you already gave it to him?'

'Try and make sense, darling,' said Mum. 'You're sounding manic.'

'Sorry,' I said, the tension in my body subsiding. 'I'm a bit all over the place.'

'So am I. Astrid and Aziz off. Hottest day of the year. And, I haven't paused.' Mum stopped for a second and took a deep breath. 'Doesn't the old house look magnificent in the evening sun, Alice? I still miss it.'

'Me too, Mum.'

In a rare moment, she rested her head against mine and we both looked over to the far end of the paddock where the arched wrought iron gates offered a perfect vista of the avenue beyond, which led through the gardens before giving way to the star of the show: the old house itself. Sunlight honeyed its grey stone façade and roses clambered every which way, immodest in their luxurious, heavy beauty. The house tugged something deep inside me like it always did, but even that was nothing compared to the way I was drawn towards the foreground and the old apple trees flanking the gates, where Matthew was stretching up to fix a lantern in the gnarled bough. His T-shirt was damp and sticking to the muscles of his back and the indent of his spine. His triceps were flexing as he reached above and that tattoo was snaking out the sleeve. He made the roses look chaste. If I was still lusting after the house that hadn't been mine for over a decade, I had no chance of getting over Matthew Lloyd.

'Darling, you're unpleasantly clammy,' said Mum. 'Ironic given you've done nothing to help apart from get embarrassingly drunk. Probably a good job that chap of yours didn't make it yesterday. What's his name?'

'Guy,' said Arrie, coming over. 'With the hairy back.'

'He's not mine,' I said.

'Good grief.' Arrie took one look at me and baulked. 'Honestly, Alice, the least you could have done after sleeping all day is make an effort. You look like you've been let loose on the bad orange squash.'

'I ran here,' I said defensively. 'I'll cool down.'

'Why?' said Arrie. 'You never run anywhere.'

'I thought I'd lost something.'

'What? Besides a sense of pride in your appearance.'

'She's looking for an envelope,' said Mum.

'I'm not,' I replied.

'For Matthew,' said Mum.

'What's that?' said Dad, joining us.

'Nothing,' I said quickly. 'Is it time for that toast yet?'

'Alice has lost an envelope addressed to Matthew,' said Arrie. 'Have you seen it?'

'No,' said Dad, 'maybe Aziz has. Aziz?' he called. 'Aziz, have you—'

'Dad! Dad!' I grabbed his arm, my heart racing with panic. 'It's fine. I haven't lost it. It's fine. Please.'

'What?' shouted Aziz.

'So you haven't lost it?' said Arrie.

'But you kept asking me where it was,' said Mum. 'You're making no sense today, Alice.'

'Yes,' said Dad, looking puzzled, 'why are you writing to Matthew? He's just over there if you want to speak to him. I can call him if you want. Matthew?' he shouted.

'Dad!' I nearly cried. 'Please! Leave it.'

'No problem, darling. They're coming over now,' said Dad, looking pleased. 'We can have that toast to Astrid and Aziz before the other guests arrive.'

473

I looked over and there they were, Aziz, Drunk Stephen and Matthew Lloyd, coming across the grass towards us.

'I've got to say,' said Dad. 'I've only ever been attracted to women myself, primarily your mother of course, but Matthew really is an extraordinarily attractive young man. Remarkable. I mean it almost jolts to look at him really.'

If I thought I was sweating before, that was nothing compared to now. Obviously part of it was the treacherous bodily response to Matthew that most other humans clearly shared, including Dad. But the bulk of it was down to the fact that I potentially had about ten seconds of life remaining. I mean, it didn't seem like Mum or Dad had given Matthew the letter, but the fact remained that it hadn't been in the bureau, where I left it, and until that letter was back in my possession, I was in danger.

Dad pressed a bottle of champagne into my hands and busied himself getting glasses.

'Jesus, Alice,' said Astrid, who'd just wandered over, settling herself on a hay bale. 'You still look rough. Is something wrong?'

Eight seconds.

'I'm fine,' I said, removing the foil and untwisting the metal.

Seven.

'You don't look fine,' said Edwin, running up.

Six.

'You look like Mrs Hutchinson did after she told Verity to piss off. Did you know teachers aren't allowed to tell children to piss off?'

Five.

'She's fretting because she lost an envelope,' said Dad. 'Open the bottle, please, Alice. You're the expert.'

474

Four.

'What envelope?' said Roger, lugging over a final crate of beer.

Three.

'How about not sweating all over the beer, Roger?' snapped Arrie. 'Rather than fussing about Alice's envelope for Matthew.'

Two.

'Oh that,' said Astrid. 'Don't worry, Alice. I found it on the bureau this morning.'

One.

'I dropped it off for him after my run.'

The champagne cork popped and arced into the air, making everyone jump.

'Woah!' said Edwin. 'Did you see that?'

'Build-up of pressure,' said Roger. 'Could have taken an eye out.'

'You did what?' I said, staring at Astrid in total horror.

Time froze. Or stopped. There was no time anymore. What was time?

'I delivered it for you. Why, has he not got it?'

A trickle of icy champagne ran down my hand.

'There's the man himself,' said Mum. 'We can ask him.'
I closed my eyes and swayed slightly; I could feel the smooth glass of the champagne bottle sliding from my desperate grip.

'Do you want a hand with that?' said a familiar deep voice, and suddenly the bottle was steadied. 'Let's get some glasses,' said Matthew, and just like that everyone was distracted and fetching glasses and Mum was saying, 'Yes, we must do a family toast before the guests get here.'

Matthew leant a little closer; apple and earth and the faint tang of sea mocked me. 'If you let go of the bottle now it would help,' he said.

I started to relinquish my hold, my hands shaking.

'Gosh,' he said quietly, taking the bottle from me. 'You must have been seriously slaughtered last night.' Our fingers touched and my eyes snapped open, as if he'd triggered an electric circuit. He was looking right at me. I froze, trying to read him. Oh my god. Did he know? His face was a mask of neutrality but I could see the faint crease at the side of his mouth, tantalising.

'Here we go, Matthew,' interrupted Dad, pushing glasses in front of us. 'Fill these.'

Dumbly, I watched as Matthew filled the flutes Dad was holding, and then the others on the trestle table. Astrid handed me a glass, and Drunk Stephen nudged me.

'Fuck, Alice,' he said in a low voice. 'You look terrible. Have you not noticed Matthew Lloyd's here? Couldn't you have made an effort? Have I taught you nothing?'

I looked at him, still stupefied.

'Okay,' said Arrie, 'everyone's got a glass, so let's keep this short and sweet. Mum, do the honours.'

'To Astrid and Aziz,' said Mum. 'May you have a gap year to rival Alice's.'

'Except without the multiple sexual partners,' said Arrie.

'And no drugs,' said Dad. 'I've not forgotten that phone call from Holland, Alice.'

'And no ill-advised tattoos,' said Astrid.

'You've got a tattoo?' said Matthew, his eyes flicking over me.

'You've got a tattoo, Alice?' said Mum in horror. 'Astrid, are you saying Alice has a tattoo and you've never told me? Alice Carver?!'

'Don't worry,' Astrid smirked. 'I don't think you'll ever set eyes on it, Mum.'

'Oh dear,' said Dad. 'It's not one of these intimate tattoos, is it? I've heard about those on—'

'To us!' interrupted Aziz.

'To Aziz and Astrid!' everyone chorused, obediently.

We all raised our glasses and Aziz smiled at me. I was going to miss Aziz so much. He's what makes family occasions more bearable. For a fraction of a second, with the heat of the sun and the fizz of the champagne and the warmth of the people I loved best around me, I forgot everything else.

Until Mum spoke.

'So, Matthew,' said Mum, 'we're all in suspense. Did you get Alice's envelope?'

I was mid-sip and the shock rendered me incapable of swallowing, so the bubbles went up my nose, making me splutter.

Drunk Stephen patted me none too gently on the back and whispered, 'If you want Matthew Lloyd to fancy you, maybe stop acting like some kind of beef-wit.'

I wiped my mouth, straightened up and looked at Matthew; his expression was inscrutable.

'This one?' said Matthew, casually, pulling out my letter from the back pocket of his jeans. 'Yes, I did, thank you.'

My champagne flute dropped and bounced on the ground, spraying my legs and Drunk Stephen's, and nearly getting Astrid.

'Alice!' said Astrid. 'Careful!'

Drunk Stephen quickly retrieved my glass, and widened his eyes at me. 'You're acting like someone they rolled out in a cage in medieval times,' he hissed.

'Well, there we go, all delivered, maybe you can relax now, Alice, darling,' said Dad, putting his arm round my shoulders.

I risked glancing over at Matthew again. He held my gaze, his eyes glinting in the sun as he slowly stuffed the letter back in his pocket.

'She doesn't look very relaxed, Grandpa,' said Ernie helpfully. 'She looks a bit like Maud does when she gets caught in her lead. Sort of bulgy eyed.'

'What on earth is in the envelope anyway, Alice?' asked Mum. 'You're being rather odd.'

'Nothing,' I said, my voice high.

'You don't send someone an empty envelope,' said Arrie.

'Yeah,' agreed Matthew. 'It doesn't feel like nothing.'

I looked at him hopefully. Maybe he hadn't opened it yet.

'No,' said Matthew, thoughtfully. 'It definitely feels like something to me.'

He slowly and deliberately raised his eyebrows at me. He was toying with me. Matthew Lloyd was fucking with me.

'Maybe I should check now,' he challenged, the corners of his mouth lifting with amusement. 'Are you sure there's nothing in it, Alice? Nothing carefully stained with tea, like the envelope?'

I watched in slow motion as he reached towards his back pocket and my instincts took over. Luckily Dad moved back, only losing a little of his champagne, as I leapt towards Matthew, trying to grab the letter.

'Alice!' Mum exclaimed. 'What is wrong with you?'

'For goodness' sake, Alice,' Astrid sighed.

'Give it back,' I said. 'Give it back, you big fucker.' If I could get it back, everything would be okay. He probably hadn't even read it. I still had a chance.

Matthew was fielding me with ease and my insult only made him laugh, which made my ears ring with frustration and embarrassment and my temper broke.

'Mummy!' said Ernie. 'Aunty Alice is trying to kick Matthew. Am I allowed to?'

'Disgraceful behaviour, Alice,' said Arrie.

And then suddenly Matthew's arms were around me and he was holding me so close and tight that I was unable to move. I was just contained in uncompromising, solid muscle and strength. 'Stop fighting,' he said quietly.

Even now, when I wanted to kill him, my perfidious body responded to his proximity.

'What on earth is going on, Matthew?' asked Mum.

'Nothing,' said Matthew loudly, from above my head. His voice reverberated through me.

'I just need my letter back,' I gasped, my voice muffled against his chest. 'You're not meant to read it. I wrote it to the Universe. Give it back.'

Then Matthew bent his head so his mouth was against my ear, making sparks tango down my skin. 'Too late,' he whispered. 'I already read it.'

I went limp. He had read it. I whimpered softly. 'All of it?'

'Every. Single. Word.'

'What's happening, Matthew? Why are you both whispering?' said Mum crossly. 'Is Alice having some kind of fit? The guests are about to arrive!'

'She's okay,' called Matthew. He returned his attention to me. 'I'm going to let go,' he said quietly. 'But if you try and take my letter I won't be happy. Understood?'

'I accept defeat,' I muttered. 'Humiliate me. Tell them what I did. I don't care. I was drunk.'

Matthew chuckled and released me. 'Is this how you're playing it? You were drunk? The letter isn't for me? You didn't mean it?'

I stared at an ant crawling up a blade of a grass and wondered if it was possible to manifest swapping bodies.

'Matthew, why is your barman here?' said Mum.

Matthew's head jerked up. 'Hey, Troy. I take it you didn't get my message, then?'

I looked over, the sun eye-wateringly bright after the protection of Matthew; Fit Barman from yesterday was walking through the grass towards us, carrying some kind of heavy bubble-wrapped package.

'Er, what message?' asked Fit Barman Troy.

'About leaving it at the house?'

'Sorry.' Fit Barman Troy stopped in his tracks. 'Do you want me to take it there instead?'

Matthew glanced back at me and rubbed his jaw. 'No. I guess it's here now.'

'Let me help,' said Drunk Stephen, practically vaulting over.

'The other thing I asked, Troy,' said Matthew, 'all in hand?'

'Yep.' Fit Barman Troy nodded, wiping sweat from his brow. 'So where do you want this, Matthew?'

'It's actually for Alice.' Matthew shrugged. 'I was going to give it to her later. So, wherever she wants it.'

'Ooh, it's massive, Matthew,' said Mum, perking up. 'Is it a present?'

'No, it's a prize. She won it.'

'Sounds exciting, Alice,' said Dad. 'What is it?'

'I've no idea,' I said, my voice croaky.

'You can probably work it out,' Matthew said, his eyes enigmatic.

I shook my head, and stared at him obstinately, trying to keep calm. What was this about? Some other way of making me look stupid? This was awful – waiting for public rejection. All I needed now was for Ebba to turn up too. 'I don't want it,' I said.

'No returns I'm afraid.' Matthew folded his arms. 'A win is a win.'

'Well, I jolly well want to know what it is,' said Astrid, 'and I'd also like to know why you two are being so peculiar.'

'Yes,' said Mum. 'Open the parcel, Alice. It's rude to look a gift horse in the mouth.'

'If you don't want it, I'll have it,' said Astrid.

'Fine, you open it then,' I retorted. 'But I want to see what it is before I give it to you.'

'At last,' said Astrid, grabbing a pair of scissors from the trestle table.

Matthew moved pretty swiftly. 'No scissors,' he said firmly. 'I'll open it, seeing as Alice won't.' He gave me an annoyed glance.

Carefully he peeled off the bubble wrap. The muscles in Matthew's arms were further contoured by the sunlight as he worked.

'Looks like a painting,' said Mum.

Slowly, Matthew flipped the rectangular object around till it was facing us.

'That's a lot of red,' said Mum.

'Gracious,' breathed Astrid.

'Wow,' said Aziz.

Drunk Stephen just covered his mouth with his hand. 'Is that, is that an *actual* Yayoi Kusama?'

'Who?' I said.

'Your favourite artist, Alice,' said Matthew wryly. 'Remember? We had a bet. Outside your old house. On Boxing Day?'

I thought back to the scene I'd replayed many times. Me, Aziz, Astrid and Matthew. Arguing about my new copy of *The Guide*. Matthew telling me I was vulnerable and stupid. And I told him he was closed-minded. His arrogant, certain, beautiful smile. I swallowed. 'You mean the bet where if I could prove to you that manifesting really worked . . .'

'. . . I'd not only admit that I was wrong, but also give you my Yayoi Kusama painting,' said Matthew.

I stared at Matthew, open-mouthed, and then at the painting again.

'Because he's my favourite artist,' I finished for him.

'*She*, Alice.' Matthew shook his head. '*She* is supposedly your favourite artist. Which we both know is total bollocks. Anyway. A bet is a bet. And now the painting is yours to do with as you wish.'

Drunk Stephen looked up from where he'd been searching on his mobile phone, his face a cartoon of shock. 'Oh my god, Alice, do you know how much that painting is worth? You're rich.'

'Where would you put it, Alice?' Mum looked dubious. 'It's very red indeed.'

Astrid put her hands up. 'Hang on. Back up here a minute, Matthew. Are you trying to say that Alice has "proved" to you manifesting works?'

Matthew nodded. 'She has.' He cleared his throat. 'I would like to publicly admit, I was wrong. Manifesting works.'

I looked at him dazed. 'Did you just admit you were wrong?'

'Come on,' scoffed Astrid. 'No way. As you said yourself, manifesting is simple nonsense for simple minds.'

Matthew smiled.

'And you're smiling,' said Astrid. 'You're blatantly lying.'

I was totally with Astrid here.

'Or I've changed my mind,' said Matthew mildly.

'What's manifesting?' said Mum.

'It's pseudo-scientific nonsense,' said Astrid. 'Where delusional people, like Alice, convince themselves that by believing something will happen, you actually make it happen. It's all because of that ridiculous journal you got Alice for Christmas.'

'It's not ridiculous . . .' I began, and then trailed off. 'Why would you change your mind, Matthew?'

'I realised manifesting works.'

I shook my head. 'I don't believe you.'

'Don't be so closed-minded,' he said. 'This is all down to you, after all.'

'We both know I haven't manifested our old house, so how have I made you believe in manifesting all of a sudden?' I thought back to our conversation on Boxing Day. 'You told me it was exploitative. And how it was effectively magic beans for vulnerable people like me who wanted things that were out of reach. Like relationships . . . Oh my god,' I said, a wave of fresh, nausea-inducing mortification washing over me, knowing what he'd read in my letter. 'You haven't changed your mind at all! You're just going to prove that you always win.'

Matthew rolled his eyes. 'Fine.' He sounded exasperated. 'I was hoping to do this part privately, but here you go, Alice.' He handed me an envelope.

'What is it?' said Mum.

'Not this game again,' snapped Arrie. 'It's another envelope. Bloody open it *now*, Alice.'

I opened the envelope and inside was a receipt. I recognised it immediately – it was one of my Margarita Monday receipts and on the back was Matthew's scrawl in eyeliner.

'Is this from our trip to Dartmoor?' I asked.

Matthew nodded. He looked nervous.

'When did you go to Dartmoor?' said Mum. 'No one tells me anything!'

'Alice let me manifest under the Capricorn moon with her.'

'No way,' said Astrid. 'You've definitely lost it, Matthew.'

I smoothed out the receipt. My hands were trembling.

Matthew, for once, seemed to hesitate. 'You see . . . when I read your letter, Alice, I realised that manifestation does work.'

An entire universe resting on one receipt. I took a deep breath and took the leap.

In Matthew's scrawl was written:

I manifest Alice Carver feeling the same way about me as I do about her.

Matthew Lloyd
12 January

I felt like the world had tipped slightly so that everything was at a new angle. I looked up at Matthew. Well, I'd finally wiped that cocky grin off his face. I don't think I'd ever seen him look so serious before: his dark eyes warm; vulnerable in their hope.

'But what about Ebba?' I checked.

Matthew shook his head. 'Never stood a chance.'

'All the other models?'

'Distraction.'

'I'm not a model,' I pointed out.

'Precisely.' A glimmer of Matthew's smile returned.

'Frieda? She made you smile.'

'*You* make me laugh.'

I paused. 'What about the fact you think I'm selfish and spoilt and frivolous?'

He shrugged. 'I also think you're kind and fun and irresist-ible.'

'Irresistible? Since when?'

'Since you rode that pony into the fence. But I suppose it was the summer we worked at the Lamb, I knew for certain; it was like living in technicolour for the first time. You were my Wonderland.'

'Aw,' said Astrid. 'That's sweet. See what he's done?'

'We did actually name Alice after the novel.' Dad sounded tearful. 'Didn't we, Nell?'

'She is fun,' said Mum proudly. 'She gets that from me.'

I tuned them out.

'What about now?' I asked. 'How do you feel now?'

I stood for a second and a lifetime, staring up at Matthew, and the world paused; a blue butterfly seemed to hover in mid-air; the goldfinch listened silently; even the breeze skipped a beat.

'Well, I'm in love with you, Alice Carver,' said Matthew. 'Just like I always have been.'

And as the world started spinning, and the butterflies spiralled, and the goldfinches fluted, and the breeze meandered around us – Matthew Lloyd finally kissed me.

Later, as the sun was setting in a flamboyant display of reds and oranges and purples, Matthew pulled me away from the talking, laughing groups of family and friends, and the congratulations and well-wishes, and Mum telling everybody she always knew about us, and towards the far end of the paddock, under the apple trees, where the volume was turned down. My hand tingled from him holding it. If he had that kind of physical effect on my hand, what was going to happen if we took it further? Correction. *When* we took it further. There was a genuine risk of combustion.

Even thinking about it cranked my thermostat to super high. It almost hurt. I swallowed. Matthew paused by the wrought iron gates which led through to the garden of our old house. 'Dirty thoughts, Alice?' Matthew sounded amused.

'Always.'

'Well, keep manifesting,' he said, backing me up against the stone gate posts.

'I am.' I shivered in anticipation.

Matthew trailed his gaze over me. Deliberately. Slowly.

I reached my arms round his neck and pulled him down towards me. As our mouths found each other's and the weight of his body crushed against mine, the universe exploded in a kaleidoscope of colour, and I think I actually groaned out loud.

Matthew pulled back, and ran his hand through his hair. 'Alice,' he said, his eyes black. 'We're in full view of everyone.'

'I don't care.' I caught his top and dragged him towards me again, ignoring the cheers in the background. 'They like it. They can watch.' I ran my hands down his chest and stomach, marvelling, longing.

A snippet of Dad's voice carried over. '. . . he's like a son to me already . . .'

'Yeah,' said Matthew, pushing me away firmly. 'Not doing this in front of your parents. Already declared my love. I think that's enough for public consumption.'

'Matthew! I can't wait any more. Be reasonable. What about under the trestle table if you're too prudish to do it here?'

Matthew chuckled. 'What about doing it somewhere on our own?'

'But I've waited years.' My voice caught with desperation and frustration. 'I can't wait until later.' And I really couldn't; I was on the verge of detonating.

'I didn't say you had to,' said Matthew steadily, his composure only increasing my feverishness. Then suddenly he pushed open the gates to our old house, and tugged me through them.

'We can't just barge in here!' I looked back over my shoulder as the gates closed behind us, to see if anyone had noticed. 'This is trespassing!'

Matthew glanced sideways at me without breaking his stride. 'Interesting. So you're worried about your parents seeing *that*?'

'What are you doing?' I whispered as he led me up the avenue of lawns.

'Getting us some space.'

'You do know I haven't actually manifested this house, right?' I hurried to match his purposeful pace.

'I do know,' said Matthew, laconically.

'It's been sold to some wanker who gets to spend Christmas in it. In fact, what if they're in there right now? Calling the police?'

'It's empty. Trust me.'

The approach was so beautiful I was almost momentarily distracted from lusting after Matthew; someone had threaded fairy lights through the lavender and beneath the pergola dripping with roses, tea lights in jam jars lit the path. As our old house came fully into view, the songbirds were singing goodnight like it was the only goodnight that ever mattered; the air was filled with the heady scent of rose and honeysuckle.

Almost.

'Let's go inside,' said Matthew, picking up a rock on the window ledge by the back door. The movement made his shoulder muscles undulate under his T-shirt; he'd turned me into a shameless lech.

'We can't!' I said. I couldn't let him break into someone else's house.

'I thought you didn't want to wait?' he said, raising his eyebrows at me.

He had me there. I took a steadying breath. 'I don't. Fine. Let's break in!' My heart was pounding in excitement. Sex with Matthew Lloyd would be worth six months in prison. 'Give me the rock and I'll smash the window myself.'

'Easy tiger,' said Matthew, handing me a key and putting the rock back. 'How about just going in the normal way?'

I looked at the key in my hand. 'Why have you got the key, Matthew? Do you know the owner?'

'Er, yeah.' Matthew looked sheepish. 'And, so do you. In fact, that key is your copy I asked Troy to get made and leave there . . .'

He bit his lip and waited for the penny to drop.

'You?'

'Yeah . . . the thing is,' said Matthew, unlocking the back door, 'I'd kind of already made an offer when you talked about manifesting it on Boxing Day.'

'What? You let me promise to manifest a house you had under offer? Not just *a* house. Our old house that I love.'

'Well, *technically*. But no money had changed hands and it's been a slow . . . ow!'

'You twat!' I tried to kick him again. 'No wonder you were laughing in my face. You bloody knew I had no chance! You allowed me to bet against you knowing I'd lose.'

'Alice!' Matthew folded his distractingly powerful arms around me. 'Less violence, please. I only wanted the house in the first place because of you. Same reason I wanted the Lamb. Don't be cross. Besides, I did warn you: I always win.'

And there it was. That insufferably smug grin.

'Well, you're not winning when it comes to me.'

'Okay,' agreed Matthew, his eyes gleaming. 'If you're sure.'

'Totally sure. You let me manifest spending Christmas in there knowing I wouldn't.' I tried to sound cross, but my body had a mind of its own, giving into Matthew's, and he wasn't even doing anything, other than existing.

'But you will spend Christmas here, Alice.' Matthew tucked a strand of hair behind my ear and ran his thumb down my cheek leaving a shimmering, static trail. 'If you want to.' He could tell perfectly well I wanted to. 'In fact,' he suggested casually, 'if you want to, we could spend some time in there, together, right now. Just you and me. On our own. I'll let you win anything you want . . .'

'I don't know, I heard the owner was a bit of a wanker,' I said, immediately pressing closer to him, my hands searching for him under his T-shirt, trying ineffectively to get it off him. 'Obsessed with winning.'

'Yeah, but you love him anyway,' said Matthew, kissing up my neck agonisingly slowly, and setting my skin on fire. 'And I'll make sure you win too.'

I gasped at his touch and tried to stay upright before I started winning right now. 'I'd love him a lot more if he took his T-shirt off and stopped teasing me. I've been waiting lifetimes for this.'

Matthew paused and gave me that knowing, cocky smile. 'Oh. I haven't even *started* teasing you yet, Alice,' he said. 'But it'll be worth the wait.'

And it was.

(FYI: Technically we both won. A lot.)

I ask the Universe:

To give herself a massive pat on the back – thank you so much.

Guide Post™

Take the time to revisit and reflect on your manifestations by completing the table below. Be sure to add any extra manifestations you've been working on since last time.

MANIFESTATION	REFLECTION	PROGRESS RATING 1 – 10 1 – I can see very little or no progress 10 – I have manifested with complete success
I manifest . . . the perfect man (~~Guy Carmichael~~ Matthew Lloyd) falling in love with me	So did this. Obviously, the perfect man was actually Matthew Lloyd. Manifested the fuck out of this.	10++++++

I manifest . . . having a gorgeous flat to live in from 4 January (preferably central and cheap, or ideally free, and no rats)	Done. Manifested Astrid's house. And whilst maybe technically resident for now in Sidcup which is not central, it is cheap.	*10*
I manifest . . . not getting fired (I may not *love* my job, but I need the money)	Kept job and like it now (even have a spider plant on desk).	*10*
I manifest . . . getting a better job (more money, not boring, people bring me coffee rather than the other way round, no one gets my name wrong, etc.)	Running imprint and everyone calls me Alice, including Lydia.	*10*
I manifest . . . respect and admiration from friends, colleagues and family (preferably with high levels of envy, veneration of my social media output, and general sense of shame for having doubted me)	The other day Annabel sent me flowers just to say she cares. Matthew and I reckon she wants a discount on a function at the Lamb.	*10*
I manifest . . . a perfect wedding (everyone whose wedding I've had to sit through can sit at mine and endure, knowing how much better mine is. Plus there will be many comments about how young and beautiful a bride I am)	Rolling this one over. But suddenly it doesn't seem as urgent or important now.	*TBC*

I manifest . . . wiping that smug smile off Matthew Lloyd's face	Did it. It keeps coming back. But I wouldn't want it any other way	Out of the park
I manifest . . . having our old house and spending next Christmas in it	Don't ask me how, but I've done it . . .	*10++++*

Have you made the progress you were hoping to?

Not in the way I imagined. Not in the way I tried to. But in a way that exceeded every dream I didn't dare to have.

How do you feel about your manifesting journey?

I've got to hand it to the Universe. I am so on board with manifesting.

I got everything I asked for and more: limited became limitless; little hopes grew shoots and leaves and forests.

If I want, I can reach across and touch Matthew Lloyd's chest, run my fingers along that tattoo . . . I've just done it now. He barely raised an eyebrow. I'm probably going to be naked under that chest later, looking up at those reality-defying muscles, offering prayers of gratitude up to the Universe. Or, I might be looking down at that chest, or facing—

'Alice,' cut in Matthew. 'You're dribbling.'

'I'm manifesting actually.'

Matthew's mouth curved in a decidedly self-satisfied way. 'Is that what you call it?' he said drily, pulling me towards him.

'Call it what you want, Matthew,' I said, 'so long as it happens.'

His eyes grew dark. 'It's going to happen.'

Yeah. I'm a big fan of manifesting.

So, I guess the real question is, once I've manifested that, what do I manifest next . . . ?

Guide Post™

'Hope' is the thing with feathers –
That perches in the soul –
And sings the tune without the words –
And manifests it all . . .

*Emily Dickinson**

Congratulations!

You've reached the end of **The Guide**™. *But just because you've completed this manifesting journal, that's not to say you've reached the end of your manifesting journey. You may wish to continue that journey solo, but many choose to upgrade to* **The Second Guide**™* *for their next leg – we guarantee we won't disappoint.*

For more inspiration and free content, visit www.the-guide-journal.com

Please note, any purchases made through the website are non-refundable and non-exchangeable and may be subject to import duty

Read the guidelines before you manifest!

* Please note that The Second Guide™ retails at more than The Guide™; this is reflective of the updated and repurposed content, and the luxury choices of cover.

Acknowledgements

So this is the bit I've been waiting for. . .

I'd like to start by acknowledging my neighbours. Sometimes I don't in real life, but this is a book. And I'd like to acknowledge the post lady who wears shorts and a smile, plus the Amazon delivery people (who I intend to give good reviews to, but then forget) as well as the various Ocado delivery drivers who never judge me for being too lazy to go to the shop. And the people on my walk who smile but also don't want to talk. These people are my writing friends. (They may not know it but they are).

To all my other friends (the ones that should be aware we are friends) who have supported me with this: thank you. Jenny, you'd better be listening on audio – it's vital to have that one sale. I hope I've reflected some of the poshness elements correctly, and thank you for making risk-taking seem fun, and for letting me bore you through the whole writing thing, and for believing for me. Trevor, remember this when you're writing my reference / your own acknowledgments, and thank you for unfailingly finding humour alongside despair: never has negativity been more positive or competitive; in fact, I almost look forward to rejections so I can share them with you – and Jenny. (FYI Jenny you're still in the lead based on the feedback that nurse gave you after your last internal.) And thank you, Emma and Giovanna, for motivating me to step outside my comfort zone and try, and for sticking with me still. (I'm also going to thank Greg, even though he's unlikely to read this, for being an inspiration – talk about knocking it out of the park…) Thanks: Tom, for the silliness and empathy; Caroline, for the confidence; Laraine, for being a rude cowgirl; Anna for the encouragement; Helen for reliable equanimity (and for starting my own romcom). Thank you, Jane, for reading this and giving spot-on suggestions, and for bringing your creativity, wisdom and positivity. A special thanks to lovely Vickie for uncovering the dreams and sparkle that sometimes get lost in the throes of baby-time, and for the quiet coaxing. I took too long, and I haven't got to tell you, but I reckon you'd be proud, and I am glad that I got to share what I did with you. Can't tell you how much I wish you were here for that glass of Bollinger.

I'd also like to acknowledge my parents and the big, somewhat chaotic, never-boring family you've created; I'm lucky to be part of it and lucky to have you. Now, as discussed, you're not allowed to read this story, due to unsuitable content and graphic swearing. Therefore, best not to mention it to your siblings, Dad, or to any Oxford Old Codgers. Mum, even though this isn't one for you, happy for you to share it with some of your Zumba crowd (not Wednesday's), or select members of Tai Chi, but I doubt it's suitable for fellow speed-watchers. (Schwester, you may read it – it was written with you in mind. And I know you think that laughing at one's own jokes doesn't necessarily correlate with comic ability, but you're wrong.)

Many thanks to the team at HQ digital for bringing *Alice Carver* to life, and for everything everyone has done to make it the best it could be. Thank you to: Lou Nyuar and Joanna Rose for their inventive marketing campaign; Georgia Hester for being a dedicated publicist; and Emily Scorer and Brogan Furey for their tenacious approach to sales. Thank you also to Design and Maren Landsnes who have created such a cool cover, and to all in Production who have brought this book into being. I'd like to sincerely thank Lisa Milton for seeing potential in the story and for championing it, as well as Georgina Green for taking it on and improving it. I really appreciate all your expertise and encouragement, George, as well as your collaborative and ambitious approach – it's a complete pleasure to work with you.

Also, a huge thank you to Claire Wilson, for giving me a reason to write a novel; for the support, advice, humour, editing, ingenuity, optimism etc; and for continuing to back me. You're not only intimidatingly successful but kind too. It's good to know that there are people like you who have reached influential positions they absolutely deserve – it's like a real-life children's book or rom com where the world is as it should be.

Finally, I'd like to thank Dude for setting this story in motion (did I manifest you?). Biggest thanks and love goes to my dearest friends, Neverending P Ness, Beetroot Bandus and Hilmanella Von-Skvitschi for being entirely awesome.

And, to Nick. Of course.

Everything starts and ends with you.

(P.S. *Finally* finally, if you're still reading, then thank YOU!)

Dear Reader,

We hope you enjoyed reading this book. If you did, we'd be so appreciative if you left a review. It really helps us and the author to bring more books like this to you.

Here at HQ Digital we are dedicated to publishing fiction that will keep you turning the pages into the early hours. Don't want to miss a thing? To find out more about our books, promotions, discover exclusive content and enter competitions you can keep in touch in the following ways:

JOIN OUR COMMUNITY:

Sign up to our new email newsletter: http://smarturl.it/SignUpHQ

Read our new blog www.hqstories.co.uk

𝕏 https://twitter.com/HQStories

www.facebook.com/HQStories

BUDDING WRITER?

We're also looking for authors to join the HQ
Digital family! Find out more here:
https://www.hqstories.co.uk/want-to-write-for-us/

Thanks for reading, from the HQ Digital team

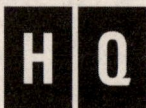